THE LADY OF SHALOTT IN THE VICTORIAN NOVEL

THE LADY OF SHALOTT IN THE VICTORIAN NOVEL

Jennifer Gribble

First published 1983 by
THE MACMILLAN PRESS LTD
London and Basingstoke
Companies and representatives
throughout the world

ISBN 0 333 35019 7

Printed in Hong Kong

Contents

Acknowledgements

The outline of this book was presented as a paper to the Sydney conference of the Australasian Victorian Studies Association in 1975, and parts of Chapter 2 to its Newcastle conference in 1980. Thanks are due to the editors of the conference papers for permission to use this material, and to the editor of the *Critical Review* for permission to reprint passages from a commentary in the 1982 number.

I am indebted to the Special Studies Committee of the University of Sydney for leave which enabled me to complete research and writing in Oxford, and to attend John Bayley and Stephen Wall's seminar on Henry James. I thank them for the stimulus of those discussions, and for introducing me to the work of Todorov.

Many other teachers and friends, colleagues and students, have contributed to the evolution of these chapters. In particular, I am grateful to Margaret Walters, Philip Martin, Peter Shrubb and Rob Jackson for comments and suggestions that encouraged me to continue. Throughout the writing, the practical support of my mother, E. M. Dallimore, has been, as ever, unfailing.

A Note on the Texts

Page references in the text relate to the following editions of the novels and shorter fiction cited.

Jane Austen, *Sense and Sensibility*, Penguin edn (Harmondsworth, 1969).
Charlotte Brontë, *Shirley*, Shakespeare Head edn (Oxford, 1931).
——, *Villette*, Everyman edn (London, 1952).
Charles Dickens, *Little Dorrit*, Penguin edn (Harmondsworth, 1973).
George Eliot, *Daniel Deronda*, Zodiac edn (London, 1971).
——, *Felix Holt, the Radical*, Penguin edn (Harmondsworth, 1972).
——, *Middlemarch*, World's Classics edn (London, 1956).
Thomas Hardy, *Jude the Obscure*, Penguin edn (Harmondsworth, 1981).
——, *A Pair of Blue Eyes*, Wessex edn (London, 1938).
Henry James, *The Bostonians*, Penguin edn (Harmondsworth, 1966).
——, 'In the Cage', in *The Complete Tales of Henry James*, ed. Leon Edel (London, 1964) vol. x.
——, *The Portrait of a Lady*, World's Classics edn (London, 1955).
——, *The Wings of the Dove*, Bodley Head edn (London, 1969).
D. H. Lawrence, *The Rainbow*, Heinemann edn (London, 1955).
——, *Sons and Lovers*, Heinemann edn (London, 1972).
——, *Women in Love*, Heinemann edn (London, 1954).
Leo Tolstoy, *Anna Karenina*, Penguin edn (Harmondsworth, 1967).
Virginia Woolf, *A Haunted House and Other Stories* (London, 1967).
——, *Mrs Dalloway*, Penguin edn (Harmondsworth, 1964).
——, *To the Lighthouse*, Penguin edn (Harmondsworth, 1964).

Introduction

'Who is this? and what is here?' asks Sir Lancelot. But Tennyson's
Lady of Shalott carries her mystery into death. Her imprisonment is
mysteriously ordained, and yet she seems a willing, even a cheerful,
prisoner. The placid rhythms of the verse express obedience to the
whispered threat ('A curse is on her, if she stay/To look down on
Camelot'), and acceptance of the world as it is reflected in her
mirror and recreated in her web.

The various damsels of Tennyson's juvenilia, Claribel and Lilian
and Isabel and Madeline, indicate his early interest in the
emblematic lady of romantic heritage, and prefigure the Blessed
Damozel and other Pre-Raphaelite ladies, living and partly living,
in the decline of Victorian romanticism. Shakespeare's 'Mariana in
the moated grange' provides Tennyson with the occasion for a more
lingering look at the figure of the lady. Enclosed upon her own
ennui, shut away from a world in which not even the passing of the
hours and seasons brings hope of change, Mariana waits in vain for
the lover who might furnish her with a destiny. Stasis pervades the
poem's langorous cadences and repeated refrain, holding Mariana
forever within her literary picture-frame. In 1833, however, in 'The
Lady of Shalott', Tennyson gathers together his developing poetic
preoccupations to create an arresting and memorable fable that is to
fascinate the Victorian imagination.

Whether or not Tennyson had read of Malory's 'Lily maid of
Astolat' before he wrote the poem (he was unable, later in life, quite
to recollect),[1] his medieval Italian source, the romantic novella of
the *Donna di Scalotta*, is yet another Arthurian variant, telling of how
a damsel dies of love for Lancelot du Lac.[2] And it provides, as
Malory's *Morte d'Arthur* was to provide, a legendary dimension for
what are recognisably contemporary concerns. Tennyson's lady is
sealed off from the outside world with all the authority of fairy-tale,
but her imprisonment is no more inexplicable or irrevocable than
that of many another Victorian lady. The diary of Henry James's

sister Alice,[3] for example, or the early life of Elizabeth Barrett Browning, or the plangent songs of Christina Rossetti, make eloquent testimony to the reality on which Tennyson's fable touches. In addition, however, Tennyson introduces details about the lady's setting and task, notably the symbolic mirror, web and curse, that transform courtly romance into allegory – an allegory that reflects on the individual consciousness in its relationship with society, and on the nature and role of creative imagination.

The Lady of Shalott's imprisonment, unlike Mariana's, is set in the midst of an expansive landscape that sustains a working community. The world she must not look at has a changing, detailed life in the poem, stirred by breezes, heavy barges and passers-by. The delight of catching its mirrored reflections in her web begins to falter as handsome knights and young lovers suggest a realm of experience beyond her comfortable solitude. Nothing can match the energy with which, 'A bow-shot from her bower-eaves', Sir Lancelot is launched into the poem, as if in answer to the aim of her own wistful yearning for something more than 'shadows'. And so the lady looks out; the web breaks and the mirror cracks. But there is no place for her in the world inhabited by Sir Lancelot. In fulfilment of the curse, she drifts down the river into her inevitable 'decline'. The elegiac ending completes the drift away from the poem's more interesting reflections, back again into the world of fairy-tale.

Long before he was invited to illustrate the poem for the Moxon edition of Tennyson in 1857, Holman Hunt had made the first of a series of 'Lady of Shalott' drawings and paintings, the last of which, begun in 1887, was among the works he completed, with failing eyesight, at the turn of the century.[4] Tennyson complained that Hunt's illustration showed an unwelcome degree of artistic licence: ' "My dear Hunt . . . I never said that the young woman's hair was flying all over the shop." "No", said Hunt; "but you never said it wasn't." '[5] In Hunt's view, Tennyson's poem, dealing with 'a romantic story which conveys an eternal truth'[6] offered a parable for all to interpret: the more or less Victorian–moralising interpretations in Hunt's successive versions suggest what that 'truth' meant to him. While the entangling masses of web-like hair and the mirrored Camelot world recur in each of the Lady of Shalott pictures, *The Awakening Conscience* of 1852 sets out the parable in contemporary terms. The lady who looks towards the world beyond her window, beyond the arms of the man who encloses her within a meticulously detailed Victorian interior, looks away from the mirror that reflects that world, and the skeins of her embroidery lie unravelled at her feet.[7] For Millais, too, an interest in the Tennysonian fable predates the invitation to illustrate the Moxon edition. His *Mariana* of 1851 suggests the fairy lady as well as the Shakespearean: the figure who leans away from a window half obscured by pictured saints has woven a tapestry that nevertheless reflects the shapes and colours of the world outside. By the time of the Moxon edition, however, Millais's preoccupation with the fable has visibly waned. The miserably huddled Mariana of his illustration has none of the commanding presence and allegorical suggestiveness of the earlier painting.[8] D. G. Rossetti, the third of the Moxon artists, who had particularly set his heart on illustrating 'The Lady of Shalott', was in the end allowed to provide a tail-piece for the poem. His drawing precisely indicates the appeal the fable was to have for him, as poet and painter, throughout his career. His beatified Lady of Shalott is Rossetti's Blessed Damozel, dreamily contemplative in her funeral barque, surrounded by the venerating lords and ladies of Camelot.

In Victorian painting, poetry and novels, the enclosed lady is pictured again and again, sometimes at her window or her mirror or her embroidery, but always locked in contemplation.[9] This is not to suggest that later artists are all consciously quoting Tennyson. The figure is to be found as well in European painting and literature in the same period, and has famous and venerable antecedents.[10] It is rather to suggest that Tennyson's poem, touching as it does on such Victorian romantic concerns as the emblematic lady, the social position and rights of women, and the nature and function of creative imagination, articulates a myth in that sense of the word defined by de Rougement as 'a symbolic fable as simple as it is striking – which sums up an infinite number of more or less analogous situations'.[11] For Tennyson himself, as for his Pre-Raphaelite illustrators, the fable resonates still in works that deal with more overtly domestic subjects. In 'Edwin Morris', or 'The Gardener's Daughter' or 'The Miller's Daughter', the fable promotes lifeless idealisations of love, in which the lady is framed by time and memory, perpetuating her emblematic significance in the stasis of romantic portraiture. But the myth is sufficiently pervasive, a century later, to preoccupy one of the most innovative of modern novelists, for whom it represents what it is in his Victorian romantic heritage that he goes on debating with, and defining himself against:

> 'It's all that Lady of Shalott business', he said, in his strong abstract voice. He seemed to be charging her before the unseeing air. 'You've got that mirror, your own fixed will, your immortal understanding, your own tight conscious world, and there is nothing beyond it. There, in the mirror, you must have everything. . . .'   (D. H. Lawrence, *Women in Love*, p. 35)[12]

The charge is yet another move in Birkin's continuing argument with Ursula, and in Lawrence's argument with romanticism, Victorian and modern. A younger Ursula, the Ursula of *The Rainbow*, waits in her solitary room for Sir Lancelot to ride by, 'while she, ah, she would remain the lonely maid high up and isolated in the tower, polishing the terrible shield, weaving it a covering with a true device, and waiting, waiting, always remote and high' (p. 263). A gust of romanticism sweeps across *Sons and Lovers* as Paul Morel, in a lyrical moment with Miriam and Clara among the bluebells, moves rapidly from a vision of knight-errantry and ladies shut up safely in pavilions, 'singing at their "broidery"'', to an argument that anticipates Birkin's. The emancipated and belligerent Clara, he contends, is as much the captive of her self-enclosed and endlessly self-conscious world as the lady of the legend, 'like a dog before a looking-glass, gone mad with fury at its own shadow' (p. 233). The Lawrence of *Women in Love* is sufficiently detached from his male protagonist, and sufficiently self-aware, to see in 'all that Lady of Shalott business' not only the woman's sense of herself and of her place in the world, but also the sense of her held by men, and in the general cultural tradition each inherits. Birkin is clearly threatened by Ursula's sense of self, but the passage registers a certain 'fixed will' and 'tight consciousness' in the sermonising of her antagonist as well. The Birkin who compulsively shatters the emblematic lady he finds mirrored by the moon on water is the same Birkin who believes that 'If there isn't the woman, there's nothing.' She is 'Cybele . . . . The accursed *Syria Dea*' (*Women in Love*, p. 238), as alien and as powerful as the moon, an anima, the very source and embodiment of creativity.

'All that Lady of Shalott business' is, for Lawrence, a complex of literary and social conventions and attitudes that form the characteristic subject and shape of the novel of Tennyson's contemporaries. The self-enclosed protagonist, seeing the world mirrored by the consciousness, conscious above all of individual needs and wants, is not only the characteristic protagonist of the Victorian novel, but an image of its very form. Whether angels of the house, emergent feminists, or mere ordinary men, Victorian protagonists, conceived within a 'certain moral scheme' in terms of which they are to be made consistent, are unable, in Lawrence's view, to venture beyond the limits set by the insistently conscious 'knowable' self or the walled-in dwelling constructed by society.[13] 'Don't look in my novel for the old stable ego of the character', he warned – though even for a novelist whose development lies in the discovery of 'lines unknown', relationships between the knowable self of individual consciousness and the world within and beyond its mirror must be fathomed still.

The purpose of this study is not, however, to trace that development, but to explore 'all that Lady of Shalott business' in the work of some representative Victorian novelists. To explore the figure is, I think, to find illumined the distinctive course of romanticism in Victorian England, and developments in the English novel from the nineteenth to the twentieth century. The presence of the enclosed lady in nineteenth-century novels has been noted often enough, though her relationship with Tennyson's lady has not been explored, as far as I know.[14] A substantial anthology of extracts could indeed be compiled in which the heroine's plight is pictured with a symbolic suggestiveness that recalls the *tableau vivant* of 'The Lady of Shalott'. Within the discussion that follows there will be found the beginnings of such an anthology. In George Eliot's novels, most memorably, characters as different as Mrs Transome in *Felix Holt* and Gwendolen Harleth in *Daniel Deronda* experience that self-enclosed gentility that confines the serious Dorothea Brooke so frequently within the blue-green boudoir of *Middlemarch*. They gaze into their mirrors or stand at their windows, seeing only the reflection of their own thoughts, but seeking in that reflected expanse some enlightening interpretation of their mysterious life-sentence. Charlotte Brontë's heroines restlessly tread out their confines, their imagination at its weaving work, creating pictures of a compensating 'reality'. In the narrow darkened rooms of the Dickens world are women held by the paralysis of their 'mind-forged manacles': Miss Havisham in the bride-chamber at Satis House, where the stopped clocks and the arrested wedding-feast make the world her imprisoned mind projects, her particular 'spot of time' held perversely forever; or Mrs Clennam, for whom the passing hours and seasons have been stilled by the repressive unrelenting vision which has become her only reality. Hardy images the compelling, mysterious 'otherness' of 'womankind' in glimpses calculated to tantalise and bewilder their onlookers – in Elfride Swancourt's or Bathsheba Everdene's moments of private self-absorption before a mirror, or Sue Bridehead, glimpsed through her window, enclosed by reverie. Henry James's Isabel Archer is, like the older Madame Merle, the portrait of a lady closed in, repeatedly and irrevocably, on wonderful tasks of rich imaginative embroidery. And in all these pictured ladies, and in the pictures they themselves create, there is elaborated the picture in which the novels have their origin and their destination. Isabel's return, at last, to that state of enclosure from which, early on, in Albany, 'she had no wish to look out', is inherent not only in James's conception of her character, but in the very art of his novel. From the 'simple corner-stone, the conception of a certain young lady affronting her destiny', James begins to erect 'the large building of *The Portrait of a Lady*' which has to be put up around his young woman while she stands there 'in perfect isolation': 'Place the centre of the subject in the young woman's own consciousness [he tells himself] and you get as interesting and as beautiful a difficulty as you could wish.'[15] It is an approach to the novelist's art that clearly enough anticipates Joyce and Virginia Woolf. But it also leads back, to Charlotte Brontë, Dickens, George Eliot, and beyond, to Jane Austen,[16] as they explore the potentialities and the limits of a central reflecting consciousness.

Views of the impact of romanticism in the nineteenth-century novel differ widely – from John Bayley's claim that it is the novelists, rather than the poets, who are the real inheritors of romanticism,[17] to Northrop Frye's, that 'romanticism is difficult to adapt to the novel, which demands an empirical and observant attitude; its contribution is rather, appropriately, a form of romance'.[18] Peter Coveney's *The Image of Childhood in Nineteenth-Century Literature* finds in the image of the child, in both novels and poetry, a symbolisation and exposition of the romantic interest in the subjective, and of the romantic protest against the experience of society:

> If the central problem of the artist was in fact one of adjustment, one can see the possibilities for identification between the artist and the consciousness of the child whose difficulty and chief

source of pain often lie in adjustment and accommodation to environment. In childhood lay the perfect image of insecurity and isolation, of fear and bewilderment, of vulnerability and potential isolation.[19]

The image of the lady makes a similarly appropriate focus for the novel's characteristic interest in the problems of accommodation to an oppressive social environment, and in the challenge to creativity. But she becomes, in the art of Tennyson's contemporaries, a 'figure' in the rhetorical meaning of that word: male or female, artist or weaver of domestic webs, part of the configuration of romantic symbols – the imprisoning room, the web, the mirror and the 'curse' – that together comprise the symbolic fable or myth.

Aspects of this figure have been variously discussed by literary theorists in pursuit of structural myths, or sociological data, or the defining of a 'poetics of prose'. The distinctive romantic protagonist represents for Harold Bloom an 'internalisation' of Frye's 'quest myth'.[20] For George Lukács, the internalising of the quest indicates the very failure of what he sees as the nineteenth-century novel's search for something resembling the 'totality' of myth. Unlike the hero of epic, at one with his society and its shared and living traditions, the novel's protagonist is conscious only of being a separate 'interiority', estranged from nature as from society, doomed to experience the world as a prison instead of a parental home. The quest for meaning yields only the flickering of isolated lyric moments.[21] In his discussion of Flaubert, in *Writing Degree Zero*, Barthes argues, furthermore, that this 'all-embracing subjectivism', or 'Bovarysme' of the novel's protagonist reflects the 'bad faith' of his creator, who refuses to admit the imaginary nature of the created world by which he consoles himself for his own estrangement from the real world.[22] Todorov, in search of 'the figure in the carpet' of Henry James, and as an exercise in 'the structural analysis of literature', carries the idea of the unrealisable quest even further. In his view, the task of reconciling the Jamesian protagonist's vision of things with what lies beyond it can never succeed because James's tales are founded in what Todorov describes as the paradox of 'the quest for an absolute and absent cause': 'only the quest for truth can be present; truth itself, although the cause of this movement, remains absent'.[23] Later in this chapter, in discussing Todorov's reading of 'In the Cage', I shall attempt to elucidate, and to disagree with, this approach. It is perhaps worth noting here, however, that Todorov's analysis elicits what he takes to be 'a law of criticism': 'it is the search for truth, not its revelation – the quest for the treasure rather than the treasure itself, for the treasure can only be absent'.[24] The 'truth', as Todorov conceives it, is something from which protagonist, tale and teller remain alike shut away. Tennyson's lady does indeed remain shut away from the 'truth': her death indicates her inability to reconcile the world of her solitary imagination with the world beyond her tower. But the great Victorian novelists, however fascinated they are by the gap between individual consciousness and the world it creates, have a much firmer grasp than their protagonists can command on a dense quotidian world.

Clearly, not all Victorian novels display Tennyson's fable, or display it with equal clarity. By looking closely at a group of novels in which it seems most plainly, and suggestively, exemplified, however, it is possible to demonstrate its value in illuminating the particular works themselves, as well as tendencies in the Victorian novel generally, and to indicate the sense in which it might usefully be thought of as a 'myth'. It is not consciously 'used' in these novels as myths are used by romantic poets and modern novelists, or by George Eliot most notably among nineteenth-century English novelists, in her reference to myths like the Theseus–Bacchus–Ariadne story, in *Romola* or *Middlemarch*.[25] It operates as myth in de Rougement's general sense, a sense which leads Northrop Frye, by extension, to see all literature as 'displaced mythology': as a recurrence of images and patterns that seem to define prevalent social and cultural beliefs and traditions.[26] Inherent in Barthes's study of 'modern myths' is the view that the individual artist represents little more than an involuntary response to dominant modes and embedded ideologies that 'think themselves' through him. The novelist is simply 'obeying' the structuring effects of the conventions and habits of feeling distinctive of the novel as a form of discourse.[27] Individual novelists, however, and, indeed, the novel's history of parody and imitation, suggest a high degree of self-awareness about the nature of fiction, and the subtle interplay between literary convention and literary creation. Gwendolen Harleth's life takes a shape not unlike that of the genteel romances that limit her horizons, but George Eliot's horizons are significantly larger. The conventions of fiction she inherits shape her individual talent to produce, in *Daniel Deronda*, a work which is in its turn to suggest new possibilities for her successors. From Jane Austen's

Catherine Tilney to Flaubert's Madame Bovary and Tolstoy's Anna Karenina, heroines are seeking between the covers of the popular novel the image of their own lives, weaving a fanciful web that not only images the complex web that contains them, but also the 'discourse' of fiction itself. From novel to novel, shared patterns of thinking and feeling are indeed reiterated, but not simply repeated.[28] As in all myths, the reiterated story or situation recreates its meaning with each new telling; it touches sources deep within the consciousness of its age, shapes and is shaped by the cultural traditions of which it is part. In the novels to be discussed, the figure of the Lady of Shalott appears sometimes as allegory, but at best as the very centre and source of creative imagination. Coleridge makes the necessary distinction:

> Now an allegory is but a translation of abstract notions into a picture-language, which is itself nothing but an abstraction from objects of the senses; the principal one being more worthless even than its phantom proxy, both alike insubstantial, and the former shapeless to boot. On the other hand a symbol . . . is characterized by a translucence of the general in the special, or of the universal in the general; above all by the translucence of the eternal through and in the temporal. It always partakes of the reality which it renders intelligible; and while it enunciates the whole, abides itself as a living part of that unity of which it is the representation.[29]

Myth might well be described as the eternal renewal and rediscovery of the general and the universal. In exploring the symbolic fable of the Lady of Shalott, my purpose will be to distinguish between its allegorising dimension in the most weakly romantic writing, and that 'translucence of the general in the special' to which Coleridge refers, and to pursue questions raised by the views of critics to whom I have referred in this section. What relationship is there between the 'lyric' moments that celebrate the individual consciousness, when life seems held still, as in a picture-frame, and the exploration of the picture's meaning in the larger, and more overtly 'dramatic' context of the novel? For how many novelists is it true that a preoccupation with the isolated consciousness expresses that protest against 'the experience of society' that Coveney finds? To what extent does the Lady of Shalott fable entail a deterministic vision that condemns the protagonist to a circumscribed life? Are novelists exemplifying, or offering a critique of, that strain of aestheticism that develops in Victorian romantic poetry? Does the interest in sustained analysis and contemplation weaken the novel's distinctive exploration of the structure and texture of social life?[30] Where does such a focus lead the novel at the turn of the century and beyond?

The elements of the symbolic fable are so interdependent that it is difficult to discuss them separately at all. A brief survey of each of them, however – the lady, the room, the web, the mirror and the curse – within the general context of nineteenth-century literature and thought, will indicate, in a preliminary way, their characteristic co-presence and interpenetration.

I   THE LADY

> And by the moon, the reaper weary
> Piling sheaves in uplands airy,
> Listening, whispers, ' 'Tis the fairy
> Lady of Shalott.'

Tennyson's imprisoned figure, in keeping with the tradition of courtly love on which his early poems draw, is a 'lady', with all that the word implies of gentility, aloofness, veneration, 'fairy' powers: the *princesse lointaine* rather than the more sinister Belle Dame sans Merci. Essential to the lady's aloofness is that she occupies a special place, a situation that sets her apart. And, indeed, Tennyson's poetry must be accounted highly influential in domesticating the romanticism that produces for the Victorians their Angel in the House. Ruskin, at the end of the era, exhorting young ladies to appropriate domestic virtues and values, reminds them that the feudal meaning of 'lady' is 'bread-giver' (and 'lord' is 'maintainer of laws').[31] It is the rights of 'woman' that are being vindicated by Mary Wollstonecraft, and in the development of feminist thought that follows her. The high Victorian regard for domestic life and the family readily absorbs from the literary traditions of Mariolatry and courtly love[32] an idealised and emblematic lady who represents, and is custodian of, moral values and special qualities of intuition and insight. Her sequestered life protects her and safeguards what she represents. In Tennyson's poem, she is an emblem, an object of interest and speculation to 'Knight and burgher, lord and dame', as well as the humble 'reaper'. But she is also a viewpoint, a way of seeing and shaping the world:

'I am half sick of shadows', said
The Lady of Shalott.

Shut away from the fulfilments and perils of life beyond her window, she suffers Mariana's ennui and narrowly circumscribed existence.

In each of the novels to be discussed in subsequent chapters, the lady and her imprisoning circumstances makes the *raison d'être* for the novel that contains her. It is demonstrably the special qualities and circumstances represented in Lucy Snowe, Little Dorrit, Dorothea Brooke, Sue Bridehead and Milly Theale that motivate, for varying reasons, the creativity of their authors. The structure of the novel, in James's terminology, is put up around these young ladies, and their prevailing consciousness is essential to its texture – a means whereby, at best, personal feeling informs and gives an inner meaning to the exploration of public issues and events. But in each case the source of inspiration, being directly and deeply personal, gives rise as well to an idealising and sentimentality at odds with what is most finely achieved. The lady is by turns the emblematic lady of romance and that lady whose viewpoint on the world commands some of the most interesting and exploratory nineteenth-century prose. We have, on the one hand, the Dorothea Brooke poised soulfully in the Vatican museum for the venerating onlooker, and, on the other, the Dorothea who struggles in the meditations of the blue-green boudoir at Lowick, for an understanding of the world beyond her confines. These ladies of Shalott then, do not simply image a 'dissociated' nineteenth-century sensibility: at best they make part of a fruitful exploration of the role of feeling and imagination at a time when social pressures and literary and social conventions increasingly separate feeling from thought and fact, but when, conversely, it is only through the fullest resources of that consciousness which, as James believed, held one 'in one's place'[33] that a mechanistic and impersonal society could feel the importance of individuality and creativity.

'But why always Dorothea?' asks the narrator of *Middlemarch* (p. 296). A variety of answers have been given to the question of why the consciousness and the situation of women should occupy so much of the nineteenth-century novel's attention. Recent feminist criticism, emphasising the emergence of women writers and the development of feminist thought, has claimed the phenomenon as part of 'a distinctively female literary tradition', often by dealing less than adequately with male protagonists and writers, and with the complexity of literary tradition.[34] A burgeoning interest in the inner life, and in the formal study of psychology, has been seen as distinctively 'feminine'.[35] Clearly, many factors interrelate and need to be considered, together with the many qualities the lady is held, by both male and female writers, to embody: beauty, morality, 'sensibility', love, imagination, confinement, endurance, rebellion. The lady is characteristically as imprisoned by the values ascribed to her as she is by the deprivations of a diminished life.

The immediate source of nineteenth-century idealisation of the lady is to be found in the distinctively Victorian amalgam of medievalism, Christianity and protective veneration of 'the weaker sex'. 'Feminist' issues preoccupied Tennyson and his friend Arthur Hallam during the 1830s in Cambridge at the same time as they were steeping themselves, as D. G. Rossetti was to do, in Petrarch and Dante. The work of the Italian poets, they believed, had been perfected by Christianity to bring about 'an increased respect for the female character, which tempered passion with reverence, and lent an ideal colour to the daily realities of life. . . . The worship of the Virgin soon accustomed Catholic minds to contemplate perfection in a female form.'[36] 'Can it be doubted', asks Hallam in 1831,

> that the spirit of revealed religion, however little understood, wrought in the heart of man a reverence for the weaker sex, both as teaching him to consider their equality with him in the sight of God, and the privileges of Christian life, and as encouraging in himself those mild and tender qualities which are the especial glory of womanhood.[37]

In the early poems of Tennyson, the 'high-born maiden' represents not only the sanctifying of 'love', but also a version of the Jungian anima, an image of the poetic self.[38] Between 'A Dream of Fair Women', in 1832, and *The Princess* in 1847, however, Tennyson more consistently attempts to see the lady as a viewpoint, rather than simply as an emblem – admonished, perhaps, by a Benthamite reviewer of his 1830 volume:

Upon what love is depends what woman is, and upon what
woman is, depends what the world is, both in the present and the
future. There is not a greater moral necessity in England than
that of a reformation in female education. . . . How long will it
be before we shall have read to better purpose the eloquent
lessons, and the yet more eloquent history, of that gifted and
glorious being, Mary Wollstonecraft?[39]

The masculine feminists of Tennyson's Cambridge, to do them
justice, were committed to social and educational improvements
that would demonstrate women's equality 'in the sight of God'. The
gifted and glorious Mary, however, saw idealisation and liberation
as uneasy bedfellows. The valuing of 'mild and tender qualities' and
'perfection' of form signifies just that emphasis on women's capacity
to inspire pleasing sensations in the beholder, rather than on her
capacity for rational satisfaction and moral sense, of which
Wollstonecraft had accused Edmund Burke in *A Vindication of the
Rights of Man*.[40] Furthermore, it is the burden of *A Vindication of the
Rights of Woman* that women themselves accept and foster the image
that imprisons them:

Ah! why do women – I write with affectionate solicitude –
condescend to receive a degree of attention and respect from
strangers different from that reciprocation of civility which the
dictates of humanity and the politeness of civilization authorise
between man and man? And why do they not discover, when 'in
the noon of beauty's power', that they are treated like queens only
to be deluded by hollow respect, till they are led to resign, or not
assume, their natural prerogatives? Confined, then, in cages like
the feathered race, they have nothing to do but to plume
themselves, and stalk with mock majesty from perch to perch. It is
true that they are provided with food and raiment, for which they
neither toil nor spin, but health, liberty, and virtue are given in
exchange. . . .
   The passions of men have thus placed women on thrones, and
till mankind becomes more reasonable, it is to be feared that
women will avail themselves of the power which they attain with
the least exertion, and which is the most indisputable.[41]

Wollstonecraft argues that such views of women will be abandoned
by both sexes if women are educated 'like men':' "Educate women

like men," says Rousseau, "and the more they resemble our sex the less power will they have over us." This is the very point I aim at. I do not wish them to have power over men but over themselves.'[42]

Reviewing the work of Wollstonecraft, George Eliot echoes her contempt for 'the doll-madonna in her shrine';[43] in her study of Tertius Lydgate, in *Middlemarch*, she shows with a delicate perceptiveness how such an image of womanhood may be nourished by a certain kind of masculine tenderness and conventionality, and, being answered to by the 'feminine radiance' of a Rosamond Vincy may find itself over-powered. Rosamond's education at Mrs Lemon's academy has made her a model of all that Mary Wollstonecraft criticises in the late eighteenth-century education of women, 'brimful of sensibility, and teeming with capricious fancies'.[44]

Grace Melbury, in Hardy's *The Woodlanders*, and Estella, in Dickens's *Great Expectations*, are educated to become the 'lady' of Victorian convention, with predictable consequences. The 'masculine' knowledge for which Dorothea Brooke yearns, however, is conceived in terms of its 'usefulness'. Charlotte Brontë's exhortation to the 'men of England' to cultivate the minds of women, and to give them scope and work, promises that in return 'they will be your gayest companions in health, your tenderest nurses in sickness, your most faithful prop in age' (*Shirley*, p. 81). Even the education of Hardy's 'new woman', Sue Bridehead, in the books and ideas that constitute masculine knowledge at the end of the nineteenth century, simply confirms in her the habits of feeling of the Victorian lady. Something more than mere 'knowledge' is entailed, as Wollstonecraft intermittently realises, if the lady is to become more than an emblematic creature, representing and perpetuating social ideals and literary conventions:

> The world cannot be seen by an unmoved spectator: we must mix in the throng . . . we must attain a knowledge of others at the same time that we become acquainted with ourselves. Knowledge acquired any other way only hardens the heart, and perplexes the understanding.[45]

In the novels that follow Wollstonecraft, however, as in Tennyson's poem, the lady is poised uneasily between her role as 'unmoved spectator' and the discovery that she must mix in the throng.

If 'sensibility' becomes almost synonymous with femininity in this period, it denotes a wide and shifting range of qualities and experiences, both idealising and potentially emancipating. It ranges, at the outset of the century, from the shrinkings and heroics of Gothic ladies to that remarkable control of feeling that distinguishes Jane Austen's heroines.[46] And it includes not only 'that which expands the soul in contemplation of beauty or goodness' apostrophised by the heroine of Mary Wollstonecraft's novel *Mary* (an expansiveness by which both heroine and novel are finally swamped), but also the fineness and quickness of perception and intuition exemplified rather later by the heroines of Henry James (Merton Densher reflects that women have so much more imagination), and, above all, the experiencing and inspiring of 'love' in its many varieties.

'Those who constantly employ their sensibility', remarks Wollstonecraft, 'will have most; for example poets, painters and composers.'[47] In George Eliot's capacity to be finely aware and richly responsive and to create those qualities in her protagonists at best, sensibility is employed in a way that differs strikingly from the overstrained nerves and emotionalism that marks the 'sensibility' of many of her letters. The strong personal pressures, however, that motivate 'literary women' to understand and at the same time transcend their situation by writing about it make quite as potent a source for the idealised lady as the more literary sources of Tennyson and Hallam. The lady's situation is sometimes only mirrored, and not transcended, as the distinctive 'throb' that pulsates in the voices of George Eliot's heroines,[48] or Charlotte Brontë's, suggests. Charlotte Brontë, in *Shirley* (p. 81), momentarily abandons fiction altogether:

> Men of England! look at your poor girls, many of them fading around you, dropping off in consumption and decline; or, what is worse, degenerating to sour old maids – envious, backbiting, wretched, because life is a desert to them, what is worst of all, reduced to strive, by scarce modest coquetry and debasing artifice, to gain that position and consideration by marriage, which to celibacy is denied.

It was the suffering sensibilities of Charlotte Brontë's heroines, and their preoccupation with the emotional life, that drew Harriet Martineau's stern protest:

> all the female characters, in all their thoughts and lives, are full of one thing . . . love. . . . It is not thus in real life. There are substantial, heartfelt interests for women of all ages, and under ordinary circumstances, quite apart from love.[49]

But her friend George Eliot makes a somewhat different emphasis in a well-known letter to John Morley:

> as a fact of mere zoological evolution, woman seems to me to have the worse share of existence. But for that very reason I would the more contend that in the moral evolution we have 'an art which doth mend nature'. It is the function of love in the largest sense to mitigate the hardness of all fatalities.[50]

What 'the largest sense' might be, and how it relates to the somewhat smaller sense Harriet Martineau has in mind is a continuing preoccupation in Eliot's novels, most ambitiously perhaps in her last novel, *Daniel Deronda*.

As part of its many-faceted study of the position and nature of women, there is advanced, in that novel, through the Judaic piety of Mordecai, a version of the Lady of Shalott's story:

> 'women are especially framed for the love which feels possession in renouncing. . . . Somewhere in the latter *Midrash*, I think, is the story of a young Jewish maiden who loved a Gentile king so well, that this was what she did – she entered into prison and changed clothes with the woman who was beloved of the king, that she might deliver that woman from death by dying in her stead, and leave the king to be happy in his love which was not for her. This is the surpassing love, that loses self in the object of love.'
>
> 'No, Ezra, no,' said Mirah, with low-toned intensity, 'that was not it. She wanted the king when she was dead to know what she had done and feel that she was better than the other. It was her strong self, wanting to conquer, that made her die.'
>
> Mordecai was silent a little, and then argued –
>
> 'That might be, Mirah. But if she acted so, believing the king would never know?'
>
> 'You can make the story so in your mind, Ezra, because you are

great, and like to fancy the greatest that could be. But I think it was not really like that. The Jewish girl must have had jealousy in her heart, and she wanted somehow to have the first place in the king's mind. That is what she would die for.'

'My sister, thou hast read too many plays, where the writers delight in showing the human passions as indwelling demons, unmixed with the relenting and devout element of the soul. Thou judgest by the plays, and not by thy own heart, which is like our mother's.'

'Mirah made no answer. (*Daniel Deronda*, p. 640)

The lady of Mordecai's tale, like Tennyson's lady, can never claim her knight. 'The surpassing love, that loses self in the object of love' seems to thrive on its denial of any fulfilment but the perverse fulfilment of death. In a strikingly similar tale, Little Dorrit's story of the princess and the tiny woman,[51] Dickens, too, ponders the connection between Victorian ideals of feminine self-renunciation and the romantic convention of unrequited love. George Eliot's passage is visibly divided between approving the 'larger sense' of love in Mordecai's religiose romanticism, and promoting Mirah's critique of it. There is little to choose between Mordecai's notion of love as self-renouncing and Mirah's equally notional and operatic passionate assertiveness. The hint that Mirah has impulses that might challenge her brother's pietism and paternalism scarcely redeems her from the self-abnegating role in which she is cast for most of the novel. Dorothea Brooke's 'moral evolution', in *Middlemarch*, towards a love that 'looses self' is closely succeeded by love that is much more self-assertive, and, one assumes, more biologically determined. 'Love in the largest sense' represents a persistent moralising strain in George Eliot the novelist. Her own emancipation from familial pieties, and her resolutely educating herself 'like a man', does not prevent her from seeing her heroines, sometimes, through the eyes of a Tertius Lydgate. Even the refreshingly and unashamedly self-centred Gwendolen Harleth, the most interesting study of feminine sensibility in *Daniel Deronda* (or in any George Eliot novel, perhaps) can prompt in her creator such reflections as the following:

Could there be a slenderer, more insignificant thread in human history than this consciousness of a girl, busy with her small inferences of the way in which she could make her life pleasant? –

in a time too, when ideas were with fresh vigour making armies of
themselves, and the universal kinship was declaring itself
fiercely . . . a time when the soul of man was working to pulses
which had for centuries been beating in him unheard, until their
full sum made a new life of terror or of joy.
    What in the midst of that mighty drama are girls and their
blind vision? They are the yea or nay of that good for which men
are enduring and fighting. In these delicate vessels is born
onward through the ages the treasure of human affections.

(*Daniel Deronda*, p. 109)

For, while it is Eliot's distinctive achievement to show the unique
importance of 'girls and their blind vision' in the general context of
human history, the tone and diction of this passage anticipates the
Ruskin of *Sesame and Lilies*. Fortunately, for the most part, the consciousness of Gwendolen Harleth shows little sign of the
emblematic virtues with which it is here endowed. Something of the
same protective and condescending tone creeps into Henry James's
reference to this passage, in the Preface to *A Portrait of a Lady*, in
support of his wonderment at 'how inordinately the Isabel Archers
and even much smaller fry, insist on mattering'.[52]
    In asking himself, in 1883, what it was that most characterised his
age, James's answer was 'the situation of women, the decline of the
sentiment of sex, the agitation on their behalf'.[53] *The Bostonians* is not
simply 'an American tale'; the agitation for women's rights makes
part of James's analysis of a sexual malaise that, well before
Lawrence, he found distinctive of contemporary life and literature.
In *The Portrait of a Lady*, which immediately precedes it, James
creates a heroine whose most disabling ignorance is an ignoring of
her own sexuality. As a young man James was fascinated by
portraits of beautiful women. Early stories present the 'pictured
lady' with a painterly idealising, progressively tempered, though
never perhaps entirely relinquished, throughout his development as
a novelist. At the same time, he was critical of the passionless
protagonists of the English novel:

Miss Austen and Sir Walter Scott, Dickens and Thackeray,
Hawthorne and George Eliot have all represented young people
in love with each other; but not one of them has, to the best of my
recollection, described anything that can be called passion – put
it into motion before us, and shown us its various pieces.[54]

How successfully James himself, or Dickens, or George Eliot, render 'passion' is a question to be pursued in later chapters. In *The Bostonians*, however, and again in *The Wings of the Dove*, James further explores the connection between 'portraits of ladies' and the thwarting and constraining of passion. Olive Chancellor quivers with a passion the more intense because it is denied sexual expression. It is a passion moulded, and indeed warped, by an image of womanhood. And Basil Ransome, her rival for the love of Verena Tarrant, is set in notions of womanhood scarcely different from those of the young Hallam and Tennyson:

> He had the most definite notions about their place in nature, in society, and was perfectly easy in his mind as to whether it excluded them from any proper homage. The chivalrous man paid that tax with alacrity. He admitted their rights; these consisted in a standing claim to the generosity and tenderness of the stronger sex. (*The Bostonians*, p. 167)

Olive and Verena too have 'the most definite notions': Verena's rhetorical vision of an emancipated womanhood, like the caricaturing account of woman's role in history fostered by Olive's 'education', just as inevitably emblematises and enthrones women. Verena and Basil, in their separate 'boxes', Olive in her back parlour, are each constrained by notions of sexual and social identity that prove inadequate as they find themselves caught up in actual relationships. The novel establishes incisively and often movingly, its view that in a real world, as in the world of social and literary convention, the lady is not, and never can be, 'free'. Some 'mere zoological' facts cannot be ignored, and, for lovers of either sex, fulfilment brings yet another kind of containment and commitment.

As the epitome of the circumscribed life, the lady of nineteenth-century novels has frequently been described as 'tragic'. Julian Moynahan for example, argues that it is implicit in the very valuing of the lady that she is unable to be assimilated by the world beyond self. In identifying what he describes as the English novel's 'maiden cult', he advances the theory that, from Jane Austen to Hardy, the female is seen as embodying the pastoral values of 'a wholesome sense of community'. In Jane Austen's 'high pastoral comedy', the 'maiden' is, he claims, 'assimilated'; with George Eliot and Hardy, there develops 'a type of tragedy' in which the perceived values are not incorporated, but alienated.[55] Jeanette King accounts for the

predominating importance of women in Victorian novels in terms
not only of the enshrining of communal values, but also of the
determining effect of those biological factors to which George Eliot
referred, and which condemn women passively to suffer their fate:
'the subjection of women to a limited conventional role is symbolic
of the universal tragedy – the stifling of individual intuitions and
emotions by organised social structures'.[56] Whether tragedy can be
defined as the 'alienation' or 'stifling' of a protagonist by a hostile
society is a question to be taken up more fully in Chapter 4. But
demonstrably, in the best of nineteenth-century novels, the relationship between protagonist and society is more complex, and finally
more 'valuing' of individual aspiration than either of these
conceptions of 'tragedy' allows. At this point the discussion moves
inevitably towards issues that make up the next section. To
summarise briefly, however, it is clear that the 'stifling', or potential
stifling, of individual intuitions and emotions that claims the
attention of Victorian novelists of both sexes is shared by protagonists both male and female – by Dorothea and Lydgate, Little Dorrit
and Arthur Clennam, by Jude as well as Sue – although in each case
a distinctive and special value seems invested in the female
protagonist. To call her situation 'tragic', however, is to mistake
what is the nineteenth-century novel's characteristic achievement:
its holding in balance the values of the enclosed but contemplative
consciousness, its sensibility, its creativity, and the challenging
variousness of a society within which these values must, as
Wollstonecraft notes, be tested. This is the implication of that
'certain moral scheme', that network of social circumstances
within which Lawrence believed nineteenth-century characters
to be conceived, and in terms of which they were to be made
consistent.

Tennyson's lady delights to weave her mirror's magic sights.
'Love in the largest sense', is, for the romantic imagination, the
artist's love of his creation – a love which not only mitigates the
hardness of all fatalities, compensating for a limited life, but which is
widely held to transcend them as well. As Shelley memorably puts
it,

> The great secret of morals is love, or a going out of our own
> nature, and an identification of ourselves with the beautiful
> which exists in thought, action or person, not our own. A man, to
> be greatly good, must imagine intensively and comprehensively;

he must put himself in the place of another and of many others; the pains and pleasures of his species must become his own. The greatest instrument of moral good is the imagination.[57]

The values associated with imagination here, 'the beautiful which exists in thought, action or person', recall the emblematic lady of courtly tradition and Victorian convention. But in the more than emblematic ladies of Charlotte Brontë, George Eliot, Dickens, Hardy and James, is exemplified that creative power of imagination Shelley associates with 'moral good'. The capacity to see and feel creatively (to anticipate the discussion in section IV) is for all these novelists the highest achievement of the individual consciousness, and the means by which it transcends the bounds of self.

II THE ROOM

> Four gray walls, and four gray towers
> Overlook a space of flowers,
> And the silent isle imbowers
> The Lady of Shalott.

The setting is dour and forbidding, like all prisons, but the prospect is surprisingly pleasant, and the bower itself secure if sequestered. The meditative passages of nineteenth-century novels are mostly set in boudoirs, or favourite withdrawing-rooms, though 'bowers' as humble as Mrs Boffin's, or as coyly domestic as Bella Wilfer's 'doll's house', or as functional as the wire enclosure James makes for the telegraphist of 'In the Cage', as diverse as Little Dorrit's prison, Lucy Snowe's convent, or Milly Theale's Venetian palace, vividly evoke the 'shut-in' life in its many aspects.

Feminist critics, following Erik Erikson's exposition of 'inner space' as the psycho-sexual determinant of women's social role, have annexed 'the room' as the centre-piece of a distinctively female iconography, the favourite symbol of a 'separatist literature' in refuge from 'the harsh realities and vicious practices of the male world'.[58] Women authors, it is often argued, use images of enclosure differently from male authors, to 'reflect the literal reality of their own confinement in the constraints they depict . . . secretly working through and within the conventions of literary texts to define their own lives'.[59] This kind of argument tends, furthermore, to see the room as 'negative space', darkened by anxieties about biological functions and domestic roles, rather than as the 'felicitous space' of mind or womb, source of creativity and fulfilment.[60]

Images of enclosure, however appropriately they come to evoke the situation of women in the nineteenth century, have a long and diverse history. Romanticism gives renewed currency to those images of gardens, islands, towers and prisons that make part of literature's general mythological store, and which are as often associated with freedom as with incarceration and withdrawal from the world. The caged birds of Mary Wollstonecraft, 'stalking with mock majesty from perch to perch', or of Shelley and the Brownings, of Dickens's Miss Flite, as well as the emblematic dove dear to Pre-Raphaelite painting, have their antecedents in the revolutionary iconography of eighteenth-century literature and painting, where the freed bird perched on its cage represents the triumph of liberty.[61] The prison that haunts Dickens's imagination – the Bastille, Newgate, the Marshalsea – is the source of regeneration, the liberating and redemption of a buried past.[62] Male writers and female writers undoubtedly experience 'imprisonment' in different ways, but to assert that it is a more 'real' experience in the nineteenth century for women than for men reflects a very partial reading of the many dimensions of imprisonment explored by the novels of the period. And the assertion that, whereas male writers grasp the 'epistemological' and 'political' aspects of imprisonment metaphors,[63] women writers speak through them of 'social and actual' pressures, makes for a sexism that does less than justice to some impressive women writers.

Feminist criticism has yet to give adequate attention to the question of how social or personal pressures might be detected in women's prose and poetry or distinguished from such pressures in the writing of men, or indeed, to whether such pressures are likely to manifest themselves as strength or as weakness in the writing. In discussing the work of Dickens, Hardy and James in subsequent chapters, I shall look closely at their tendency to idealise their heroines, and at its personal and social sources. They are demonstrably neither more nor less prone to such idealisation than their female contemporaries are, and neither more nor less enabled, in my view, by their not being women, to write movingly and with insight about women's lives. What is most significant about the Victorian novel's interest in the enclosed lady is, I think, what it suggests about the romanticism of the novel's concerns and its form.

'For all are caged birds; the only difference lies in the size of the cage', Hardy once wrote.[64] In its sustained exploration of the 'caged bird', *The Mayor of Casterbridge* challenges the view that the metaphor 'truly deserves the adjective "female" '.[65] Like many another Victorian novel, it is dense with images of the imprisoned lady and the defining room. And the genesis of the novel lies in an actual incident that lodges in Hardy's imagination – the selling of a wife at a rural fair. Henchard's disposal of his wife, like any chattel, nakedly exposes the materialist basis of the 'contract' that joins them, and the woman's dependence on her owner for her 'establishment', her status, her social authentication. But, in that very opening scene in which the sordid and drunken transaction takes place, the swallow that flits across the human drama, with Hardy's characteristic noticing of such things, to suggest the brief illusory freedom of all lives, images Henchard's fate as clearly as it images the fate of the women who depend on him. Elizabeth-Jane's successive 'rooms' define successive vantage-points on the world, and stages in her inward journeyings. For Lucetta, status and a sense of self are established by the purchase of her vantage-point overlooking the market. At the close of the novel, however, Henchard's gift for his daughter's marriage, the caged goldfinch that dies neglected in its cage, symbolises not so much the gilded cage in which the newly married Elizabeth Jane is to sing happily enough, but, more poignantly and finally, the lonely heath cottage where he is himself to find his end, as the impetuous, wasted energies of a nature chafing at its bounds at last extinguish themselves.

Like Victorian genre painting, Victorian novels delight in lovingly described domestic interiors.[66] George Eliot and Hardy emulate the honest 'realism' of Dutch painting, Henry James adapts 'the method of picture-making' and of many painters to his novelist's purpose, to catch 'the look of things', to arrest 'a moment of life in all its shimmering evanescence'.[67] As a young art-critic, however, he was critical of 'the story-telling quality which marks the maximum of much of the English art of today . . . the vulgarity of feeling which has prompted the painter to twist into a pictorial effect a subject altogether moral and dramatic'.[68] There are in the novels of George Eliot occasional passages, like the passage of *Middlemarch* discussed in Chapter 3, where enclosure is depicted with the soulful allegorising intent of genre painting. But there are also more dynamic and suggestive passages: Gwendolen Harleth's self-allegorising tableaux are viewed by an ironic, if kindly, eye. Mrs Transome, in *Felix Holt*, is held momentarily within a room that evokes, in its painterly detail, not only her situation and state of mind, but the novel's whole structure and meaning:

> Each time she returned to the same room: it was a moderate-sized comfortable room, with low ebony book-shelves round it, and it formed an anteroom to a large library, of which a glimpse could be seen through an open doorway, partly obstructed by a heavy tapestry curtain drawn on one side. There was a great deal of tarnished gilding and dinginess on the walls and furniture of this smaller room, but the pictures above the bookcases were all of a cheerful kind: portraits in pastel of pearly-skinned ladies with hair-powder, blue ribbons, and low bodices; a splendid portrait in oils of a Transome in the gorgeous dress of the Restoration; another of a Transome in his boyhood, with his hand on the neck of a small pony; and a large Flemish battlepiece, where war seemed only a picturesque blue-and-red accident in a vast sunny expanse of plain and sky. Probably such cheerful pictures had been chosen because this was Mrs Transome's usual sitting-room: it was certainly for this reason that, near the chair in which she seated herself each time she re-entered, there hung a picture of a youthful face which bore a strong resemblance to her own: a beardless but masculine face, with rich brown hair hanging low on the forehead, and undulating beside each cheek down to the loose white cravat. Near this same chair were her writing-table, with vellum-covered account-books on it, the cabinet in which she kept her neatly-arranged drugs, her basket for her embroidery, a folio volume of architectural engravings from which she took her embroidery patterns, a number of the *North Loamshire Herald*, and the cushion for her fat Blenheim, which was too old and sleepy to notice its mistress's restlessness. For, just now, Mrs Transome could not abridge the sunny tedium of the day by the feeble interest of her usual indoor occupations. Her consciousness was absorbed by memories and prospects, and except when she walked to the entrance-door to look out, she sat motionless with folded arms, involuntarily from time to time turning towards the portrait close by her, and as often, when its young brown eyes met hers, turning away again with self-checking resolution.

(pp. 87–8)

Mrs Transome is found here, at the outset of the novel, in the room that makes vivid both her ambition and the slowly destructive incarceration it entails. Two cycles of hopeful writing are now coming to an end. The faded splendours of the furnishings and the Transome portraits are all that remain of the youthful hopefulness with which she married herself to the Transome estate. Her restless wandering to the doorway expresses the hopefulness so passionately centred on the son returning after fifteen years. The image worshipped in this mother's private room is that picture of 'a youthful face which bore a strong resemblance to her own'. The hopes woven around him sustain her in that 'gentlewoman's lot' detailed in the embroidery, the engravings, the *North Loamshire Herald*, the Blenheim: 'for thirty years she had led the monotonous narrowing life which used to be the lot of our poorer gentry, who never went to town'. She is enclosed by a tedium as unchanging as that of Tennyson's Mariana, yearning for the love that remains beyond her grasp:

> She only said, 'My life is dreary,
> He cometh not', she said;
> She said, 'I am aweary, aweary,
> I would that I were dead!'

The husband whose name she desired has become a child-like old man. The beautiful boy returns as a plump politician of uncongenial views, to wage bitter dispute with lawyer Jermyn (whose son he discovers himself to be), a man whose middle-aged greed and vulgarity mock Mrs Transome's brief passionate attachment to him. Mrs Transome's emotional isolation is made visual in this moment, which foreshadows the development of her story as part of that larger development in which inevitable social change lays waste a valued past. The room enshrines both the woman's need to hold time still, and her experience of domesticity as monotonous and stifling. The framed generations of Transomes that line the walls, like the portraits of ladies in Dorothea Brooke's boudoir in *Middlemarch*, extend the visual irony evoked by the lady framed within her room: that the capturing of a moment in which time is held still also serves to chronicle time's passing. In choosing her room and her destiny, in becoming the lady of Transome Court, Mrs Transome has become transfixed, like Dorothea, or Isabel Archer, or Gwendolen Harleth, the portrait of a lady in whom unacknowledged or unappeased passions are to be slowly drained away. In the darkened rooms inhabited by Dickens's more eccentric ladies, divergent passions and strident will flourish unchallenged within their narrow confines. To be shut away from the world beyond the window is to be denied the fullest realisation of the self, but the state of enclosure fosters remarkable imaginative energies.

The room comes to represent, in Victorian novels, not only a moment in which the novel pauses to contemplate the enclosed figure and to see the world from that vantage-point, the study of a state of mind and the outline of a life. It comes to represent the very shape of novels themselves. Fiction is, for Henry James, not the 'narrow room' of Wordsworthian sonnet form, but a 'house', a spacious and ample structure put up to contain 'the posted presence of the watcher'.[69] The watcher is the creative consciousness at the heart of the novel, reflecting the creativity of the novel and the novelist. The image of enclosure recurs in James's notebooks and prefaces, in the 'loved threshold' or 'high chamber' from which, as he writes, he surveys the streets of London or Paris, and 'the light of achievement flashes over all the place, and I believe, I see, I do'.[70]

It is the picture of the enclosed figure of Isabel Archer that James takes as representative of the growth of a novel from its 'compositional centre'. Like the heroines of Turgenev, she hovers before him making

> the single small corner stone, the conception of a certain young lady affronting her destiny . . . all my outfit for the large building of *The Portrait of a Lady*. It came to be a square and spacious house – or has at least seemed so to me in this going over it again; but, such as it is, it had to be put up round my young woman while she stood there in perfect isolation.[71]

To call this the generating and imprisoning of the female within the text as patriarchal structure[72] is to obfuscate the point that any work of art is, in anyone's hands, a containment, a structure that holds pictures that are none the less potentially dynamic, and figures endowed with creative power. There must always be a circle, or frame, drawn around relationships and possibilities that, 'ideally', as James knew, 'stop nowhere'.[73]

Containment is as inherent in the novel's fable as in its texture of repeating scenes and the generic idea of the contained protagonist.

The plots of nineteenth-century novels repeatedly turn on the lady's choosing of her room and taking its dimensions. 'What will she do?' Ralph Touchett and Henry James ask of their pictured lady:

> Most women did with themselves nothing at all; they waited, in attitudes more or less gracefully passive, for a man to come that way and furnish them with a destiny. Isabel's originality was that she gave one the impression of having intentions of her own. (*The Portrait of a Lady*, p. 273)

Isabel's originality leads her to commit herself to Osmond's villa: 'it looked as if, once you were in it, it would take an act of energy to get out', she reflects, on first seeing it. The shape of Isabel's life and the shape of James's novel are implicit in that picture of a young lady shut in her room in Albany, from which 'she had no wish to look out'. This conception of a young lady affronting her destiny would take on a bitter irony were it not for the fact that she has, by the end of the novel, more fully taken the measure of the self and of its limiting habitation.

James is the most explicit of all nineteenth-century novelists about the genesis of his novels, not only reconstructing them *ex post facto* in the Prefaces, but also, as Ian Gregor has pointed out, building into their structures the ways in which they should be read.[74] Although the actual sequence and process of a novel's composition remains mysterious, it is possible, as James shows, to think about the generative intention of a work. Even before James develops so explicitly his theories of the organic nature of the novel's art, there are, in the novels that precede his, discernible 'small corner stones' shaping whole structures. In the following chapters, discussion will proceed by close analysis of moments and states of enclosure that hold implicit the shape and meaning of the novels in which they are set. The moment defined by the room may be contemplate, creative, self-realising, or that egoistic taking of the world as 'an udder to feed our supreme selves' observed by the wise narrator of *Middlemarch* (p. 225).[75] It may be a moment of soulful allegorising, in which the imaginative urgency of the work slackens, or, like the 'lyric moments' to which Lukács refers, it may release the spontaneous overflow of powerful feelings. At best, however, the moment is not one of subjection or passivity or idealisation, but control – a space and a moment in which the conditions of Isaiah Berlin's 'positive' sense of 'liberty' may be met:

The 'positive' sense of the word 'liberty' derives from the wish on the part of the individual to be his own master. I wish my life and decisions to depend on myself, not on external forces of whatever kind. I wish to be the instrument of my own, not of other men's acts of will. I wish to be a subject, not an object, to be moved by reasons, by conscious purposes, which are my own, not by causes which affect me, as it were, from outside. . . . I wish, above all, to be conscious of myself as a thinking, willing, active being bearing responsibility for my choices and able to explain them by references to my own ideas and purposes.[76]

This is the kind of freedom the 'imprisoned' heroines of Charlotte Brontë's and George Eliot's novels, the disillusioned Arthur Clennam of *Little Dorrit*, or Hardy's enigmatic and confused Sue Bridehead strive to find. It is what so many of James's protagonists, 'caught, caged or pinioned in situations that bring them to defeat, tragedy, or a liberating disillusionment' discover in their 'exclusion from experience': 'a capture of the trophy of the spirit's vitality and self-knowledge, "qualities making for life" '.[77]

For Pater, by the end of the century, 'the moment' caught from the flux of experience promises 'nothing but the highest quality of your moments as they pass', and 'the love of art for art's sake':

if we continue to dwell in thought on the world, not of objects in the solidity with which language invests them, but of impressions, unstable, flickering, incontinent, which burn and are extinguished with our consciousness of them, it contracts still further: – the whole range of observation is dwarfed into the narrow chamber of the individual mind. . . . Every one of those impressions is the impression of an individual in his isolation, each mind keeping as a solitary prisoner its own dream of a world.[78]

It is an image echoed in a comment of Virginia Woolf on Joyce's style which might apply equally well, at times, to her own. She writes of 'our sense of being in a bright yet narrow room, confined and shut in . . . centred in a self which . . . never embraces or creates what is outside it and beyond'.[79]

Robert Kiely in *The Romantic Novel* advances the view that for those novelists he takes to be 'romantic' – Walpole, Scott, Emily Brontë – the task of exploring 'spots of time' within 'a coherent, comprehensible and sustained narrative' entailed strategies like separating the central consciousness, by imprisonment, 'from society's reckoning of time' or creating 'an inset story that interrupts the chronology of the main narrative and creates a new temporal dimension'.[80] But it is surely the great Victorians who bring the 'romantic novel' into being, precisely because they are able to find 'equivalents of the sonnet or the ode' in the elaboration of moments of individual thought and feeling held within the limits defined by the narrative that contains them. By the time of Virginia Woolf, and following Pater, the individual moment has expanded to become the structure of the whole, if not its whole significance, and to have a very different value from the value it has for Dickens or George Eliot. This development of the novel's form is foreshadowed, and, I shall argue, resisted, by Henry James.

III THE MIRROR AND THE WEB

There she weaves, by night and day
A magic web with colours gay.

Within the imprisoning room made by the self, by individual visions and societal circumstances, there is a continuing 'task' or 'process' inseparable from, indeed enabled by, being enclosed. Charlotte Brontë's web is 'the homely web of truth' (*Villette*, p. 423). For George Eliot, the 'weaving work' of the imagination is a manifestation of that same web that makes 'the net-work of our subtlest nerves' (cf. p. 110). Hardy set himself to show the human race as 'one great network or tissue which quivers in every part when one point is shaken, like a spider's web if touched'; Henry James thought of himself as an embroiderer of the canvas of life': what a Jamesian character like Kate Croy sees and spins becomes 'a wondrous silken web' (*The Wings of the Dove*, p. 292). In the lady's picture of the world outside her window there is, for James and other nineteenth-century novelists, as for Tennyson, a manifestation of their own creative activity: 'till the world is an unpeopled void there will be an image in the mirror'.[81] Whether the Lady of Shalott's mirror is set behind the tapestry to show its effect from the right side,[82] or directly reflects the outside world which is to be recreated in the tapestry, the lady's picture of that world is at more than one remove, the shadow of a shadow.

> And moving through a mirror clear
> That hangs before her all the year
> Shadows of the world appear,
> There she sees the highway near
>   Winding down to Camelot.

Like images of enclosure, these images of creativity have a long history – one that goes at least as far back as Penelope's web or Plato's 'mirror'. During the nineteenth century their recurrence and co-presence as metaphors for the perceiving mind and the creative consciousness suggests a high degree of self-consciousness and even unease about the relationship between art and life, individual imagination and worlds that challenge and test its solipsistic tendencies. Characteristically, as in Tennyson's poem, the web does not replace the mirror: there is an attempt to relate and reconcile the two. The protagonist does not simply hold the mirror up to nature, or, like Locke's *tabula rasa*, simply accept impressions. What she sees takes the shape her perceiving consciousness weaves, leading at its extreme of self-enclosure to Tennyson's 'The Palace of Art' and at its height of imaginative richness to the later novels of Henry James. In *The Ambassadors*, for example, experience is reflected not directly but indirectly, through what Lambert Strether ('he a mirror verily of miraculous silver'[83]) makes of it. In 'The Lady of Shalott', the shattering of the mirror expresses the lady's direct confrontation of experience. There is an interaction between self and world in which the self alters, and is altered by, what is confronted for the first time. The self is not created anew, however, but destroyed. Lambert Strether's confrontation with the reality beyond his web alters, not destroys, the self – a characteristically Victorian adaptation of Tennyson's symbolic fable to be observed in most, though not all, of the protagonists discussed in succeeding chapters.

It is in *Middlemarch* that George Eliot speculates most directly and sustainedly on the significance (for that novel, and for her view of the novel as a form) of 'mirror' and 'web'. Her views are at least as likely to have been shaped by earlier creative writers – Wordsworth, Coleridge, Jane Austen – as by her philosophical reading. Nevertheless, a critique of Spinoza in the *Westminster Review* in 1843 by George Henry Lewes suggests a more precise source for the famous pier-glass metaphor in Chapter 27. In rejecting Spinoza's view of the mind as 'a mirror reflecting things as they are', Lewes quotes from Bacon's *Novum Organum*:

> There can be no doubt that – *as regards myself* – consciousness is
> the clear and articulate voice of truth; but it by no means follows,
> therefore, that – *as regards not-self* – consciousness is a perfect
> mirror reflecting what is, *as it is*. To suppose the mind such a
> mirror, is obviously to take a metaphor for a fact. 'The human
> understanding', as one of the greatest thinkers finely said, 'is like
> an *unequal* mirror to the rays of things, *which, mixing its own nature
> with the nature of things, distorts and perverts them.*'[84]

Put beside Wordsworth's 'What they half create / And what perceive'
(in 'Tintern Abbey'), and the poems that reflect that perception,
Bacon's view, with its emphasis on distortion and perversion, seems
crude indeed. Eliot is to make use of her eminent philosophers, but
to move beyond them:

> An eminent philosopher among my friends, who can dignify even
> your ugly furniture by lifting it into the serene light of science, has
> shown me this pregnant little fact. Your pier-glass, or extensive
> surface of polished steel made to be rubbed by a housemaid, will
> be minutely and multitudinously scratched in all directions; but
> place now against it a lighted candle as a centre of illumination,
> and lo! the scratches will seem to arrange themselves in a fine
> series of concentric circles round that little sun. It is demonstrable
> that the scratches go everywhere impartially, and it is only your
> candle which produces the flattering illusion of a concentric
> arrangement, its light falling with an exclusive optical selection.
> These things are a parable. The scratches are events, and the
> candle is the egoism of any person now absent – of Miss Vincy, for
> example. (*Middlemarch*, p. 281)

The pier-glass recalls Bacon's 'unequal mirror to the rays of things',
and within the mirror, 'mixing its own nature with the nature of
things', George Eliot locates the web, the 'concentric arrangements'
each mind makes for itself from those rays. These are the webs we
have seen the characters weaving, 'gossamer links' (p. 368) and
'masses of spider-web' (p. 661) by which they are themselves
entangled. It is the light the individual mind brings to bear on
reflected reality that transforms its actuality, its seeming randomness, into the 'flattering illusion' of order. In so far as the candle

represents 'ego', and Rosamond's ego in particular, the Baconian emphasis on distortion is not inapposite. But the parable reminds us as well of the imaginative and creative aspects of the mind's processes. The making of order is constructive and aesthetically pleasing: the web may entangle but it may also be a tapestry. An earlier passage of *Middlemarch* anticipates the problem of relating the webs the characters make to the larger web the novel itself creates:

> I have so much to do in unravelling certain human lots and seeing how they were woven and interwoven, that all the light I can command must be concentrated on this particular web, and not dispersed over that tempting range of relevancies called the universe. (p. 148)

For the narrator too, there is illumination, concentration, the making of a 'particular web'. But the novel is an 'unravelling', a seeing how the individual webs were woven and interwoven. This passage, like the pier-glass passage, not only sees the individual web, and a pattern in which the scratches seem to go everywhere, but also sees them as contained within the larger ordering vision. The ordering and arranging of experience is shared by the egoistic Rosamond and by the learned and contemplative narrator whose reflections over such a range of 'seeming relevancies' form so important a part of the novel's texture, and direct us to its significance. The creative self is this novel's, and, Eliot would suggest, any novel's, very subject.

Gwendolen Harleth, in *Daniel Deronda*, has something of the egoism of Rosamond (whose eyes swerve repeatedly to images of herself in the glass), and of Dorothea Brooke, whose moral idealism sees only 'the reflections she herself brought' (*Middlemarch*, p. 19). Gwendolen is presented, from the outset, as a consciousness more than usually dependent on the reflected sense of self she finds even in the anonymous eyes of Deronda. Always 'the princess in exile', her ambition is 'to do what is pleasant to herself in a striking manner: or rather, whatever she could do so as to strike others with admiration and get in that repeated way a more ardent sense of living' (*Daniel Deronda*, p. 26). Eliot, like Wollstonecraft, emphasises the connection between such reflected images and an imprisonment appeased only by the imposition of its will on the world it encounters. Gwendolen's life becomes literally a search for lodgings adequate to her reflected self (and, which will provide as well, perhaps the 'dear perpetual place' that might have nourished a more securely rooted self). The successive scenes in which she sees herself reflected, both literally and metaphorically, in charming settings, culminate in the rooms provided by her marriage to Henleigh Mallinger Grandcourt. Condemned to an endlessly repeating vista, she walks about 'like an imprisoned dumb creature, not recognizing herself in the glass panels, nor noting any object around her in the painted gilded prison':

> Gwendolen seemed at the end of nine or ten hours to have gone through a labyrinth of reflection, in which already the same succession of prospects had been repeated, the same fallacious outlets rejected, the same shrinking from the necessities of every course. (p. 453)

Cut off from the world by her very eminence, she achieves a moral isolation as complete 'as a man in a lighthouse' (p. 455). As the novel moves towards her final imprisonment on Grandcourt's yacht, the restless energies and unfulfilled needs and ambitions in her are compared with those of Deronda's mother, the princess, chafing still restlessly within the self-imposed prison of a destiny that commits her to a narrowing universe. The chapter that introduces the princess, as the Grandcourts are drifting on the Mediterranean, carries a distinctly Tennysonian epigraph:

> She held the spindle as she sat,
> Erinna with the thick-coiled mat
> Of raven hair and deepest agate eyes,
> Gazing with a sad surprise
> At surging visions of her destiny –
> To spin the byssus drearily
> In insect-labour, while the throng
> Of Gods and men wrought deeds that poets wrought in song.

For Gwendolen, however, as for the Lady of Shalott, a world beyond the reflected self, and the reflections made by that self, begins to impinge upon her as she sees, in the drowning Grandcourt, the mirror-like reflection of a dead face that has haunted her imagination. In George Eliot's fable, the cracking of the mirror entails not death, but a different kind of Victorian denouement. The impulses of Gwendolen's unpredictable, barely known self are suppressed, together with its myopic and destructive impulses. And with them are suppressed both the sombre atmosphere of gathering tragedy, and that brilliant, experimental writing that takes from Gwendolen's vivacity and rebelliousness a quality found nowhere else in Eliot. The assumption that the lady's 'ego' isolates her from the world beyond it in such a way that wholeness can only be found within its 'certain moral scheme' makes that defining circle of the nineteenth-century novel's achievement beyond which a writer like Lawrence was to move.

'It was George Eliot who started it all, for the novel . . . it was she who started putting all the action inside', Lawrence once said.[85] Henry James was further to develop Eliot's interest in the perceiving consciousness – to make it the very centre and medium of his later novels. He came to call such centres 'reflectors', or 'mirroring consciousnesses', 'that provision for interest which consists in placing advantageously, placing right in the middle of the light, the most polished of possible mirrors of the subject'.[86] He saw them as he saw novelists themselves, each set squarely in his house of fiction, each looking out from his window on 'the spreading field, the human scene', each receiving and creating 'an impression distinct from every other', a consciousness of 'at once . . . boundless freedom and . . . "moral" reference'.[87]

In the Preface to *The Portrait of a Lady*, James sees Isabel Archer's night-long vigil in her lonely room as a high point in his placing the very centre of the novel's action inside the reflecting consciousness:

> Reduced to its essence, it is but the vigil of searching criticism; but it throws the action further forward than twenty 'incidents' might have done. It was designed to have all the *vivacity of incident and all the economy of picture*. She sits up, by her dying fire, far into the night, under the spell of recognitions on which she finds the last sharpness suddenly writ. It is a representation simply of her motionlessly *seeing*, and an attempt withal to make the mere still lucidity of her act as 'interesting' as the surprise of a caravan or the identification of a pirate. It represents, for that matter, one of the identifications dear to the novelist, and even indispensable to him: but it all goes on without her being approached by another person and without her leaving her chair.[88]

Such identifications depend on the lady's being 'finely aware and richly responsive', as able to untangle as to weave her web, and to interpret its pictured reality. And Isabel, despite her capacity for self-deception, has remarkably fine and sharp responsiveness – intuiting the inner struggles of so composed a lady as Madam Merle, for example, in her weakness, 'as distinctly as if it had been reflected in a large clear glass' (*The Portrait of a Lady*, p. 602). The moment of her vigil is contemplative and creative. But the truth it recognises is the truth Isabel has helped to create: its 'recognitions' are circumscribed still by the perceiver's enclosing situation. Furthermore, James's novel, too, progressively retreats from the confident embracing of opening possibilities to the privacy of the self-sustaining consciousness.[89] As James moves the nineteenth-century novel further away from its rendering of the incidents and the many-stranded texture of social experience towards the interior drama of the consciousness, the relationship between the web woven by that consciousness and the web which is the novel, becomes more problematic.

A short story contemporaneous with the later novels, 'In the Cage', has, at its centre, one of the more striking of James's ladies of Shalott. 'The action of the drama', he explains, 'is simply the girl's "subjective" adventure – that of her quite definitely winged intelligence; just as the catastrophe, just as the solution, depends on her winged wit.'[90] The unnamed girl is given the opportunity to shape events without so much as stirring from her 'cage', the telegraphist's wire enclosure that sets the Jamesian consciousness at the heart of the turn-of-the-century communications system. In comparison with other Jamesian reflectors, this young lady is not particularly lucid or polished. The cage in which she must earn her living makes manifest the limited opportunities available to a girl of her social class. Reduced, with her family, from gentility to genteel poverty, she is cut off from the 'larger life' of the fashionable world, which offers her tantalising glimpses of freedom, luxury and mystery which 'beat every novel in the shop': 'It had occurred to her early that in her position – that of a young person spending, in framed and wired confinement, the life of a guinea-pig or a magpie – she should know a great many persons without their recognizing the acquaintance' ('In the Cage', p. 139). Deprivation brings envy, pettiness, the urge for a compensatory power, which she appeases by imposing her will in small ways on the genteel bringers of telegrams:

She had, at moments, in private, a triumphant, vicious feeling of mastery and power, a sense of having their silly, guilty secrets in her pocket, her small retentive brain, and thereby knowing so much more about them than they suspected or would care to think.   (p. 154)

And thus, James observes of this somewhat uncongenial centre of consciousness, 'she liked her torment'. Like her friend Mrs Jordan, who 'does the flowers' in the homes of the wealthy, 'the only member of her circle in whom she recognized an equal', she finds the intimations of high life a source of inexhaustible interest. Unlike Mrs Jordan, however, she is 'imaginative'. 'Combinations of flowers and greenstuffs forsooth! What *she* could handle freely, she said to herself, was combinations of men and women' (p. 143); 'she read into the immensity of their intercourse stories and meanings without end', 'everything might mean almost anything' (p. 155).

'Shadows of the world appear', and from within the safety of her cage, she has an artist's delight in making patterns, in ordering the myriad impressions, 'the flashes, the quick revivals'; 'what she did retain stood sharply out: she nipped and caught it, turned it over and interwove it' (p. 143). Immersed as we are in her consciousness from the start of the tale to its end, her limitations become the more clearly apparent – her absurd social pretensions, her small triumphs, her odd mixture of shrewdness and naïveté. To suggest that she is a comic parody of the artist is to put the point crudely, though her self-importance and her enthusiastic commitment to her fictional web are subject to a measure of self-aware irony. So proletarian and so limited a reflector provides a much more distant echo of the Jamesian creative consciousness than Lambert Strether. But she is an echo none the less, and there is in the tale too much delicate feeling for the bleakness of her impoverished life and the excitements of her imagined world for her to seem a comic or parodic figure.

As the tale develops, the world beyond the cage is to challenge her role of detached observer: 'her greatest comfort, on the whole, was her comparative vision of the men' (p. 155). She selects, from the general procession of lords and ladies, her own particular knight. Captain Everard, in his chivalric devotion to his lady's service, is to awaken in her an awareness of romantic and sexual possibilities in a world beyond the cage. Tennyson's fable suggests the imprisonment of the lady's sexuality, and the suppression of sexuality in society at large. In James's fable, the lady's indulgence of an obsession at once 'romantic' and prurient, 'knowing' and curiously innocent, with the clandestine affair between Captain Everard and Lady Bradeen makes a more suggestive comment still on the suppressed passions of Victorian society. Charlotte Brontë, Dickens, George Eliot, Hardy and James register, in the unawakened or unrecognised sexuality of their heroines a fundamental aspect of their self-enclosure. The tendency in Lucy Snowe, or Little Dorrit, or Dorothea Brooke, or Milly Theale, for example, to retreat from masculine challenges for which they imagine 'heroines' more vital or self-assured than themselves, is symptomatic. But the activity of the consciousness entails process, discovery, self-assertion. Over all the months during which James's young lady facilitates the telegraphed urgencies of meetings and partings and misunderstandings between the Captain and Lady Bradeen, 'the thing in all this she would have liked most to put to the test was the possibility of her having for him a personal identity that might in a particular way appeal' (p. 151). Putting to the test the power of her 'knowledge' decisively to influence the relationship between the Captain and his lady involves her in putting to the test her own relationship with the Captain and with the larger life beyond the cage.

For Todorov, it seems to follow from James's use of 'the indirect vision' that all we can see are the 'appearances' encompassed by that vision. Because James 'never gives a clear and full representation of the object of perception' 'the cause of all the characters' efforts' 'There is no truth, there is no certainty'.[91] And indeed it is the *donnée* of 'In the Cage' that beyond the limits of the lady's consciousness there beckons alluringly, in hints and guesses, a 'truth' her imagination cannot fully or accurately grasp. She perfectly well knows that the Captain and his lady exist in a world of 'not at all guessable thoughts' (which 'directly added to their splendour' – p. 180). She has a limited success in deploying the 'code' made available by their telegrams. She does, by her 'winged wit', and in a moment of high drama, help to avert some kind of catastrophe, after which it transpires that the shady relationship achieves respectability, enclosing the debonair Captain, with telling irony, squarely in the cage of matrimony. But, circumscribed by her cage, the girl sees only what she needs and is able to see. As in *Middlemarch*, attention is drawn to the fact that the imagination, however much or little narrowed by ego, does not deal in verifiable 'truths' and has power only to reflect on, not to alter, events.

To see the point of the tale as the mirroring of its own fictional status, however, is to see it as a rather sterile, if ingenious, exercise in self-consciousness. Beyond the limits reached by the developing consciousness of the protagonist there is created that web which is the object of perception of the tale itself – a delicate and finely observed study of class relationships.

At the climax of the tale, conjecture gives way to confrontation. The lady needs to test her vision in the world beyond the cage – a test not of its 'truth' but of its adequacy to the demands of that world. Inevitably, the 'personal identity' she discovers herself to have in relationship with Captain Everard is conditioned by her being in the cage. The large vows exchanged – 'I'd do anything for you', 'I'd find you anywhere' (pp. 194, 196) – take their meaning from, and are enabled by, the barriers so surely and economically drawn. It is a meeting that reveals enough of the Captain's character to establish that he is prepared, politely, and even with an ambiguous warmth, to meet the girl's sense of their relationship, and equally prepared, as he does at the end, to walk out of her life without a backward glance. (This, for the purposes of the tale, is the Captain's 'essence', and it is surely enough[92]). And her feeling for him depends absolutely, in fact, on his being the hero of popular romance. He recommends himself by what he doesn't do for her, rather than by what he might, threateningly and embarrassingly, seem about to do. When, tired and overwrought, she confesses her hunger to him, he is slow to suggest not that they might eat, but that she should, perhaps, 'take something': 'she had known he wouldn't say "Then sup with *me*!" but the proof of it made her feel as if she had feasted' (p. 189). When he returns, months later, in the grip of some nameless trouble, she alternates between hoping and fearing that he seeks a more tangible fulfilment of her promises than the efficient sending of messages: 'he practically proposed supper every time he looked at her' (p. 214). Hungers more profound and threatening than the hunger for food are hinted at, and she retreats from them even as she recognises their existence. 'To be in the cage had suddenly become her safety and she was literally afraid of the alternate self who might be waiting outside' (p. 213).

This is the 'truth' the tale embodies, and part of it, at least, is brought home to James's young lady by the collapse of Mrs Jordan's grandiose pretensions to knowledge of the fashionable world into no more than her own hints and guesses, and her dwindling into marriage with Mr Drake the butler:

What our heroine saw and felt for in the whole business was the vivid reflection of her own dreams and delusions and her own return to reality. Reality, for the poor things they were, could only be ugliness and obscurity, could never be the escape, the rise. (p. 236)

Even at the height of mysterious imagining, a shrewd grasp of social 'reality' joins with her timorously awakening sexuality to prevent the licensing of 'the alternate self'. She sees the inevitable fate of a girl of her class in relation to a Captain Everard as clearly as she sees, stretching ahead of her, an endless dreariness in Chalk Farm, as the wife of Mr Mudge the grocer. The self-delighting imagination must come to terms with the whole context of social relationships within which it is set. The lady's vision moves towards the tale's vision – a vision implicit in the *donnée* of the enclosed figure in the tale, and in the *donnée* of the nineteenth-century novel as a form.

IV THE CURSE

> She look'd down to Camelot.
> Out flew the web and floated wide;
> The mirror crack'd from side to side;
> 'The curse is come upon me', cried
> The Lady of Shalott.

There is an ambiguity about the curse: it lies in the lady's being unable to look out, and in her looking out. It comprehends the state of being cut off, by class or by sex or by sensibility, from the very world in which significance must be discovered, and ultimately, of being condemned by, and to, the irrevocable condition of mortality. It is the state of persons like Emma Bovary, in James's words, 'romantically determined',[93] destroyed by the failure of their imagined world to find any correspondence with a larger world, and the state of persons like Lambert Strether, endowed with a sensibility that would seem to condemn him to a vicarious life. It is the state not only of Tennyson's emblematic ladies, but also of Wordsworth's Margaret, who waits in vain for the return of her husband, as the sources of domestic comfort visibly decay around her and beyond her, in troubled and desolating times. It is the momentary state of every Victorian protagonist who pauses to experience the gratifications and limits of solipsism. It is the dilemma and tension of romantic imagination in the nineteenth century, the preoccupation of philosophers as of artists.

The stirrings of a restlessness that foreshadows the romantic tension are clearly registered in the novels of Jane Austen. As Emma looks out at Highbury, in Chapter 27 of *Emma*, noting the tedium of even its liveliest incidents, 'she knew she had no reason to complain, and was amused enough; quite enough still to stand at the door. A mind lively and at ease, can do with seeing nothing, and can see nothing that does not answer.' In *Emma*, lively imagination is not quite at ease in its confinement. But nor does there develop, in the novels of Jane Austen, the Victorian novelists' interest in indulging and celebrating individual sensibility in its self-enclosed and private moments. A century of feeling separates the delicately modulated ironies of Jane Austen from the energetic despair of Nietzsche's individualism:

> And do you know what 'the world' is to me? Shall I show it to you in my mirror? This world, a monster of energy, without beginning, without end; . . . a sea of forces flowing and rushing together, eternally changing, eternally flooding back . . . as a becoming that knows no satiety, no disgust, no weariness: this, my Dionysian world of the eternally self-creating, the eternally self-destroying, this mystery world of the twofold voluptuous delight, my 'beyond good and evil', without goal, unless the joy of the circle is itself a goal; without will, unless a ring feels good will towards itself. . . . *This world is the will to power* – and *nothing besides*! And you yourselves are also this will to power – and nothing besides![94]

Between the two lies the distinctively Victorian reconciliation of individual creative energy with a world whose stability and authenticity trembles, but still holds good. Victorian writers do not pursue the paradoxes and ironies inherent in romanticism to that brink of ontological chaos Nietzsche contemplates.

'Ein Roman ist ein romantisches Buch', Schlegel wrote. The appropriateness of his claim surely rests not, as he thought, in the novel's 'arbitrary mixture of all known literary genres', but in its engrossment with that irony he finds characteristic of romantic poetry. In Schlegel's view, romantic poetry, 'a mirror of the whole surrounding world . . . constantly reinforcing this reflection and multiplying it as in an unending series of mirrors', is characterised by an authorial consciousness simultaneously affirming and mocking its own creation.[95] This is the kind of emphasis that enables recent critics to see so many of the achievements of nineteenth-century literary art 'deconstructing' themselves. There is a significant difference between self-awareness, self-consciousness and 'mockery'. As the twentieth century progresses, however, and as Nietzsche envisaged, self-mockery becomes a prevailing tone. In Thomas Mann's Doctor Faustus, D. C. Meucke has suggested, the concept of romantic irony furnishes a *modus vivendi* for writing in the modern world:

> It recognized, to begin with, man's ironic predicament as a finite being, terrifyingly alone in an infinite and infinitely complex and contradictory world for which he and particularly the artist, the artist as God since there was no other, had nevertheless to accept responsibility and give it meaning and value. It went on to recognize that implicit even in the artist's awareness and acceptance of his limitations there lay the possibility, through the self-irony of art, of transcending his predicament, not actually yet intellectually and imaginatively.[96]

Whether Mann's novel transcends its predicament is open to question; arguably, its self-irony merely reflects unmitigated despair.[97]

The sense of consciousness as 'finite . . . in an infinite and infinitely complex and contradictory world' is diffused through German and English romanticism throughout the nineteenth century. It is the source, as Carlyle notes early on, of the individual's most urgent self-questioning and solitary contemplation:

> Man stands as in the centre of Nature; his fraction of Time encircled by Eternity, his hand breadth of Space encircled by Infinitude: how shall he forbear asking himself, What am I; and Whence; and Whither? How too, except in slight partial hints, in kind asseverations and assurances such as a mother quiets her fretfully inquisitive child with, shall he get an answer to such enquiries?[98]

These are the questions that torment Tolstoy's Levin, and Anna Karenina, at their most anguished: 'and in everything he sought a bearing on his questions: "What am I? Where am I? And why am I here?" ' And Anna, as the light is extinguished for her, utters the cry that has led her from the security of her comfortable establishment to the exposure of a world beyond the bounds of society as she knows it: 'Where am I? What am I doing? Why?' More than any English novel of the nineteenth century, *Anna Karenina* foreshadows the 'ontological chaos' that preoccupies twentieth-century writers. No Victorian heroine steps out of the enclosing room in the way Tolstoy's Anna does when she moves from her warm carriage (where she has been contemplating the illicit passions of 'romance' between the covers of a novel) to encounter Vronsky in the icy wind outside. She leaves her 'nice ordinary life', with its domestic predictability and security, and the conventional sense of self these have made for her. She enters the unknown and uncontrollable world inhabited by 'the alternate self', 'the possible self, not to be predicted', only glimpsed by James's telegraphist, or George Eliot's Gwendolen, and quite beyond the scope of Tennyson's Lady. For Levin, and at last, less than satisfactorily for Tolstoy's novel, some answer to the unanswerable questions is found in terms of Levin's accommodation to the 'ordinary life' of social relationships (see *Anna Karenina*, p. 853).

Like Tolstoy, Carlyle thought of society as the 'genial soil' that nourishes human life,[99] but as a soil that must in turn be fertilised by the insights of individual thought and feeling. For Matthew Arnold, at mid century, it is only through individual contemplation that the demands of the larger world will be met:

How does one get to feel much about any matter whatsoever? By dwelling upon it, by staying our thoughts upon it, by having it perpetually in our mind. The very words *mind, memory, remain,* come, probably, all from the same root, from the notion of staying, attending. Possibly even the word *man* comes from the same, so entirely does the idea of steadying oneself, concentrating oneself, making order in the chaos of one's impression, by attending to one impression rather than the other. The rules of conduct, of morality, were themselves, philosophers suppose, reached in this way; – the notion of a whole self as opposed to a partial self, a best self to an inferior self, to a momentary self a permanent self requiring the restraint of impulses a man would naturally have indulged; because – by *attending* to his life, man found it had a scope beyond the wants of the present moment.[100]

In the novels of his contemporaries, it is just such a 'whole self' that the momentary self pursues. It is by 'steadying', 'concentrating', 'making order' and, above all, 'requiring the restraint of impulses' that the romantic imagination finds congenial soil in Victorian society. The curse that imprisons the Lady of Shalott, glimpsed in Lucy Snowe's solitary self-enclosure, in Little Dorrit's imprisonment, in Dorothea's isolation from the world beyond her window, in Sue Bridehead's impenetrable privacy, in Milly Theale's 'never going down', is set within a confidently created social world that nourishes, and is nourished by, individual sensibility.

1 Sense and Sensibility: Lucy Snowe's Convent Thoughts

> Those who live in retirement, whose lives have fallen amid
> the seclusion of schools or of other walled-in and guarded
> dwellings, are liable to be suddenly and for a long while
> dropped out of the memory of their friends, the denizens of a
> freer world. Unaccountably, perhaps, and close upon some
> space of unusually frequent intercourse – some congeries of
> rather exciting little circumstances, whose natural sequel
> would rather seem to be the quickening than the suspension
> of communication – there falls a stilly pause, a wordless
> silence, a long blank of oblivion. Unbroken always is this
> blank; alike entire and unexplained. The letter, the
> message, once frequent, are cut off; the visit, formerly
> periodical, ceases to occur; the book, paper, or other token
> that indicated remembrance, comes no more.
>
> (Charlotte Brontë, *Villette*, p. 241)

Lucy Snowe's convent thoughts find her once again shut away from
the world, imprisoned as completely by the peculiarities of her own
sensibility, as by social circumstances. That her solitude has
profound psychological sources is evident in the way she retreats
even from the comfort of recognising what the passage
comprehends – that her imprisonment is both explicable and
temporary, the inevitable result of an occupation which cuts her off
from 'the denizens of a freer world' preoccupied, in turn, by their
own concerns. For Lucy, at this moment, her state is predestined
and inexplicable, 'a fiat of fate, a part of my life's lot, and – above
all – a matter about whose origin no question must ever be asked, for
whose painful sequence no murmur ever offered' (p. 243). It has no
foreseeable end.

44

Such moments of retreat into the isolated self recur in *Villette*, in Charlotte Brontë's other novels, and, though in varying tones, in novels throughout the nineteenth century. Sometimes, as here, the moment explores the view from the prison, revealing the protagonist only in what she sees. In other moments, the lady is, like George Eliot's Mrs Transome, both emblem and viewpoint, pictured in her tableau of imprisonment, her thoughts interwoven with the objects that surround her, making a web in which she becomes a visual centre. 'Picture me then', Lucy Snowe invites (p. 28), but her narrative characteristically directs attention to pictures of other ladies, especially to the emblematic ladies of social and artistic convention, to Polly, the Victorian Angel in the House, or Ginevra, the coquette, or the actress Vashti, or the 'Cleopatras' and 'Jeunes Filles' of the art gallery. Of Lucy herself we have only the most fleeting mirror-glimpses. Or we see her as she is reflected in the pictures others make of her, or catch impressions of her through the pictures she makes of others. Nevertheless, she is one of the most notable ladies of Shalott in fiction. She moves from one imprisoning circumstance to the next, weaving the web which is her narrative, reflecting within it that 'freer world' beyond her confines. The powers of the solitary imagination are as consolatory for Lucy as for Jane Eyre, for all Charlotte Brontë's protagonists, for Charlotte herself. If Lucy rails against her imprisonment, she is as often acquiescent: 'thinking meantime my own thoughts, living my own life, in my own still, shadow-world' (p. 146).

Clearly enough, the repetition in all Charlotte's novels of the moment of solitude, and of the pattern of retreat from and engagement with life that flows from it, has its source in her own experience. And, whereas Jane Eyre's solitude is finally dispelled by her marriage with Rochester, Lucy Snowe is promised no such happy ending. By 1852, while writing *Villette*, Charlotte Brontë had come to believe that for certain beings, suffering and solitude are preordained:

> The evils that now and then wring a groan from my heart – lie in position – not that I am a *single* woman, and likely to remain a single woman – but because I am a lonely woman and likely to be lonely. But it cannot be helped and therefore imperatively must be borne.[1]

The successive blows fate delivers Lucy in the course of the novel seem to record all too directly the blows by which Charlotte was bereft of those dearest to her. Her letters express a sense of her destiny in sentences that, like Lucy's, drive inexorably to conclusions of frustration and disappointment bravely endured. But, if the distinction between heroine and creator is sometimes blurred, and the autonomy of the novel's vision called in question, few nineteenth-century writers register with such inwardness (though the case of Dickens's Miss Wade in Chapter 2 will make an interesting comparison[2]) the anguish of a sensitive woman forced to find her own way in the world, without hope of emotional support or fulfilment.

Recent criticism has found it no less difficult to disentangle the Brontë novels from the Brontë legend than Henry James found it in 1905: 'the attendant image of their lives, their tragic history, their loneliness and poverty of life. That picture has been made to hang before us as insistently as the vividest page of *Jane Eyre* or *Wuthering Heights*.'[3] More completely than any other English novelists, the Brontës themselves lived out the myth of the Lady of Shalott, writing of the social isolation that nourished their own creative energies. If they 'domesticated' the Gothic elements of their literary inheritance, it was as much because they encountered them in life, as in art. Branwell Brontë (or the Reverend Patrick, in some moods) is as credibly the source for a Rochester or a Heathcliff as anything in Byron, or in the Angrian 'web of childhood' they themselves composed.[4] The setting of *Villette* in the strange land of Labassecour, the convent and its legends, have their origin not in Gothic romance but in Charlotte Brontë's own sojourn in Brussels. Her life and letters remind us of what a reading of Foucault's account of eighteenth-century disorders of the nerves,[5] or Mary Wollstonecraft's account of women's 'sensibility' or the opium experiences of de Quincey or Coleridge suggest – that the age produced a 'Gothic' sensibility quite as distinctive, and persistent, as the stylised representations of sensibility between the covers of the romances. 'If my master withdraws his friendship from me entirely I shall be altogether without hope',[6] Charlotte Brontë wrote to Mr Héger in 1845. 'If I cannot be with you I shall die',[7] George Eliot wrote to Herbert Spencer in 1852. George Eliot, interestingly enough, found *Villette* 'a still more wonderful book than *Jane Eyre*. There is something almost preternatural in its power.'[8] Charlotte Brontë's exploration of heightened emotional states entails a self-indulgence in the prose and a certain contrivance in the plot, as well as 'wonder' and 'power', but it does indeed open up for the English novel the 'private' realm of the suffering self.

Early in *Villette*, there is a story within Lucy's story – a version of the Lady of Shalott fable that draws attention to conventionally romantic aspects of the novel's larger fable. Miss Marchmont, the recluse who provides Lucy with a home and occupation after she is cast adrift in the world, also provides an exemplum of unfulfilled love and neurotic self-enclosure. The lover for whom Miss Marchmont has waited, as a young and hopeful girl one Christmas Eve, falls from his horse and dies in her arms. Now she waits still, as she tells Lucy, 'a woe-struck and selfish woman', confined to her room and dwelling on memory, for the death that will reunite them. Miss Marchmont's story, like the legend of the nun whose ghost is said to haunt the Villette convent, prefigures the essential elements of Lucy's story: a retreat from the world, a suppression of painful feeling, a blighting of hope and love, a lingering neurosis. Lucy's readiness to identify with Miss Marchmont grows daily:

> a crippled old woman my mistress, my friend, my all. Her service was my duty – her pain, my suffering – her relief, my hope – her anger, my punishment – her regard, my reward. I forgot that there were fields, woods, rivers, seas, an ever-changing sky outside the steam-dimmed lattice of this sick-chamber.   (p. 30)

It is a relationship, and a state of being, that echoes Miss Marchmont's relationship with her doomed lover, the commitment to an ideal of devotedness that destroys the selfhood. In the first of many moments of solitary self-analysis, Lucy looks inward to discover and assert a self that will lead her out into the world beyond her narrow room. Despite the reflected self the mirror shows, she is conscious of promptings that will dispel the numbing effect of self-enclosure: 'I saw myself in the glass, in my mourning dress, a faded, hollow-eyed vision. Yet I thought little of the wan spectacle. The blight, I believed, was chiefly external: I still felt life at life's sources' (p. 29). This confidence and energy distinguishes Lucy from the emblematic ladies of romantic fable, giving her a decisive, individual voice, and the courage to venture out in search of an independent life. She resists the drift into resignation and retreat, braving the vastness of London and crossing the Channel to make a new life for herself in a strange land. In Lucy's repeated, resolute movement out of solipsism, Charlotte, like her heroine, resists the romantic self-indulgence inherent in Miss Marchmont's fate. Nevertheless, Miss Marchmont's story retains an indisputable fascination for her. Charlotte's temptation to see Lucy, too, as Lady of Shalott, is what inspires and necessitates the novel's searching critique of its own fable. The novel pauses again and again to present and explore an imprisoned Lucy, but the coda to Lucy's steady progress out of solitude into action and relationship is a return to her most stoic and despairing note of self-enclosure. Each of the novels to be discussed in succeeding chapters is similarly intermittent and uncertain in its appraisal of the romantic fable at its heart. This is the tension and the dilemma represented in the myth of the Lady of Shalott: the creative consciousness is constrained by the law of romantic irony, to mirror itself in a continuous process of critique and affirmation. Or, to recall the finer emphasis of Wallace Stevens, to make 'The poem of the mind in the act of finding/What will suffice' ('Of Modern Poetry').[9]

George Eliot thought of her novels as 'a set of experiments in life – an endeavour to see what our thought and emotion may be capable of'.[10] Lawrence wrote memorably, 'one sheds one's sicknesses in books – repeats and presents again one's emotions, to be master of them'.[11] *Villette* is highly self-conscious about the sickness at its heart, and 'sickness' is not too strong a word for the crisis of sensibility that brings Lucy, in her convent, to that point of breakdown where all ties with the real world are cut. In her letters, as well as in the novel, Charlotte Brontë underlines an intended detachment from her 'cold' and 'morbid' heroine: 'I am not leniently disposed to Miss *Frost*',[12] the name Frost being chosen, initially, because of the need for 'a cold name'. If the savagery with which Lucy is treated (and treats herself), suggest self-identification rather than detachment at times, it remains true that, through Lucy, Charlotte explores not only the disabling qualities of her own sensibility, but its creative powers as well. The alternations between 'cold Lucy' and 'the distraught governess' that puzzle some readers,[13] between the public and private selves, are part of the very texture and purpose of the novel. But to distinguish the novel's strengths from its weaknesses, the controlled writer from the self-identifying, intensely reverberating, confessional 'I', requires a continuous effort of discrimination. 'I still felt life at life's sources.' It is not only the resoluteness in that conviction, but also the confident offering, and searching out, of deeper sources of feeling in the individual sensibility that makes the distinctive interest of Lucy

Snowe, and of Charlotte Brontë's writing. The Brontë novels were going 'a stratum deeper' well before Lawrence, if not quite so far. In this area of experience, Charlotte Brontë found the writing of her great predecessor notably lacking: 'What throbs fast and full, though hidden, what the blood rushes through, what is the unseen seat of life and the sentient target of death – this Miss Austen ignores.'[14] Comparison is as interesting as the familiar contrast, however, and it is worth a short digression to consider the different contributions made by each of these novelists, the one Augustan–Romantic and the other a romantic Victorian, to the on-going debate between 'sense' and 'sensibility'.

Jane Austen, a 'single' woman, though not, it would seem, a 'lonely' or a dependent one, writes nevertheless of a society in which economic circumstances are powerful determinants in the life of women. The opening of *Sense and Sensibility* makes the situation of the Dashwood girls quite clear: they must marry, and marry well, if their futures are to be happy. But in addition their survival depends on qualities of character – as much on the capacity for warm and generous feeling, as on the judicious control of feeling. In the sequestered pockets of social life in which, as for so many girls their lot is cast, it is only through such inner resources that they will be enabled to find their place in society, and to endure the tedium, insensitivity, and pettiness of the milieu in which they find themselves. Jane Austen's early heroines, as D. W. Harding pointed out,[15] characteristically endure their social lives as their creator must have done, 'regulating' their intensities of feeling. Their heroism lies in their having more control, more intelligence, more self-awareness, more capacity to bear their burden and deal with it in private, than seems called for in those around them. Lucy Steele's friendly persecution of Elinor Dashwood with the details of her secret engagement to Elinor's much-loved Edward is so blatant as to call to mind Ginevra Fanshawe's callous taunting of Lucy Snowe for her lack of beauty and prospects. There is more than a hint, on such occasions, in both Jane Austen's and Charlotte Brontë's writing, of an intensity of authorial feeling finding an element of relief in dramatisation. Intense feeling requires a measure of containment.

Among the many shifts in meaning of the word 'sensibility'[16] is the shift that enables T. S. Eliot, for example, in discussing its

nineteenth-century 'dissociation', to denote the general responsiveness and disposition of the culture of an age, and enables in modern
usage generally the notion of sensibility as the thinking–feeling
capacities and dispositions of individuals. In referring to Lucy
Snowe's 'sensibility' I have contemporary usage in mind, while
retaining, necessarily, something of the emphasis made in the
central popular meaning – 'a more than ordinary degree of responsiveness or reaction'.[17] This is the emphasis that writers like
Johnson and Fanny Burney and even Mrs Radcliffe make in the use
of adjectives like 'wayward' or 'heightened' or 'excessive'. And, side
by side with novels that celebrate 'sensibility', and often within the
same works, there develops a censorious belief that sensibility and
what Dr Johnson in *Rasselas* describes as the 'hunger of imagination
which preys incessantly on life'[18] must be checked by reason,
judgement and good sense. Lucy Snowe's internal debate on the
rival claims of 'reason' and 'fancy', although it differs in important
respects from Jane Austen's debate in *Sense and Sensibility* some forty
years earlier, reflects similar impulses, a not dissimilar literary
education,[19] and certain similarities in social position and
temperament.

In Jane Austen's novels, however, sensibility is kept firmly in
check. Moments of solitary self-enclosure are few. Certainly
Marianne Dashwood retreats to her chamber, like Miss
Marchmont, following her disappointment in love, and Jane
Austen is far from underestimating the emotional sources of her
debilitating illness. Yet the private feelings are endured rather than
explored. Or they erupt only in lyric attitudinising that provides
easy targets for deflation, as in Marianne's account of solitary
moments among autumnal leaves:

> 'Oh!' cried Marianne, 'with what transporting sensations have
> I formerly seen them fall! How have I delighted, as I walked, to
> see them driven in showers about me by the wind! What feelings
> have they, the season, the air altogether inspired! Now there is no
> one to regard them. They are seen only as a nuisance, swept
> hastily off, and driven as much as possible from sight!'
> 'It is not everyone', said Elinor, 'who has your passion for dead
> leaves.'   (*Sense and Sensibility*, p. 80)

The yoking together of Marianne's romantic impulses with conventional notions of the picturesque, the rhapsodic tone and language,

and the dryness of Elinor's nicely paced rejoinder make the simpler intent of the novel's dialectic perfectly plain. Jane Austen's view of Marianne's 'sensibility' is in fact more complex than passages like this suggest. For one thing, Marianne has a refreshing capacity to speak her mind on occasions when the sensible Elinor is unbearably tactful and even dissembling. And, for another, Marianne's feeling is not always in excess of the object, or self-preoccupied, as her tenderness for her mother and sister, and her quick sensitivity to others, indicates. But, if the novel as a whole calls in question a too simple opposition between 'sense' and 'sensibility', the very need to weigh those abstractions and those personalities suggests the potential interest in and perhaps the threat of a sensibility like Marianne's to the stability of Jane Austen's writing in this period of her development. *Sense and Sensibility* is clearly most at ease with Elinor's 'sense'. Her feelings for Edward are shaped by, and expressed in terms of, what is socially correct; her grief at news of his engagement to Lucy Steele is silently borne:

> Without shutting herself up from her family, or leaving the house in determined solitude to avoid them, or laying awake the whole night to indulge meditation, Elinor found every day afforded her leisure enough to think of Edward, and of Edward's behaviour, in every possible variety which the different state of her spirits at different times could produce; – with tenderness, pity, appro-bation, censure and doubt. There were moments in abundance, when, if not by the absence of her mother and sisters, at least by the nature of their employments, conversation was forbidden among them, and every effort of solitude was produced. Her mind was inevitably at liberty; her thoughts could not be chained elsewhere; and the past and the future, on a subject so interesting, must be before her, must force her attention, and engross her memory, her reflection, and her fancy.   (p. 95)

As Marianne reflects, 'her self-command is invariable. When is she dejected or melancholy? When does she try to avoid society, or appear restless and dissatisfied in it?' (p. 30). A hint of sententious-ness in the passage commends Elinor's fortitude, and parallels a pointing the moral in Marianne's loss of self-command. Elinor's moment of rapture when Edward at last and unexpectedly becomes hers is, like Emma Woodhouse's similar moment, off-stage. Her burst of seemingly unquenchable tears might just perhaps be

overheard, but the question 'How are *her* feelings to be described?'
returns the answer that 'it required several hours to give sedateness
to her spirits, or any degree of tranquillity to her heart' (p. 353).
These are the hours that remain private. It is not simply that Elinor,
or any of Jane Austen's capable heroines, cannot find the time and
space 'to indulge meditation', interminable though the presence of
other people always seems. It is that she not only accommodates to
society, but that her 'sensibility' embodies society's best values:
control, decorum, restraint, 'elegance of mind'. Passages that find
Fanny Price in the East room of Mansfield Park or Anne Elliot in
Persuasion 'tranquillising' themselves and subduing agitation,
record inner lives as achieved self-mastery, not as a chaos of
ungovernable feelings. There is no doubt that Elinor's mind is
intensely active, observing and ordering her experience, forming
conclusions that affect her behaviour. She has evidently spun a web
of hopeful and 'engrossing' thoughts about her future. But she feels
free to let her thoughts range only when her attention is not required
elsewhere, and certainly not to the point of obsessiveness, sleepless-
ness, or any kind of unsociableness. And they occupy little of the
novel's space. Marianne's web of hopeful dreams is no more
available to us than is Elinor's, but its effects indicate Jane Austen's
retreat from the more private areas and processes of the personality.
In Marianne's projection of that web, as in the delusive and self-
gratifying fancies of Emma Woodhouse, directions are taken in
which the individual sensibility finds itself at odds with what is
acceptable and with what, in terms of the Jane Austen world, is
actually the case. Necessary social bearings are lost in unpredictable
and uncontrollable impulses from within the centre of self.

In the novels of Charlotte Brontë, such impulses are 'indulged' and,
at best, explored. In Lucy Snowe's moments of solitude, in her
irremediable loneliness, is expressed that shift in the perspective of
the nineteenth-century novel that is the romantic 'curse'. A world is
unfolded in which the protagonist's estrangement from society is a
necessary condition of life. Lucy alternates between deliberate
avoidance of society and something like Dorothea Brooke's effort, in
which 'connection' with it must be 'painfully kept up'. And,
although Charlotte Brontë frequently disapproves of the impulses
springing from 'sensibility', her urge to reconcile them with 'sense'

and with the exigencies of social life reflects the very dislocation
between self and world explored in her protagonist's experience. If
Jane Austen's heroines embody the social and moral values their
creator most admired, and dramatise their continuing relevance
and power, Charlotte Brontë's heroines display their creator's high
valuing of 'imagination', that 'strong restless faculty that demands
to be heard and exercised'.[20] The social disorder entailed in
'indulging meditation' yields new modes of order and insight. The
enclosed, contemplative protagonists of nineteenth-century novels
discover something of the novelists' capacity to make, from
reflections in the mirror of consciousness, an 'order' that is
distinctively their own. But, whereas in *Bleak House*, for example,
Dickens sets Esther Summerson's first-person narrative, her innermost thoughts and feelings, in the larger context of the novel's
narrative, the interior life of Charlotte Brontë's protagonists seems
to occupy the whole space of her novels. Critics continue to find no
distinction between Jane Eyre's web, or Lucy Snowe's, and the
vision of the novel that contains it.[21] The case is repeatedly made
that Brontë's heroines have in fact no properly realised social
dimension, but exist largely as the wish-fulfilling fantasies of their
creator.

Discussion of what, if any, social dimension Lucy Snowe has, and
the related question of how adequately *Villette* realises a sense of
social life either through Lucy's perspective or beyond it, may
usefully begin by noting Terry Eagleton's Marxist reading,[22] Kate
Millett's feminist reading,[23] and Mary Jacobus's structuralist
reading.[24] For Eagleton, Lucy Snowe provides an example of what
he takes to be the Brontë 'myth of power', in which an oppressed
and isolated, yet powerful, romantic ego asserts itself in the struggle
for bourgeois security:

At the centre of Charlotte Brontë's novels, I am arguing, is a
figure who either lacks or deliberately cuts the bonds of kinship.
This leaves the self a free, blank, 'pre-social' atom: free to be
injured and exploited, but free also to progress, move through the
class structure, choose and forge relationships, strenuously utilize
its talents in scorn of autocracy and paternalism. The novels are
deeply informed by this bourgeois ethic, but there is more to be
said than that. For the social status finally achieved by the
déraciné self is at once meritoriously won and inherently
proper.[25]

For Millett, Lucy's progress exemplifies the ambition of 'every conscious young woman'. Millett sees her goal not as the bourgeois social status Eagleton postulates, but as the achievement of 'individualist humanity'. '*Villette* reads like one long meditation on a prison break', but at the last 'Lucy is free. Free is alone.'[26]

The novel has no such simple notion of 'freedom', however, and no such notion, therefore, of its being Lucy's motivation or goal. The opening section of *Villette*, the three chapters dealing with her childhood at Bretton, establish tone and texture precisely. 'One child in a household of grown people is usually made very much of, and in a quiet way I was a good deal taken notice of by Mrs Bretton' (p. 1). Displaced in the notice of Mrs Bretton (and, more important, of her son John Graham) by the arrival of Polly, a younger and more winning child, Lucy experiences the feelings of any sibling. She watches the childish games between Polly and John Graham with the shrewd eye of jealousy, and sees defined for herself the role that is hereafter to become her 'defence', that of 'life's onlooker'. Her resentment, not overtly stated, is none the less apparent: Lucy is as capable of witholding her feelings as of luxuriating in them. But the novel is not, I think, 'silent about the true nature and origin of Lucy's oppression' in the way Mary Jacobus finds it to be: 'the novel's real oddity', she writes, 'lies in its perversely witholding its true subject, Lucy Snowe, by an act of repression which mimics hers'.[27] What is being unfolded in *Villette* is the culmination of Charlotte Brontë's developing art of autobiographical narration. There is present from the beginning a shrewder eye on Lucy than Lucy's own. If the world as it moves through the mirror of Lucy's self-enclosed, fallible and often deliberately deceptive vision is a shadowy one, that is because it reflects Lucy in what she sees. But there is, demonstrably, an autonomous Lucy revealing herself to us in the way Charlotte Brontë admired in the writing of Balzac, by 'the subtle perceptions and the most obscure and secret workings of the mind'.[28] What she sees, and what she withholds, reflect her own deepest needs, needs the novel grasps clearly from the outset. Lucy's alternation between retreating from life and reaching out for it, her steady progress in search not of social status or independence, but of emotional commitment and sexual fulfilment, expresses Charlotte Brontë's conception of Lucy's desperate need to be loved and to belong. The long stay at Bretton fosters her need for loving, stable relationship; the unnamable disaster by which her own family is lost to her and which her godmother has seen shaping, buries that need deep within the psyche:

> It will be conjectured that I was of course glad to return to the bosom of my kindred. Well! the amiable conjecture does no harm, and may therefore be safely left uncontradicted. Far from saying nay, indeed, I will permit the reader to picture me, for the next eight years, as a bark slumbering through halcyon weather, in a harbour still as glass – the steersman stretched on the little deck, his face up to heaven, his eyes closed: buried, if you will, in a long prayer. A great many women and girls are supposed to pass their lives something in that fashion; why not I with the rest?
>
> (p. 28)

The sources of Lucy's depression are here. Unable to confront the pain of that 'shipwreck', in which 'all hope that we should be saved was taken away' she retreats even from articulate narration. The lurid metaphors of rushing briny waves, of sunless and starless days and nights, of battling against tempest, elaborate the conventional romantic landscape that characterises Lucy's most intense moments. Unlike the comparable passage at the end of the novel, however, Lucy's retreat into the suffering self is here registered as the indulgence and elaboration of 'sensibility'; it brings Lucy no strength or insight; its stoic 'self-sufficiency' barely disguises her longing to belong to the happy world held at arm's length by caricature. The tone is that of Lucy's convent thoughts; the assumption that life beyond her own pain is uniformly blissful is a measure of her self-enclosure. It is the bitterness not of a 'pre-social atom', but of one who loves to be 'with the rest'.

Lucy's 'curse' is not, then, the mysteriously ordained 'fiat of fate' for which she, and Terry Eagleton, take it. In so far as it is a *donnée* of the novel, it demonstrates not a denial of the social dimensions of personality, but the opportunity to explore them more fully. And so the novel juxtaposes Lucy's moments of solitary self-enclosure against a pattern of events that forces her engagement with life. A discussion of four such representative moments will suggest Charlotte Brontë's distinctive interest in *Villette*, in the nature of the individual sensibility, and in its relationship with the world on which it feeds.

In Chapter 11, 'The Casket', the novel pauses to contemplate Lucy's reverie as she seeks out the solitude of her favourite retreat,

'l'allée défendue' in the convent garden. This garden setting – a
retreat within a retreat within the convent – is as suggestive as any
domestic interior in its evocation of Lucy's 'imprisonment':

> I was sitting on the hidden seat reclaimed from fungi and mould,
> listening to what seemed the far-off sounds of the city. Far off, in
> truth, they were not: this school was in the city's centre; hence, it
> was but five minutes' walk to the park, scarce ten to buildings of
> palatial splendour. Quite near were wide streets brightly lit,
> teeming at this moment with life: carriages were rolling through
> them to balls or to the opera. The same hour which tolled curfew
> for our convent, which extinguished each lamp, and dropped the
> curtain round each couch, rang for the gay city about us the
> summons in festal enjoyment. Of this contrast I thought not,
> however: gay instincts my nature had few; ball or opera I had
> never seen; and though often I had heard them described, and
> even wished to see them, it was not the wish of one who hopes to
> partake of pleasure if she could only reach it – who feels fitted to
> shine in some bright distant sphere, could she but thither win her
> way; it was no yearning to attain, no hunger to taste; only the
> calm desire to look on a new thing.
>
> A moon was in the sky, not a full moon, but a young crescent. I
> saw her through a space in the boughs overhead. She and the
> stars, visible beside her, were no strangers where all else was
> strange: my childhood knew them. I had seen that golden sign
> with the dark globe in its curve leaning back on azure, beside an
> old thorn at the top of an old field, in Old England, in long past
> days, just as it now leaned back beside a stately spire in this
> continental capital.
>
> Oh, my childhood! I had feelings: passive as I lived, little as I
> spoke, cold as I looked, when I thought of past days, I *could* feel.
> About the present, it was better to be stoical; about the future –
> such a future as mine – to be dead. And in catalepsy and a dead
> trance, I studiously held the quick of my nature.   (p. 95)

'I studiously held the quick of my nature.' For Lucy, this is a
moment of solitude in which the last of the evening is to be savoured,
a secret place of the self enabling the release of feeling. But the
passage is not just lyric utterance. There is an attempt, as in other
such passages, to answer Ginevra Fanshawe's question, 'Who *are*
you, Miss Snowe?' (p. 280), both in terms of Lucy's understanding

and in terms of the novel's exploration of her distinctive sensibility. Lucy's reverie is in fact a dramatic monologue – more than a shade self-pitying, and totally self-absorbed. Like the other seemingly stock romantic elements in this chapter, however – the moon, the garden, the legend of the nun, the creaking casement that opens suddenly to drop a casket at her feet, containing a *billet-doux* – the reverie is part of Charlotte Brontë's exploration of romantic sensibility. In tone and detail it makes interesting comparison with the near-contemporary Pre-Raphaelite painting of Charles Allston Collins, *Convent Thoughts*. The detailed recording of plants (praised by Ruskin), the wistfully contemplative lady in her nun's garb, surrounded by a high wall, the evocation of a vicarious life in the book she holds and in the pool's reflections, are all elements of Charlotte's picture too. That picture frames Lucy for our contemplation. Unlike Collins's picture, however, Charlotte's is the occasion for penetrating beyond the stasis and surface of allegory. It is framed as such moments in Victorian novels characteristically are, poised between the indulgence of feeling and the attempt to evaluate it, between 'affirmation' and 'critique'. It seeks to reconcile that larger perspective on Lucy with the perspective she herself offers, by which the novel is shaped.

Lucy thinks of herself as one who repudiates the exciting, unknown, busy world beyond the convent walls, and who discovers compensatory gratifications in solitary imagining:

> I seemed to hold two lives – the life of thought, and that of reality; and provided the former was nourished with a sufficiency of the strange necromantic joys of fancy, the privilege of the latter might remain limited to daily bread, hourly work, and a roof of shelter. (p. 66)

For the life of reality she cultivates a 'passive', 'cold', serviceable identity. She follows the dictates of 'Reason' in her own behaviour, exemplifying 'the very pink and pattern of governess correctness', and preaches them to others – to Ginevra, or, on occasion, to Polly. And yet her good sense cannot constrain the intensities of fancy and feeling that seek outlet in the privacy of her 'life of thought'. Like the Lady of Shalott, her curse is twofold: in the circumstances that shut her away from the world, and in the quiescence with which she accepts her imprisonment, transforming it by the delights of her imagination.

'Of an artistic temperament, I deny that I am; yet I must possess something of the artist's faculty of making the most of my present pleasure', Lucy declares early on (p. 51). She describes her garden retreat in profuse detail: 'the perfumed snow' and 'honey-sweet pendants' of the pear tree, the 'verdant' turf and 'sun-bright clusters of nasturtiums', the vines gathering their tendrils in 'a knot of beauty', which 'hung their clusters in loving profusion about the favoured spot where jasmine and ivy met and married them' (p. 93). The effect, as in Collins's painting, is of nature decoratively composed: the diction reflects currents of sensuousness and emotionalism that make part of her 'present pleasure'. The clustering and gathering, the physicality of pears and tendrils, the 'loving profusion' and meeting and marrying brings to the surface feelings and needs of which Lucy's conscious, articulate self is barely aware, but of which the passage takes account. Lucy's 'picture' of nature reflects the self that composes it. Literary and sentimental recollection shapes the world Lucy contemplates. The very sweetness of the garden at evening prompts the picture of moonlit 'Old England' which is superimposed on it.

Lucy's fancy is of a stock romantic variety here, but made interesting by what it reveals of Lucy. Even when she breaks into her Wordsworthian rhapsody – 'Oh my childhood! I had feelings' – her romanticism is not parodied, however. Lucy in this vein is taken seriously as Marianne Dashwood can never be, because the exercise of her fancy directs attention beyond the conventional, to aspects of Lucy's self that exact respect. For Lucy (as for the Wordsworth of the 'Immortality' Ode), this passage suggests, wholeness of self depends on acknowledgement of the individual's needs for love and for belonging, and for the assurance of a continuity between past and present.

The suppression of those needs is the point, after all, of the somewhat laboured irony that spells out the equivocal nature of Lucy's repudiation of the outside world. Her evocation of it 'teeming with life', sending out its 'summons in festal enjoyment', her protest that she doesn't wish for it, or think of the 'contrast' it makes with her own dull life, convey the yearning she denies. It is in the act of withholding herself that Lucy is revealed.

A more subtle and witty comment on Lucy's self-enclosure is made by the novel's 'new Gothic'[29] use of the legendary nun. Lucy is conscious, within her garden, of the legend that beneath it lie 'the bones of a girl whom a monkish conclave of the drear middle ages had here buried alive for some sin against her vow' (p. 93). Lucy's grey-clad figure is to haunt 'l'allée défendue' (out of bounds for Mme Becke's pupils), like the nun of the legend. It is here that she is to come, and to bury forever, with his letters. her love for Dr John. But a 'realist' reading of the novel does not need to relegate the nun to 'Gothic machinery', as Jacobus argues, nor to see the later 'appearances' of the nun as 'that phantom or psychic reality which representation represses'.[30] The nun's story, like Miss Marchmont's, is another version of the Lady of Shalott fable, against which Lucy's story is to define itself. In so far as Lucy represses her own sexuality and feels excluded from a world that might gratify her social needs, the novel suggests a clear resemblance between Lucy and the stereotype of romance. The extreme point of that burial of the self is marked by her fear that the 'phantom' nun is a supernatural visitation. The nun Lucy sees, however, is no 'psychic reality', but a practical joke which has the healthy, if somewhat malicious, effect of parodying Lucy's own nun-like role. Ginevra and her lover de Hamal, 'resurrecting' the nun as a disguise for de Hamal's clandestine visits, underline the contrast between their happy liaison and Lucy's solitary life when they leave the 'nun' in Lucy's empty bed, on the night of their elopement. They make cruelly explicit a view of Lucy that the novel holds as potentiality.

Catherine Tilney, in Jane Austen's *Northanger Abbey*, creates Gothic mysteries out of the heightened literary sensibility she brings to bear on her new experiences. Lucy is to debunk the Gothic mystery mischievously set up for her, and to distinguish, in the process, the 'conventional' from the 'real' in the love relationships that now begin to involve her. The *billet-doux* that drops at her feet as she sits here in the garden addresses its recipient as 'angel of my dreams'. Lucy protests that, while 'all the teachers had dreams of some lover', 'suitor or admirer my very thoughts had not conceived' (p. 97). Nevertheless, the satiric references to her own grey figure 'revêche comme une réligieuse' make the implications of her solitude vivid to her. That solitude is now punctured, and in a way that forwards the subtle critique of Lucy as emblematic lady of romance. What intrudes is a somewhat equivocal 'reality', in the form of romantic intrigue. Lucy's involvement in this kind of romanticism follows directly from the kind of romanticism explored in her reverie. No longer an onlooker, Lucy is transformed, by the next turn of the novel, into the romantic heroine who waits desperately for her own *billets-doux*. The handsome figure who enters the garden to intercept the casket finds the solitary Lucy. Dr John is the Sir Lancelot who will encourage Lucy's participation in the world beyond the convent walls and whose carriage will take her to 'festal enjoyment'. A critique of this new phase of Lucy's romanticism is already suggested, however, in the jealous attention of M. Paul Emanuel, who overlooks Lucy's garden solitude with dedicated interest. Hard upon the heels of Dr John, the ever-watchful Mme Becke enters what has changed from a reverie into a 'scene'. Lucy infers that she interprets the scene as a lovers' tryst. And a close reading of Lucy's interest in Dr John during the preceding chapters (characteristically expressed in her noting the sexual attractiveness he has for Mme Becke) makes it clear that, as far as Lucy is concerned, that interpretation is not entirely far-fetched. The unexpected arrival of Dr John not only answers to, but helps to explain, needs and feelings Lucy's solitude discovers.

Lucy's moment of solitude demonstrates the limitations and indeed the impossibility of solitude. It registers what the preceding chapters have made vivid – that the life of the convent, like the recessive personality of Lucy Snowe, is not separable from a larger social life in the way the solipsism of this passage would have it to be. Mme Becke's mediation of the social values of Villette is sharply registered through Lucy's early impressions. Between Mme Becke and Lucy there develops a relationship whose complexities exceed Lucy's shrewd grasp of it, and through which is charted Lucy's attempt to come to terms with the foreignness of her new environment, and with her own reticence and prejudice. Forced out of the nursery and into the schoolroom, Lucy is further involved in social interaction, and in testing her decided views on education, and moral values even more decided.

Lucy is 'framed' by the passage, then, as part of Charlotte Brontë's exploration of her role as emblematic lady of romance. In the process Charlotte explores what are clearly aspects of her own romantic heritage and habits of mind. There is an intelligent self-awareness in the writing. The contemplative moment is dynamic, opening up Lucy's necessary, developing relationship with a world beyond self. Lucy is seen to suppress feelings of which she herself is barely conscious, and the tone of the passage holds in balance a measure of sympathy, and a measure of ironic detachment.

During the long vacation, the solitude Lucy seeks in the garden, and thinks of as her proper medium, becomes unendurable. The deserted convent holds her, 'crushing as the slab of a tomb', as she experiences her isolation at its most extreme point. The complete removal of the network of social relationships entails the loss of her developing sense of identity. The solipsistic illusion of being all-powerful is succeeded by the illusion of not existing at all. At her most dejected, Lucy characteristically feels herself invisible, attracting from Dr John, for example, 'just that degree of notice and consequence a person of my exterior habitually expects, that is to say, about what is given to unobtrusive articles of furniture, chairs of ordinary joiner's work, and carpets of no striking pattern' (p. 86). Now it is as though she exists only as a mirror of the lives of others, as she imagines the *dramatis personae* of her narrative, notably the charmed Ginevra, basking in affection and blessed by fate:

> I pictured her faithful hero half conscious of her coy fondness, and comforted by that consciousness: I conceived an electric chord of sympathy between them, a fine chain of mutual understanding, sustaining union through a separation of a hundred leagues – carrying, across mound and hollow, communication by prayer and wish. Ginevra gradually became with me a sort of heroine. One day, perceiving this growing illusion, I said, 'I really believe my nerves are getting overstretched: my mind has suffered somewhat too much; a malady is growing upon it – what shall I do? How shall I keep well?'
> Indeed there was no way to keep well under the circumstances. At last a day and night of peculiarly agonizing depression were succeeded by physical illness – I took perforce to my bed. About this time the Indian summer closed and the equinoctial storms began; and for nine dark and wet days, of which the hours rushed on all turbulent, deaf, dishevelled – bewildered with sounding hurricane – I lay in a strange fever of the nerves and blood. Sleep went quite away. I used to rise in the night, look round for her, beseech her earnestly to return. A rattle of the window, a cry of the blast only replied – Sleep never came.
> I err. She came once, but in anger. Impatient of my importunity she brought with her an avenging dream. By the clock of St Jean Baptiste, that dream remained scarce fifteen minutes – a brief space, but sufficient to wring my whole frame with unknown anguish; to confer a nameless experience that had

the hue, the mien, the terror, the very tone of a visitation from eternity. Between twelve and one that night a cup was forced to my lips, black, strong, strange, drawn from no well, but filled up seething from a bottomless and boundless sea. Suffering, brewed in temporal or calculable measure, and mixed for mortal lips, tastes not as this suffering tasted. Having drank and woke, I thought all was over: the end come and past by. Trembling fearfully – as consciousness returned – ready to cry out on some fellow-creature to help me, only that I knew no fellow-creature was near enough to catch the wild summons. . . . I rose on my knees in bed. Some fearful hours went over me: indescribably was I torn, racked and oppressed in mind. Amidst the horrors of that dream I think the worst lay here. Methought the well-loved dead, who had loved *me* well in life, met me elsewhere, alienated: galled was my inmost spirit with an unutterable sense of despair about the future. Motive there was none why I should try to recover or wish to live . . . .   (p. 143)

Lucy's outpouring of sensibility knows no restraint. The 'strange joys' of burgeoning fancy plague the enclosed consciousness. In charting its lyric overflow, however, Charlotte uncovers sources deep within Lucy's psyche. The passage opens with a 'picture' that projects Lucy's emotional hungers and frustrations. It closes with a dream that articulates her long-suppressed grief.

The tone in which Lucy imagines Ginevra's happy romance is quite at odds with the dry irony of her usual response to Ginevra and her *amours*. Her fiction of Ginevra's lover as 'half-conscious of her coy fondness, and comforted by that fondness' transforms Dr John's actual discomfort and Ginevra's coquetry into an achieved, physical responsiveness, 'an electric chord of sympathy', and a magic spiritual expansiveness that withstands separation. This extraordinary distortion leads us back to the enclosed lady herself: to an idealising romanticism, the yearning for her Sir Lancelot, the envious but mostly generous tribute to her rival's vitality and attractiveness. 'No other woman in the novel has any identity except as Lucy herself bestows it', Jacobus claims.[31] Lucy here becomes aware of such all-consuming and all-powerful fancy as a 'malady'. The passage depends, for its fullest understanding, on the autonomy of people and events beyond Lucy's fanciful vision.

Most immediately, Lucy's delirious fantasy draws on her discovery, as an actress in M. Paul's play, of the painfulness of her role

as 'life's onlooker'. Never easily able to find public expression for her
deepest feelings, Lucy warms to those who can express them for her,
as it were – to the young Polly, or the girl who sobs unrestrainedly at
M. Paul's leave-taking, or to the actress Vashti. When she does 'act',
it is within the conventions of art that she asserts herself, and, as in
the garden, as the protagonist of a romantic intrigue. Lucy discovers
an appetite and a capacity for taking part, but what she participates
in on stage, and, by extension, in the intrigue the 'little comic trifle'
echoes, is a romantic fiction. Again, Charlotte Brontë makes use of
convention to expose the conventional romanticism which is, at this
point, Lucy's only mode of self-assertion. The play, which has
Ginevra ideally cast as the coquette between two suitors, sets the
tone and identifies the nature of the feelings acted out. Like
Ginevra, who acts as much to her two suitors in the audience as to
her two suitors on the stage, Lucy takes her cue from the 'real'
intrigue. Dr John's expression inspires her to make the text a vehicle
for her personal drama:

> It animated me. I drew out of it a history; I put my idea into the
> part I performed; I threw it into my wooing of Ginevra. In the
> 'Ours', or sincere lover, I saw Dr John. Did I pity him, as erst?
> No, I hardened my heart, rivalled and out-rivalled him. I knew
> myself but a fop, but where he was outcast, I could please.
>
> (p. 125)

Public performance enables the expression of 'contradictory
. . . inward tumult', and of a sexual potency she feels denied in
actuality.

Lucy's picture of Ginevra the romantic heroine, then, simply
extends the imaginative exercise of M. Paul's play, and Lucy's part
in it, extinguishing any but a reflected self. For, while the fiction
Lucy acts out has acknowledged Ginevra's attractiveness, it has also
sought to deny and vanquish Dr John's role in Ginevra's life, freeing
him from his enthralment. The needs of the solitary self are reflected
in the exercise of fancy, making love dramas in which wish-
fulfilment magically transforms what is difficult or intractable in
real life.

In private, as this passage makes clear, suppressed feelings find
release in a strange kind of exultation, rousing the repressed self to
act out a new kind of self-assertion. The 'equinoctial storms' that
rage outside Lucy's window are echoed within her by a 'strange

fever of the nerves and blood', recalling Lucy's earlier account of being roused by storm, perched on her window-ledge to savour the 'terribly glorious' spectacle, while the Catholics rise in terror 'to pray to their saints' (p. 96). Lucy's sensitivity to nature's more violent moods resembles her admiration for the art of the actress Vashti. Both 'performances' draw out of her an intensity of response, expressed in images of strong natural energies breaking all bounds. The absence of restraint is welcomed, whatever its source, because it gives free reign to 'the being I was always lulling', 'the craving cry I could not satisfy' (p. 96). Vashti's power, 'like a deep, swollen winter river thundering in cataract . . . bearing the soul, like a leaf, on the steep and steely sweep of its descent' (p. 235), enables Lucy to experience those passionate intensities vicariously. The violence of nature prompts in her a more immediate response, which the rhetoric and movement of the writing attempts to render, in crescendo after crescendo: 'the hue, the mien, the terror, the very tone', 'black, strong, strange, drawn from no well, but filled up seething from a bottomless sea'. It is the mood of Hopkin's terrible sonnets, 'Pitched past pitch of grief', of 'pangs . . . schooled at forepangs' (from 'No worst, there is none'). But in Hopkins there is the utmost precision of imaginative evocation. Lucy's storm is quite unspecific in its characterisation of suffering. Throughout the novel, metaphoric storm imagery conveys both Lucy's inability to articulate her suffering and that element in her personality in which Charlotte Brontë signifies her critique of such *Angst*. As Lucy sits beside Dr John, noting his dispassionate response to Vashti, and giving voice to her own quivering intensities, there is a wryly observed contrast between his not-unjustified detachment from the melodrama, and Lucy's histrionic responsiveness. 'Anybody living her life would necessarily become morbid', Charlotte told her publisher.[32] The 'seething', 'nameless', 'bottomless', 'boundless', 'indescribable', 'unutterable', 'unendurable' sensations with which Lucy experiences romantic agony take the tone as close as possible to parody, without ever quite losing sympathy for her suffering.

The reason for this is that in and behind the vague helpless buffeting of Lucy's suffering sensibility the passage locates its quite specific sources: 'methought the well-loved dead . . . met me . . . alienated'. The loss of love goes on reiterating itself. The dream fantasy, as is common in such experiences of grief, transforms the subjective sense of loss into an act of deliberate forsaking. Once again, the power of the enclosed consciousness to make its picture of the world is elaborated and analysed. As Lucy hovers between sleep and delirium, the shape of known things begins to change: 'the ghastly white beds were turning into spectres – the coronal of each became a death's head, huge and sun-bleached' (p. 144). At the end of this remarkable passage of psychoanalysis, Lucy has acknowledged her need of counselling. The effort to articulate and deal with her feeling in the presence of the nearest counsellor she can find, the Catholic Père Silas, is the first step in the process of healing.

As Lucy comes to consciousness, after the collapse that follows her 'confession', her gaze takes in not the expected surroundings of the white-washed dormitory, with its two-dozen stands and beds, and its long line of windows, but a pleasant parlour

> with a wood fire on a clear-shining hearth, a carpet where arabesques of bright blue relieved a ground of shaded fawn; pale walls over which a slight but endless garland of azure forget-me-nots ran amazed and bewildered amongst myriad gold leaves and tendrils. A gilded mirror filled up the space between two windows, curtained amply with blue damask. In the mirror I saw myself laid, not in a bed, but on a sofa. I looked spectral; my eyes larger and more hollow, my hair darker than was natural, by contrast with my thin and ashen face. It was obvious, not only from the furniture, but from the position of windows, doors, and fireplace, that this was an unknown room in an unknown house.
>
> Hardly less plain was it that my brain was not yet settled; for, as I gazed at the blue armchair, it appeared to grow familiar; so did a certain scroll-couch, and not less so the round centre-table, with a blue covering, bordered with autumn-tinted foliage; and, above all, two little footstools with worked covers, and a small ebony-framed chair, of which the seat and back were also worked with groups of brilliant flowers on a dark ground.
>
> Struck with these things, I explored further. Strange to say, old acquaintance were all about me, and 'auld lang syne' smiled out of every nook. There were two oval miniatures over the mantelpiece, of which I knew by heart the pearls about the high and powdered 'heads'; the velvets circling the white throats; the swell of the pale muslin kerchiefs; the pattern of the lace sleeve-ruffles. Upon the mantel-shelf, there were two china vases, some

relics of a diminutive tea service, as smooth as enamel and as thin as egg-shell, and a white centre ornament, a classic group in alabaster, preserved under glass. Of all these things I could have told the peculiarities, numbered the flaws or cracks, like any clairvoyante. Above all, there was a pair of handscreens, with elaborate pencil-drawings finished like line engravings: these, my very eyes ached at beholding again, recalling hours when they had followed, stroke by stroke and touch by touch, a tedious, finical, school-girl pencil held in these fingers, now so skeleton-like.

Where was I? Not only in what spot of the world, but in what year of our Lord? For all these objects were of past days, and of a distant country. Ten years ago I bade them goodbye; since my fourteenth year they and I had never met. I gasped audibly, 'Where am I?' (p. 149)

That transformation of familiar sights into strange and threatening shapes that marked Lucy's breakdown gives way here to the discovery, in strange surroundings, of a reassuring familiarity. She now experiences what Coleridge (in his account of the writing of the *Lyrical Ballads*) describes as 'the sudden charm' given to the 'known and familiar' by changed circumstances of perception.[33] Whereas the Lucy of the previous passage was unable to articulate her feelings, and lost any adequate sense of her self and her surroundings, Lucy here observes, with a cataloguing precision and control, her reflected self and the objects around her. The deliberation of the contrast between these two 'enclosed' moments is a measure of Charlotte Brontë's probing exploration of Lucy's 'sensibility'. Each of Lucy's solitary passages marks a stage in the exploration of that self, drawing on what has happened in the larger dramatic context of the novel, and throwing the action forward yet again. Just as Lucy's fanciful romance of Ginevra extended insights made by her participation in M. Paul's play, so this reawakening at La Terrasse extends the effort towards articulation made in the confessional.

Lucy finds herself returned to the womb-like security of Bretton, and to all the emotional and material comforts of that childhood world. In the re-creation of this early environment, the passage uncovers further the sources of Lucy's self-enclosure. This room, the room of the self and of memory, contains a sense of self that is both reassuring and radically disturbing, questioning Lucy's grasp on where, and who, she is. The self it reflects in its mirror is 'spectral'.

The web of memory both is, and is not, home. She retraces here that earliest formative process in which the familiar objects of perception shape in the child's mind its sense of identity and its concepts. Charlotte Brontë anticipates the opening pages of Joyce's *A Portrait of the Artist as a Young Man*, in seeing this process as analogous with the workings of the artist's imagination.

As in the two previous passages, attention is drawn to the way in which Lucy's perspective, with its distinctive needs, shapes her seeing. And, again, these are needs that establish her as no 'pre-social' atom, but as continually reaching out to recapture and extend relationship with the world beyond self. Her delight in the cheerful domestic comfort of this room is registered in her verbal caressing and possessing of it, piece by piece – the 'arabesques' of bright blue, the 'clear-shining hearth', the 'ample' curtains. Surprise and bafflement are registered too: the forget-me-nots which run 'amazed and bewildered amongst myriad gold leaves and tendrils' make an image of her effort to discern significance in the patterns of memory. She re-enacts with her eyes the care with which, 'stroke by stroke' and 'touch by touch', she has given expression to her loving feelings for her godmother. Bretton has furnished Lucy's mind with objects that make part of her continuing identity, the passage suggests, and Lucy has found assurance in the reciprocal process in which she has herself engraved the hand-screens and worked the foot-stools and ornamented the pin-cushions that make part of Bretton. There is here, as well, a world of elegance, taste and sensual gratification that answers to other needs than those of the fourteen-year-old self. The oval miniatures, 'the velvets circling the white throats; the swell of the full muslin kerchiefs', recall Lucy's attention to Mme Becke's ample bosom set off by her perfectly cut French clothes, and make a painful contrast with that hollow-eyed oval miniature, thin and pallid, that stares at Lucy from the gilded mirror.

The room as an imprisoning circumstance made for, and by, the self here takes on a new dimension. Of course it is a coincidence that Mrs Bretton should be living in Villette, that Lucy should be found in the street by Dr John and taken to his mother's house, that Dr John should be none other than the attractive John Graham of childhood days. The chain of coincidence is justified, as in Victorian novels generally, only when it establishes a significance beyond the merely mechanical. Lucy's recuperation enables her living out again, and reassessing, the formative experience of her childhood, and the reconciliation of her past self with her present self. (Charlotte Brontë had been faced with just such an effort of reassessment and reconciliation when she met her girlhood friends, the Taylors, in Brussels.)

This passage makes vivid the novel's perception that there can be no detachment from such formative experiences, however they may be forgotten or suppressed, and that they contain the potentiality both for psychic growth and for neurosis. As in the opening chapters of the novel, Bretton nurtures and yet frustrates Lucy's needs. The recovery of the warm relationship with her godmother brings joy to both of them. The world beyond the convent walls opens up for her – a Villette of galleries and concerts and dinners. She becomes part of a social circle, no longer a 'nobody', as Ginevra observes, but somebody. She becomes the chosen companion of Dr John, and her love for him, and dependence on him, is fostered by his solicitous attention.

It is only in the weeks that follow her return to the convent, after her convalescence at La Terrasse, that the full significance of the episode emerges. Lucy is plunged into a grim battle of sense and sensibility. She entreats 'Reason' to help her control the rush of 'importunate' feelings released by her being made much of. Her continuing check on feeling is, of course, an instinctive defence against hurt. (Characteristically she has retreated from her recognition of each of the Brettons until they first recognise her.) As she desperately awaits Dr John's promised letters, her 'strange sweet insanity' touches again the intensities of self-exultant suffering. It is Mrs Bretton's letter, after months of silence, that most helps her towards a detachment that is neither willed nor defensive. 'I dare say you have been just as busy and as happy as ourselves at La Terrasse', writes her godmother, and Lucy reflects, 'their feelings for me too were – as they had been' (p. 247). Mother and son respond to a view of Lucy's self-sufficiency that her manner encourages, and make up a self-sufficiency of their own, not ungenerously observed by the always sharp Lucy, as is Dr John's complacent self-preoccupation: 'consciousness of what he has and what he is: pleasure in homage, some recklessness in exciting, some vanity in receiving the same' (p. 178). To say that he has flirted with Lucy would be to put it too crudely. There is a delicate registering of Dr John's kindness alternating with forgetfulness, and Lucy's gradual relinquishing of infatuation. The novel does not bury Lucy's love, though Lucy does. For, when she accepts her godmother's holiday invitation to La Terrasse she finds that the pretty parlour of her convalescence is occupied: 'a full wax-light stood on each side of the great looking-glass: but between the candles, and before the glass, appeared something dressing itself – an airy, fairy thing – small, slight, white – a winter spirit' (p. 250). The return to childhood has been completed by Polly's again usurping Lucy's place at Bretton, and in Dr John's affections.

The pattern completes itself with a difference this time, however. While Lucy acknowledges needs fostered by the Brettons, she is also learning that they cannot be met by a return to familial security or by the potent romanticism of unrequited love. Her sojourn at La Terrasse suggests that the patterns of experience made for the individual identity, and made by it, are inevitably repetitions, and yet always contain possibilities for growth.

There is one final, striking moment in the novel in which Lucy's self-enclosure is explored. In her desolation at the supposed departure of M. Paul she confines herself to the convent: 'What bodily illness was ever like this pain? This certainty that he was gone without farewell. . . . What wonder that the second evening found me like the first – untamed, tortured, again pacing a solitary room in an unalterable passion of silent desolation' (p. 409). Mme Becke's sleeping-potion arouses, not sedates, Lucy:

Instead of stupor, came excitement. I became alive to new thought – to reverie peculiar in colouring. A gathering call ran among the faculties, their bugles sang, their trumpets rang an untimely summons. Imagination was roused from her rest, and she came forth impetuous and venturous. With scorn she looked on Matter, her mate –

'Rise!' she said; 'Sluggard! this night I will have *my* will; nor shalt thou prevail.' . . .

Entering on the level of a Grande Place, I found myself, with the suddenness of magic, plunged amidst a gay, living, joyous crowd.

Villette is one blaze, one broad illumination; the whole world seems abroad; moonlight and heaven are banished: the town, by her own flambeaux, beholds her own splendour – gay dresses, grand equipages, fine horses and gallant riders throng the bright streets. I see even scores of masks. It is a strange place, stranger than dreams. But where is the park? – I ought to be near it. In the midst of this glare the park must be shadowy and calm – *there*, at least, are neither torches, lamps, nor crowd?

I was asking this question when an open carriage passed me filled with known faces. Through the deep throng it could pass but slowly; the spirited horses fretted in their curbed ardour. I saw the occupants of that carriage well: me they could not see, or, at least, not know, folded close in my large shawl, screened with my straw hat (in that motley crowd no dress was noticeably strange). I saw the Count de Bassompiere. I saw my godmother, handsomely apparelled, comely and cheerful. I saw, too, Paulina Mary, compassed with the triple halo of her beauty, her youth, and her happiness. In looking on her countenance of joy, and eyes of festal light, one scarce remembered to note what she wore; I know only that the drapery floating about her was all white and light and bridal: seated opposite to her I saw Graham Bretton; it was in looking up at him her aspect had caught its lustre – the light repeated in *her* eyes beamed first out of his. It gave me strange pleasure to follow these friends viewlessly, and I *did* follow them, as I thought, to the park. I watched them alight (carriages were inadmissible) amidst new and unanticipated splendours. Lo! the iron gateway, between the stone columns, was spanned by a flaming arch built of massed stars; and, following them cautiously beneath that arch, where were they, and where was I?

In a land of enchantment, a garden most gorgeous, a plain sprinkled with coloured meteors, a forest with sparks of purple and ruby and golden fire gemming the foliage; a region, not of trees and shadow, but of strangest architectural wealth – of altars and of temple, of pyramid, obelisk, and sphinx; incredible to say, the wonders and the symbols of Egypt teemed through the park of Villette.   (pp. 409, 412)

As in Lucy's reawakening at La Terrasse, the border between dream and reality is blurred: there is the same experiencing of familiar things rendered strange and even enchanted, the same suppression of Lucy's personality and the same bewilderment about a self cast adrift from the expected and familiar. The bejewelled landscape opened up by the heightened sensory awareness induced by opium makes a climax in that web of colour and incident Lucy's narrative has woven. Although she is here represented as travelling forth, she moves in and out of the convent with the strange ease of dream movement, drifting through the crowded scenes of the fête as though she is indeed invisible. Contained, still, within her own solitary imagination, set apart, like any dreamer, from the scene she projects, she travels 'viewlessly'. The *dramatis personae* of her narrative appear and vanish 'like a group of apparitions'; 'on the whole scene was impressed a dream-like character: every shape was wavering, every moment floating, every voice echo-like – half-mocking, half-uncertain' (p. 413).

And, as in dream, the significance of the day-time world is pictured forth in visual images that resonate with meaning – the family group from Bretton bespeaking self-contained happiness, the love between Polly and Dr John reflected in their eyes. The dream-like figures act with symbolic significance, articulating meaning to the invisible watcher, the dreamer. Lucy's exclusion from the Bretton family is underlined by her overhearing their regret that they have not invited her. She is excluded by the circle that gathers around Mme Becke, and from the circle M. Paul makes, in enfolding the young Justine Marie 'carefully from the night air' (p. 425). She sees pass her on the road the carriage containing the eloping pair, Ginevra and de Hamal. She alone is shut away from the world's happiness, but delighting in the sights her imagination reveals to her. Indeed, it is by virtue of her role as 'life's onlooker' that the heightened perceptiveness of fanciful imagination becomes available to her. The narrow focus of Lucy's self-enclosed vision is alike reflected in the formal tableaux that exclude her, and in the moonlit transformation of Villette that delights her inward eye. The dream logic returns Lucy to the convent to find her bed occupied by the sinister black-and-white figure of the nun.

What has seemed, to Lucy's disordered senses, a mirrored self, reflecting her own despair of life, is proved to be a trick perpetuated by the eloping lovers to enable their secret meetings. Lucy's determined unveiling and destruction of 'the mystery' rejects the symbolic portent, and the malice with which the self-satisfied lovers have made their comment on the solitary Lucy: 'all the movement was mine, so was all the life, the reality' (p. 429). The episode completes Lucy's 'dream' and underlines its significance. The 'nun' is as real a visitant as the enchanted people and scenes in moonlit Villette are 'real'. But the mind makes of them meanings that question that 'reality', reflecting the perceiver's face in what is perceived. The pale dead nun loved by M. Paul and the living Justine Marie are real enough, also, but the significance they take on for Lucy, and the wasted sense of herself they convey, are discovered to be similarly legendary and spectral.

But Lucy's looking out on 'the real world' is still not completed. The curse that imprisons her within her solitary viewpoint is broken only when the declaration of M. Paul's love recognises her distinctive identity, and frees it for the establishing of an independent life outside Mme Becke's convent. The writing that explores the growing relationship between Lucy and M. Paul is quite different from the soulful moments with which this chapter has been largely concerned, and intending just such a contrast. M. Paul draws Lucy into relationship, into explosive confrontation and inexplicable affection. Lucy does not relinquish her habits of private contemplation, but she discovers that she is now herself the object of someone else's continuing scrutiny. M. Paul spies upon her, admonishes her, is always happening upon her when she least expects him. Seated before a voluptuous nude in the picture gallery in Villette she is surprised by a sharp tap on her shoulder:

> Starting, turning, I met a face bent to encounter mine; a frowning, almost a shocked face it was.
>
> 'Que faîtes vous ici?' said a voice.
>
> 'Mais, monsieur, je m'amuse.'
>
> 'Vous vous amusez! et à quoi, s'il vous plaît? Mais d'abord, faîtes-moi le plaisir de vous lever; prenez mon bras, et allons de l'autre côté.'
>
> I did precisely as I was bid. M. Paul Emanuel (it was he), returned from Rome, and now a travelled man, was not likely to be less tolerant of insubordination now, than before this added distinction laurelled his temples.
>
> 'Permit me to conduct you to your party', said he, as he crossed the room.
>
> 'I have no party.'
>
> 'You are not alone?'
>
> 'Yes, monsieur '
>
> 'Did you come here unaccompanied?'
>
> 'No, monsieur. Dr Bretton brought me here.'
>
> 'Dr Bretton and Madame his mother, of course?'
>
> 'No; only Dr Bretton.'
>
> 'And he told you to look at *that* picture?'
>
> 'By no means; I found it out for myself.'
>
> M. Paul's hair was shorn close as raven down, or I think it

would have bristled on his head. Beginning now to perceive his drift, I had a certain pleasure in keeping cool, and working him up.

'Astounding insular audacity', cried the professor. 'Singulières femmes que ces Anglaises!'

'What is the matter, monsieur?'

'Matter! How dare you, a young person, sit coolly down, with the self-possession of a garçon, and look at *that* picture.'

'It is a very ugly picture, but I cannot at all see why I should not look at it.'   (p. 181)

Lucy's silent reflections on the Cleopatra – 'fourteen to sixteen stone', 'strong enough to do the work of two plain cooks', 'out of abundance of material . . . she managed to make insufficient raiment' (p. 180) – suggests her private contempt for this image of womanhood. M. Paul's objections are more narrowly moral still, however, and he directs her instead to the pious and decorously conventional paintings of 'La vie d'une femme'. Yet again, Charlotte Brontë's art is intelligently self-aware. For Lucy's reflections on these paintings, like her reflections on the images of womanhood presented by the various women characters of the novel, make part of her own, and the novel's reflections on the social and sexual role of Lucy Snowe. And here she asserts to M. Paul a feminine nature that both affronts and attracts him. And, although she is sufficiently detached to enjoy irritating him, this is not an untrue 'image' of herself. Crisp repartée, trenchant judgement, and a very firm sense of her own rightness are the attributes of 'cool Lucy' in all her conversations. Her rejoinders show her registering M. Paul's magisterial manner as overbearing and a shade comic, as indeed his self-important portentousness shows him to be. But she obeys him, none the less; she abhors the prejudices but respects the sincere beliefs and generous feelings of his uncongenial Catholicism. She withholds herself from him, frequently mocks and opposes him, refuses to gratify his vanity, yet trusts and begins to understand him, and he her. She hides the birthday present she has made for him: he is wounded to the quick, but still searches her desk for what he feels he must find. He is fiercely jealous of Dr John, but sits in silent forbearance as Lucy weeps, in her misery and loneliness, over one of his letters. Lucy's model of the romantic hero is being replaced by an unexpected, inexplicable response to a man not in the least conventionally attractive. Her changing impressions of him register changing feelings. Fierce quarrels and gentle reconciliations play out sexual tensions and an unorthodox courtship ritual. We hear less of his tyranny and irascibility and more of his surreptitious acts of kindness, the books and the comfits. For, as M. Paul recognises, there is an affinity between these two 'crabbed and crusty' personalities that will dissolve their differences – a strong *amour-propre* warring with an outgoing kindness, a passionateness of feeling and belief, a straightforwardness of speech and manner, an impatience of humbug and deceit, a blending of sense and sensibility. The very 'passions and hurricanes' which make M. Paul seem a ridiculous little man, frequently the object of Lucy's amused contempt, manifest a volatility not dissimilar from the feelings that pour out of Lucy in her most private moments.

M. Paul intrudes on, and at last invades, Lucy's privacy. His tenderness breaks down the last barrier, Lucy's 'haunting dread' about her 'outward deficiency'. As they walk together for the last time before his voyage, he comments that her pallor troubles him, and she nerves herself to ask 'Do I displease your eyes *much*?' (p. 440). The 'short, strong answer' which silences and profoundly satisfies her makes a satisfying conclusion to the novel's exploration of Lucy's self-reflections. Her painful sense of her own plainness is of course apparent throughout in her shrinking into the background, and her sensitivity to the attractiveness of other women. The fleeting mirror-glimpses of her 'grey shadow', and the more prolonged mirror comparison prompted by Ginevra in playful mood return to Lucy that unattractive self she feels herself to be. Now she confesses what for so long has remained unspoken, and in M. Paul's physical reassurance she finds a self defined in relationship replacing the self confirmed in the mirrors of her self-enclosure. Dialogue has succeeded monologue, and there begins, for Lucy, 'a wonderfully changed life, a relieved heart. . . . Few things shook me now; few things had importance to vex, intimidate, or depress me' (p. 449).

This gratification of Lucy's need for relationship is the point of self-discovery towards which the novel has moved with progressive insight. Each of the 'moments' studied in this account of *Villette* (and there are, of course, many more of them), marks a stage in this movement. On each occasion, Lucy's retreat into the contemplative mode is explored, and its significance clarified, before the moment gives way to the demands of a world whose autonomy lies beyond Lucy's reflecting consciousness. From the repeated image of the imprisoned Lucy flows the novel's whole design, and there is a sense in which that image circumscribes it at the last.

The novel by no means denies the need for containment and definition that is appeased by self-enclosure. The little house in Faubourg Clothilde is finally to enclose Lucy within the domestic and professional environment lovingly created by M. Paul, satisfying needs discovered or reaffirmed by her teaching work at the convent, with the family at La Terrasse, and in her love for M. Paul. Lucy is independent, but she is certainly not 'free'. The ending of *Villette*, however, returns to that more limiting romantic self-enclosure that has been subjected to continuing critique. The storm that overtakes the returning M. Paul is evoked in the lurid images and feverish intensity of Lucy's suffering and solipsistic fancy. Sunny imaginations are allowed to hope, and relegated to a different world. The narrator retreats from it into silence. Unlike her earlier retreats into the inarticulate, this one remains unchallenged, not even by that perspective of a white-haired Lucy who appears close to the start of the narrative, to remind us that it is all 'emotion recollected in tranquillity'. The pain of that feverish close lingers. Charlotte Brontë's decision that Lucy should be denied that membership of the happy outside world towards which she and the novel have steadily moved doubtless springs from her own personal commitment to 'the real'. She had, after all, to relinquish M. Héger and continue life without him. And that exercise of 'reason' is just as romantic as Lucy Snowe's grimly reasonable impulses. The personal sources that give such urgency to the novel's exploration reverberate too nakedly, at the last. That is not a large failure, however, given its remarkably penetrating study of the beleaguered and solitary consciousness, and of the necessary relationship of that consciousness with the world it reflects.

2 Little Dorrit's Prison

In Chapter 24 of *Little Dorrit*, Army Dorrit entertains the child-like Maggy with a fairy-tale that provides a clue to the change that has stolen 'almost imperceptibly' over 'the patient heart'. 'Every day found her something more retiring than the day before.' Gazing out at the world from her prison garret, she sees it, as she always does, through the Marshalsea bars:

> Many combinations did those spikes upon the wall assume, many light shapes did the strong iron weave itself into, many golden touches fell upon the rust, while Little Dorrit sat there musing. New zig-zags sprang into the cruel pattern sometimes, when she saw it through a burst of tears; but beautified or hardened still, always over it and under it and through it, she was fain to look in her solitude, seeing everything with that ineffaceable brand.
>
> (Charles Dickens, *Little Dorrit*, pp. 337–8)

Dickens shared George Eliot's view of Charlotte Brontë's 'preternatural power'. As the novels of the 1850s suggest, he was himself increasingly preoccupied by the kind of feminine sensibility the Brontë novels unfold – a sensibility in retreat from the world, sustained in its isolation by the power to create its own self-enclosing vision. Miss Wade frequently strikes Lucy Snowe's note of intense controlled bitterness. There is in Little Dorrit something of Lucy's acceptance of imprisonment as 'life's lot', and, occasionally, of her indulgence of fancy. As in Lucy's case, there is a measure of authorial support for such quiescence. It can be heard here in the patterns and cadences into which the narrative voice falls. The fancy that sustains Little Dorrit makes part of her special value for Dickens, reflecting a disposition, and a view of creative imagination, more surprising in the gregarious Boz, perhaps, than in the daughter of a clergyman in remote Yorkshire. 'I can see others in the sunlight', Dickens wrote. 'But I myself am always in the shadow looking on. Not unsympathetically – God forbid! – but looking on alone.'[1] Little Dorrit, like Lucy Snowe, is unobtrusive to the point of invisibility. Her first appearance is noted only in Arthur Clennam's afterthought ('what girl was that in my mother's room just now?' – p. 79). She lingers in the shadow, in an imprisonment she is inclined to see as an 'ineffaceable brand', making for her life a 'cruel pattern'. From within the prison, sunlight makes only a shifting, abstract picture, fitfully evoking the natural world that lies beyond the prison and the city, source of a thousand fresh scents and beautiful forms of 'growth and life'.

It is only in her private moments that Little Dorrit indulges in anything like self-pity or self-absorption. Nevertheless, such moments are crucial to the novel's purpose and achievement, revealing its heroine as by no means exempt from that warping and constricting of feeling in which Dickens identifies the malaise of Victorian society. There is some local unsteadiness in Dickens's valuing of Little Dorrit, but his guiding sense of her is apparent if she is seen as the novel's most delicate study of sensibility: of its strengths and weaknesses, and the conditions that nourish and thwart it. A novel that undertakes to explore with such range and variety the sensibility of its age, responding with Dickens's characteristic delight to possibilities for the comic and the ironic, provides fewer moments of introspection than a novel like *Villette*. And such moments have not generally been regarded as the novel's strengths. It is not easy to detach them from the dense texture of the whole, and impossible to discuss them without considering in some detail the adequacy of Dickens's characterisation of Little Dorrit. This chapter will focus on four of the novel's introspective moments, then: first a comparison of Miss Wade's 'History of a Self-tormentor' with Little Dorrit's fairy-tale, and secondly a discussion of two passages that explore Little Dorrit's inner life. These passages will be discussed, however, within the context of psychological exploration and social analysis in which the novel sets them, and in the context of critical debate about Dickens's treatment of women, and of Little Dorrit in particular.

'We are all partly creators of the objects we perceive', Dickens wrote,[2] defending his belief in 'fancy'. This after all, was the very charter of romantic writing: 'the appropriate business of

poetry . . . is to treat of things not as they are, but as they appear'.[3]
Villette reveals a deep unease about the creative powers, with their
'strange necromantic joys' (p. 66). In *Little Dorrit* there is a
confident, though never uncritical, acceptance of imagination as
the shaping and sustaining power of human life. From the poignant
comedy of 'fancy's fair dream', in which Flora Finching celebrates a
past that never was and a future that never will be, or Mrs Plornish's
evocation of a pastoral world in the shabbiness of Bleeding Heart
Yard, to the tragi-comic illusions that sustain Mr Dorrit's imprisoned gentility or the castle-building that continues them into
prosperity and 'freedom', to society's golden fiction of Mr Merdle,
these are people individually, and communally closed in and
buoyed up by myths of their own making. Little Dorrit in her prison
garret finds consolation, as she has done since her childhood, in the
play of fancy. The little girl who sits with Bob the turnkey is not
'thinking of the fields' as he supposes in his kindly sentimental way,
but enjoying that visual illusion that stamps the sunlit bars on
succeeding images. That picture is recalled as an older Little Dorrit
projects her prison bars in a more extended fancy. Also recalled,
perhaps, are stories told by a boy to a waif from the Chelsea
workhouse, as he waited to join his family inside the Marshalsea
gates.[4]

Little Dorrit's fairy-tale catches the story-telling relish of the
inimitable Boz himself: the rhetoric of the story-teller, the shaping of
suspense and climax, the consciousness of audience, that are as
essential to the texture of this as of any other Dickens novel. George
Eliot's narrative voice is quite as strongly characterised. But it
persuades us to broader intellectual and moral perspectives by
analysis, and by argument illumined by metaphor. The voice of Boz
persuades us to share a distinctive way of seeing, in which pictures
often do the work of analysis, repeating and gathering meaning as
the images in a poem probe and generate significance. And so Little
Dorrit's inner turmoil is expressed in terms of a palace and a cottage,
a carriage and a passer-by. Her picturing, like the Lady of Shalott's,
reflects her sense of the world, and her creator's faith in the power of
the visual. Pictures tell stories in the Dickens world, weaving a web
quite distinctive in its patterning and order. Inevitably, the story-
teller falls into exhortation or gratuitous emphasis when the
pressures of imagination slacken. And Little Dorrit's fairy-tale is a
fanciful, and to some extent a self-preoccupied echo, merely, of
what the novel takes to be the most impressive qualities of her
imagination. It is imagination as 'the greatest instrument of moral

good' that she manifests – at best, empathic and outward-reaching, taking as its own, as the novel does, the pains and pleasures of its species. The cover-design visualises this confidence at its heart. The small figure who clings to the shadows at the centre of the page, looking out from her prison, is seen in a shaft of sunlight that illumines the impotent miseries encircling her. She is, in Jamesian terminology, the novel's compositional centre, that place 'where all the rays meet and from which they issue'.[5] As Dickens's sense of the meaning and direction of his novel grows, he abandons the title that expresses impotence, 'Nobody's Fault', in favour of a title that simply names the heroine, *Little Dorrit*.[6]

That illuminated and illumining glow, Garis trenchantly affirms, is merely 'the work of the lighting technician'.[7] His general conviction that Dickens is unable adequately to render 'the inner life' is widely shared, as is the extremity of his reaction to Little Dorrit's goodness. On the one hand there are mystical or at least quasi-religious 'explanations' of her – 'the paraclete in human form',[8] 'the kind of miracle that happens: the flowering of love or energy which is inexplicable by the ways of describing people to which . . . we have got used'.[9] On the other, she is simply seen as the expression of those Victorian conventions of womanhood much admired by Dickens the essayist and letter-writer: 'Little Dorrit's character is one of complete self-abnegation: in a long line of Dickens heroines who live for others, she carries the principle furthest.'[10] F. R. Leavis's sensitive attention to her characterisation[11] seems to me to give too little attention to her surely very palpable limitations. And John Bayley's perceptive account of those limitations sees them as an involuntary manifestation, beyond Dickens's 'conscious control', the product of Dickensian 'dream intensity' rather than a fully grasped and articulated 'human nature':

> With nothing to hide, Little Dorrit has Cordelia's blandness: nothing for author and reader to overhear and look in at. For Dickens and his public such a heroine must be outside the conversation of criticism, and portraying her in this way actually augments – as it does with the complementary Clennam – the large shadows of the pressures which have moulded them into what they are.[12]

I would argue that in *Little Dorrit* Dickens apprehends more 'consciously' and more critically than ever before the limitations of the good little woman of Victorian convention. One sign of this is that he explores those pressures which have moulded Little Dorrit into what she actually is, pressures that she is felt inevitably to share with the rest of the novel's world, and which leave her, despite her impressiveness, in some ways stunted, timorous, lacking a necessary measure of self-assertion.

That distinctive moulding is quite clearly revealed in her fairy-tale, as clearly as Miss Wade's particular moulding is exposed in her remarkable 'History of a Self-tormentor', in Chapter 21 of Book the Second. The philanthropic Mr Meagles offers, for the benefit of his ward Tattycoram, a moralistic reading of the two life-histories, Miss Wade's exemplifying selfishness and destructive passion, Little Dorrit's exemplifying selfless devotion to 'duty'. The reading the novel offers, particularly in the sense of her own history each projects, is altogether more subtle. And it forwards questions that increasingly claim Dickens's attention in the novels that precede and follow *Little Dorrit*, questions that have to do with the nurturing and blighting of the sensibility of women in Victorian England. What are the formative influences that make for women 'a happy temperament' or its reverse? What are the consequences for those they seek, in turn, to form? In *Bleak House* the inquiry centres on Esther Summerson, whose 'history' runs parallel to the novel's narrative. In Esther's continuously projected self Dickens evokes (only too vividly perhaps[13]) a personality imprisoned by impervious defensive niceness. Her irksome blend of the self-effacing and the self-congratulatory gives appropriate voice to a society which, suppressing all pain and guilt and passion, have made her what she is. Little Dorrit's voice, in her fairy-tale and in her two long letters to Arthur Clennam, occasionally comes close to Esther's tones. Miss Wade responds more forcibly than the mild Esther ever could, to a history that closely resembles hers. Dickens, who has none of Charlotte Brontë's first-hand experience of the fate of the 'un-provided for' women of Victorian society, finds in it an equally important focus for the malaise of that society. The Doras and Agnes and Little Nells of earlier novels give way to more complex and more deeply pondered studies of women. Born into their bleak houses, law suits, stern philosophies and neuroses, compelling figures like Lady Dedlock, Louisa Gradgrind, Mrs Clennam, Miss Wade and Miss Havisham recur and dominate.

Like Tennyson and Charlotte Brontë, Dickens borrows from convention to probe the relationship between the heritage of popular imagination and urgent contemporary concerns. The legendary girl of Bleeding Heart Yard, 'closely imprisoned in her chamber by a cruel father for remaining true to her own true love' (p. 176), is, like the legendary nun of *Villette*, the popular romantic version of the novel's more searching romanticism. Whether she represents the historical actuality the 'gentler and more imaginative inmates' of the Yard see in her, or 'the invention of a tambour worker, a spinster and a romantic', she emblematises the yearning, imprisoned love at the heart of *Little Dorrit*. Her refrain, 'Bleeding Heart, Bleeding Heart, bleeding away' is echoed in many tones and voices. She is the lovelorn girl of the chivalric song 'Compagnons de la Majolaine'.[14] She is the mother of Arthur Clennam, 'always writing, incessantly writing' (p. 852), a prisoner until she dies of Mrs Clennam's moralistic vengeance, a haunting presence in the decaying house. She is the tiny woman and the princess of Little Dorrit's fairy-tale. In Little Dorrit herself, and in the women who surround her, there are explored aspects of this potent romanticism.

In the diverse context the novel provides for its study of maimed, imprisoned sensibility, Arthur Clennam is no less important a protagonist than the novel's women. 'Trained by main force; broken, not bent; . . . always grinding in a mill' (p. 59), he is left, at the outset, in his middle years, without 'will, purpose, hope' as he returns to the prison which is London and 'home'. And there is Mr Dorrit, 'the impurity of his prison worn into the grain of his soul' (p. 273). The first two chapters of *Little Dorrit* make a proem in which imprisonment is, for men and women alike, the inescapable condition of life; 'journeying by land and journeying by sea, coming and going so strangely', now captive, now forced onwards in illusory freedom, 'we restless travellers through the pilgrimage of life' endure the physical and mental discomforts of our confinement (p. 67). Aspects of the novel's large theme are glancingly noted – in the 'caged beasts' and the angelic child who feeds them; in the snatch of chivalric song hinting at the fabulous freedom of a Sir Lancelot ('Of all the king's knights 'tis the flower' – p. 45) and at the eternal faithfulness of the lady at her window; in the heat and odour of the Marseilles prison that links the criminals with the English travellers on their Grand Tour, and the French quarantine with the stifling atmosphere of London. But, if we must all see the world through prison bars, what hope is there that an Arthur Clennam, or a Little Dorrit, or a Miss Wade, can change themselves or the world they create? Critics for whom the novel provides no adequate answer to its own insistent question inevitably describe *Little Dorrit* as 'static'.[15]

The question is sharpened for Dickens, during this decade, by his work for Urania Cottage.[16] He must have interviewed hundreds of Miss Wades and Tattycorams in his 'nightly wanderings into strange places', destitute and fallen women of London condemned to their fate by a law far more inexorable than the law of romantic legend:

> It is dreadful to think how some of these doomed women have no chance or choice. It is impossible to disguise from one's self the horrible truth that it would have been a social marvel and miracle if some of them had been anything else than what they are.[17]

In Little Dorrit, in Miss Wade, in Tattycoram, in Society's matriarchs, Dickens explores what chance or choice there may be within imprisoning circles that seem inevitably, endlessly, to repeat themselves. These are circles made by and for the self, by men and by women alike, but the novel finds a special significance in the female and the maternal, as a comparison of Little Dorrit's story with Miss Wade's makes clear.

Little Dorrit's fairy-tale provides us with something as patently to be overheard and looked in on as the more overtly autobiographical confession Miss Wade writes for Arthur Clennam. Each narrative depicts its Lady of Shalott, though in Little Dorrit's story she assumes two forms: that of the 'Princess' and the 'poor tiny little woman'. The story begins with a fine king who had everything he could wish for, and a great deal more, including a daughter who is, Little Dorrit tells Maggy

> . . . the wisest and most beautiful Princess that ever was seen. When she was a child she understood all her lessons before her masters taught them to her; and when she was grown up, she was the wonder of the world. Now, near the Palace where the Princess lived, there was a cottage in which there was a poor little tiny woman who lived all alone by herself.'
>
>   'An old woman', said Maggy, with an unctuous smack of her lips.

'No, not an old woman. Quite a young one.'

'I wonder she warn't afraid', said Maggy. 'Go on, please.'

'The Princess passed the cottage nearly every day, and whenever she went by in her beautiful carriage, she saw the poor tiny woman spinning at her wheel, and she looked at the tiny woman, and the tiny woman looked at her. . . .'   (p. 341)

That 'staring habit' that infects the novel's world, from its opening in Marseilles to the grand dinners at Harley Street, Cavendish Square, is broken in the world of fairy-tale. For when the Princess stops her carriage one day she is shown the tiny woman's secret. Alone in her cottage, she keeps watch over 'a great, great treasure', the shadow of someone who has passed by and is quite out of reach. It transpires that the Princess already knows the cause of the tiny woman's solitary vigil, for she simply says, 'Remind me why.' To which the tiny woman replies, 'that no one so good and kind had ever passed that way and that was why in the beginning. She said, too, that nobody missed it, that nobody was the worse for it, that someone had gone on to those who were expecting him – ' (p. 342). In the end the wheel stops, and the tiny woman carries her treasured shadow into the grave.

Put beside the uncompromising toughness of Miss Wade's self-revelation, Little Dorrit's story seems more than a little sentimental. The nursery-tale language and assumptions ('no one so good and kind had ever passed that way') establish with the easy fluency of the practised story-teller the mode in which children like Maggy are told stories. There is more in Little Dorrit's tale than the evocation of childish simplicities, however. It is dramatic utterance.[18] The plangency of its cadences reveals that aspect of its teller that lies hidden by her habitual selflessness. There is an unmistakable note of self-pity in this self-projection. For a Tattycoram, the over-charged heart finds release in sobbing and raging and pluckings at her lips 'with all the force of her youth and fulness of life' (p. 65). For Little Dorrit, suffering finds no vent in action, except that of weaving a web that reflects the imprisoned consciousness in its wistful yearnings, its underlying resignation. It is a 'cruel pattern' that Little Dorrit's story makes, this vision of life seen through the Marshalsea bars. The tiny woman is content to retreat from the world and from the promise of love it offers, transforming her real feelings and needs into a sentimentally-conceived vigil that has its appropriate outcome in death. Just as the Lady of Shalott's drift towards extinction is the appropriate sequel to her solitary vigil, so Little Dorrit's retreat from life is projected in the tiny woman's retreat from the claims of identity and responsibility into a world of anonymity ('nobody missed it . . . nobody was the worse for it . . . someone had gone on to those who were expecting him'). Her story echoes that hopelessness with which Arthur Clennam surrenders his love for Pet Meagles, and with which all the irremediable pain of the world is 'nobody's fault'. In making this fable of her response to Arthur Clennam, Little Dorrit attempts to explain and understand why, instead of allowing herself the pleasure of meeting him, she retreats to her prison garret and composes her feelings into a tale about the sorrows and the sad fate of a tiny woman.

Between the tiny woman and the Princess is fixed an insuperable gulf, reflecting that gulf the novel explores between the 'Poverty' of Book the First, and the 'Riches' of Book the Second. Through Little Dorrit's fairy-tale, Dickens lays bare not only her private dreams, but also the assumptions on which the fantasies and hopes of 'Society' are based, in which great happiness is inevitably associated with wealth and status. Little Dorrit's Princess is the emblem of social success, the Pet Meagles of Arthur's poor dream, 'round and fresh and dimpled and spoilt' (p. 54), whose father can provide the wealth that makes a princess to match the knight who rides past the palace and cottage. The novel is to develop more sombre implications in the Princess's story, in which her wealth makes her prey to the insouciant charm of knights, and her sheltering parental castle deprives her of the worldly knowledge with which to defend herself against such charm. The pastoral episode at Twickenham invites comparison with Tennyson's 'The Gardener's Daughter', except that for Dickens the rural sequestering and nurturing of such a conventional pattern of Victorian womanhood entails precisely the kind of 'happy ending' Pet makes for her life. Little Dorrit is to find the solitary Pet, in yet another vividly pictured imprisonment, on her wedding-journey in Book the Second, in a dingy room, gazing out at the sky through the tops of blocked-up windows. The eligible young lady, formed by a 'prunes and prisms' education to take her due place in the world of 'Riches' is as much imprisoned by her castle as the tiny woman is by her cottage.

The Princess and the tiny woman are, of course, not simply rivals: they are allies, and even, as their instinctive knowledge of one another suggests, aspects of the same imagining consciousness. If the little woman is the self in which Little Dorrit takes refuge, the princess is the self she imagines she would like to be if the world were indeed a fairy-tale – good and wise and her father's chief delight, but also free to come and go in her carriage, and likely, in the end, to be claimed by the knight. And here Little Dorrit's tale, like Panck's 'fortune-telling', foreshadows the fairy-tale outcome in which she becomes first a princess, and at last a poor tiny woman who nevertheless claims the knight. The roles of the little woman and the princess find reconciliation in a 'real' world, in a way that raises questions about the relationship between Little Dorrit's tale and the novel as a whole.

Little Dorrit's fairy-tale, like the story of Miss Marchmont in *Villette*, provides a simple outline of the novel's more complex and subtle fable. And her act of imagination, like comparable imaginings of Lucy Snowe's, reveals the creative consciousness of the novelist reflecting on the shape and meaning of his narrative. It is from the imprisoned figure of Little Dorrit, at once victim and visionary, that shape and meaning flow, bringing into relationship all the novel's self-enclosed centres of consciousness and community. (This surely, is the 'unifying' idea in which Dickens discovers the inner relationship of the mass of material 'clamouring for inclusion' as he labours at the novel in its early stages.[19]) When Little Dorrit becomes the Princess, coming and going in her carriage, she feels herself as much a prisoner as ever. The gratification of fairy-tale dreams in *Great Expectations*, which is to follow immediately after *Little Dorrit*, leads to a similar discovery that happiness is not to be found in the world of 'Riches', but in the giving and receiving of generous, disinterested love. *Little Dorrit* is the novel in which Dickens most searchingly explores the questions of how and why this should be so. Little Dorrit herself, like Pip, is the neglected child of the Dickens world and of Victorian society.[20] But this 'Child of the Marshalsea' is also 'Little Mother', exemplifying from the beginning a capacity to love which Pip is only to glimpse in his painfully achieved maturity. The fairy-tale Little Dorrit imagines for Maggy shows not only a maternal caring for this grotesque child–woman, but also an ability to inhabit her world, a moral strength that enables the growth and development of the self as well as of others. In this way, Little Dorrit stands in sharp contrast to the stunted and eccentric ladies of this and later Dickens novels, imprisoned and imprisoning others.

Dickens's presentation of Society's great 'mother', Mrs Merdle, recalls Mary Wollstonecraft's striking image of nineteenth-century womanhood confined in cages 'like the feathered race', with nothing to do 'but to plume themselves and stalk with mock majesty from perch to perch'.[21] Composed in her bower with attendant parrot, Mrs Merdle's extensive bosom harbours neither maternal nor sexual feelings, but opulently displays its true values. And the Society that Mrs Merdle regards is a projection, quite simply, of her own attitudes. Her conversations with that other great social mother, Mrs Gowan, concerning the marriages of young men, makes delightfully plain the process by which, like all the novel's enclosed consciousnesses, she sees a world that reflects only the self:

> we know it is hollow and conventional and wordly and very shocking, but unless we are Savages in the Tropical seas (I should have been charmed to be one myself–most delightful life and perfect climate, I am told), we must consult it. It is the common lot. Mr Merdle is a most extensive merchant, his transactions are on the vastest scale, his wealth and influence are very great, but even he–Bird, be quiet!   (p. 285)

The vast mansion in Harley Street holds Mr and Mrs Merdle captive as all the great dreary gaols of Society's houses hold their owners captive, and indeed stamp their imprisoning materialism on their owners' faces, 'all approachable by the same dull steps, all fended off by the same pattern of railing' (p. 292). Dickens's caricaturing art sparkles on the unchanging surfaces cultivated by these fixed attitudes, in which there is no possibility of naturalness, savage or delightful, no possibility of growth or flowering of real feeling.

Mrs Clennam, from her vantage-point of professed other-worldliness, incarcerated in the room that gives her neurosis such vivid actuality, has an equally loveless notion of 'mothering' the illegitimate child born to her husband and the girl he loves, a notion that reflects the 'wholesome repression, punishment and fear' (p. 843) of her own childhood. And here the writing is trenchant as it gives voice to the vision that has made Arthur Clennam's world:

> I was stern with him, knowing that the transgressions of the parents are visited on their offspring, and that there was an angry mark on him at his birth. . . . I have seen him, with his mother's face, looking up at me in awe from his little books, and trying to soften me with his mother's ways that hardened me.   (p. 859)

The room Mrs Clennam inhabits, beyond the reach of seasons, weather, feelings, like Mrs Merdle's, however, contains nothing but the mirrored reality of the enclosed consciousness itself:

> To stop the clock of busy existence at an hour when we were personally sequestered from it, to suppose mankind stricken motionless when we were brought to a stand-still, to be unable to measure the changes beyond our view by any larger standard than the shrunken one of our own uniform and contracted existence, is the infirmity of many invalids, and the mental unhealthiness of almost all recluses. (p. 388)

Dickens is already envisaging *Great Expectations*. Miss Havisham's neurosis translates its vision with an even more grotesque literalness than Mrs Clennam's, into a shrunken and contracted world. And, more irrevocably than Mrs Clennam, Miss Havisham creates, in the child she mothers, a life in which the springs of generous feeling are stricken motionless. In Miss Wade's history, Dickens gives a chilling account of the 'mental unhealthiness' that encloses her.

In writing Miss Wade's 'History of a Self-tormentor' Dickens saw his task as 'making the introduced story so fit into surroundings impossible of separation from the main story, as to make the blood of the book circulate through both'.[22] In fact Miss Wade's part in those surroundings, from her very first appearance, fully justifies Dickens's organic metaphor. She is the 'solitary young lady', among the quarantined fellow-travellers of Chapter 2, who sits, silent and remote, in 'shadow':

> on a couch in a window, seeming to watch the reflection of the water as it made a silver quivering on the bars of the lattice. She sat, turned away from the whole length of the apartment, as if she were lonely of her own haughty choice. And yet it would have been as difficult as ever to say, positively, whether she avoided the rest, or was avoided. (p. 62)

The passage prefigures Little Dorrit's indulgence of 'reflections' through the Marshalsea bars in Book the First, and her gazing down into the waters of Venice in Book the Second. In the histories of both young women, Dickens is to explore the question of whether such a retreat into silent contemplation and seclusion can be thought of as a matter of 'choice'. But, when Miss Wade speaks, it is in a tone very different from Little Dorrit's. Stung out of silence by the complacencies of her fellow travellers, she finds inexorable meaning in their common journey and their temporary imprisonment, delivering herself of the view that there is no escape from one's destiny, and that the prisoner 'never forgives his prison' (p. 61).

In Arthur Clennam she recognises a fellow prisoner, and it is to him that she addresses her 'History'. There is nothing quite like this dramatic monologue elsewhere in Dickens, nor indeed, in Victorian fiction. While its intensity of bitterness recalls Lucy Snowe's more painful moments, there is in Miss Wade an icy control, expressing a final inflexibility Lucy never has, as well as a greater degree of authorial detachment. Miss Wade speaks out of the centre of her solitude, 'unconsciously laying bare all her character'.[23] Her lonely diatribe expects no answer or exchange. Through her own eloquent expression of suppressed needs, Dickens analyses the psychological processes that entrap her, through which her sense of social deprivation is perpetuated in barriers of her own making and, subsequently, in the life of Tattycoram.

The 'History of a Self-tormentor' chronicles Miss Wade's reaching out, from childhood onwards, for friendship and affection, and her inability to receive the offered love. Of her first, 'chosen friend' she reflects,

> I loved that stupid mite in a passionate way that she could no more deserve than I can remember without feeling ashamed of, though I was but a child. She had what they called an amiable temper, an affectionate temper. She could distribute, and did distribute, pretty looks and smiles to every one among them. I believe there was not a soul in the place, except myself, who knew that she did it properly to wound and gall me!   (p. 726)

Cool detachment is belied by the extremity of reaction. And again Charlotte Brontë's Lucy Snowe comes to mind, a heroine whose suppressed feelings must be played out for her by a Polly or a Ginevra. There is a greater deliberation and manipulativeness in Miss Wade, however. Her 'passionate way' of loving is to provoke in her small friend the passion she cannot allow herself to express:

I would reproach her with my perfect knowledge of her baseness; and then she would cry and cry and say I was cruel, and then I would hold her in my arms till morning: loving her as much as ever, and often feeling as if, rather than suffer so, I could hold her in my arms and plunge to the bottom of a river – where I would still hold her after we were both dead.   (p. 727)

This is a pattern of behaviour we have seen her repeat with Tattycoram, who has left her 'dependent' position in the Meagles' household for the promise of freedom held out by Miss Wade. Chapter 2 glancingly pictures the girl's attraction to the woman who views her 'with a strange attentive smile' shut in on her paroxysm of weeping (p. 65). It is not only Tattycoram's providing a history like her own, but her capacity to give vent to the feelings of envy, frustration and ignominy it creates, that make Miss Wade 'adopt' and further imprison her. In the conversation that precedes Miss Wade's history, the two natures are seen 'tearing each other to pieces', enclosed in their 'dead sort of house, with a dead wall over the way and a dead gateway at the side' (pp. 724, 716).

Miss Wade's 'History', then, unfolds a disposition already elaborated in her behaviour throughout the novel. What this chapter explores and develops is the tone in which Miss Wade accepts and indeed exults in her solipsism. There is no room for doubt about the motivations of others, no self-scrutiny about the 'unhappy temper' ascribed to her. She writes for herself in her monologue the history the novel has shown her making for herself, to perpetuate her loneliness and rejection. She tells of the kind young mistress in her first post as governess:

When she pressed me to take wine, I took water. If there happened to be anything choice at table, she always sent it to me: but I always declined it, and ate of the rejected dishes. These disappointments of her patronage were a sharp retort, and made me feel independent.   (p. 728)

Unlike Little Dorrit's self-mortification (poor kind Flora has to press her again and again to eat, wanting to bridge the gulf that makes her guest a social dependent), Miss Wade's is calculated to offend. The society her beleaguered vision creates is given no quarter. One by one the possibilities for development and fulfilment in childhood, in her work as governess, in her betrothal, and in her free liaison with Henry Gowan are blighted because of her refusal to be appeased by them. Through her narrative is glimpsed a figure analogous to Little Dorrit's Princess, for whom life holds a different destiny – 'my Mistress', 'my friend', 'the fair Gowanna' – scorned and deeply envied by Miss Wade. Henry Gowan feeds in her a cynicism that, matching her own, enables her to reject him. But the affair destroys any chance of escaping the vicious circle that entraps her, in which deliberate 'choice' compounds the chance that makes her social deprivations. Her seduction of Tattycoram (even Mr Meagles is 'old enough to have heard of such perversions' – p. 379) confirms her role as social outcast.

What makes for Miss Wade her 'unhappy temperament' is explained to Arthur Clennam by Pancks, with a directness Miss Wade's narrative, for all its apparent candour, can never manage:

> 'I expect . . . I know as much about her as she knows about herself. She is somebody's child – anybody's – nobody's. Put her in a room in London here with any six people old enough to be her parents, and her parents may be there for anything she knows. They may be in any house she sees, they may be in any street, she may make chance acquaintance of 'em at any time and never know it. She knows nothing about 'em. She knows nothing about any relative whatever. Never did. Never will.'
>
> 'Mr Casby could enlighten her, perhaps?'
>
> 'May be', said Pancks. 'I expect so, but don't know. He has long had money in trust to dole out to her when she can't do without it. Sometimes she's proud and won't touch it for a length of time: sometimes she's so poor that she must have it. She writhes under her life. A woman more angry, passionate, reckless and revengeful never lived. . . .'   (p. 595)

' . . . somebody's   child – anybody's – nobody's': Dickens   here sounds his keynote. In the neglected child, fiercely denying and suppressing needs that might make for wholeness of being and a proper self-assertion, 'love' takes only manipulative and destructive forms. Passion becomes vengeful.

Each of these extended narratives, then, permits the exploration of feelings habitually suppressed. Miss Wade's exults in its repetitious, savage self-sufficiency, a poem of lonely suffering that illumines her terse utterance and hostile behaviour throughout the novel. Little Dorrit's lyricism is more whimsical, its tone finely balanced between defeatism and the faint stirrings of wistful hope. Dramatic monologue, it might be argued, is the natural resource of a novelist whose preferred mode of psychological exploration is dramatic. Undoubtedly Dickens is most at ease with revelations of the inner life in terms of speech and behaviour, or in terms of images that make for it objective correlatives, or in the celebration of people who have no inner lives at all. But as well, in the later novels, Dickens experiments more successfully with passages of sustained introspection that explore the development of thought and feeling in characters like Little Dorrit and Arthur Clennam. Two such passages, Little Dorrit's reverie at the end of Chapter 19 of Book the First, and the comparable reflections in Chapter 3 of Book the Second, suggest how our inhabiting of her inner life is essential to an understanding and a proper valuing of Little Dorrit's way of seeing the world.

In preparing for a discussion of these passages, it is necessary to pursue the question of what more there is to Little Dorrit's goodness than the assertion of a rather tiresome, and, to modern readers, distinctly alienating, Victorian stereotype. How is that Little Dorrit's goodness flowers while the lives of so many of society's neglected children are blighted? Her dual role as 'child of the Marshalsea' and 'Little Mother' raises the further question of how adequately Dickens deals with the feelings appropriate to filial, maternal and sexual love, and with the relationship between them.

Chapter 14 of Book the First, 'Little Dorrit's Party', suggests some answers. On the pretext of a 'party', Little Dorrit gives herself an evening away from the Marshalsea – first, an outing with Maggy to the theatre to see Fanny dance, followed by a visit to Arthur Clennam to thank him for his kindness to Tip. Locked out of the Marshalsea, she and Maggy wander about the chilly streets, waiting for dawn. As she thinks longingly of the 'home' which has closed its gates for the night, Little Dorrit imagines a party in a home that is 'light and warm and beautiful', with her father as its master, and Mr Clennam as its guest, and all of them dancing to beautiful music. There is more to this exercise of fancy than a sentimentally conceived comparison between the imagined party and the party through which Little Dorrit and Maggy actually move, among the dispossessed of nocturnal London. Little Dorrit has had her party in seeing Clennam: her tour of duty had that as its end, and her imagined party, like all her exercises of fancy, draws attention to inner needs and hopeful dreams that begin to involve Clennam as well as her father. Her sensitivity to the needs of others does not exclude a sensitivity to her own, and she here finds a way of heeding both at once. Nevertheless, her party must take account of its other guests, the waifs and strays of the uncaring city:

> Three o'clock and half-past three, and they had passed over London Bridge. They had heard the rush of the tide against obstacles; and looked down, awed, through the dark vapour on the river; had seen little spots of lighted water where the bridge lamps were reflected, shining like demon eyes, with a terrific fascination in them for guilt and misery. They had shrunk past homeless people, lying coiled up in nooks. They had run from drunkards. They had started from slinking men, whistling and signing to one another at bye corners, or running away at full speed. Though everywhere the leader and the guide, Little Dorrit, happy for once in her youthful appearance, feigned to cling to and rely upon Maggy. And more than once some voice, from among a knot of brawling or prowling figures in their path, had called out to the rest to 'let the woman and the child go by!'   (p. 217)

Arthur Clennam sees Little Dorrit as somehow separate from 'the common and coarse things surrounding her'. The force of a scene like this, however, is to show her as belonging in these streets, among the 'restless travellers' drifting towards the complete extinction of their humanity. No mystic power removes her from exposure to its dangers. Dickens's London is a world in which nature's energies threaten frail, desolate, human energies, or make a welcoming vortex for them. Slinking and prowling and galloping in terror, or 'lying coiled up in nooks', these are scarcely human lives at all. And Little Dorrit and Maggy must 'start' and slink and feign with the rest. This very night Little Dorrit has seen, with an intensity of pain so sharp that she can scarcely take in Clennam's lighted room, places where 'the miserable children in rags . . . like young rats, slunk and hid, fed on offal, huddled together for warmth, and were hunted about' (p. 208). In the prison of London's streets the struggle for survival is elemental. Little Dorrit's birth, in the squalor of the Marshalsea, is part of this grim, unsentimental vision of the frailty of gratuitous human life: 'the flies fell into the traps by hundreds; and at length one little life, hardly stronger than theirs, appeared among the multitude of lesser deaths' (p. 102). These are 'nobody's children', the ciphers administered by circumlocutory bureaucracy, the births about which society does not want to know. The novel evokes again and again the inexorable drift of life into anonymity. In Chapter 31, the children are grown into creeping little old men, in coats of uncertain shape and cut, measured and lent by Fate, as to 'a long unfinished line of many old men' (p. 413). But out of that poignant, comic procession of sad old figures there emerge first poor old Nandy, an individual loved and valued, outside the workhouse, by his admiring family, and William Dorrit, the Father of the Marshalsea in his several relations. In the love that nourishes their individuality and their self-assertion, Dickens sees the reversal of that hopeless drift.

Little Dorrit and Maggy are protected from the nameless and homeless figures of London by their clinging together. They are 'the woman and the child', and their physical embrace holds a more than symbolic meaning, a response other than hopelessness, for these rejected people. The prostitute, 'strange and wilful', sees in them the bonds of love and nurture from which her exposure to a predatory sexuality excludes her. But, as she recognises with surprise, Little Dorrit is not 'the child', but a woman.

Dickens's novels show a marked fondness for 'little mothers'. Little Nell, Florence Dombey, Cissy Jupe come to mind as examples of what is often simply construed as Victorian domestic pietism, or as continuing nostalgic tribute to the memory of Mary Hogarth. Little mothers were common enough among the motherless large families of Dickens's day. And Dickens is strongly drawn to the ideal of womanhood as essentially responsible, selfless and passionless, and, as a public man, does much to promote it: 'those who are our best and dearest friends in infancy, in childhood, in manhood, and in old age, the most devoted and least selfish natures that we know on earth, who turn to us always constant and unchanged, when others turn away'.[24] This is the kind of rhetoric that mars the final coming-together of Little Dorrit and Arthur Clennam. But it does not mar this novel's more exploratory insight into idealisations of woman's role that Little Dorrit is all too ready to exemplify, or its recognition that her womanliness grows as she acknowledges and asserts her own needs and rights.

Despite Little Dorrit's ready acceptance of the maternal role, she remains in an important sense 'the Child of the Marshalsea'. Her smallness of stature emphasises, in Dickens's characteristically non-discursive way, deprivations she shares with other malnourished and imprisoned children. She starves herself to provide her father with small delicacies, a self-abnegation that makes palpable both her child-like emotional dependence and her maternal solicitude. Like Maggy, this passage reminds us, Little Dorrit is a woman whose full development has been arrested. She is content, in the threatening streets, to retreat into the protection her diminutive figure makes for her, just as she shrinks back into the familial world of childhood that makes her emotional security. If the world of those streets insistently recalls Blake's *London*,[25] the world Little Dorrit's prison makes for her within it recalls his *Songs of Innocence*. Like the nurse who shares her children's needs and delights, or the shepherd who follows the rhythms of nurture that bind ewe and lamb, where instinctive call is answered by its immediate reply, Little Dorrit's maternal loving springs directly from, and is enabled by, the needs of a child-like nature. There is strength and joy in this circumscribed world, but, as the larger context of Blake's and Dickens's London suggests, it excludes those marks of weakness and woe that belong to the more complex and assertive self discovered by experience. Little Dorrit has been distressed at Arthur Clennam's so often calling her 'child'. Her inner struggle is towards the acknowledgement of an adult love that seeks to gratify 'self'.

For Miss Wade, as for Fanny Dorrit, maternal deprivation fosters only an inability to love. Fanny continually strikes Miss Wade's note of ruthless self-assertion: 'Other girls, differently reared and differently circumstanced altogether, might wonder at what I say or may do. Let them. They are driven by their lives and characters; I am driven by mine' (p. 649). Fanny's passionate outbursts are the obverse of Amy's inability to assert her feelings, formed as she is by the unnatural and unremitting demands of her father. When, then, is Little Dorrit 'inspired to be something which was not what the rest were, and to be that something, different and laborious, for the sake of the rest' (p. 111)? Dickens does answer his question, in terms of that very relationship which begins as she sits on the high fender, 'quietly watching' not with Miss Wade's suspicious watchfulness, but with a solicitude for the parent for whom she is a 'necessary' and an 'accustomed' presence. Years later, the Little Mother who soothes the Father of the Marshalsea to sleep is still the child whose emotional needs are bound up with his, and whose life depends on his direction.

In Chapter 19 of Book the First, however, and in the grip of her unacknowledged feeling for Clennam, Little Dorrit asserts herself, against her father's expectations of compliance, by refusing to encourage the attentions of young John Chivery, son of the turnkey. Committed as she is to bolstering William Dorrit's position in the Marshalsea world – she 'boasts' to a percipient Clennam of Mr Dorrit's attainments and the high regard in which he is held – there are aspects of it that she will not countenance. She is mortified by her father's and her brother's applications to Clennam for money, seeing them not as 'tributes' or 'loans' due to their being gentlemen among gentlemen, but as the unashamed sponging it really is. Her sticking firm in the matter of John Chivery prompts a rare moment in which even Mr Dorrit sees the shabbyness of his own motives and of the pretensions that sustain him in the prison. Dicken's mastery of the rhetoric of his self-delusion enables truth of feeling to be discerned, struggling through the comfortable repetition of protective lies: 'Amy, my love, you are by far the best loved of the three; I have had you principally in my mind – Whatever I have done for your sake, my dear child, I have done freely and without murmuring' (p. 275). It is a mastery of tone, as well as of rhetoric. Mr Dorrit's claim of 'doing' for the child who does everything for him is both ridiculous and poignant, evoking that gracious gentility that is his last, hollow, resource. And yet, in this very scene, in which the ebb and flow of feeling between father and child is charted, with a sure sense of the deep sources of need from which these feelings flow, Mr Dorrit's claim has its own rightness. He has indeed given his favourite daughter all he could. Maudlin, self-pitying, querulous as he is here, his suffering imprisoned self elicits her tenderness and fulfils her yearnings, making a circle that contrasts with the circles of unloved and unloving children endlessly repeating themselves in society at large.

The scene ends, however, in Little Dorrit's dispirited contemplation of the view from her prison garret:

> the smokeless housetops and the distant country hills were discernible over the wall in the clear morning. As she gently opened the window, and looked eastward down the prison yard, the spikes upon the wall were tipped with red, then made a sullen purple pattern on the sun as it came flaming up into the heavens. The spikes had never looked so sharp and cruel, nor the bars so heavy, nor the prison space so gloomy and contracted. She thought of the sunrise on rolling rivers, of the sunrise on wide seas, of the sunrise

on rich landscapes, of the sunrise on great forests where the birds were waking and the trees were rustling; and she looked down into the living grave on which the sun had risen, with her father in it three-and-twenty years, and said, in a burst of sorrow and compassion, 'No, no, I have never seen him in my life!'   (p. 276)

Little Dorrit's moment of introspection makes an essential part of the scene just enacted. It is a moment in which she asserts the claims of self, but one whose tone and vision catch the very flavour of her imprisonment. The 'gloomy and contracted' view from the window makes visual the pain and shame sharply registered, but suppressed by Little Dorrit's need to cope with and relieve her father's pain. That active compassion springs from her empathy. She inhabits his own gloomy and contracted perspective as readily as she shares the simpler childishness of Maggy's world. What her moral imagination enables her to 'see' in her long vigil is what imprisonment has meant to this weak and sensitive man. And, yet, she remains 'but too content to see him with a lustre round his head', to shrink back into idealisation of him and to cling to her own child-like need of him, as he, too, retreats from his momentary perceptiveness. That idealisation is as much a part of her contracted vision as the weirdly coloured patterns the sun makes on the prison spikes. Looking from the window, she sees not the distant rolling hills, that world elsewhere so freshly evoked in the novel's pastoral moments, but a world as fanciful as the world of her fairy-tale, or the warm and beautiful home she imagines in the streets of London. The vague, unbounded freedom of 'rolling rivers, . . . wide seas, . . . rich landscapes', the rhetorical patterns that repeat the rising of the sun, bespeak large yearnings and impossible fulfilments. Chief among these rosy pictures is her picture of the father she has never seen, and who could never be.

The underlying tone we need to hear in this flow of private reflection, however, expresses an emotional reality that colours all fancy and idealisation, something tired, resigned, self-enclosing. It is the tone of Arthur Clennam's vision of a London from which there is 'no escape between the cradle and the grave' (p. 68) or of Pancks's vision of the 'Whole Duty of Man in a commercial country', 'always grinding, drudging, toiling, every minute we're awake' (p. 202), or of Mrs Clennam's view of the earthly life as 'a scene of gloom, and hardship, and dark trial, for the creatures who are made out of its dust' (p. 407). Amy Dorrit, 'drinking from infancy of a well whose waters had their own peculiar stain, their own unnatural taste', absorbs large draughts of the novel's prevailing medium.

In Book the Second, the unimaginable world of freedom opens up for the Dorrits, and in comparable moments of contemplation Little Dorrit takes the measure of this world. She has looked from a series of windows at a succession of the expansive vistas Dickens creates with such precise and varied richness. But she is as little able to see what is spread before her eyes as she was in the Marshalsea garret:

> her favourite station was the balcony of her own room, overhanging the canal, with other balconies below, and none above. It was of massive stone darkened by ages, built in a wild fancy which came from the East to that collection of wild fancies; and Little Dorrit was little indeed, leaning on the broad-cushioned ledge, and looking over. As she liked no place of an evening half so well, she soon began to be watched for, and many eyes in passing gondolas were raised, and many people said, There was the little figure of the English girl who was always alone.
>
> Such people were not realities to the little figure of the English girl; such people were all unknown to her. She would watch the sunset, in its long low lines of purple and red, and its burning flush high up into the sky: so glowing on the buildings, and so lightening their structure, that it made them look as if their strong walls were transparent, and they shone from within. She would watch those glories expire; and then, after looking at the black gondolas underneath, taking guests to music and dancing, would raise her eyes to the shining stars. Was there no party of her own, in other times, on which the stars had shone? To think of that old gate now!
>
> She would think of that old gate, and of herself sitting at it in the dead of night, pillowing Maggy's head; and of other places and of other scenes associated with those different times. And then she would lean upon her balcony, and look over at the water, as though they all lay underneath it. When she got to that, she would musingly watch its running, as if, in the general vision, it might run dry, and show her the prison again, and herself, and the old room, and the old inmates, and the old visitors: all lasting realities that had never changed. (pp. 519–20)

The passage glances at the emblematic romanticism of the isolated figure at the palace window, and sees it momentarily through eyes in passing gondolas. But it notes as well that Little Dorrit here indulges a mood of romantic melancholy. There is a longer perspective, too, in that history of wild fancy written in the stones of Venice. Little Dorrit's gentler fancy, dwarfed and incongruous though it is in this exotic setting, nevertheless composes a personal history made immediate and compelling by this exploration of her inner life. Little Dorrit's history, like the history of Venice, is a continuing one. She is as completely excluded now, from the music and dancing, as she was in the old Marshalsea days. The upward lift of her eyes to the stars signals an intrusive question which underlines the connection with 'Little Dorrit's Party' in the dark streets of London. But the impulse to solicit pity for her isolation is quickly dispelled. Little Dorrit prefers the 'realities' created by her solitude, and communion with the self created and contained by 'the old mean Marshalsea'. Buildings dissolve and shine from within, solid walls that do not imprison, but glow with the warmth they contain. The stars she sees are the stars of bitter and cheerless London. Nostalgia for the prison is there in the very tone and cadences of the prose. And, again, there is resignation and hopelessness. The Dorrits celebrate their freedom with style and splendour, while they take with them into 'freedom' those selves irrevocably formed by the Marshalsea. Moving in Society, they enter that larger prison supervised by Mrs General, a life of surface whose first rule is that nothing unpleasant should ever be looked at. But Little Dorrit's isolation is not simply a mark of moral superiority. Deprived of her old close relationship with her father – 'to occupy herself in fulfilling the functions of – ha hum – a valet' (p. 516) would be incompatible with their changed position – she is unable to develop, but remains a passively suffering consciousness. Released from the imprisoning room, she is afflicted by the contrast between the 'reality' she has made for herself, and the intractable reality that lies outside it. In these dream-like sequences of the novel, scarcely relieved by her various confrontations with her father or Fanny or Mrs General, Little Dorrit's response is to retreat into the kind of quiesence characterised in this passage. Only in her letters to Arthur Clennam, now, does she reach out beyond the private and passive centre. Like her fairy-tale in Book the First, these narratives take advantage of a conventional mode in order to express underlying feelings. Most importantly, they further the relationship through which Dickens envisages love as growth and development, the discovery of a 'reality' different from anything the prisons of the self can make.

Of all Dickens's characters, Clennam's 'inner life' is the most fully explored. If anyone in *Little Dorrit* has 'self-aware honesty', 'reflective intelligence', and the capacity for a 'full consciousness of what is happening to him',[26] it is Clennam. He shares with Little Dorrit 'a warm and sympathetic heart', and responds instinctively and warmly to that quality in her: 'He was a dreamer in such wise, because he was a man who had, deep-rooted in his nature, a belief in all the gentle and good things his life had been without' (p. 206). Through Clennam's reflections Dickens explores in him a moral imagination quickened by Little Dorrit's, as the darkened vistas of his hopelessness are gradually lit up. The 'blackened forest of chimneys' seen from the window of his old room, the 'grim home of his youth', the dreary streets of London over which it casts its shadow, make up the 'long, . . . bare, . . . blank' history of Clennam, to which he returns 'like the imaginings of a dream' (p. 75). Presiding at the heart of it all is Mrs Clennam,

> wrathful, mysterious and sad; and his imagination was suf-
> ficiently impressible to see the whole neighbourhood under some
> tinge of its dark shadow. As he went along, upon a dreary night,
> the dim streets by which he went, seemed all depositories of
> oppressive secrets. (p. 596)

That shadow continues to shape Clennam's seeing, in his more prosperous life in Book the Second, as her father's old life in prison hangs about Little Dorrit 'like the burden of a sorrowful tune' (p. 517). The youthful romanticism represented in Flora Finching is dispelled by Arthur's soberly comic reunion with her. The conventional romanticism invested in the figure of Pet Meagles proves only another version of 'fancy's fair dream'. Clennam's need for something to fill 'the empty place in his heart that he has never known the meaning of' (p. 860) is answered by Little Dorrit.

For Clennam, too, she is both 'child' and 'Little Mother'. Her fragility and courage touch that 'empty place' as he comes to know her (as they have touched the business-like Pancks, and inspired him to unravel the Dorrit history); 'So diminutive she looked, so fragile and defenceless against the bleak damp weather, flitting along in the shuffling shadow of her charge' (p. 215). In Chapter 9, 'Little Mother', the grotesque Maggy (whose hopeless idiocy is seen with honesty and compassion), makes a focus for the feelings that flow between Little Dorrit and Clennam, feelings different in kind from those that flow between Little Dorrit and her father. Little

Dorrit tells a history that changes Arthur's way of seeing the desolate streetscape in which their conversation is set, 'the piles of city roofs and chimneys among which the smoke was rolling heavily . . . the wilderness of masts and river, and the wilderness of steeples on the shore' (p. 139). In telling the story of Maggy's life, she is also telling the story of her own devotedness, so that 'the mother and the child' take on, for Clennam, an individual and a personal meaning:

> 'You can't think how good she is, sir', said Little Dorrit, with infinite tenderness.
> 'Good *she* is', echoed Maggy, transferring the pronoun in a most impressive way from herself to her little mother.
> 'Or how clever', said Little Dorrit. 'She goes on errands as well as anyone.' Maggy laughed. 'And is as trustworthy as the Bank of England.' Maggy laughed. 'She earns her own living entirely. Entirely, sir!' said Little Dorrit, in a lower and triumphant tone. 'Really does!' (pp. 142–3)

'Goodness' is registered here as surely as the oddity in Maggy which might seem more congenial to the Dickensian imagination. Arthur Clennam's yearning for 'some beautiful form of growth or life' in the dinginess of London is answered by this exchange of delicate and instinctive feelings. In Book the Second, the nosegay of choice and beautiful flowers Little Dorrit takes with her to his room in the Marshalsea makes vivid what she has come to mean to him.

Little Dorrit creates such tenderness in his thoughts that she sees it in his eyes: 'She wondered what he was thinking of, as he looked at Maggy and her. She thought what a good father he would be. How, with some such look, he would counsel and cherish his daughter' (p. 210). There is a satisfying appropriateness in the pattern of plot that brings Clennam, with his burden of unpayable debts and Calvinist guilt, to precisely that room in the Marshalsea once inhabited by Mr Dorrit. Recent criticism has been surprisingly naïve in its objection to what is surely a basic premise of Freudian psychology: the persistence, in adulthood, of the emotional dependencies and needs of the child. Clennam replaces Mr Dorrit as the object of Little Dorrit's care and love, as a counseller and cherisher who is the 'good father' her own could never be. And Little Dorrit embodies, for Clennam, the maternal love he has never had:

Clennam, listening to the voice as it read to him, heard in it all that great Nature was doing, heard in it all the soothing songs she sings to man. At no Mother's knee but hers had he ever dwelt in his youth on hopeful promises, on playful fancies, on the harvests of tenderness and humility that lie hidden in the early-fostered needs of the imagination; on the oaks of retreat from blighting winds, that have the germs of their strong roots in nursery acorns. But, in the tones of the voice that read to him, there were memories of an old feeling of such things, and echoes of every merciful and loving whisper that had ever stolen to him in his life. (pp. 883–4)

Dickens is as reticent as any Victorian novelist about sexuality. In these images of fertility and plenitude, however, nature's creativity gives intimations of a human creativity without locks or limits. Like Wordsworth in the passage of *The Prelude* echoed here,[27] and like Charlotte Brontë in *Villette*, Dickens envisages the continuity of the growing child, from 'nursery acorn' into the strong-rooted being of adulthood. And, in the continuity of the human needs for nurture and 'soothing', he finds the very sources of human vitality. These are the needs suppressed in and by Miss Wade and Society's matriarchs, but repeatedly expressed by Little Dorrit, not only in the warm embraces that enclose Maggy, or her father, but also in her offering her hand to the imprisoned Clennam. And so the pastoral world that seems to lie beyond the prison, of the meadows and fields from which Little Dorrit returns on her excursions with Bob the turnkey, laden with grass and flowers, and which she sees, in adulthood, only through the prison bars, and the romanticised pastoral of Clennam's fanciful dream, is created freshly in the world each can open up for the other.

The epithet 'Little' which has expressed Clennam's tenderness for Little Dorrit continues to express her need for tenderness. Such diminutives are, after all, part of the language of love. But Little Dorrit is no child–bride. Clennam's imprisonment provides a renewed focus for her characteristic energy and responsibility. The passivity of her retreat from her own needs gives way to an assertion of them. The tiny woman's 'secret' is revealed, and it is she who claims the knight, at last. This revelation is part of their final uncovering of the buried past. At a level more profound than plot, however, an energy of inquiry in the novel has penetrated the surfaces of life, in search of hidden sources of feeling. Arthur

Clennam's 'wanting to know' is inseparable from the awakening of his own inner resources. His is a more penetrating and a more energetic mind than Little Dorrit's, but it is her hidden history that inspires the speculations that, quite early on, take him close to an intimation of the hidden past of their two families,[28] and that makes the centre of 'the web that his mind was busily weaving' (p. 80). As he comes really to know her, however, she ceases to be the emblematic imprisoned figure of his imaginings, or the stereotype of domestic goodness. There is an appropriateness in the coming together of Arthur Clennam's resolute pursuit of what is true, and Little Dorrit's exemplification of integrity of feelings, in a marriage that recalls ideals of liberty defined in John Stuart Mill's essay on women's 'subjection':

> when each of two persons, instead of being a nothing, is a something; when they are attached to one another, and are not too much unlike to begin with: the constant partaking in the same things, assisted by their sympathy, draws out the latent capacities of each . . . by a real enriching of the two natures.[29]

' . . . inseparable and blessed', they go out of the prison, into the roaring streets, and 'a modest life of usefulness and happiness' (p. 895).

The ending of *Little Dorrit* brings the release of other captives. The fall of the house of Clennam forces its imprisoned lady to look out upon a real world, shattering 'the controllable pictures her imagination had often drawn' (p. 856). As the curse comes upon her, and she rushes out into the streets, she releases not only the haunted imagination of Affery, but also the haunting presence of Arthur's dead mother. And she takes with her Little Dorrit, whose history has been hidden, like Arthur's, in the darkened room. Thus the novel's romantic fable completes itself; the ailing life of Mrs Clennam cannot be sustained in the world that opens up before her. But for Little Dorrit, as for the novel, its sunlit vision promises a cleansed imagination:

> The vista of street and bridge was plain to see, and the sky was serene and beautiful. People stood and sat at their doors, playing with children and enjoying the evening; numbers were walking for air; the worry of the day had almost worried itself out, and few but themselves were hurried. As they crossed the bridge, the clear

steeples of the many churches looked as if they had advanced out of the murk that usually enshrouded them, and come much nearer. The smoke that rose into the sky had lost its dingy hue and taken brightness upon it. The beauties of the sunset had not faded from the long light films of cloud that lay at peace in the horizon. From a radiant centre, over the whole length and breadth of the tranquil firmament great shoots of light streamed among the early stars, like signs of the blessed later covenant of peace and hope that changed the crown of thorns into a glory.   (pp. 861–2)

Perhaps Lawrence had this passage in mind at the close of *The Rainbow*. Dickens's tone is less apocalyptic than Lawrence's and its hopefulness more modest. The prison of London lies all around, as its inhabitants take air and exercise; its streets are still filled with the uproar of 'the arrogant and the forward and the vain' (p. 895). Within this all-pervasive social atmosphere, the individual sensibility must still retreat into its own vision, awaiting a final covenant of peace and hope. The religious note, however, takes its authority from that transforming shaft of sunlight, bringing tranquillity and a heightening of the spirits to the people who play with their children. The sunlight makes for Little Dorrit, now, not lurid and cruel patterns or fanciful images, but the brightening prospect of a city from which she has no wish to escape, but within which she, too, will find her own modest domestic happiness.

3 George Eliot's Web

In Chapter 34 of *Middlemarch*, Dorothea looks down from her upper window at the procession of townsfolk and farmers on their way to Featherstone's funeral. This, we are told, is to become one of the scenes that for ever afterwards defines for Dorothea an epoch in her own history:

> The dream-like association of something alien and ill-understood with the deepest secrets of her experience seemed to mirror that sense of loneliness which was due to the very ardour of Dorothea's nature. The country gentry of old time lived in a rarefied social air: dotted apart on their stations up the mountain they looked down with imperfect discrimination on the belts of thicker life below. And Dorothea was not at ease in the perspective and chilliness of that height. (p. 346)

The vantage-point from which Dorothea contemplates the passing history of provincial life is both detached and uncomfortable; a version of that life is interwoven, nevertheless, with the deeper dimensions of private life. In Rome, the past of a whole hemisphere seems 'moving in funeral procession with strange ancestral images and trophies gathered from afar' (p. 205), and here again in Lowick, it is the poignancy of what seems lifeless, unintelligible, mysteriously 'other' that affects Dorothea, imaging the inner sorrows of her life with Casaubon. For what is 'mirrored' in Dorothea's contemplative imagination is not the scene itself, but the significance given to it by her own isolation – an isolation due as much to the unappeasable demands of her 'ardour' as to the social conditions by which she is held, like other 'country gentry of old time', ignorant and aloof from her neighbours' lives and from a larger world beyond the provincial. It is in this way, and only in this way, as the narrator is at pains to point out to us here, that such 'background' scenes of Dorothea's life become part of that fabric which is made by the selection of her 'keenest consciousness'. That consciousness, at once self-enclosed and yearning for a life beyond self, is at the very heart of George Eliot's study of interweaving provincial life. It is in the sequence of scenes that picture Dorothea's isolation in her blue-green boudoir,[1] and explore the reflected reality she creates there, that the novel pauses to study in depth its large subject, the impact of romanticism on the provinciality of Victorian England.

As in *Villette* and *Little Dorrit*, these solipsistic moments display most clearly the creative tensions in which the novel has its origins – in the high valuing of individual sensibility and the need to explore its limits. Dorothea's struggles to reach out from her centre of self towards the equivalent centre of self in others exemplifies that effort of the moral imagination towards which the learned narrator – here surely recognising the inevitable detachment of any middle-class observer from 'knowable community'[2] – continually exhorts the reader. The creative task the novelist sets herself is to place the 'Miss Brooke' material, with all the autobiographical resonances prompted by that idea of provincial largeness of soul circumscribed by narrowness of opportunity, within the context of the Featherstone–Garth–Lydgate material,[3] to become part of a larger 'web'.

Henry James perceives how the task went against her grain:

> with all its abundant and massive ingredients *Middlemarch* ought somehow to have depicted a weightier drama. Dorothea was altogether too superb a heroine to be wasted; yet she plays a narrower part than the imagination of the reader demands. She is of more consequence than the action of which she is the nominal centre.[4]

In terms of action and achievement, Dorothea's part is relatively inconsequential. That is, after all, the point of George Eliot's conception of her. Imprisoned in her 'envelope of circumstances', she takes her leading, if contentious, role in the novel's moral drama. The reflected reality she inhabits is progressively destroyed, forcing her to look outward. Like other Victorian protagonists, she never entirely escapes from the enclosing room, but neither is she destroyed by the world beyond it. George Eliot's moral fable, like those of Charlotte Brontë and Dickens, makes a comparison with, and finally a critique of, Tennyson's. Dorothea is to live the more adequately as she sees herself and the world she reflects more directly and openly.

James's admiration for the novel's 'panorama' is also qualified: 'it sets a limit . . . to the development of the old-fashioned English novel. . . . If we write novels so, how shall we write History?⁵ Eliot's instinct is that 'History' takes its most profound meaning from the individual histories that compose it, just as those histories are most fully to be understood within their larger context. Her creation of the vivid and various web formed by a whole social network is a remarkable achievement. But she is, like Dickens, fascinated by each individual's creation of his own world, by seeing how its cobwebby accretions were 'woven and interwoven'. Lydgate, Rosamond, Bulstrode, Casaubon, even the venial Featherstone, are all, like Dorothea, 'imaginative in some form or other', found, in their private moments, forming the 'gossamer links' or 'masses of spider-web, padding the moral sensibility' (*Middlemarch*, pp. 368, 661). The web Rosamond Vincy's pier-glass reflects, illumined by her self-centred egoism,⁶ makes a pleasingly concentric arrangement. The 'threads of investigation' Dr Tertius Lydgate takes up (p. 156) would seem to transcend such narrow subjectivism. The analogy he pursues is that of the living body, with its structure of 'primary webs or tissues' (p. 155), an aspect of that larger web of which George Eliot, like John Stuart Mill, believed the universe to be composed: 'the regularity which exists in nature is a web composed of distinct threads'.⁷ And the infectious excitement of the light shed on medical research by the 'gas-light' of Bichat's discovery is created in terms that evoke the creativity of the novelist as appropriately as that of the scientist. Lydgate is fired by

> the imagination that reveals subtle actions inaccessible by any sort of lens, but tracked in that outer darkness through long pathways of necessary sequence by the inward light which is the last refinement of Energy, capable of bathing even the ethereal atoms in its ideally illuminated space . . . that arduous invention which is the very eye of research, provisionally framing its object and correcting it to more and more exactness of relation; he wanted to pierce the obscurity of those minute processes which prepare human misery and joy, those invisible thoroughfares which are the first lurking-places of anguish, mania and crime, that delicate poise and transition which determine the growth of happy or unhappy consciousness. (p. 174)

The 'ideally illuminated space' of microscopic study is the pursuit of creator and characters alike; the study of those conditions that determine 'the growth of happy or unhappy consciousness' is as imperative for Eliot as for Charles Dickens. But the lights by which the texture of experience is illuminated, whether the candle-flame of all-consuming ego, or 'the serene light of science', or that light commanded by the struggling writer, fall with a certain difference for every centre of self. The image of the web reconciles the extremes of egoism with scientific truth and creative imagination; it images the expansiveness as well as the inevitable limits of the larger web which is the novel. That web, too, is only a reflected 'reality'.[8]

The contemplative activity of the self-enclosed lady is an aspect only, then, of that profound and widely ranging exploration indicated by the density of narrative speculation on mirror, web and enclosure, and the close attention given to individual mental processes. But, if the plight of a Maggie Tulliver or a Dorothea Brooke inevitably leads a writer of Eliot's imaginative and intellectual stature into a more profound exploration of the significance of her own imaginative life than that of any novelist before her, it also tempts her towards the simpler romanticism represented in Tennyson's lady. As with her predecessors, George Eliot's interest in the figure is not unequivocally critical. Dorothea's nun-like garb and penchant for renunciation can occasionally confer a halo that recalls Charlotte Brontë's Lucy Snowe or Dickens's Little Dorrit in similar postures. Like the dreaming Dorothea, Eliot is not entirely at ease in the perspective of Dorothea's romantic 'height':

> The remote worship of a woman throned out of their reach plays a great part in men's lives, but in most cases the worshipper longs for some queenly recognition, some approving sign by which his soul's sovereign may cheer him without descending from her high place. (p. 233)

Will Ladislaw is the worshipper here, his worship, as the narrator's irony suggests, making a virtue of Dorothea's inacessibility: 'What others might have called the futility of his passion, made an additional delight for his imagination' (p. 502). The attempt to show in Will a development beyond the mode of courtly love is not entirely successful, partly because the narrator herself is much inclined to be a worshipper. Like the readers she envisages with tolerant irony, she admits to feeling the attractiveness of 'the twanging of the old troubador strings' (p. 151) and they are to be heard playing rather insistently in the developing romance of Will and Dorothea. It is not only Will, in fact, who sees Dorothea as the imprisoned lady of romantic myth, 'shut up in that stone prison at Lowick . . . buried alive' (p. 234), but a sometimes indulgently romantic narrator: 'the mere chance of seeing Will occasionally was like a lunette opened in the wall of her prison, giving her a glimpse of the sunny air' (p. 386). There is often little to distinguish the terms in which the lovers think of their situation from the terms in which the narrator presents them: 'To-day she had stood at the door of the tomb and seen Will Ladislaw receding into the distant world of warm activity and fellowship – turning his face towards her as he went' (p. 507).

The significance of Dorothea's soulful pose in the Vatican museum in Chapter 19 is only flickeringly grasped by her creator. On the one hand, the novel's decisive movement, at this point, out of provincial narrowness into the large historical and cultural perspectives of Rome, ancient and modern, intends to explore the limitations of Middlemarch and of Dorothea. On the other hand, the individuality and the valuing of strong feeling that characterise Dorothea's provincial romanticism has strong affinities with the artistic credo of Will Ladislaw: 'the true seeing is within' (p. 203). Each has its due place in the cultural relativism encompassed by the broad sweep of the chapter's opening, which moves from the representative English tourist's view of the continent to the connoisseur's world of art history, to the fallibility of the most brilliant English critic of the day's mistaking 'the flower-flushed tomb of the ascended Virgin for an ornamental vase due to the painter's fancy'.[9] The 'inner light' is no certain guide, however beguilingly it shines within or upon the individual consciousness, or however valuable its insights.

Nevertheless, Dorothea is allowed to stand, a moment later, in unequivocal illumination, replicating the antique perfection of the reclining Ariadne:

> a breathing blooming girl, whose form, not shamed by the Ariadne, was clad in Quakerish grey drapery; her long cloak, fastened at the neck, was thrown backward from her arms, and one beautiful ungloved hand pillowed ·her cheek, pushing somewhat backward the white beaver bonnet which made a sort of halo to her face around the simply-braided dark-brown hair. She was not looking at the sculpture, probably not thinking of it:

her large eyes were fixed dreamily on a streak of sunlight which
fell across the floor.   (p. 201)

It is Will Ladislaw's artist friend Naumann who draws attention to
Dorothea's 'pose', and his summarising phrases 'beauty in its
breathing life, with the consciouness of Christian centuries in its
bosom' (p. 201) suggest the soulful religiosity with which he would
translate it into painting.[10] Yet Will's objection that Naumann's
'painting and Plastik' could never catch Dorothea's essential
qualities extends, not qualifies, Naumann's idealising vision. The
deliberateness with which Dorothea is posed and framed clearly
springs from theoretical as well as idealising impulses in Eliot. Not
only does her pose raise questions rehearsed in Eliot's *Westminster
Review* discussion of Lessing's *Laocoon*. It also draws on myth to
suggest a simpler version of Dorothea's story than the one the novel
offers us: the visualising of Dorothea as Ariadne, calling to mind the
abandonment by Theseus and the rescue by Bacchus,[11] sketches
roles for Casaubon and Ladislaw, as well as for Dorothea, that
would transform the subtle and sensitive interrelationship of the
three into reductive romantic fable. These impulses translate
themselves into the stasis of Victorian genre painting, in writing that
belies the characteristic delicacy of a novelist who knows that
character is not cut in marble. The phrases that elaborate
Dorothea's pose suggest that Eliot shares Naumann's vision of
her at this moment–'one beautiful ungloved hand', 'her large
eyes . . . fixed dreamily on a streak of sunlight', 'the white beaver
bonnet which made a sort of halo to her face'–create a symbolic
picture that all too simply and tenderly bespeaks largeness of soul.
As it continues, this chapter is to recognise how very far from serene
Dorothea is. The flexible, if affectionate, irony that plays over Miss
Brooke at the outset of the novel sees in her Pre-Raphaelite
simplicity of dress – 'she could wear sleeves not less bare of style than
those in which the Blessed Virgin appeared to Italian painters'
(p. 1) – a degree of self-consciousness and even affectation, express-
ive of Dorothea's 'lofty conceptions' on herself and her destiny.
Elsewhere, Dorothea's lonely dreaming, seen from within, challenges her own self-images and her creator's impulse to hold her aloof
from the complex toils that animate and hamper other lives.

   The somewhat uncertain attempt to estimate Dorothea's distinctive fineness is there, of course, from the start. The 'Prelude'
conceives of St Theresa of Avila as one whose 'largeness of soul'

transcends the limitations in which it comes to birth, forsaking 'domestic reality' and the fictional and actual romances that shape the imaginations of women, to realise a national and an epic destiny in the reform of a religious order. Subsequent Theresas, the argument runs, helped by 'no coherent social faith and order which could perform the function of knowledge for the ardently willing soul' (p. xv), are doomed to the wry or perhaps even tragic destiny of being failed saints, misunderstood and disapproved of by their contemporaries. If Dorothea's spiritual quest is a sad echo of St Theresa's, it is none the less judged worthy of comparison with it, so that a potentially mock-heroic note struggles in vain in these opening paragraphs against the valuing of 'a certain spiritual grandeur'. And Dorothea is to appear, and reappear, in the guise of the original Saint (or as the blessed Virgin, or St Cecilia, or 'a heaven-sent angel', as well as in the statuesque perfection of more ancient mythology), her inconsistencies and vagueness shed, to exemplify the triumph of spiritual grandeur over the hindrances in which it finds itself.

In asking, as Eliot's 'Prelude' is asking, 'what does the spirit need in the face of modern life', Walter Pater notes the inexorable sense modern man has of being caught, unfree. The relevant passage from the essay on Wincklemann, in *The Renaissance*, makes illuminating comparison with the inspiration for *Middlemarch*:

> The chief factor in the thoughts of the modern mind concerning itself is the intricacy, the universality of natural law, even in the moral order. For us, necessity is not, as of old, a sort of mythological personage without us, with whom we can do warfare. It is rather a magic web woven through and through us, like that magnetic system of which modern science speaks, penetrating us with a network, subtler than our subtlest nerves, yet bearing in it the central forces of the world. Can art represent men and women in these bewildering toils so as to give the spirit at least an equivalent for the sense of freedom?[12]

Pater's answer is made in the famous conclusion to these essays, as well as in *Marius the Epicurean*.[13] Like Tennyson, Pater sees a 'magic web', the wondrous subtlety of which suggests something less palpably binding than 'that magnetic system of which modern science speaks'. George Eliot takes the analogy between social and scientific laws rather more seriously, but she is nevertheless intermittently drawn towards Pater's 'magic web'. Her nostalgia for the authority of myth, like the pictorial impulse that holds dorothea's subtle nerves stilled in Grecian perfection, suggests that Dorothea's is a spirit potentially freer from bewildering toils than other Middlemarch lives. But Eliot's study of Dorothea is at its best when it reflects her conviction that 'inward needs' must find a harmony with 'outer life'. Dorothea's isolation from the general run of Middlemarch life is essential to George Eliot's conception of her, but the delicate task the novel sets itself is to establish why that isolation is felt not as freedom, but as constraint. Dorothea plays her narrow part, to come back to James's criticism, because she is conceived of as subject to that 'certain moral scheme', or network of 'inner and outer necessity' that constrains all lives. This is not to evade, but rather to pursue further the question of whether the novel's delicate task is compatible with the realisation of 'fineness of spirit', 'freedom', or indeed any adequate realisation of energies and aspirations that might challenge the dead level of Middlemarch society.[14]

Middlemarch is as much concerned to discover what makes provincial ladies prisoners within their boudoirs as it is to discover what inhibits large-scale national reforms and individual local ones. If Dorothea's marriage holds her subject to the will of her husband and the duties associated with his household, this is in accordance with a notion of her destiny that, despite her refusal to be 'the pattern of the lady', she shares with him, and with Lydgate, with the sensible Celia and her dowager mother-in-law, and with the generality of young ladies of her own time and place. The terms in which Eliot envisages the expected conventional marriage Dorothea thinks she is repudiating are not remarkably different from the actuality of the successive marriages Dorothea's independence of mind brings her to:

> With some endowment of stupidity and conceit she might have thought that a Christian young lady of fortune should find her ideal life in village charities, patronage of the humbler clergy . . . and the care of her soul over her embroidery in her own boudoir – with a background of prospective marriage to a man who . . . might be prayed for and seasonably exhorted. (p. 24)

Women as utterly different as placidly beautiful Rosamond Vincy and sharply cynical Mrs Cadwallader, faced with the dullness of

village life and husbands in need of exhortation, resort to the restless
activity of boudoir inventiveness. Their unappeased energies,
channelled into smaller and larger forms of destructiveness, are
brilliantly evoked in the drama of the novel: Rosamond, 'a romantic
heroine and playing the part prettily' (p. 317); Mrs Cadwallader,
'With such a mind, active as phosphorous, biting everything that
came near into the form that suited it' (p. 59), the ineffectual
scourge of her neighbours' pretensions. It is to 'the care of her
soul . . . in her own boudoir' that Dorothea is condemned by her
marriage. Wanting Mr Casaubon's 'knowledge' as vantage-point
for the enlargement of that soul as well as for a more effective social
usefulness, Dorothea finds herself retreating more and more into the
privacy of her own bewildered thoughts and judgements. And
Casaubon's clerical and bachelor expectations of wifely companionship, 'to supply aid in graver labours and cast a charm over
vacant hours' (p. 40), are not dissimilar from those of the
sophisticated and cosmopolitan Lydgate, in which 'an accomplish-
ed creature who venerated his high musings musings and moment-
ous labours and would never interfere with them' would create
order in the home and 'yet keep her fingers ready to touch the lute
and transform life into romance at any moment' (p. 376).

Like older Herodotus, then, George Eliot chooses 'a woman's
lot' as starting-point for her study of provincial life. Like Flaubert or
Chekhov or Ibsen, she sees the essence of provincialism as the co-
presence of a yearning for a large life with social and imaginative
limitations that must thwart such a yearning. The depressing
circularity of Dorothea's pattern of self-assertion is relieved only by
the sharpness and sympathy with which it is identified. Marrying
Casaubon follows close upon planning better housing for the poor as
the expression of Dorothea's urgent need for connection with the
world beyond her gentlewoman's horizons. Far from establishing
such a connection, of course, her marriage isolates her still further,
so that 'the sense of connection with a manifold pregnant existence
had to be kept up painfully as an inward vision, instead of coming
from without in claims that would have shaped her energies'
(p. 292). But it is 'the inward vision', after all, that has shaped the
particular circumstances of her fate. Almost at once, Dorothea has
'looked deep into the ungauged reservoir of Mr Casaubon's mind,
seeing reflected there in vague labyrinthine extension every quality she
herself brought' (p. 19). So it is with Lydgate and Rosamond, too,
that they find in each other a reflection created by their own needs

and expectation, and present a self that will in turn answer to these needs and expectations. Dorothea's nobility of nature does not prevent her from displaying, as Rosamond does, and as James's Isabel Archer is to do, her most agreeable self in answer to what she discerns of the expectations of her future husband. In fact, her anxiety to appear properly serious-minded in Casaubon's eyes causes her, in several incisive scenes early on, to be brusque with the kindly Sir James, barely civil to her uncle, and to 'show temper' with the gentle but shrewd Celia. In 'the symphony of hopeful dreams, admiring trust, and passionate self-devotion which that learned gentleman had set playing in her soul' (p. 71), there come together all Dorothea's unfocused yearnings to learn and to do good while escaping what James, in *The Portrait of a Lady* (p. 629), describes as 'the mill of the conventional'. It is these yearnings, composed of practical and religious zeal and unexamined emotional cravings, that prompt the most delicately and intelligently ironic treatment of Dorothea in Book 1 – an irony that sees Dorothea's 'ardour' as a quality of temperament, rather than the more patient and disciplined idealism that is tested in maturity. Her renunciations of worldly enjoyment like riding, or her mother's jewellery, 'those little fountains of pure colour' (p. 9), spring directly from, and take their intensity from, what is clearly a sensuous delight. As quick to anger and tears as she is to sympathy, Dorothea seems continuously swept by 'currents of feeling'. Mr Casaubon is to be baffled and repelled by her 'unaccountably darkly feminine manner' (p. 213). Mr Brooke has always a generalisation at the ready: 'Young ladies are a little ardent, you know – a little one-sided my dear' (p. 417). Sir James struggles in vain with the enigma – your sister is given to self-mortification, is she not?' (p. 13) – as does Celia, who has always lived with it. In a later discussion, it seems agreed between Dorothea and Will, and with the complicity of the narrator, that Dorothea has the soul of a poet, in which 'knowledge passes instantaneously into feeling' (p. 239). But there is no knowledge, and certainly no self-knowledge, contained in Dorothea's 'feeling' in Book 1. An occasional 'throb' in the writing suggests that element of self-identification on the writer's part to which Leavis rightly drew attention,[15] but the 'Miss Brooke' section for the most part recalls the Eliot who found in the sensibility of contemporary womanhood, and in women's education, matter for trenchant criticism: 'Women have not to prove that they can be emotional, and rhapsodic, and spiritualistic. . . . They have to prove that they are capable of accurate thought, severe study, and continuous self-command.'[16] In choosing Casaubon, and the task of amanuensis to his sterile scholarship, and the social milieu of the country manor-house, Dorothea finds herself 'from the enthusiastic acceptance of untried duty . . . plunged in tumultuous preoccupation with her personal lot' (p. 206). 'She was humiliated to find herself a mere victim of feeling, as if she could know nothing except through that medium: all her strength was scattered in fits of agitation, of struggle, of despondency' (p. 212).

Dorothea's boudoir is the appropriate setting for a series of scenes throughout the novel in which Eliot explores that preoccupation, and the relationship between 'feeling' and 'knowledge'. As in *Little Dorrit*, these private moments unfold a dimension of experience that relates to, but also contrasts with, the disillusionment and inertia of the general social life. There has been considerable disagreement, however, about the relationship between Dorothea's personality and feelings and the more generally acknowledged strengths of the novel.[17]

Dorothea's choice of the blue-green boudoir on a first visit to 'the home of her wifehood' is made with a certain deliberation: ' "Perhaps this was your mother's room when she was young." "It was", he said, with his slow bend of the head' (p. 75). An ominous note is registered in her eagerness to embrace Casaubon's history, and to repeat the histories of those women whose lives are framed around her on the walls. The faded furnishings, which Dorothea has no desire to change (' "you like them as they are, don't you?" she added, looking at Mr Casaubon'), the volumes of polite literature in calf, the pale stag in a tapestried blue-green world, the miniatures along the walls, evoke centuries of quiet and monotonous genteel existence. A girlish fancifulness transforms its sombre history: 'It was a room where one might fancy the ghost of a tight-laced lady revisiting the scene of her embroidery' (p. 74). Vivid among the framed lives is that of Mr Casaubon's aunt – the interesting face within its miniature scarcely hinting at the independent spirit that led her to marry the lover disapproved of by her family. The picture within the picture unobtrusively prefigures the stasis in which Dorothea's own impulsiveness and independence are to be held within the frame of this room – a stasis very much more fruitful for the novelist,[18] however, than the marble stasis of the Vatican museum.

From the bow window stretches that view which is to become the defining sameness of Dorothea's life 'of English fields and elms and hedge-bordered highroads' (p. 217), and the avenue of limes which now cast dark shadows. She is to become so used 'to struggle for and to find resolve in looking along the avenue towards the arch of western light that the vision itself had gained a communicating power' (p. 397). For what she sees are not the particularities of the scene,[19] any more than she perceives, or takes in the significance of, the furnishings of her new room. As the seasons transform the landscape from the uniform whiteness of her first winter at Lowick into the gradual advance of summer over the western fields, she sees only a setting and a focus for the absorbing drama of her inner life. Beyond the window is a world of activity in which she can share only as an onlooker. The ordered little village lies 'in a nutshell', as Mr Brooke points out to her with approval: 'the cottages are like a row of almshouses – little gardens, gillyflowers, that sort of thing' (p. 76), where prosperity and contentment are palpable. The disappointment of Dorothea's wish 'that her home would be a parish which had a larger share of the world's misery, so that she might have had more active duties in it' returns her to an alternative imaginative future: 'she made a picture of more complete devotion to Mr Casaubon's aims, in which she would await new duties. Many such might reveal themselves to the higher knowledge gained by her in that companionship' (p. 78).

In Chapter 28, Dorothea, newly returned from her honeymoon journey to Rome, is pictured at her bow-window, 'looking out on the still, white enclosure which made her visible world', experiencing the full meaning of her imprisonment within 'the stifling oppression of that gentlewoman's world where everything was done for her and none asked for her aid':

Her blooming full-pulsed youth stood there in a moral imprisonment which made itself one with the chill, colourless, narrowed landscape, with the shrunken furniture, the never-read books, and the ghostly stag in a pale fantastic world that seemed to be vanishing from the daylight.

In the first minutes when Dorothea looked out she felt nothing but the dreary oppression; then came a keen remembrance, and turning away from the window she walked round the room. The ideas and hopes which were living in her mind when she first saw this room nearly three months before were present now only as memories: she judged them as we judge transient and departed things. All existence seemed to beat with a lower pulse than her own, and her religious faith was a solitary cry, the struggle out of a nightmare in which every object was withering and shrinking away from her. Each remembered thing in the room was disenchanted, was deadened as an unlit transparency, till her wandering gaze came to the group of miniatures, and there at last she saw something which had gathered new breath and meaning: it was the miniature of Mr Casaubon's aunt Julia, who had made the unfortunate marriage – of Will Ladislaw's grandmother. Dorothea could fancy that it was alive now – the delicate woman's face which yet had a headstrong look, a peculiarity difficult to interpret. Was it only her friends who thought her marriage unfortunate? or did she herself find it out to be a mistake, and taste the salt bitterness of her tears in the merciful silence of the night? What breadths of experience Dorothea seemed to have passed over since she first looked at this miniature! She felt a new companionship with it, as if it had an ear for her and could see how she was looking at it. Here was a woman who had known some difficulty about marriage. Nay, the colours deepened, the lips and chin seemed to get larger, the hair and eyes seemed to be sending out light, the face was masculine and beamed on her with that full gaze which tells her on whom it falls that she is too interesting for the slightest movement of her eyelid to pass unnoticed and uninterpreted. The vivid presentation came like a pleasant glow to Dorothea: she felt herself smiling, and turning from the miniature sat down and looked up as if she were again talking to a figure in front of her. But the smile disappeared as she went on meditating, and at last she said aloud –

'Oh, it was cruel to speak so! How sad – how dreadful!'

(p. 293)

The first part of this passage, like the opening paragraphs of the chapter, has been widely discussed as exemplifying the 'moment of disenchantment' in George Eliot's novels.[20] The evocation of Dorothea's dejection in this scene, however, contends with the less searching romanticism indicated by yet another presentation of her as statuesque and emblematic lady: 'Her blooming full-pulsed youth stood there in a moral imprisonment which made itself one with the chill, colourless, narrowed landscape. . . . ' Eliot continues to resist with difficulty the idealising impulse played out in the Vatican museum. The passage is to consider the ways in which Dorothea's disillusionment, in part self-made, 'makes itself one' with a frozen world, but it is also tempted to entertain the vision of Dorothea as pathetic victim. Words like 'blooming' and 'full-pulsed' generally herald such an impulse in the writing, and indeed there is a certain tenderness in the treatment of Dorothea's physical presence from the moment she enters the room. The description of her 'breathing whiteness above the differing white of the fur which itself seemed to wind about her neck and cling down her blue-grey pelisse with a tenderness gathered from her own, a sentient commingled innocence which kept its loveliness against the crystalline purity of the outdoor snow' (p. 291) invests both the beautiful appearance and the colourless landscape with a simplifying purity. The incipient identification of Dorothea with the trees that lift their limbs towards heaven in supplication to a dun and motionless sky completes the picture.

The chapter gathers strength as it moves from this tableau of the imprisoned lady to explore what it is that has brought her to this moment of extreme dejection. The writing is enlivened by its interest in the mind's processes, as the lights and shadows fall within a particular sensibility at a particular moment in time. In the holding in balance of Dorothea's perspective and a perspective on it there is an enlargement of sympathy that necessarily involves judgement.[21] In Dorothea's very note of subjective suffering the 'toils' that imprison her in dejection are evoked in terms that recall the detailed study of Dorothea in Book I: 'the clear heights where she expected to walk in full communion', 'the delicious repose of the soul on a complete superior', 'the active wifely devotion' which was to 'strengthen' and 'exalt' (p. 292), the idealistic phrases of an emotion devoid of fulfilment, a sensousness seeking 'spiritual' gratification, an energy depending for its shaping on something outside the self, expose the sources of Dorothea's despair clearly enough.

The contrast between the hopefulness with which Dorothea has first seen the room, and the dreary oppression that looks back at her now, challenges, in its extremity, her own sense of reality. Her distress is prompted by the utter failure of Casaubon to answer to her warm and generous feelings, but it lies deeper than that.

Alienation from the self she has offered so confidently and joyfully to
Casaubon, a self defined by the room and its objects and memories,
reflects and is reflected in a larger alienation. The room, the
universe, God Himself, remove themselves from her, to make a state
of alienation Eliot herself knew well: 'her religious faith was but a
solitary cry'. Isolation in a meaningless universe is registered in
insistently physical sensations – in the cold, the claustrophobia, the
barely heightened pulse. Feelings shape perception into a vision in
which every object seems 'withering and shrinking away from her':
'narrowed', 'shrunken', 'ghostly', 'fantastic', 'vanishing'. The room
becomes an image of the mind, its images, objects, memories, unlit
by hope. Other characters in *Middlemarch* – Casaubon, Bulstrode,
Lydgate – are to undergo the despair of destroyed hope. But it is
given only to Dorothea, and, this passage convincingly suggests,
appropriately to Dorothea, most fully to feel that despair.

It is the more disappointing, then, that she is lifted out of it so
readily by wandering fancy. Despair shapes a disenchanted world:
the web of fancy is a less substantial creation. The downward
movement of the prose, from 'solitary cry', 'struggle out of
nightmare', disenchanted', 'deadened', is suddenly arrested by the
group of miniatures, illumined now by 'new breath and meaning'.
It is as though the framed imprisoned lady hears and can see her,
and then as though the face glows with vivid life, and then takes on
the masculine character of Will Ladislaw. The laborious quality of
the fancy here is indicated in Dorothea's somewhat clumsy self-
questioning and the narrator's flat expostulatory intrusion: 'What
breadths of experience Dorothea seemed to have passed over since
she first looked at this minature.' And the fancy depends on a
notion that, as it is sketched here (and in contrast with Little
Dorrit's love for Clennam), illustrates a simplifying romanticism:
that love has the power to bring to life what is passive and
unfulfilled. Dorothea's sympathetic musing on the unhappy marriage of Will's grandmother animates the dead face, recalling the
capacity of Will's sympathy to animate her own, by 'that full gaze
which tells her on whom it falls that she is too interesting for the
slightest movement of her eyelid to pass unnoticed and uninter-
rupted'. In Will's eyes, it is suggested, Dorothea is to become more
than the imprisoned lady of portrait. What is projected here, for
Dorothea's future, is a life whose limits George Eliot images, but is
scarcely willing to acknowledge – a life in which large yearnings are
quenched by the gratifications of personal relationship. In this new

direction of Dorothea's fanciful imagination, clearly marking the new direction of her feelings and her history, the unlit room is lost sight of – indeed, positively transformed. For the 'pleasant glow' is something George Eliot shares with her heroine. At its best, the passage shows how the needs and hopes that shape Dorothea's seeing inevitably shape her destiny. But Eliot turns from valuing that destiny as a grappling with the claims and demands of self entailed in moral growth, to admiring it as the appeasement of the old troubadour strains. The more testing circumstances, for Dorothea's solipsism, are those she recalls at the end of this passage, in the 'cruel', 'sad', 'dreadful' impulses that struggle within Casaubon and threaten her own hopefulness and generosity of vision.

These are the circumstances that test Dorothea in the long meditative struggle of Chapter 42, and enable Eliot's most impressive writing. For it is not only Dorothea's struggle, but also Casaubon's, and what he grapples with are the 'cruel fingers' of approaching death. He, too, is 'the centre of his own world' (p. 85), and the chapter begins by entering that world of brooding fear – a world darkened by the 'morbid consciousness' that, as his life ends, he has achieved nothing, and in which the 'affectionate ardour' and 'Quixotic enthusiasm' of Dorothea accuse and threaten, not soothe or stimulate him (p. 451). 'Suspicion and jealousy of Will Ladislaw's intentions, suspicion and jealousy of Dorothea's impressions, were constantly at their weaving work' (p. 449). Responsibility to the fullest realising of Mr Casaubon's way of seeing takes the narrator, quite consciously, to the very limits of what even the most sympathetic onlooker at the 'inward drama' of another centre of self can know: 'This is a very bare and therefore a very incomplete way of putting the case. The human soul moves in many channels' (p. 451). Lydgate's reaction, as he walks with Casaubon, is to feel 'a little amusement mingling with his pity' as he intuits 'the inward conflict implied in his formal measured address' (p. 453): 'He was at present too ill acquainted with disaster to enter into the pathos of a lot where everything is below the level of tragedy except the passionate egoism of the sufferer' (p. 454). But no one, however educated by suffering or enlarged by the insight of the moral imagination, can escape that general solipsism which it is the achievement of *Middlemarch* to explore:

Instead of wondering at this result of misery of Mr Casaubon, I think it quite ordinary. Will not a tiny speck very close to our vision blot out the glory of the world, and leave only a margin by which we see the blot? I know no speck so troublesome as self. And who, if Mr Casaubon had chosen to expound his discontents – his suspicions that he was not any longer adored without criticism – could have denied that they were founded on good reasons? On the contrary, there was a strong reason to be added, which he had not himself taken explicitly into account – namely, that he was not unmixedly adorable.   (p. 449)

To be enclosed within the narrow chamber of the self, 'the glory of the world' caught only by the web that reflects the needs and wants of that self, is, in the best scenes of *Middlemarch*, the stuff not of Arthurian legend, but of ordinary human life. Repelled by Dorothea's sympathetic effort to share his private suffering, Mr Casaubon allows 'her pliant arm to cling with difficulty against his rigid arm', before retreating to his library to 'shut himself in, alone with his sorrow' (p. 457). Dorothea, too, is condemned to the isolation of her sorrow:

She went up to her boudoir. The open bow-window let in the serene glory of the afternoon lying in the avenue, where the lime-trees cast long shadows. But Dorothea knew nothing of the scene. She threw herself on to a chair, not heeding that she was in the dazzling sun-rays: if there were discomfort in that, how could she tell that it was not part of her moral misery?

She was in the reaction of a rebellious anger stronger than any she had felt since her marriage. Instead of tears, there came words:

'What have I done – what am I – that he should treat me so? He never knows what is in my mind – he never cares. What is the use of anything I do? He wishes he had never married me.'

She began to hear herself, and was checked into stillness. Like one who has lost his way and is weary, she sat and saw as in one glance all the paths of her young hope which she should never find again. And just as clearly in the miserable light she saw her own and her husband's solitude – how they walked apart so that she was obliged to survey him. If he had drawn her towards him, she would never have surveyed him – never have said, 'Is he worth living for?' but would have felt him simply a part of her own

life. Now she said bitterly, 'It is his fault, not mine.' In the jar of
her whole being, Pity was overthrown. Was it her fault that she
had believed in him – had believed in his worthiness? – And what,
exactly, was he? – She was able enough to estimate him – she who
waited on his glances with trembling, and shut her best soul in
prison, paying it only hidden visits, that she might be petty
enough to please him. In such a crisis as this, some women begin
to hate.   (p. 458)

In Chapter 25, a wintry landscape is transformed by the pleasant
glow of fancy. Here, the 'serene glory of the afternoon' becomes a
'miserable light'. Dorothea sees nothing beyond her own despair.
The self-enclosure of the boudoir has become not only a retreat, but
also an aggressive statement. The temptation to remain shut away is
the most extreme expression of her resentment of Casaubon.

Some of the best scenes in *Middlemarch* – the vote for the
chaplaincy, for example, or the various musterings of small-town
opinion against new ideas and new people and new scandals – make
vivid the subtle process by which the larger social virtues, such as
reform, or integrity in public affairs, or neighbourly compassion, are
thwarted. The long perspective of history may reveal a 'double
change of self and beholder'; in the short term, individual self-
interest impedes it at every turn. For the interests vested in the self
are not easily set aside. The marital conflict between Lydgate and
Rosamond, like the conflict between Casaubon and Dorothea,
dramatises with compassionate insight the private dimension that
makes part of a more general social conflict. But it is again within
the solitary self-enclosed confines of Dorothea's consciousness that
the difficult actuality of looking beyond one's own centre of self is
most fully measured.

Dorothea at her human best is no saint. Anger bursts out of her as
immediately as tears, and the passage notes the relationship
between aggression and emotional frustration in this elaboration of
her feelings. Her aggressive impulses are given full play, and given
their due, as a natural resentment needing outlet and indulgence.
There is nothing to do with the feelings of blame, however
ineffectual and even inappropriate the passage shows them finally
to be, but to let them flow out and find articulation. Dorothea's
words make her 'inward' struggle immediate. Eliot more adequately articulates her hostile than her generous feelings. Like
Little Dorrit, Dorothea can express her soulfulness in an utterance

more cloying than her creator fully intends. Here, however, Dorothea moves convincingly from a sense of injustice: 'What have I done . . . ', 'he never cares', to reliving yet again the loss of her 'young hope', to envisaging the dreary stretch of her future. Bitterness, and a grim recognition of her husband's pettiness entirely extinguish her customary generosity. Her reluctance to confront him with her anger easily slides into a justification for cruelty. The weaving work of the imagination schemes destruct-ively: 'It was good that he should wonder and be hurt'. It is 'a jar of her whole being'.

In these reflections, Dorothea is oppressed not by boredom and monotony, but by the still more narrowing perspective of complete psychological isolation within her marriage. The craving for physical tenderness, both childlike and maternal, emotional and sexual, so delicately explored in the disillusioned meditation of Dorothea's honeymoon, is by now scarcely more than a notion: 'If he had drawn her towards him, she would never have surveyed him. . . .' Without the physical closeness that might break down the barriers of self, each becomes object to the other, obliged to 'survey' and to judge.

In this impasse, the passage makes plain, there is no such easy response as the apportioning of blame. Dorothea is in so sense 'victim'. Her relationship with Casaubon is seen as a mutual development in which her very ardour dams up the 'shallow rill' of Mr Casaubon's responses, so that each must walk alone, their irreconcilable and deepest needs uncomprehended and unmet. James clearly draws on this meditation in creating Isabel Archer's long vigil in *The Portrait of a Lady*: like Isabel, Dorothea has herself 'shut her best soul in prison' in order to please her prospective husband, and only now, with bitterness and without self-awareness, sees the proferred self as 'petty'.

The view from within Dorothea's boudoir is shared, but the perspective of the passage is larger. The questions 'what am I', 'And what, exactly, was he?' uttered in bitterness, find a more adequate answer than the immediacy of bitterness dictates. As evening slowly deepens into night, Dorothea begins to envisage not self-appeasing fantasies or vengeful schemes, but the image of Casaubon, no wish-fulfilling admirer, but 'a shadowy monitor looking at her anger with sad remonstrance' (p. 459). Something more palpable than duty shapes her vision now, as her energy of anger is deflected into an energy of 'submission'. It is a self-abnegation which does not deny her own needs, but which recognises the irresolvable needs her husband must bear alone. And so she waits for him to emerge from the library:

> slowly the light advanced up the staircase without noise from the footsteps on the carpet. When her husband stood opposite to her, she saw that his face was more haggard. He started slightly on seeing her, and she looked up at him beseechingly without speaking.
>
> 'Dorothea!' he said, with a gentle surprise in his tone. 'Were you waiting for me?'
>
> 'Yes, I did not like to disturb you.'
>
> 'Come, my dear, come. You are young, and need not to extend your life by watching.
>
> When the kind quiet melancholy of that speech fell on Dorothea's ears, she felt something like the thankfulness that might well up in us if we had narrowly escaped hurting a lamed creature. She put her hand in her husband's, and they went along the broad corridor together.   (p. 459)

Dorothea's generosity commands Casaubon's acknowledgement, and this time the outstretched hand is not rejected. Instead of walking apart, they walk together, out of solitude. The clasped hands tacitly accept the great gulf that divides them, separating Dorothea's youth from Casaubon's life extended by watching, and now lamed and irremediably melancholy. The opening door and the flickering taper delicately recall the knowledge each has sought – the 'Key to All Mythologies' and the lamp of learning – in the light of the knowledge they now find. The quiet cadences with which the chapter closes are to be echoed at the close of a later chapter, in a similar moment of imaginative generosity, when Harriet Bulstrode's act of physical tenderness, after her long solitary struggle in her locked room, absolves the hidden and unlovable self of her husband. In these moments, the moral grandeur envisaged in the 'Prelude' takes on an ordinary admirableness.

'Goodness' is inextricably linked, in *Middlemarch*, with the awareness of, and the acceptance of, limitations imposed on and by the self. Sensible Mary Garth has 'learned to make no unreasonable claims' on life, 'having early had strong reason to believe that things were not likely to be arranged for her peculiar satisfaction' (p. 337). Surveying her plain, shrewd, honest face in the mirror side by side with Rosamond's blonde loveliness, she is able to accept, with a pardonable sardonic note, but without dismay, that she is, as Rosamond blandly points out, 'sensible and useful' enough to manage without Rosamond's 'beauty' (p. 118). Dorothea, by contrast, delights in Celia's mirrored beauty, in Chapter 1, as a way of denying her own, together with her interest in jewels and appearances generally. Dorothea's is a moral egotism, Rosamond's the characteristic egoism of feminine attractiveness: the pier-glass reflects an equally concentric picture for each of them. Of all these young ladies on the brink of choosing their destinies, Mary seems the most aware and the most accepting of limitations: 'she neither tried to create illusions, nor indulged in them for her own behoof, and when she was in a good mood she had humour enough in her to laugh at herself' (p. 117). Her presence in the novel provides as interesting and significant a comparison with Dorothea as does Rosamond's, for she seems inherently to have a knowledge for which the novel's most overtly self-engrossed protagonists struggle so painfully. Mary's self-sufficiency is expressed in her enjoyment of her own thoughts. Her moments of solitude are enlivened by an interest in the powers of her own observation and imagination: 'a vigorous young mind not overbalanced by passion, finds a good in making acquaintance with life, and watches its own powers with interest' (p. 338). Her long vigil beside the dying Featherstone, in Chapter 33, anticipates Dorothea's vigil:

> She sat to-night revolving, as she was wont, the scenes of the day, her lips often curling with amusement at the oddities to which her fancy added fresh drollery: people were so ridiculous with their illusions, carrying their fool's caps unawares, thinking their own lies opaque while everyone else's were transparent, making themselves exceptions to everything, as if when all the world looked yellow under a lamp they alone were rosy.   (p. 337)

If Mary's inner life is not exposed to the searching light that illumines Dorothea's, this is surely because Mary's 'goodness' has no great depth or complexity. While the narrator is careful to fend off the suggestion that Mary is 'cynical', she doesn't entirely dispose of the implication that, in seeing herself as sharper and more sane than the rest of the world, Mary is more than a little inclined to share its prevailing habit of seeing the self as exceptional. Her tendency to regard life as a comedy transforms human weaknesses the novel sees as genuinely compelling and difficult into matter for amused detachment. She has her mother's trenchant dislike of pretence, and something of Mrs Cadwallader's astringent wit, qualities enjoyed and respected by the novel. But there is something closed and a shade complacent in her self-sufficiency and self-control. She has no difficulty in refusing the dying Featherstone's demands and pleas that he alter his will, being proof against the parasitic greed that fuels the comic farce gathered about his death-bed. Despite the likelihood that she will affect Fred's inheritance, Mary is resolute, characteristically sure in the knowledge of what is 'right' – in general, and for herself, and for Fred. But a goodness which makes no impulsive errors and has no need to wrestle with their results displays marked limitations. Not creating and entertaining illusions herself, Mary has none of Dorothea's tolerance of, or compassionate interest in, the comforting illusions with which people are characteristically 'wadded about'. Celia Brooke, who sees 'the emptiness of other people's pretensions' much more readily than her sister, prompts the narrator's reflection that the only guarantee against 'feeling too much' is 'to have in general but little feeling' (p. 63). Mary has maturity enough for herself and Fred, but she lacks the generous imagination that leads Dorothea, and the narrator of her story, to see the world as potentially tragic, as well as comfortably comic.

It is not until after Casaubon's death, however, that Dorothea experiences her most intense suffering. Her long vigil in Chapter 80 releases a feeling different in quality from any of her earlier inner struggles, an intensity in which passion and grief are inseparably mixed. Her accidental discovery of Rosamond and Will, hands clasped, in fervently whispered conversation, joints her into recognition of the feeling she has suppressed for so long: 'Oh, I did love him!' (p. 842). Dorothea has been quite incapable of the self-awareness or astuteness of Rosamond's pleased discovery 'that women even after marriage, might make conquests and enslave men' (p. 466). And so she is unable to see any grounds for Casaubon's jealousy of Will, just as she is unable to acknowledge the more puzzling passionate intensities in herself. The chapter begins with Dorothea's characteristic attempt to put her passion aside with her grief, in order to fulfil her dinner obligation at the Farebrothers', until, at last unable to control the 'waves of suffering', she locks herself in with 'the mysterious incorporeal weight of her anguish'. Contempt for Will's emotional betrayal ('his cheap regard'), jealous indignation, and offended pride contend within her in question and expostulation until she sobs herself to sleep in exhaustion.

Eliot's habit of seeing Will and Dorothea as 'childlike' evades some of the adult circumstances and decisions they confront. It mars the scene (dominated by a theatrical storm) in which they express, at last, their mutual love. But, in this moment of uncontrollable feeling, Dorothea's childlikeness is more than an appeal to Victorian convention. As with Little Dorrit, what is emphasised is the persistence of childhood need into adulthood: 'she lay on the bare floor and let the night grow cold around her; while her grand woman's frame was shaken by sobs as if she had been a despairing child' (p. 843). Such an abandonment in a grown woman is both natural and disconcerting, and the narrative envisages both responses. Here, as in the grief and frustration of Dorothea's honeymoon, emotional yearnings fostered in childhood, 'those childlike caresses which are the bent of every sweet woman, who has begun by showering kisses on the hard pate of her bald doll' (p. 211), make a continuity with sexual and maternal longings. The unyielding pate of Mr Casaubon traps Dorothea's emotionalism in the world of girlhood. A vivid imaging of the judgement of Solomon suggests how that element of maternal solicitude drawn from Dorothea by the rather aimless and youthfully confused Will is not only frustrated, but violently destroyed:

> two living forms that tore her heart in two, as if it had been the heart of a mother who seems to see her child divided by the sword, and presses one bleeding half to her breast while her gaze goes forth in agony towards the half which is carried away by the lying woman who has never known the mother's pang.
> (p. 843)

In the face of such fundamental physical needs as these, 'justice' and 'judgement' lose their meaning. This is a dimension of human experience that large schemes or patient research or rational inquiry can never fathom, for it underlies them all – a truth to be embodied, not known. But, in accordance with Eliot's guiding conception of her heroine, and with the characteristic logic of the nineteenth-century novel, the turning of Dorothea's thoughts from her own helpless suffering towards a world beyond 'the narrow cell of her calamity' enables her if not to escape her cell completely, at least to expand its dimensions. In the closing pages of Dorothea's history her intensities of feeling, like her unfocused aspirations for a larger life, are comfortably transformed into social usefulness and the fulfilment of 'the common yearnings of womanhood' (p. xvi).

As in the two earlier meditations, it is by dwelling on the visual images of memory that Dorothea's web changes its contours.[22] In the chill twilight of morning, she forces herself to see again the scene that torments her: 'Was she alone in that scene? Was it her event only? She forced herself to think of it as bound up with another woman's life' (p. 844). The image of Rosamond returns not as her jealously has pictured her, as the 'lying woman' who would heedlessly steal the object of another's love, but as her earlier sympathy has represented her – young, troubled in her marriage as Dorothea has been, needing support and comfort. Dorothea's capacity to transcend 'the besotted misery of a consciousness that only sees another's lot as an accident of its own' is signalled by her looking out from her boudoir to the world stirring below her:

> She opened her curtains, and looked out towards the bit of road that lay in view, with fields beyond, outside the entrance-gates. On the road there was a man with a bundle on his back, and a woman carrying her baby; in the field she could see figures moving – perhaps the shepherd and his dog. Far off in the bending sky was the pearly light; and she felt the largeness of the world and the manifold wakings of men to labour and endurance. She was a part of that involuntary, palpitating life, and could neither look out on it from her luxurious shelter as a mere spectator, nor hide her eyes in selfish complaining.
>
> (p. 845)

There is an emblematic quality in the picture Dorothea sees, however, that surely questions the extent to which she is, or ever could be, 'a part of that involuntary, palpitating life'.[23] While her refusal to be 'a mere spectator' has been reflected in her decision to go again to Rosamond, she here looks out on this landscape still from the enclosure of her luxurious shelter. And the figures she sees, although they recall those domestic relations and needs that have held their sway in her long struggle, represent them somewhat notionally. Wordsworth's evocation of ordinary suffering in 'The Old Cumberland Beggar' makes a significant comparison:

> While from door to door,
> This old man creeps, the villagers in him
> Behold a record which together binds
> Past deeds and offices of charity,
> Else unremembered, and so keeps alive
> The kindly mood in hearts which lapse of years
> And that half-wisdom half-experience gives,
> Make slow to feel, and by sure steps resign
> To selfishness and cold oblivious cares.

In the very creep of time itself, the lines insist, even a community for which the shuffling figure makes a continuing focus for kindness may find that feeling neutralised by the blurring of 'half-wisdom', 'half-experience'. Dorothea's Wordsworthian vision is closer to the Victorian Wordsworthianism of George Eliot's 'Natural History of German Life', or of Ruskin, than to the sombre and profound 'extension of our sympathies' which Wordsworth's poetry requires. For Ruskin, the unconscious expression of human suffering made for 'noble picturesque': 'nobly endured by unpretending strength of heart . . . the world's hard work being gone through all the while, and no pity asked for, nor contempt feared'.[24]

As Dorothea looks out at the villagers who process to Featherstone's funeral, it is clear that her participation in 'a wider public life' can never lie in the direction she envisages. Her very sympathy for the plight of the Downeses and the Dagleys is given in tones that utter the fixed gulf that separates Dorothea from them:

> I used to come from the village with all that dirt and coarse ugliness like a pain within me, and the simpering pictures in the drawing-room seemed to me like a wicked attempt to find delight in what is false, while we don't mind how hard the truth is for the neighbours outside our walls. I think we have no right to come forward and urge wider changes for good until we have tried to alter the evils which lie under our own hands.   (p. 416)

Dorothea senses the irony that those very estates that qualify the ineffectual Mr Brooke to stand for Parliament are the greatest indictment of him as a landlord and a 'reformer'. What Dorothea's speech to him here makes clear, however, is that her own incapacity to alter life for the Dagleys of the village has as much to do with the unfocused sensibility that gushes forth in such circumstances, as it has to do with her gentlewoman's horizon of drawing-rooms and simpering pictures. George Eliot can take us into the lives of the Dagleys and Old Timothy and grasp the patterns of rural life and attitudes within which a Caleb Garth can work effectively. Dorothea can never command such insight. What she looks out on are never more than emblematic figures, reflections of her own dimly grasped yearnings outward, or the mirror of her own solitary suffering.

Dorothea's real struggles are with that unfocused sensibility, and it is within the enclosure of her boudoir that she learns to deal with the most immediate evils that lie under her hands. She remains at the end impulsive, beneficent, a supportive but undistinguished politician's wife, still feeling 'that there was always something better which she might have done, if she had only been better and known better' (p. 893). Although the 'Finale' is inclined, however, like the 'Prelude', to find Dorothea a kind of St Theresa after all, but denied her opportunities for greatness by 'the conditions of an imperfect social state', the accumulated weight of the novel tells a different story. As with Little Dorrit, Dorothea's fineness of spirit shows itself not in terms of fame or large social achievements, but in terms of individual moral growth. Here is a moral imagination that, altering her perceptions, makes changes in her own life and in the lives of those close to her. Yet her capacity to see beyond the webs made for her and by her, by the circumstances of her time and place and temperament, is necessarily limited by those very perspectives. It is the larger web woven by the novel as a whole that translates that knowledge for which Dorothea has yearned into a significant and lasting achievement. On the other hand, however, it is the tension between inherent limitation and large yearnings that makes the novel's most exploratory, as well as its most imperfect, writing. Essential to George Eliot's incomparable rendering of the web of provincial life is her detailed study of that web within the inner, private world of individual sensibility.

4 Jude, Sue and 'Social Moulds'

' . . . I can talk to you better like this than when you were inside. . . . It was so kind and tender of you to give half a day's work to come to see me! . . . You are Joseph the dreamer of dreams, dear Jude. And a tragic Don Quixote. And Sometimes you are St Stephen, who, while they were stoning him, could see Heaven opened. O my poor friend and comrade, you'll suffer yet!'

Now that the high window-sill was between them, so that he could not get at her, she seemed not to mind indulging in a frankness she had feared at close quarters. 'I have been thinking,' she continued, still in the tone of one brimful of feeling, 'that the social moulds civilization fits us into have no more relation to our actual shapes than the conventional shapes of the constellations have to the real star-patterns. I am called Mrs Richard Phillotson, living a calm wedded life with my counterpart of that name. But I am not really Mrs Richard Phillotson, but a woman tossed about, all alone, with aberrant passions, and unaccountable antipathies. . . .'   (Thomas Hardy, *Jude the Obscure*, pp. 265–6)

Beneath Sue's window, unable to get at her, stands Jude, perpetual supplicant of the unattainable. This often-to-be repeated *tableau vivant*, in which Jude is to remain shut out, and Sue irrevocably shut away, seems at first glance, perhaps, to echo George Eliot's 'troubadour strains'. Hardy's Lady of Shalott is subject to an analysis more troubled and searching, however, than is the inaccessible lady of Will Ladislaw's (and George Eliot's) romantic imaginings. The emblematic lady is, of course, a recurring figure in Hardy's novels and in his poems – an expression of complex, compelling feelings about the nature of 'womankind'.[1] In the character of Sue Bridehead she takes on a more immediately personal, and contemporary, significance than ever before. Sue embodies, and, for Jude, becomes the focus of, 'the ache of modernism' and of all the related and confused romantic yearnings of Victorian spirituality. In Sue, Hardy attempts to relate feelings he has about the nature of women and of sexuality, to interpretations of those feelings in terms of the intellectual climate of Victorian England. Hardy gives to the little tableau Sue creates a suggestive power that recalls Blake's prophetic vision, where 'the Youth pined away with Desire/And the pale Virgin shrouded in snow' can only yearn, with a romanticism frozen into immobility, for a romantic heaven in which their human nature will find its harmony in nature's 'golden clime' ('Ah! Sun-flower'). *Jude the Obscure* is, I think, Hardy's most sustained and moving attempt to explore the 'aberrant passions' by which he is himself assailed – passions that underlie both the 'social moulds' of Victorian domesticity and the 'conventional shapes' of nineteenth-century romantic imagination.

Imprisoned within the home of her 'wifedom', and the social identity that goes with it, Sue sees herself as Jude sees her – as a mysterious being whose essential nature can never quite be caught. The tableau makes visual the paradox Sue gives voice to, of a union of thought and feeling between the cousins that is at once enabled, and prevented by, the barriers between them. It is in terms of their shared belief in an 'actual shape' free of social constraints that Sue here expresses her loving kinship with Jude. But Sue's 'actual shape' eludes Jude, as it eludes Sue herself. There is a characteristic detachment in what she says, a detachment not only from Jude, but from herself. It is an impression she often gives – that of an ill-equipped voyager into the hinterland of an unfathomable psyche. Hardy, like Jude, pursues the enigma of Sue, but with a greater understanding of the psychological barriers that enclose her. Her verbal caressing of the devoted and outcast Jude is finely registered. Tenderness is incalculably mingled with satire and a strange kind of gloating. Jude comes to think of her, despairingly, admiringly, as an 'epicure in emotions' (p. 229). Sue's ready intellectualising of her brimming feeling makes it into a weapon with which she joins in the stoning of St Jude, her 'poor friend and comrade'. Still the feeling remains aberrant, however, and Sue continues to be buffetted by it, not an agent in her own destiny, but a helpless object. In Jude's rueful acceptance of his position there is something equally chilling:

'Now that the high window-sill was between them, so that he could not get at her, she seemed not to mind indulging in a frankness she had feared at close quarters.' In moments of this kind, Hardy suggests, what holds them in the stasis of courtly love is not a matter of literary or social conventions, but, as D. H. Lawrence observed, of their 'last and deep feelings'.[2]

That claim seems to lie somewhat against the bias of Lawrence's argument that it is transgression of the social code that dooms Hardy's protagonists. And indeed the conflict between 'nature' and 'civilisation' so wistfully entertained by Sue lies uneasily at the heart of *Jude the Obscure*. For, as Lawrence in fact perceives, there is an unresolved tension in Hardy's own vision, between a tragic sense of life, in which the individual is pitted against 'the vast un-comprehended and incomprehensible morality of nature or life itself ', and a sense of life as answerable to 'the established system of human government and morality'. There are in the novel, as there are in Sue, two dimensions of experience: the one conscious, pondering 'civilisation' and its 'social moulds', and the other registering the bafflement of reason, the failure of intellect and judgement to explain, or to cope with, the unfathomable prompt-ings of 'nature'. In Charlotte Brontë, Dickens and George Eliot, such promptings are glimpsed only as part of that moral struggle by which rebellious sensibility discovers its social destiny. The 'certain moral scheme' within which protagonists are conceived, and in terms of which they are to be made consistent, has a much more equivocal force for Hardy. There is a strong impulse, in *Jude the Obscure*, to see Sue's vulnerability, and Jude's, as part of that inexorable law of nature that condemns Tess of the d'Urbervilles. Sue's plight is imaged sometimes in ways that suggest not the entrapment of social circumstances and romantic conventions, but a poignancy in 'nature' itself. Like the doomed rabbit Jude releases from its trap, Sue is caught by her timorous sensitivity in a succession of vividly imaged traps. It is Hardy the narrator, however, who draws a prosaic general reflection from the 'pretty, suggestive, pathetic sight' of rows of 'tender feminine faces' in the cubicles of Sue's training college; 'every face bearing the legend "The Weaker" upon it, as the penalty of the sex wherein they were moulded, which by no possible exertion of their willing hearts and abilities could be made strong while the inexorable laws of nature remain what they are' (p. 194). Jude, too, is part of that same vulnerable human nature for which fiendish traps are set, suffering the weakness of a sensibility in which 'flesh' is at odds with 'spirit'. And, like his creator, he feels impelled to question the nature and structure of society for some explanation of his sufferings: ' "Is it", he said, "that the women are to blame; or is it the artificial system of things, under which the normal sex-impulses are turned into devilish domestic gins and springes to noose and hold back those who want to progress?" ' (p. 279). The need to question the 'system of things' links Hardy with his great Victorian predecessors. As with Dickens, however, his questions have their most telling power when they are at their least rhetorical and explicit.

Hardy's Preface to the first edition describes the novel as an attempt to tell of 'the strongest passion known to humanity . . . of a deadly war waged between flesh and spirit: and to point the tragedy of unfulfilled aims' (p. 39). In the story of Sue and Jude, Hardy is to show unfulfilled aims inextricably bound up in that war between flesh and spirit, and is to give the connection he grasps between personal and societal 'aims' a quite specific contemporary setting. A tall neo-Gothic church has replaced the quaint old hump-backed, wood-turreted church in Jude's village, and Jude is envisaged, from the outset, as a protagonist of that drift of civilisation away from its roots in the soil that was to preoccupy Lawrence in *The Rainbow* (written at the same time as his 'Study of Thomas Hardy'). In the centre of the hamlet of Marygreen, ancient as the village itself, stands the well, and Jude's peering down into the timeless depths of the earth is as strong an impulse as his climbing a barn to catch a glimpse of the towers of Christminster. The spire that summons Lawrence's generations from the teeming life of the farm is surely an acknowledgement of Hardy's influence. But the spires that make Jude a 'dreamer of dreams' are the dreaming spires of Arnold's and of Newman's and Pater's Oxford, repository of 'culture', epitome of 'civilisation', home of lost causes. Jude is to encounter at Christminster not those challenges of the modern world that confront Lawrence's Ursula Brangwen, but only his own unfocused and yearning spirituality. In his life there, as hopeful student or as artisan of the new culture, he sustains only the most precarious livelihood restoring its Gothic fabric. He is to discover not the medieval wholeness envisaged by Ruskin or William Morris, nor the heightened imaginative moment of Pater, but only the failure of such visionary dreams to support either the questing spirit or the weakness of the flesh. In this quest, Sue is not only Jude's companion: she becomes the very embodiment of the quest itself.

The great drama of Hardy's Wessex narrows, in his last novel, to focus, as Lawrence increasingly does, on the relationship between man and woman. And within *Jude the Obscure* the focus is further narrowed, as Sue becomes Jude's all-engrossing object, an embodiment of the unattainable heart of Christminster.

'I see what you are doing, you are leading me on' is the plaintive, jubilant, bewildered cry with which the lover pursues the ghostly beloved in Hardy's poem 'After a Journey'. It is Hardy the poet who pictures what eludes explanation – the compelling, mysterious 'otherness' of the woman and of this woman in particular, as Jude goes back again to gaze up at Sue's window:

> A glimmering candle-light shone from a front window, the shutters being yet unclosed. He could see the interior clearly – the floor sinking a couple of steps below the road without, which had become raised during the centuries since the house was built. Sue, evidently just come in, was standing with her hat on in this front parlour or sitting-room, whose walls were lined with wainscoating of panelled oak reaching from floor to ceiling, the latter being crossed by huge moulded beams only a little way above her head. The mantelpiece was of the same heavy description, carved with Jacobean pilasters and scrollwork. The centuries did, indeed, ponderously overhang a young wife who passed her time here.
>
> She had opened a rosewood work-box, and was looking at a photograph. Having contemplated it a little while she pressed it against her bosom, and put it again in its right place.
>
> Then becoming aware that she had not obscured the windows she came forward to do so, candle in hand. It was too dark for her to see Jude without, but he could see her face distinctly, and there was an unmistakable tearfulness about the dark, long-lashed eyes.   (pp. 226–7)

The scene is detailed in the manner of a Hardy poem: the interior of the house with its sunken floor measuring the centuries, the panelled wainscoting, the huge moulded beams, the heavily carved wood of the mantelpiece expressing the ponderous, enduring weight of an impersonal, inescapable tradition of domestic quietude. Here is the 'social mould' that encloses Sue. Human figures give the scene its individual meaning, however. The moment evokes that inner constraint of tender beleaguered nature that encloses these lovers, one from the other, and from a world beyond their private dreaming. Sue as she contemplates Jude's picture, Jude as he contemplates his window-framed image of Sue, make a tableau in which immobility is not finally explicable in terms of 'artificial systems' or of the stereotypes of courtly love. It has its deepest source in the paradox that is to provide the twists and turns of the novel's plot – the paradox of a kinship in nature that irrevocably separates.

It is not often, in *Jude the Obscure*, that the narrative pauses to dwell on Sue's moments of privacy. The two passages already discussed suggest why this is so, and the ways in which the characteristic 'Lady of Shalott' moments in Hardy's novel differ from those moments in which we see Lucy Snowe or Dorothea Brooke, for example, held in focus. Sue is not, like Lucy or Dorothea, the central consciousness of the novel that contains her. It is Jude who occupies that space. But Sue's is the consciousness he seeks to penetrate, and the elusive object of the novel's pursuit. In Sue's moments of self-analysis, Hardy has an interest comparable with Charlotte Brontë's or George Eliot's, and an insight no less compassionate and convincing that theirs, into the interweaving of conscious and sub-conscious. In the moments in which we see Sue not through her perspective on the world, but as she is in a private world of self-enclosure, she is tantalisingly enigmatic, an embodiment of romantic yearning, for the onlooker who is Hardy as well as Jude. Dickens's Little Dorrit embodies values as important to her male creator as the values embodied by Charlotte Brontë and George Eliot in their protagonists: in the end these are values that are felt to be susceptible of understanding, if not always of analysis, by male and female writers alike. But for Hardy (and this is the particular interest of *Jude the Obscure* in the present context) Sue's very fascination lies in her failure, fluently articulate though she is, to reveal herself. The challenge to his creativity is to capture her 'actual shape' in all its elusiveness.

Hardy described her as 'a type of woman which has always had an attraction for me, but the difficulty of drawing the type has kept me from attempting it till now'.[3] In fact though, there is something of Sue's elusiveness in one of Hardy's earliest heroines, Elfride Swancourt, in *A Pair of Blue Eyes*.[4] Elfride is not quite 'the intellectualized, emancipated bundle of nerves' (p. 42) Sue's modernity makes her. But she is intellectually adventurous, physically daring, given to perplexing currents of feeling and impulsive action. Her coquetry seems, like Sue's, unconscious, yet powerful enough, like Sue's, to enthrall three suitors and to destroy one of them. Elfride presents, as Sue does, a baffling picture to the suitor who stands outside her window, looking in:

> Elfride's dressing-room lay in the salient angle in this direction, and it was lighted by two windows in such a position that, from Knight's standing-place, his sight passed through both windows, and raked the room. Elfride was there; she was pausing between the two windows, looking at her figure in the cheval-glass. She regarded herself long and attentively in front; turned, flung back her head, and observed the reflection over her shoulder.
>
> Nobody can predicate as to her object or fancy; she may have done the deed in the very abstraction of deep sadness. She may have been moaning from the bottom of her heart, 'How unhappy I am!' But the impression produced on Knight was not a good one.   (*A Pair of Blue Eyes*, p. 378)

Knight rakes the room because, tantalised by the ambiguities of Elfride, he must assure himself that she satisfies his ideals of womanly behaviour. It is through his watchful eyes that Elfride becomes here, potentially, the vain coquette, preening herself before her mirror. And there is enough in her behaviour throughout the novel to confirm that the need to make a good effect overrules her candour, sometimes, and her good sense. On the other hand, Elfride is young, and has lived all her life in retirement. Her self-contemplation, the passage suggests, might express self-doubt and even melancholy. The young Thomas Hardy seems himself in doubt about whether Elfride's desire to please and her love of being liked is innocent and artless, or the manifestation of 'woman's ruling passion – to fascinate and influence those more powerful than she' (p. 215). Elfride remains ambiguous – a somewhat uncertain tribute to the mysteriousness of womankind.

Hardy's command of his heroine's 'womanliness' is altogether more assured when he comes to write *Tess of the d'Urbervilles*. It is Tess's stumbling integrity, that very inability to defend and explain herself, that makes her, like Elfride, both victim of masculine demandingness and involuntary coquette. She is compelled, despite herself, to lead her lovers on to mutually destructive consummations. Lascelles Abercrombie long ago noted how the women of Hardy's novels seem to embody a fatal and inevitable force:

> For this womanly caprice, with all its tragical result, becomes at last the very type of the impersonal, primal impulse of existence,

driving forward all its various forms of embodiment, profoundly working even within their own natures to force them onward in the great fatal movement of the world, all irrespective of their conscious desires.[5]

In *Jude the Obscure* it is not only Sue, but Arabella as well, who obeys that prompting of nature to set in motion the 'deadly war waged between flesh and spirit'. The Apocryphal epigraph from Esdras which prefaces Book I refers most immediately to the marriage with Arabella: 'Yea, many there be that have run out of their wits for women, and become servants for their sakes. Many also have perished, have erred, and sinned, for women. . . . O ye men, how can it be but women should be strong, seeing they do thus?' (p. 46). Nevertheless it stands appropriately enough as an epigraph for the whole course of Jude's brief life, drawing attention to the novel's real emphasis. It is Sue, after all, who comes to represent Jude's 'unfulfilled aims' in their most compelling form, and it is the failure of his relationship with her, followed by the savage irony of his return to Arabella, that finally destroys him. Against the bitter and Apocryphal note, however, must be weighed the tenderness of Hardy's dealing with the fragile 'strength' of Sue Bridehead. If women forward 'the impersonal, primal impulse of existence' this is an involuntary process in which they are, like Tess and Sue, forced onward to their own destruction.

In the preceding chapters, attention has been drawn to novels in which the self-enclosed consciousness, reflecting the creative consciousness of the novelist, makes a centre from which, in James's image, all the rays of the novel's form flow. It has been possible, by discussing the novel's contemplative pauses, to elucidate the form and significance of the larger 'web'. In that aspect of *Jude the Obscure* that explores self-enclosedness, most particularly Sue's, in terms of its social and psychological circumstances, there is a potential Victorian novel that resembles the novels already discussed, and a form that moves towards a similar kind of closure and self-containment. But in that aspect of the novel that registers the patterns and paradoxes made by individual sensibilities following the promptings of their natures, there is a more wayward and inconclusive shape. In the twists and turns of plot to which 'the impersonal primal impulse of existence' gives rise, Arabella and Sue interweave in Jude's destiny, not only as contrasting, but also as comparable, figures. So that, in elucidating the relationship between the figure of the lady and the form of the novel, it is necessary to begin where Hardy begins, with Arabella, and with Marygreen.

As the novel opens, Phillotson the schoolmaster starts out from the ancient village on his journey to Christminster, in pursuit of his 'scheme, or dream' eventually to become an undergraduate and then to be ordained. He leaves the young Jude with the instruction to be kind to animals and birds, and to read all he can. For Jude, the brown fields of Marygreen with their 'history of village life', 'echoes of songs from ancient harvest days', and of 'Love-matches that had populated the adjoining hamlet . . . made up there between reaping and carrying' (p. 53), are lonely and inhospitable. His relationship with his aunt and with the village is unfolded in a chorus of folk-wisdom that establishes his 'difference': 'It would ha' been a blessing if Goddy-mighty had took thee too, wi' thy mother and father, poor useless boy! . . . Why didn't ye get the school-master to take 'ee to Christminster wi' un, and make a scholar of 'ee?' (pp. 51–2). Jude, with his strange introspectiveness and love of books, sets his sights on the 'distant halo' of the city, determined in his own person to recreate the course of civilisation by learning to build as well as to read. Nevertheless, his 'unnecessary life' finds an affinity with that of the birds, 'living in a world which did not want them'. The lad whose tender care of the birds prevents his caring for the crops, who carefully picks his way on tip-toe among the earth-worms, who, wooed by a provocatively thrown pig's pizzle, could never kill a pig, discovers early that 'Nature's logic was too horrid for him to care for. That mercy towards one set of creatures was cruelty towards another sickened his sense of harmony' (p. 57). Jude succumbs to 'Nature's logic' all too readily, however, as Arabella draws him out of his dreams of Christminster, back into the recurring rhythms of village life, with its love-matches made up between reaping and carrying.

Arabella's seduction of Jude, like Alec d'Urberville's seduction of Tess, is felt as a profound fulfilment of 'Nature's logic', as consummation as well as violation. Jude's response to Arabella is immediate and instinctive: 'there was a momentary flash of intelligence, a dumb announcement of affinity *in posse*, between herself and him' (p. 81). 'Nature' presents its mysterious imperative, and the narrative tone registers a certain clumsy unease when faced with it: 'She saw that he had singled her out from the three, as a woman is singled out in such cases, for no reasoned purpose of further acquaintance, but in commonplace obedience to conjunctive orders from headquarters . . . .' Hardy's awkwardly phrased speculations sort oddly with Arabella's unthinking obedience to instinct: the problem of how the essentially natural can entail consequences so much the reverse is one that Hardy fathoms no more successfully than Jude does. This is not to admit Lawrence's criticism, however, that there is animus in Hardy's portrayal of Arabella. He sees her as 'a complete and substantial female animal – no more, no less': 'a fine dark-eyed girl, not exactly handsome, but capable of passing as such at a little distance, despite some coarseness of skin and fibre. She had a round and prominent bosom, full lips, perfect teeth, and the rich complexion of a Cochin hen's egg.' Abundance, fecundity, a coarseness that scarcely detracts from a natural bloom and ripeness – these are the physical manifestations of interest in, and interest for, a potential mate. They effect a relationship that has no place for 'reason' or those visionary claims of the spirit that distinguish Jude from his surroundings. Lawrence's conviction that 'Arabella gives Jude to himself'[6] makes that self a much simpler, more univocal being than Hardy conceives Jude to be. Jude is led as inevitably by the instinctive coquetry of Arabella as he is led by the more subtle coquetry of Sue. And, as Arabella woos Jude to her bed, she, too, is led by instinct cunningly to ensnare him:

> 'Don't touch me, please', she said softly. 'I am part egg-shell. Or perhaps I had better put it in a safe place.' She began unfastening the collar of her gown.
> 'What is it?' said her lover.
> 'An egg – a cochin's egg. I am hatching a very rare sort. I carry it about everywhere with me, and it will get hatched in less than three weeks.'
> 'Where do you carry it?'
> 'Just here.' She put her hand into her bosom and drew out the egg, which was wrapped in wool, outside it being a piece of pig's bladder, in case of accidents. Having exhibited it to him she put it back, 'Now mind you don't come near me. I don't want to get it broke, and have to begin another.'
> 'Why do you do such a strange thing?'

'It's an old custom. I suppose it is natural for a woman to bring live things into the world.'

'It is very awkward for me just now', he said, laughing.

'It serves you right. There – that's all you can have of me.'

She had turned round her chair, and, reaching over the back of it, presented her cheek to him gingerly.

'That's very shabby of you!'

'You should have catched me a minute ago when I had put the egg down! There!' she said defiantly, 'I am without it now!'

(pp. 99–100)

Arabella's 'Don't touch me . . . I am part egg-shell' anticipates, in near-parody, Sue's shrinking fragility. And, indeed, the scene sets a pattern for both relationships. Arabella's withholding of herself, like Sue's, is a conscious challenge to Jude's response. The cochin's egg, recalling Arabella's own rich complexion and plenitude, perfectly emblematises an artfulness in her that takes its cue from nature. Nestling in her bosom, the egg tells of promptings that have their origins in what is 'natural for a woman', and that make part of Arabella's visibly compelling womanliness. The rituals of courtship are enacted at a level below conscious apprehension, but, Arabella's cunning suggests, likely to be at odds with it. The 'old custom' she here enacts prefigures the other old custom to which social considerations lead her. The playful game with the egg takes on an altogether different aspect when the egg becomes the feigned pregnancy that traps Jude in 'the gin which would cripple him' (p. 107). There is set in motion a 'social ritual which made necessary a cancelling of well-formed schemes involving years of thought and labour, of foregoing a man's one opportunity of showing himself superior to the lower animals'. There is a 'superior' fastidiousness in Jude's gradual awareness that Arabella is not the natural village maiden she had seemed (Angel Clare's disenchantment with Tess makes a resonant echo here). But Jude's indignation, and Hardy's, is no repudiation of satisfied instinct, and seems tediously beside the point made with such brilliant economy and evocativeness in the writing that describes Jude's pursuit of Arabella. Nevertheless, it has also been established that there are instincts and aspirations in Jude that Arabella can never satisfy, and that compel Jude to leave her, and the village life of Marygreen, behind him.

Sue becomes almost at once the focus of those spiritual yearnings that have led Jude to Christminster. The photograph that he takes from his aunt to bear him company among the dreaming spires invests his cousin with a radiance that, for Jude, she is never to lose: 'a pretty girlish face, in a broad hat with radiating folds under the brim like the rays of a halo' (p. 124). It is not only Aunt Drusilla's superstitious dread of this meeting that prevents Jude from making her acquaintance. He delights to think of her as 'an ideal character, about whose form he began to weave curious and fantastic day-dreams' (p. 136). Occasional glimpses of her in the street or at church, or in the neo-Gothic frame of her bookseller's shop, at her 'sweet, saintly, Christian business' (p. 135) satisfy Jude's rhapsodic imagination:

> She looked right into his face with liquid, untranslatable eyes that combined, or seemed to him to combine, keenness with tenderness, and mystery with both, their expression, as well as that of her lips, taking its life from some words just spoken to a companion, and being carried on into his face quite unconsciously. She no more observed his presence than that of the dust-motes which his manipulations raised into the sunbeams.
>
> (p. 136)

The connection between Jude's heightened feeling and the remoteness of the unknown Sue is delicately made, recalling as it does the contrasting, instinctive recognition that flows between Jude and Arabella. There is only an illusion of communication here, as Sue looks 'right into his face' with her 'liquid untranslatable eyes'. But Jude's 'manipulations' and Sue's innate obliviousness of what lies beyond her immediate range make a complicity that seems as much in the nature of things as Arabella's more palpable allure: 'She no more observed his presence than that of the dust-motes which his manipulations raised into the sunbeams.' These early chapters present Sue's inaccessibility as answering precisely to the idealising needs of Jude's imagination. Already he has made her 'his' – part of his family history, his own flesh and blood, part of himself: 'he recognized in the accents certain qualities of his own voice: softened and sweetened, but his own' (p. 135). Even when they meet at last, Sue remains in the romantic realm to which he has consigned her:

> Though they had talked of nothing more than general subjects Jude was surprised to find what a revelation of woman his cousin

was to him. She was so vibrant that everything she did seemed to have its source in feeling. An exciting thought would make her walk ahead so fast that he could hardly keep up with her; and her sensitiveness on some points was such that it might have been misread as vanity. It was with heart-sickness he perceived that, while her sentiments towards him were those of the frankest friendliness only, he loved her more than before becoming acquainted with her . . .   (p. 151)

Sue is 'a revelation of woman': what she reveals is a nervous intensity that seems to Jude the epitome of fineness. He marvels that 'one of his cross-grained, unfortunate, almost accursed stock' should 'have contrived to reach this point of niceness' (p. 137). Sue's 'otherness', associated with the intellectual refinements of 'civilisation', is a different kind of otherness from Arabella's, and it leads him on more inexorably than Arabella's more overt sexual attractiveness.

Hardy's sense of sexual attractiveness as a force that draws lovers towards one another while entailing their fateful divisiveness has clearly discernible autobiographical promptings. In the case of Jude, as of Angel Clare before him, Hardy relates this paradox of feeling to distorting elements in the Victorian cultural milieu. But in Jude's love for his cousin, so insistently recalling Hardy's 'lost love' for his cousin Tryphena, there is an attempt to explain that divisiveness in terms of a paradox at the heart of nature itself. A blood relationship becomes an expression of the natural law whereby like will seek out like. The sensibilities of Jude and Sue are formed by childhood emotional deprivations, and that shared sense of family doom so amply dispensed by Aunt Drusilla. Jude's consciousness of it is a most eloquent testimony to its power: 'in a family like his own where marriage usually meant a tragic sadness, marriage with a blood relation would duplicate the adverse conditions, and a tragic sadness might be intensified to a tragic horror' (p. 137). As Jude and Sue begin to seek and to find in each other familial tenderness denied them by the previous generation of Fawleys, their kinship expresses itself in similarities of nature that reinforce each in the other a tendency towards hyper-sensitivity and melancholy. They become, in fulfilment of Jude's own foreboding, two bitters in the one dish. To Phillotson, the outside observer, 'They seem to be one person split in two!' (p. 293). His account of them recalls the doomed love of Emily Brontë's Catherine and

Heathcliff: 'Their supreme desire is to be together – to share each other's emotions and fancies, and dreams' (p. 295). A relationship in which the feelings that seek expression and fulfilment are of such a nature that they can only find bafflement and self-destruction may properly be thought of as 'tragic'. If *Jude the Obscure* lacks tragic stature in the end, it is because Hardy relinquishes his tragic perception in favour of social explanations, and because he is unable to imagine for his protagonists anything more eloquent than the despairing inertia that follows the gratuitous blow delivered by little Father Time.

Jude and Sue's vexed kinship is brilliantly realised in terms of the complex action that flows from it. It is Jude's desire to have Sue near him that prompts him to give her into the charge of Phillotson, who falls in love with her. As Sue's 'frank friendliness' begins to suggest to Jude the possibilities of a more than cousinly interest between them, the strong tender feelings she arouses in him are explained, and sometimes explained away, by their cousinly relationship. That peculiar immunity for sexual commitment Sue is to explain to Jude is matched by Jude's awareness that the hidden fact of his marriage to Arabella prohibits such a commitment. These further barriers augment the barrier of their blood-relationship perversely to sanction feelings they are intended to prevent. A protracted courtship of approach and recoil is acted out. Each seeks to penetrate the other's separateness. Jude, in the drunken bout that follows the disappointment of his academic hopes, stands beneath Sue's window, calling plaintively until she hears him. Sue leaps from her college window and wades through a river to call beneath Jude's window. These large romantic gestures bring them into a chaste closeness, as they sleep together but apart, in a foreshadowing of the relationship that is to come. The tensions of their ambiguous loving proximity begin to be reflected in a barely conscious, and then a more deliberate battle between them. Sue's announcement that she is to marry Phillotson seems to Jude a reprisal for his drunken visit: he fails to see that his shame-faced retreat from Sue's solicitude makes her stronger motive. Sue is gratified to detect in Jude a reproach belying his acceptance of the news ('Oh Sue! . . . But of course it is right – you couldn't have done better' – p. 186), and still peeved that no stronger expression of feeling has been aroused. Jude is aware both that he has no right to protest, and that Sue's engagement to the schoolmaster will safeguard and more clearly define the cousinly relationship in which they take refuge from feelings they cannot acknowledge. The social context in which they find themselves proves unable to accommodate their ambiguous relationship: their night together in the peasant's hut, 'Outside all laws except gravitation and germination', Sue believes (p. 191), brings about expulsion from her college and Jude's confession that he would be unable, anyway, to make their relationship acceptable to society. Sue's rejoinder is a decision to marry Phillotson at once.

It is worth elaborating the details of this courtship of attraction and recoil that gives its shape to the middle phase of the novel, because it so vividly dramatises what the *tableau vivant* of the lovers pictures. More inexorably than the long arm of fate or coincidence that frequently strikes down Hardy's protagonists, the very nature of Jude and Sue's relationship sets in motion the fatal process within which they are locked. And so their ritual of courtship continues in the repudiation of it: 'He tried to take her hand but she withdrew it. Their old relations of confidence seemed suddenly to have ended, and the antagonisms of sex were left without any counterpoising predilections' (p. 221). 'When she saw how wretched he was she softened, and trying to blink away her sympathetic tears said with all the winning reproachfulness of a heart-hurt woman: "Ah, you should have told me before you gave me the idea that you wanted to be allowed to love me! . . ."' (p. 222). Further barriers – Sue's marriage and Jude's theological aspirations – only increase a longing for each other that begins to demand physical expression: 'his kiss of that aerial being had seemed the purest moment of his fateful life' (p. 278). Jude burns his theological books in recognition that his hopes and needs are centred on Sue.

The little ceremony in which Sue compels Jude to accompany her up the aisle on the morning of her marriage to Phillotson nicely catches the flavour of the cousins' perverse, ambiguous love. Sue tantalises herself and Jude, and exacts his complicity in a 'mock marriage' which declares their utter separation. Moments of this kind emphasise how Hardy's tableaux in this and other novels take their cue from his notion of 'womankind'. Sue's creation of a public form that visualises complex private feeling (like Elfride's or Bathsheba's striking attitudes before their mirrors) may be deliberated or it may be spontaneous: 'I like to do things like this', Sue confides (p. 229). Elegiac, punitive, experimental feelings mingle. The scene rehearses Sue's 'marriage' with both men – both the formal marriage to Phillotson in which she shrinks from sexual commitment, and the vexed union with Jude which she feels unable formally to ratify. The paradoxes of approach and retreat continue even after Sue leaves Phillotson to live with Jude. It is only the unexpected return of Arabella that coerces Sue into a fully sexual relationship with Jude. The social difficulties that stand in the way of their marrying each other are quite removed as Jude's divorce is followed by Sue's. Even after their family begins, however, with the arrival of little Father Time, melancholy son of Jude and Arabella, and the birth of Jude and Sue's children, their inability to bring themselves to the public commitment of marriage creates fresh social difficulties. The exhausting pattern reaches a grotesque conclusion when Sue, remarried to Phillotson, feels compelled to consummate the marriage only when she has allowed herself to be clasped once again by the lover she has repudiated.

What *is* Sue's 'actual shape'? How convincingly does Hardy, as distinct from Jude or Phillotson, or Sue herself, ever fully articulate it? Recent attempts to answer this question,[7] emphasising Sue's role as 'New Woman', have given, I think, undue authority to the accounts she offers of herself. I have been drawing attention to Sue's habit of 'performing' herself in moments of self-analysis as in her more visual poses. However persuasive Hardy finds some of Sue's ideas, he never sees them as 'explaining' Sue's vexed and perplexing nature. Jude and Phillotson are dazzled and daunted by her intellectual 'superiority' and radical views: 'She's one too many for me!' says the schoolmaster (p. 293). Jude describes her as 'a woman whose intellect was to mine like a star to a benzoline lamp' (p. 481). Their enthusiasm for Sue's smatterings of culture and somewhat uncertain attitudinisings reflects their own hard-won struggle for the life of the mind and their amazement that a young woman should compete in it, against the barriers of sex as well as of class. Intriguingly, her 'gender' makes her an intellectual companion about whom it is possible also to feel emotional stirrings: 'If he could only get over the sense of her sex, as she seemed able to do so easily of his, what a comrade she would make', Jude reflects (p. 208). Interpenetrating Sue's explanation of her attitude to 'gender' (as she sits in Jude's armchair seductively dressed in his clothes), is Hardy's view of what that explanation actually means:

> My life has been entirely shaped by what people call a peculiarity in me. I have no fear of men, as such, nor of their books. I have

mixed with them – one or two of them particularly – almost as
one of their own sex. I mean I have not felt them as most women
are taught to feel – to be on their guard against attacks on their
virtue; for no average man – no man short of a sensual savage –
will molest a woman by day or night, at home or abroad, unless
she invites him. Until she says by a look 'Come on' he is always
afraid to, and if you never say it, or look it, he never
comes.   (pp. 201–2)

Hardy creates the barely conscious provocativeness of this as surely
as he registers the effect of Arabella's stratagem with the cochin's
egg. Sue's confession is a subtle 'Come on', in its inevitable
challenge to, and tantalising of, male response: she tells the story of
her non-sexual liaison with the young undergraduate to Phillotson
as well as to Jude, and she tells Jude that she has told it to Phillotson.
But the provocativeness is barely conscious just because Sue's
retreat into the ideal of purely intellectual and platonic friendships
is not a 'transcendence' of sex, but the consequence of sexual
timidity and ignorance. Jude rightly intuits that only a sexually
ignorant girl could will herself into marriage as Sue does, and the
girlish naïveté of her tone here is symptomatic. She has manifestly
no notion of what it is that women are taught to 'guard against': her
very terms reduce the subtle potency of sexuality (as the novel shows
it at work in Arabella for instance) to a power-struggle amenable to
the control of the will. Passionate ecstasy is something Sue delights
to find safely contained between the covers of books. She defends
herself against the charge of coldness by stating that 'Some of the
most passionately erotic poets have been the most self-contained in
their daily lives' (p. 203). The 'curious unconsciousness of gender'
Jude notes in her is a product of what Hardy repeatedly underlines
in her: the extraordinary detachment from her own and others'
emotional lives as well as from importunate physicality. That
quality is caught in the account of her relationship with her
undergraduate companion:

> He said that I was breaking his heart by holding out against him
> so long at such close quarters; he could never have believed it of
> woman. I might play that game once too often, he said. He came
> home merely to die. His death caused a terrible remorse in me for
> my cruelty – though I hope he died of consumption and not of me
> entirely.   (p. 202)

Hardy is inclined to underline the moral here: 'I might play that game once too often, he said.' John Goode's recent argument that Sue's withholding herself from a man she doesn't love is completely natural[8] misses Hardy's continuing emphasis on the destructive effect of Sue's habit of behaving as though there were no sexual dimension and therefore no problem. Sue is to play this game, which she scarcely apprehends, with Phillotson and with Jude, who is finally destroyed by it in his turn.

Nevertheless, she becomes a poignant figure as the game she plays with Jude arouses feelings in her that have a good deal to do with gender, and which can't be vanquished by fearlessness. Their interaction gradually delineates the 'actual shape' that underlies the masculine toughness and iconoclasm of her discourse. The intellectual attitudes Sue strikes represent not the emancipation of an independent selfhood from constricting social moulds, but the protective covering of new moulds. Ideas become weapons, aggressively and defensively deployed in reaction to her growing emotional dependence on Jude:

> 'I have no respect for Christminster whatever, except, in a qualified degree, on its intellectual side', said Sue Bridehead earnestly. 'My friend I spoke of took that out of me. He was the most irreligious man I ever knew, and the most moral. And intellect at Christminster is new wine in old bottles. The medievalism of Christminster must go, be sloughed off, or Christminster itself will have to go. To be sure, at times one couldn't help having a sneaking liking for the traditions of the old faith, as preserved by a section of thinkers there in touching and simple sincerity; but when I was in my saddest, rightest mind I always felt,
>
> O ghastly glories of saints, dead limbs of gibbeted Gods!' . . .
>
> 'Sue, you are not a good friend of mine to talk like that!'
> 'Then I won't, dear Jude!' The emotional throat-note had come back, and she turned her face away.   (pp. 204–5)

Despite his capacity for self-deception, Jude is altogether more straightforward than Sue, and the more susceptible to and bewildered by her manipulative, confused, emotions: 'He felt that she was treating him cruelly, though he could not quite say in what way. Her very helplessness seemed to make her so much stronger than he' (p. 204). Jude's understanding lingers well behind Hardy's here. Sympathy is retained for 'tiresome little Sue' because she, like Jude, is felt to be in the grip of uncontrollable and unfathomable feeling, helplessly 'tossed about'. What seems like childish cruelty has its source in Sue's intuiting the very point at which Jude's confusion drifts into unspoken criticism. And so she seizes on the vulnerability in Jude: 'I did want and long to ennoble some man to high aims; and when I saw you, and knew you wanted to be my comrade, I – shall I confess it? – thought that man might be you. But you take so much tradition on trust that I don't know what to say' (p. 207). Hectoring, cajoling, Sue hovers between playing the defenceless female – 'I *wish* I had a friend to support me; but nobody is ever on my side!' (Jude is 'surprised at her introducing personal feeling into mere argument') – and attempting a tone of strident aggression. At one point the discussion pauses while they shake hands 'like cronies in a tavern'. But, all the while, Sue's keenness of response to Jude's response bespeaks a quite different kind of relationship.

Sue's account of her 'woman's nature', then, is neither an understanding of herself nor a platform for new womanhood, but a desperate attempt to provide a rational basis for feelings inherent in that nature (and for the nature of her relationship with Jude) that lie beyond the reach of such 'explanations':

> I should shock you by letting you know how I give way to impulses, and how much I feel that I shouldn't have been provided with attractiveness unless it were meant to be exercised! Some women's love of being loved is insatiable, and so, often, is their love of loving; and in the last case they may find that they can't give it continuously to the chamber-officer appointed by the bishop's licence to receive it. But you are so straightforward, Jude, that you can't understand me!   (p. 265)

This is a line of social protest that Sue, and after her, Jude, are to develop as the marriage with Phillotson becomes intolerable to Sue. Undoubtedly her defiance of law and convention, supported as it is by selected quotations from J. S. Mill on liberty, carries a measure of authorial approval. So too does the more conventional notion that women's attractiveness compels them to attract – an echo of that conviction about womanhood Mary Wollstonecraft attacked in

Edmund Burke.[9] It is a notion in which Sue takes refuge again, seeing in this 'craving to attract and captivate, regardless of the injury it may do to the man', a 'reason' for the disasters that befall her. But the novel's view of 'the inexorable laws of nature' (p. 194) as they utter themselves through Sue is altogether more subtle and tender.

After the successive barriers between the cousins have been removed, the happiness they find together is intense, fleeting, equivocal. Its quality is brilliantly caught in a further *tableau vivant* of courtly love, refracted through the shrewd eye of Arabella. Oblivious of all eyes, Jude and Sue nevertheless make public their private 'moment', isolated by Hardy but held in focus by Arabella, as they attempt to interest little Father Time in their excursion to the rural fair:

> But they soon ceased to consider him an observer, and went along with that tender attention to each other which the shyest can scarcely disguise, and which these, among entire strangers as they imagined, took less trouble to disguise than they might have done at home. Sue, in her new summer clothes, flexible and light as a bird, her little thumb stuck up by the stem of her white cotton sunshade, went along as if she hardly touched the ground, and as if a moderately strong puff of wind would float her over the hedge into the next field. Jude, in his light grey holiday-suit, was really proud of her companionship, not more for her external attractiveness than for her sympathetic words and ways. That complete mutual understanding, in which every glance and movement was as effectual as speech for conveying intelligence between them, made them almost the two parts of a single whole.
>
> The pair with their charge passed through the turnstiles, Arabella and her husband not far behind them. When inside the enclosure the publican's wife could see that the two ahead began to take trouble with the youngster, pointing out and explaining the many objects of interest, alive and dead; and a passing sadness would touch their faces at their every failure to disturb his indifference.
>
> 'How she sticks to him!' said Arabella. 'O no – I fancy they are not married, or they wouldn't be so much to one another as that. . . . I wonder!' . . .
>
> 'He's charmed by her as if she were some fairy!' continued Arabella. 'See how he looks round at her, and lets his eyes rest on

her. I am inclined to think that she don't care for him quite so much as he does for her. She's not a particular warm-hearted creature to my thinking, though she cares for him pretty middling much – as much as she's able to; and he could make her heart ache a bit if he liked to try – which he's too simple to do. . . .'   (pp. 360–1)

'. . . external attractiveness' and 'complete mutual understanding' present, as Hardy's phrases suggest, an harmonious picture. Sue's delicacy is made much of by Hardy as by Jude. But it requires the folk wisdom of Arabella fully to interpret the picture. That wisdom is inevitably coloured by Arabella's prejudices. Envy for the grace and all-consuming mutual tenderness of the cousins is clearly to be heard in her commentary. On the other hand, it is Arabella's shrewdness and sense, and her easy sensuality, that the cousins lack. The perceptiveness of Arabella's reading has behind it the novel's recurrent emphasis on the definitive tableaux of courtly love: 'See how he looks round at her, and lets his eyes rest on her.' This, Arabella intuits, is a potent substitute for 'marriage', by which she means not just the formal commitment the pair can never make, but also the confident sexual gratification that eludes them still. Sue has wanted to remain Jude's 'dear, sweet, tantalizing phantom' (p. 309), embodying the pretty lines from Shelley's *Epipsychidion* she has Jude repeat. And so he has subdued his passion, accepting the bitter disappointment of her refusal to consummate their unconventional liaison until fear of Arabella coerces her, and the still more bitter one when grief is to make her repudiate their sexual relationship altogether. Hers, he accuses, has never been 'a passionate heart': 'your heart does not burn in a flame! You are, upon the whole, a sort of fay, or sprite – not a woman!' (p. 429). Sue is to confess to Widow Edlin, as she tears to shreds the silk nightgown in which she has slept with Jude, before putting on the calico in which she will give herself to the husband whose physical being she abhors, 'Jude has been here this afternoon, and I find I still love him – O, grossly!' (pp. 473–4). The word catches perfectly the ambivalent sexual responsiveness Hardy found himself unable to be explicit about in Victorian England:

> her intimacies with Jude have never been more than occasional, even when they were living together. (I mention that they occupy separate rooms, except towards the end, and one of the reasons for

fearing the marriage ceremony is that she fears it would be breaking faith with Jude to withhold herself at pleasure, or altogether, after it, though while uncontracted she feels at liberty to yield herself as seldom as she chooses.) This has tended to keep his passion as hot at the end as at the beginning, and helps to break his heart. He has never really possessed her as freely as he desired.[10]

The passing sadness that touches their faces at the fair becomes a recurrent note in their shared life. Living as 'two parts of a single whole' they find no resources, beyond their shared sensitivity, to combat the difficulties their unconventional life makes for them. Keenly attuned to each other's moods, neither has the power to avert in the other the drift towards fatalistic endurance of suffering that is apparent long before little Father Time destroys their fragile happiness irrevocably.

In his childish way, this child of Arabella and Jude articulates the social implications of their liaison that Jude and Sue keep evading, in an attempt, as Ian Gregor points out, to cheat time itself.[11] Their solicitude for him at the fair only momentarily deflects their mutual absorption. He provides an object for their sensitive concern, but their passing sadness acknowledges failure to cope with his intrusive presence. Hardy makes the connection between the child's destruction of himself and the other children psychologically as well as symbolically appropriate. It is Jude's nostalgic return to crowded Christminster on Remembrance Day, and his staying too late at the procession to find adequate lodgings, followed by Sue's self-preoccupied treatment of the child's questions about their continuing plight, that provide the occasion for the child's action. In the end, Sue and Jude are destroyed, and their children are destroyed, because the life brought into being by their romantic imagination is unable to sustain itself within a society whose more prosaic exigencies it seeks to exclude.

This, I think, is the conclusive emphasis the novel makes in its exploration of the relationship between Jude and Sue. It is not their defiance of society's conventions that destroys them, but their embodying so purely its attenuating spirituality. In pursuing the insoluble paradoxes made by their natural affinity, Hardy is feeling his way towards an account of their relationship that touches a timeless and potentially tragic dimension of experience. But, in seeking an explanation of those paradoxes of feeling in terms of the role of feeling in Victorian culture generally, Hardy clarifies a more limited conception of Jude and Sue. One last picture makes vivid the connection between Jude and Sue's aspirations, and their particular phase of Victorian cultural history. Searching for the grieving distracted Sue, Jude finds her at last in the deserted church of St Silas:

> High overhead, above the chancel steps, Jude could discern a huge, solidly constructed Latin cross – as large, probably as the original it was designed to commemorate. It seemed to be suspended in the air by invisible wires; it was set with large jewels, which faintly glimmered in some weak ray caught from outside, as the cross swayed to and fro in a silent and scarcely perceptible motion. Underneath, upon the floor, lay what appeared to be a heap of black clothes, and from this was repeated the sobbing that he had heard before. It was his Sue's form, prostrate on the paving.
>
> 'Sue!' he whispered.
>
> Something white disclosed itself; she had turned up her face.
>
> 'What – do you want with me here, Jude?' she said almost sharply. 'You shouldn't come! I wanted to be alone! Why did you intrude here?'   (p. 425)

The details are sharply delineated. That vast bejewelled cross held up by 'invisible wires', faintly illuminated and set in motion by what little light and air it can catch from the darkened world outside, seems inevitably to draw to itself the prostrate black-robed figure who here renounces that world. The theatricality of Sue's renunciation scarcely minimises the suffering she is undergoing in this final phase of the novel. In creating so Pre-Raphaelite a setting for it, Hardy underlines the representativeness of Jude and Sue's various spiritual yearnings. Even the stolid and decent Phillotson is touched by the prevailing climate, and the hedonistic Arabella undergoes a fleeting religious conversion in the wake of bereavement. Jude's anguished protest against Sue's 'Christianity or mysticism or Sacerdotalism or whatever it may be called' is painfully ironic in view of Sue's earlier deflation of Jude's 'Tractarian stage' (pp. 426, 205). From the unfolding of their tale to its close, each of them is to remain a supplicant of the veiled mysteries, inhaling the pagan air 'that blew . . . from Cyprus' (p. 139) or the heavier incense of Oxford Anglo-Catholicism.

'I wanted to be alone!', Sue cries, as indeed she has done throughout the novel. As Sue retreats from the experience of womanhood into a notional womanhood, this representative woman of the new feminist movement looks equally representative of that phase of Victorian culture ushered in by Keats's 'La Belle Dame sans Merci' and Tennyson's 'The Lady of Shalott'. In taking on again the silent martyrdom of her marriage to Phillotson she becomes, irrevocably, the emblematic lady of Jude's unattainable dream. Jude's collapse into the 'grossness' of drunken despair that gives him back to Arabella makes its final comment on the destructive potency of that emblem. The domestic gin is sprung on Jude as Arabella claims him for a life devoid of dreams:

> She pulled off his boots. 'Now,' she whispered, 'take hold of me – never mind your weight. Now – first stair, second stair – '
>
> 'But, – are we out in our old house by Marygreen?' asked the stupefied Jude. 'I haven't been inside it for years till now! Hey? And where are my books? That's what I want to know?'
>
> 'We are at my home, dear, where there's nobody to spy out how ill you are. Now – third stair, fourth stair – that's it. Now we shall get on.'   (p. 455)

The house of Jude's 'husbandom' encloses him as the house of Sue's 'wifedom' once more encloses her, and he is laid out in it as the bells of Christminster once again celebrate 'Remembrance Week'.

5 Portraits of Ladies: *The Wings of the Dove*

> She made now, alone, the full circuit of the place, noble and peaceful while the summer sea, stirring here and there a curtain or an outer blind, breathed its veiled spaces. She had a vision of clinging to it; that perhaps Eugenio could manage. She was *in* it, as in the ark of her deluge, and filled with such a tenderness for it that why shouldn't this, in common mercy, be warrant enough? She would never, never leave it – she would engage to that; would ask nothing more than to sit tight in it and float on and on.
>
> (Henry James, *The Wings of the Dove*, p. 350)

The 'place' is the upper room of Milly Theale's Venetian palace, one of the 'high florid rooms' where

> hard cool pavements took reflexions in their life-long polish, and where the sun on stirred sea-water, flickering up through open windows, played over the painted 'subjects' in the splendid ceilings – medallions of purple and brown, of brave old melancholy colour, medals as of old reddened gold, embossed and beribboned, all toned with time and all flourished and scalloped and gilded about . . . (p. 341)

The world presents itself to Milly as a gallery of pictures; her painter's eye responds as her creator's does, to a social texture in which both settings and relationships are composed of impressions given and received, mirrored by and reflecting the interpreting consciousness. In Milly's feeding on its visual delights, James registers the sense of her confinement not as limitation, but as granting her, as she is to tell Densher, 'the freedom of all the centuries' (p. 371). Densher, in his turn, is to reflect that her setting 'gained from her, in a manner, for effect and harmony, as much as it gave' (p. 379). In this splendid room, the portrait of Milly that has been made by Milly herself, by the encircling social world, and by James, finds its completion.

Milly's resolution that 'She would never, never leave it' comes well before that point in her story when the discovery of Kate and Densher's deception causes her to 'turn her face to the wall' and die. From the beginning, she is presented as inevitably, finally 'alone', set apart and raised aloft, mysteriously but inexorably doomed. And, as this passage reminds us, Milly clings to her solitude. She has a 'tenderness' for it, and for the 'romance' of sitting there for ever, as in a portrait which is also a 'fortress'. She builds for herself, or conspires with Eugenio, Susie, Sir Luke Strett and all her 'court' in the building of, that 'impenetrable ring fence, within which there reigned a kind of expensive vagueness made up of smiles and silences and beautiful fictions and priceless arrangements, all strained to breaking' outside which 'all the world', Densher perceives, is made to 'hover' (p. 461). Like Isabel Archer, that earlier American heiress so close to James's heart,[1] whose high hopes of 'life' lead her into a room from which there is no exit, and into the final deadness of portrait ('framed in the gilded doorway . . . the picture of a gracious lady' – *Portrait of a Lady*, p. 398), Milly's doom is inherent in the very conception of the novel that contains her.

That conception is foreshadowed as early as 1894; in a year that produced many general reflections and some fine stories about death, there comes the Notebook jotting about 'some young creature . . . who, at twenty, . . . on the threshold of a life that has seemed boundless, is suddenly condemned to death'.[2] And the Notebook entry that envisages Isabel Archer's destiny is even more inexorable than Ralph's summary of it in Chapter 54 of *The Portrait of a Lady*: 'the idea of the whole thing is that the poor girl, who has dreamt of freedom and nobleness, who has done, as she believes, a generous, natural, clear-sighted thing, finds herself in reality ground in the very mill of the conventional'.[3] Both heroines clearly enough reflect James's preoccupation with the 'will to live' of his beloved, ailing cousin, Minnie Temple:

the very figure and image of a felt interest in life, an interest as magnanimously far-spread, or as familiarly and exquisitely fixed, as her splendid shifting sensibility, moral, personal, nervous, and having at once such noble flights and such touchingly discouraged drops, such graces of indifference and inconsequence, might at any moment determine. She was really to remain, for our appreciation, the supreme case of a taste for life as life, as personal living.[4]

It is a comment that catches equally well, of course, James's responses to the qualities and circumstances of his ailing sister Alice. But the complexity of Minnie's 'case' for James is suggested in his confiding to his brother William: 'it's almost as if she had passed away – as far as I am concerned – from having served her purpose, that of standing well within the world, inviting and inviting me onward by all the bright intensity of her example'.[5] Leon Edel argues that in fact her death was a psychological relief to James, converting her 'into an object to be serenely contemplated, appreciated and even loved – through the opaque glass of memory'.[6]

That is to put too baldly the point that aesthetic preoccupations inevitably mingle with personal urgency in James's pursuit of the figure he sees as 'inviting and inviting me onward'. That phrase interestingly recalls the figure that compels Hardy, both as unresolved personal feeling and as emblem, or 'object to be serenely contemplated'. An important difference is suggested, however, in James's dislike of Hardy's women, 'of the inconsequential, wilful, mettlesome type . . . the type which aims at giving one a very intimate sense of a young lady's womanishness . . . a flirt'.[7] Milly's 'taste for life', many would feel, involves too little sense of distinctive 'womanishness'. Feminist critics, in particular, are inclined to see both Sue and Milly as male 'stereotypes' rather than as adequately realised women.[8]

I have argued that in Sue, and with impressive insight, Hardy explores his own and his culture's pursuit of the emblematic lady, and reveals the essential woman she really is. The charge is more difficult to answer in the case of Milly, who of all fictional heroines surely most closely resembles Tennyson's Lady of Shalott.[9] For women writers as for men, exploration of the emblematic figure makes the focus of urgent personal questions as well as of more general cultural questions about the 'framing' and isolating of feeling and of passion in nineteenth-century society. But for no other heroine is the 'curse' experienced as so unequivocal a death-sentence. Milly takes to an extreme point that sacrifice of life that distinguishes the 'artist figures' of James's later stories and novels.[10]

Like George Eliot's Dorothea or Dickens's Little Dorrit, Milly is well qualified to be her author's 'concrete deputy or delegate'. But for neither of those protagonists does their 'splendid shifting sensibility', however it may temporarily necessitate private reflective moments that isolate them from the texture of social life, entail so complete and final an isolation as Milly's.

Her emblematic aspect is underlined in the novel's very title, especially if we bear in mind not only the prevalence of the dove as a symbol of womanhood in many Pre-Raphaelite paintings,[11] but also the currency given the psalmist's dove in this period by Pater's epigraph for *The Renaissance*: 'yet shall ye be as the wings of the dove'.[12] Milly's brief life may indeed be seen as a dramatising of Pater's famous conclusion:

> we have an interval, and then our place knows us no more. Some spend this interval in listlessness, some in high passion, the wisest, at least among 'the children of this world', in art and song. For our one chance lies in expanding that interval, in getting as many pulsations as possible into the given time. Great passions may give us this quickened sense of life, ecstasy and sorrow and love, the various forms of enthusiastic activity, disinterested or otherwise, which come naturally to many of us. Only be sure it is passion – that it does yield you this fruit of a quickened, multiplied consciousness.[13]

In Milly James certainly celebrates the 'quickened, multiplied consciousness'. But the poignancy of her case is that this does not sufficiently illumine her brief interval. Her death becomes an equivocal triumph indeed in a world where the 'taste for life' comes to mean so much more than the gratifying of the imagination. The aesthetic ideals continually tested out in the experience of Milly lead James to the most searching of all his inquiries into the value of imaginative gratification. Essential to this purpose is the making for his novel of twin protagonists. Milly's 'case' is inseparable from Kate Croy's: the living lady is seen to occupy the same 'box' as the dying. And both are at the centre of the social composition, held in that act of portraiture by their own contrivance, by society, and by the novelist. Kate's 'one chance', dominated by 'the beauty of what I see' (p. 267), discovers the paucity of an imaginative gratification that becomes an end in itself. As in Millais's interpretation of Tennyson's fable, the 'wondrous silken web' Kate spins at last enmeshes her completely. That Kate, in her robust vitality, comes so thoroughly to experience Milly's 'case' is not only a check on the potential aestheticism of that case, but also clearly underlines James's recognition of the weaknesses inherent in the conception of his ailing heroine.

In the Preface to *The Wings of the Dove*, James, with his habitual self-awareness, puts the fundamental question: 'Why had one to look so straight in the face and so clearly to cross-question the idea of making one's protagonist "sick"' ' (p. 14). He is conscious of the fact that it is 'by the act of living' that characters have their appeal, and that he needs to justify the compelling power his 'motive' has had for him for so long. In confessing his 'painter's tenderness of imagination' for Milly (recalling the tenderness acknowledged by the narrator of Isabel Archer's story), he speaks of her in ways that indeed suggest the idealisation and veneration many critics have found in his presentation of her. His 'merciful indirection' in approaching her, 'as an unspotted princess is ever dealt with', indicates in James the writer of prefaces, if not James the novelist, a tendency to share 'the view' of Milly as dove. And any critical account of *The Wings of the Dove* must come to grips with the question of whether the novel itself penetrates 'the impenetrable ring fence' to establish for Milly a convincing, and convincingly feminine, presence.

Dickens's Little Dorrit, who also finds a vantage-point at the window of a Venetian palace, descends to mingle where she is most at home, with the crowd of people in the common streets, to marry and to make a life of modest usefulness. For Milly Theale, as for the majority of Jamesian protagonists, there is no such descent. 'What should one do with the misery of the world in a schema of the agreeable for one's self?' Isabel jauntily asks in an early self-analysis. The essentially rhetorical nature of the question is underlined in Henrietta Stackpole's criticism of her friend: 'You live too much in the world of your own dreams. You're not enough in contact with reality – with the toiling, striving, suffering, I may even say *stirring* world that surrounds you' (*Portrait of a Lady*, p. 233). James is aware, as George Eliot is, that being a 'lady' entails just such an embowered life as Dorothea Brooke's, and he is to bring Milly only briefly face to face, in Regent's Park, with the 'toiling, striving, suffering' world of London poverty. Nevertheless, this is the world that makes Milly's destiny, and the novel opens by surveying it. Again, it is through the interweaving 'case' of Kate Croy that Milly is brought to confront its exigencies and its miseries.

James's defence, in the Preface, against the anticipated charges of Milly's being passive and aloof, emphasises first the creative challenge and excitement provided by the very conception of her apparent isolation. The figure of Milly makes the compositional 'centre' of an unfolding story, and he describes that centre in terms of the dynamic action inherent in it: 'It stood there with secrets and compartments, with possible treacheries and traps; it might have a great deal to give, but would probably ask for equal services in return, and would collect this debt to the last shilling' (p. 13). It is just the passivity of Milly's case that is to draw the world to itself, in an action that makes Milly as vital a protagonist as Kate and Densher. If Kate is Milly's 'doom', 'laying a trap for the great innocence to come', the other implication James discovers in his design is that Milly is Kate's 'doom': that Kate (and Densher) are 'drawn in as by some pool of a Lorelei', 'terrified and tempted and charmed; bribed away, it may even be, from more prescribed and natural orbits, inheriting from their connexion with her strange difficulties and still stranger opportunities, confronted with rare questions and called upon for new discriminations' (pp. 27, 16)

And so the novel begins with Kate. She waits in her imprisoning room not simply because of James's confessed desire to approach Milly indirectly, but because, as we see, Kate's destiny is being conceived of in terms that curiously resemble, as well as involve, Milly's. The two girls share a destiny because they share a predicament – that general state of being each in her 'box' that Milly is to see in all the poor girls around her in Regent's Park. Like them, Kate Croy has her 'rent' to find, but she also has her social identity to keep up. The novel opens, as it is to close, with Kate framed in a meagre room, irrevocably and in every detail, the portrait of a lady. The portrait comes in two parts, the first an evocation of Kate's sensibility in terms of what she 'sees', followed by a picture of Kate as she is seen, and as she sees herself:

> She waited, Kate Croy, for her father to come in, but he kept her unconscionably, and there were moments at which she showed herself, in the glass over the mantel, a face positively pale with the irritation that had brought her to the point of going away without sight of him. It was at this point, however, that she remained;

changing her place, moving from the shabby sofa to the armchair upholstered in a glazed cloth that gave at once – she had tried it – the sense of the slippery and of the sticky. She had looked at the sallow prints on the walls and at the lonely magazine, a year old, that combined, with a lamp in coloured glass and a knitted white centre-piece wanting in freshness, to enhance the effect of the purplish cloth on the principal table; she had above all from time to time taken a brief stand on the small balcony to which the pair of long windows gave access. The vulgar little street, in this view, offered scant relief from the vulgar little room; its main office was to suggest to her that the narrow black house-fronts, adjusted to a standard that would have been low even for backs, constituted quite the publicity implied by such privacies. One felt them in the room exactly as one felt the room – the hundred like it or worse – in the street. Each time she turned in again, each time, in her impatience, she gave him up, it was to sound to a deeper depth, while she tasted the faint flat emanation of things, the failure of fortune and of honour. If she continued to wait it was really in manner that she mightn't add the shame of fear, of individual, of personal collapse, to all the other shames. To feel the street, to feel the room, to feel the table-cloth and the centre-piece and the lamp, gave her a small salutary sense at least of neither shirking nor lying. This whole vision was the worst thing yet – as including in particular the interview to which she had braced herself; and for what had she come but for the worst? She tried to be sad so as not to be angry, but it made her angry that she couldn't be sad. And yet where was misery, misery too beaten for blame and chalk-marked by fate like a 'lot' at a common auction, if not in these merciless signs of mere stale feelings?   (pp. 31–2)

The contrast between 'the vulgar little room' and Milly's Venetian setting is marked in every anticipated particular. Milly's chamber, adorned with splendid paintings, illumined by the sun on stirred sea-water, overlooking the changing spectacle of a Venetian canal, offers imaginative delights commensurate with its cost. In Mr Croy's room, the passing of time has made not mellowness, but the sallowness of faded prints and furnishings that proclaim the tastelessness of poverty. Lit by a cheap lamp in coloured glass, it overlooks the endlessly repeating reflection of its own bleakness, in the drab, uniform, exposed backs of England's working-class cottages. The sensibility evoked through Kate's consciousness of her surroundings is, like Milly's, acute. But Kate's is a sensibility cramped, restless, irritated by what it takes in: the 'knitted white centre-piece wanting in freshness', the armchair upholstered in a glazed cloth, the whole faded accumulation of ugly objects, are successive notations of the affront to her taste and spirits. In Kate's forcing herself 'To feel the street, to feel the room, to feel the table cloth', to taste 'the faint flat emanation of things', there is a certain resilience, a potential fineness of spirit as well as a fineness of taste. Kate's family has broken down, not quite as literally as Milly's, but more painfully, leaving her as exposed, in her circumstances, to the 'common auction' as Milly is to feel. Like Milly, Kate is dependent on the inner resources unfolding here, in the self-sufficient, self-sustaining capacity to confront and ponder what she sees. Spread out before her are the boxes inhabited by those who live an existence she sees at first hand in her widowed sister's small house in Chelsea, and in the even deeper 'hole' in which the Misses Condrip dwell. Kate is to recognise, in her Aunt Maud's mansion at Lancaster Gate, 'how material things spoke to her' (p. 50). And her consciousness is created here by a writer whose sympathy for that mode of discourse is quite apparent. Mr Croy's surroundings do bespeak 'stale feelings' and a 'beaten spirit'. The figure of Kate, struggling for mastery against her own feelings of defeat and despair, is poised with careful deliberation against these unlovely surroundings. Hers is a mind that is energetic, speculative, constructive. In her not surrendering to feeling there is a steady resilience. Her 'small salutary sense at least of neither shirking or lying' suggests a potential fineness that is larger than a fineness of taste or the need for material comforts. On the other hand, she has (like Isabel Archer) a view of herself that, while it is proof against sordid surroundings, highly values 'the look of the thing'. Kate is never simply 'villainous'. In presenting her first through what she sees, James enlists a measure of sympathy and trust in her that is to be progressively qualified but never entirely lost. Kate's vision of the world inevitably shapes her picture of herself, and the passage looks now in some detail at the self-portrait that emerges as she contemplates herself in the mirror:

> She stared into the tarnished glass too hard indeed to be staring at her beauty alone. She readjusted the poise of her black closely-feathered hat; retouched, beneath it, the thick fall of her dusky hair; kept her eyes aslant no less on her beautiful averted than on

her beautiful presented oval. She was dressed altogether in black, which gave an even tone, by contrast, to her clear face and made her hair more harmoniously dark. Outside, on the balcony, her eyes showed as blue; within, at the mirror, they showed almost as black. She was handsome, but the degree of it was not sustained by items and aids; a circumstance moreover playing its part at almost any time in the impression she produced. The impression was one that remained, but as regards the sources of it no sum in addition would have made up the total. She had stature without height, grace without motion, presence without mass. Slender and simple, frequently soundless, she was somehow always in the line of the eye – she counted singularly for its pleasure. More 'dressed', often, with fewer accessories, than other women, or less dressed, should occasion require, with more, she probably couldn't have given the key to these felicities. They were mysteries of which her friends were conscious – those friends whose general explanation was to say that she was clever, whether or no it were taken by the world as the cause or as the effect of her charm. If she saw more things than her fine face in the dull glass of her father's lodgings she might have seen that after all she was not herself a fact in the collapse. She didn't hold herself cheap, she didn't make for misery. Personally, no, she wasn't chalk-marked for auction. She hadn't given up yet, and the broken sentence, if she was the last word, *would* end with a sort of meaning. There was a minute during which, though her eyes were fixed, she quite visibly lost herself in the thought of the way she might still pull things round had she only been a man.

(pp. 32–3)

Kate's mirror returns not 'shadows of the world', quite, but a confirmation of her sense of her own value, which she both elicits from, and imposes on, the social world she inhabits. She *is* beautiful, but also 'beautiful[ly] presented': the impeccable taste with which she expresses herself helps explain the intensity of her reaction to her father's shabby circumstances. Unlike Hardy's Elfride, Kate surveys herself with an unambiguous candour. She is taking account of material advantages. But, as her impressions of herself give way to the impressions she makes, the passage registers a view of Kate that admires, without completely trusting or liking her. Her acts seem to conceal her essence; as with Hardy's Elfride, 'impression' is what remains. Her friends associate her mysterious impressiveness with 'cleverness'. James's balanced cadences suggest that the mystery lies in her capacity to sustain illusions – 'stature without height, grace without motion, presence without mass' – and to sustain them without visible 'aids'. He so far forgets himself, before returning to the centre of her consciousness, as to underline the subtleties of a self-portrait in which even her lying 'somehow always in the line of the eye', counting 'singularly for its pleasure', suggests an element of the consciously composed. The source of Kate's impressiveness lies in her not holding herself cheap, and this capacity in her to present herself beautifully is what must see her through – given that she is not a man. For the costs of being a woman are as clearly held in view here (promoting what is seen throughout the novel as distinctively feminine cleverness and contriving), as the costs of meeting the requirements of imagination.

The novel's opening sets its pattern, moving between Kate's 'web' or vision (and later Milly's, and to a lesser extent, Densher's) and the 'portrait' the protagonist presents to the world. The room, or 'box', or envelope of circumstances that contains her, shapes her 'seeing', as it shapes Milly's. The figure of the enclosed lady provides from the outset, then, an image of social experience as James sees it: it is through the flow of consciousness, and, interweaving with it, the receiving and creating and interpreting of pictures that the individual's and the novel's narrative composes itself. 'Picture', in James's characteristic way, is extended by 'scene'. So now the choices confronting James's imprisoned lady are explored in Kate's conversation with her father.

Like Isabel Archer, Kate wants not only to look well, but also to be seen to behave, if possible, 'even better'. Her offer to share her life and her small annuity with Mr Croy, rather than accepting the support of her wealthy aunt (whose offer is conditional on her cutting all ties with her father), sounds extraordinarily self-sacrificing, especially in view of his manifest cynicism and detachment: 'It's simply a question of your not turning me away – taking yourself out of my life. . . . We won't worry in advance about how or where; we'll have a faith and find a way' (p. 45). There is a particular quality of intimacy between father and daughter – a tone and rhetoric in which shrewd and knowing appraisal masquerades as moral grandeur. They perfectly understand one another. Kate is not devoid of feeling for him, despite his unnameable disgrace and his irresponsibility; her feeling for the difficulties of her widowed sister and her children is similarly demonstrated in her sharing with them the other half of her small inheritance. But it is Croy who immediately perceives the element of self-interest in Kate's offer to him: the matter with you is that you're in love, and that your aunt knows and . . . hates and opposes it' (pp. 45–6). And it is Croy who has the effrontery to proclaim, echoing Marx, 'The family sentiment, in our vulgarised brutal life, has gone utterly to pot' (p. 42). Croy's 'family sentiment' is revealed in the sordid bargaining that makes his real exchange with his daughter. And, indeed, conversation after conversation, between Kate and her father, Kate and her sister, Kate and Aunt Maud, reduces itself to this kind of blackmail. For all of them, as she is to tell Densher, she is *'the* value – the only one they have' (p. 81). Aunt Maud sees Kate as an appreciating 'investment', a key to improving her own social connections. 'Poor Marian', like her father, sees that a marriage between Kate and the penniless Densher would effectively prevent any improvement in her bleak circumstances. And Kate herself finds a 'provisional citadel' at Lancaster Gate. She is pictured, in a passage that echoes, and contrasts with, the novel's opening, in the handsome room allotted her by Aunt Maud, with its silk-covered sofa, the warmth of fire-light, the whole 'great grey map of Middlesex spread beneath her lookout':

> She had a dire accessibility to pleasure from such sources. She liked the charming quarters her aunt had assigned to her – liked them literally more than she had in all her other days liked anything; and nothing could have been more uneasy than her suspicion of her relative's view of this truth.   (p. 50)

The tacit bargain she has begun to strike with Aunt Maud is to live with her on what seem to be Mrs Lowder's terms, in return for surroundings so visibly the antithesis of Mr Croy's: 'It wouldn't be the first time she had seen herself obliged to accept with smothered irony other people's interpretations of her conduct. She often ended by giving up to them – it seemed really the way to live – the version that met their convenience' (p. 48).

Kate's sensibility, shrewd as well as delicate, permits a measure of self-awareness, though we see it from the start formed by, and pitted against, uncompromising economic and social circumstances. It is through her own honest self-appraisal that we glimpse a self that underlies the social 'version': 'she saw herself as handsome, no doubt, but as hard, and felt herself as clever but as cold; and as so much too imperfectly ambitious, furthermore, that it was a pity, for a quiet life, she couldn't decide to be either finely or stupidly indifferent' (p. 71). When Densher admires the 'high beauty' of her reported approach to her father, she is anxious to dispel the illusion she has begun by wanting to give: 'It wasn't courage – it was the opposite. I did it to save myself – to escape' (p. 79).

The question of whether Kate can escape her 'box' is inextricably bound up with the question of whether Milly can escape hers; inherent in the symmetry of their mutual 'case' is that Merton Densher should be the Sir Lancelot who makes vivid the possibility of escape for each of them. Densher elicits for Kate, as for Milly, a quality of feeling not appeased by 'material things'. Analysis may usefully proceed, then, as the novel does, by focusing on a series of pictures in which, as in the opening sequences, rooms become not only the setting, but also a complex metaphor for the self in its whole imprisoning envelope of material circumstances. Aunt Maud's room is no more adequate to the needs of the self awakened by Kate's love for Densher than Mr Croy's room is adequate as a setting for her imaginative hungers. Kate recalls her first meeting with Densher in terms that catch the ambiguity of her escape; to find a way out of one box is only to experience the need for another:

> She had observed a ladder against a garden-wall and had trusted herself so to climb it as to be able to see over into the probable garden on the other side. On reaching the top she had found herself face to face with a gentleman engaged in a like calculation at the same moment, and the two enquirers had remained confronted on their ladders. The great point was that for the rest of the evening they had been perched – they had not climbed down; and indeed during the time that followed Kate at least had had the perched feeling – it was as if she were there aloft without a retreat.   (pp. 67–8)

For a lady who experiences society as habitually distorting or suppressing intensities of feeling, such a meeting, not only with 'eyes', but also with all other sensations, is overwhelming in its impact. The moment makes a ladder that transcends all that anchors Kate within the rooms that Society provides for her. And it defines the way in which Kate and Densher are to remain together, in a tableau that brings to mind Jude and Sue, suspended and dispossessed, until the end of the story and beyond, the eyes continuing to meet, and the understanding never quite meeting. Densher is to feel, again and again, 'perched' by Kate; Kate is always to be as she is here, not so much joined in her solitariness, as confirmed in it, by the compelling scrutiny of another pair of eyes. In Kate's case, as in Milly's, the potentialities of love can be glimpsed on the high vantage-point from which ladies of Shalott survey their world. But the attempt to fulfill and complete the self is inevitably doomed, this, and all such metaphoric moments in the Victorian novel suggest, from the very beginning. Marriage glimmers before Kate and Densher 'like a temple without an avenue'. (p. 72). Their problem, from the instant they recognise each other, is one of reconciling the public form with the private passion, of 'squaring Aunt Maud', of finding places to walk and to meet, ways of 'seeing' and presenting their relationship, and of finding, quite literally, a 'room'.

Critics of latter James novels often complain of 'a kind of epistemological vertigo'[14] in which distinctions and values, and the sense of what is 'true', are blurred, and in which we are left only with

> different images of the passive but highly responsive self trying to find its way in a maze of demands being made on it by the external social world. . . . *The Wings of the Dove*, is, then, largely about relations among different aspects of the narrator's mind . . . the conflicts among these aspects are resolved by purely mental processes, through reflection, assimilation, and rejection.[15]

Certainly James's interest in the relationship between consciousness and 'external demands' is explored, as it is with earlier novelists, in the experience of the novel's protagonists. In *The Wings of the Dove*, even comparatively minor characters such as Susan Stringham and Aunt Maud, in their different ways, create versions of 'reality' that reflect what we learn to recognise as their distinctive ways of seeing things. So that, as Kate and Densher's story develops, we are surely aware that it does so in terms of clearly discernible differences between their ways of thinking and feeling, and that it is driving towards painful conflict that goes far deeper than 'mental processes'. Those differences establish themselves even as the lovers, wandering about in parks and public places, explore their sense of expansive possibilities:

He saw after a little that she had been following some thought of
her own. . . . Suddenly she said to him with extraordinary
beauty: 'I engage myself to you for ever.'

The beauty was in everything, and he could have separated
nothing – couldn't have thought of her face as distinct from the
whole joy. Yet her face had a new light. 'And I pledge you – I call
God to witness! – every spark of my faith; I give you every drop of
my life.' That was all, for the moment, but it was enough, and it
was almost as quiet as if it were nothing. They were in the open
air, in an alley of the gardens; the great space, which seemed to
arch just then higher and spread wider for them, threw them back
into deep concentration. They moved by a common instinct to a
spot, within sight, that struck them as fairly sequestered, and
then, before their time together was spent, they had extorted from
concentration every advance it could make them. They had
exchanged vows and tokens, sealed their rich compact, solem-
nised, so far as breathed words and murmured sounds and lighted
eyes and clasped hands could do it, their agreement to belong
only, and to belong tremendously, to each other.   (pp. 98–9)

At such moments, James dramatises the consciousness of each, as
well as that 'practical *fusion* of consciousness' of which he writes in
the Preface. There is, early in Book Second, an authorial promise to
show us what it is that draws and holds the lovers together – marked
differences of temperament and experience creating the sense 'of
being poor where the other was rich. (p. 65). The abundant 'life'
Kate vivifies, for Densher, is rendered here in the rapt intensity of
her distinctively heightened rhetoric. Kate's capacity for fulsome
declarations of feeling is to strike the more reticent Densher as
'beautiful' again and again, and to prompt in him, as here, an
answering, confused, physical response that sometimes calms,
sometimes stirs, his dissatisfaction with Kate's controlling voice. For
it is Kate, always, who speak for the relationship, envisaging its
shape and plotting its course. Strong feelings generate trust,
moments of joy dispelling doubt and difficulty, sustaining an energy
that is gradually to ebb, distort and miscarry. This very scene in
which the lovers seal themselves each to the other with such moving
solemnity ends in Densher's detecting a note of falsity in Kate, and
Kate's resenting this. Her protestation that her letters to him in New
York will travel independently of her aunt's mail not for 'anything
so vulgar as to hide them' (p. 102) plainly fails to take account of the

fact that she *is* hiding them. Subterfuge is defended by Kate as 'refinement' – 'of consciousness, of sensation, of appreciation . . . men *don't* know. They know in such matters almost nothing but what women show them' (p. 102). It is a lame defence, a confession of weakness masquerading as a superior awareness that recalls Sue Bridehead's appeals to 'woman's nature'. Like Hardy, James sees the strategy as a response to feelings of impotence inherent in the social role enjoined on women. The beauty of what Kate sees is the product of those mysterious arts that make the beauty of what she herself seems to be – a portrait beside which Densher feels the blundering 'crudeness' of the merely male. Furthermore, what is required of him is not that he see what Kate sees, but that he act as though he does.

Nevertheless, Densher's 'passivity' is rather more interesting than it has seemed to many critics, and, indeed, integral to the novel's developing design. He shares with the two female protagonists a certain vulnerability. He, too, has his rent to pay. His consciousness, like theirs, is remarkably active and sensitively aware. Seen at first, however, moving somewhat aimlessly about Kensington Gardens, he suggests 'that wondrous state of youth in which the elements, the metals more or less precious, are so in fusion and fermentation that the question of the final stamp, the pressure that fixes the value, must wait for comparative coolness' (p. 64). The process through which Densher finds that final stamp, and a value rather different from Kate's 'value', transforms openness into a decisiveness that confronts and is alienated by her final inflexibility. Densher, introspective and even romantic, not wanting to read 'the romance of his existence in a cheap edition' (p. 373), as a journalist handling facts 'with deplorable ease' (p. 75), is nevertheless a man of conscience. He is troubled by 'the question of whether it were more ignoble to ask a woman to take her chance with you, or to accept it from your conscience that her chance could be at the best but one of the degrees of privation'. His plea to Kate – 'will you take me just as I am' (p. 259 – impractical though it comes to seem in the light of Kate's subtle strategies, expresses urgencies of feeling as Kate never does, and an impulse to honour them straightforwardly. But his is, above all, the insecurity of a man who has 'nowhere to "take" his love' (p. 248). On his return from New York, he suppresses the impulse to provoke the question of whether Kate would come to his rooms. His passion, the need to possess the 'life' Kate promises, is less readily accommodated now by social arrangements he finds 'maddening', 'an impatience that, prolonged and exasperated, made a man ill' (p. 250).

A series of 'rooms' make vivid the material considerations that shape what Kate 'sees' and, with it, constrain the lovers' passion. In Aunt Maud's opulent boudoir, and Milly's hotel, in the great salon of the National Gallery, in Milly's Venetian ball-room, they hurriedly and furtively seize a fragmentary independence from the public world to which they are increasingly answerable. In response to Aunt Maud's expectations and demands, and the dazzling promise of Milly's wealth, Kate becomes manipulative in turn, in accordance with that law of the social jungle she explains so candidly to Milly, 'where the worker in one connection was the worked in another' (p. 158). It is not until Milly's ball that Densher at last grasps the implications of the 'wondrous silken web' that enmeshes him, at the end of its intricate process of hints and half truths and subtle directives. During this process, it is only through Kate's web that we, too, are able to read her; in this way James conveys Kate's losing touch with her own innermost thoughts and feelings. The gaiety, charm, quickness and poise of her social self begins to do duty for a larger self, glossing over the ugliness of her plan and the deflection of Densher's feeling. Densher is to face the paradox that to possess Kate he must sustain the ambiguities of behaviour she requires of him, and turn his fullest attention to Milly.

Surrounded by the 'Veronese' scene of Milly's ball, the beauty of her smile, the lustre of her priceless pearls, Densher's questioning of Kate begins to elicit the ugliness of her 'web' and his own repugnance to the twist by which Kate will return to London, leaving him to woo the dying girl:

'You leave her here then to die?'

'Ah she believes she won't die. Not if you stay. I mean', Kate explained, 'Aunt Maud believes.'

'And that's all that's necessary?'

Still indeed she didn't break down. 'Didn't we long ago agree that what she believes is the principal thing for us?'

He recalled it, under her eyes, but it came as from long ago. 'Oh yes. I can't deny it.' Then he added: 'So that if I stay –'

'It won't' – she was prompt – 'be our fault.'

'If Mrs Lowder still, you mean, suspects us?'

'If she still suspects us. But she won't.'   (p. 411)

Kate doesn't 'break down' in her confident justification of what is believed and what is necessary to make all aspects of her picture 'fit', although the stilted, blunt exchange establishes the costs, in terms of Kate's fineness, of her violation of candour and decency. She is chillingly able to speak of Milly, in her very radiant presence, as 'object'. ('Her fortune's absolutely huge', she has earlier told Densher. 'I shouldn't care for her if she hadn't so much' – p. 283.) As Densher notes here, with incredulity, she is prepared to leave Milly to die, and to evade the accusation of callousness by turning the question not once, but twice: 'she believes she won't die . . . . Aunt Maud believes.' The conversation now encloses Densher, too, in that process of bargaining blackmail that has engulfed Kate from the outset. There is an ironic contrast between the splendour of the room Milly so fittingly inhabits and the ugly space within it established by the lovers' dialogue. Their intensity has transformed itself from rapt lyricism to the most basic of sexual power struggles: 'there glowed for him in fact a kind of rage at what he wasn't having' (p. 372); whereas he had done absolutely everything that Kate had wanted, she had done nothing whatever that he had' (p. 374). His 'price' for continuing the courtship of Milly set up by Kate is also a revenge for his 'so manipulated state': that Kate will come to him in his rented room.

Densher's room not only defines the essential privacy of his passion, and the urgency of his need to consummate it. He has been aware, in renting this Venetian retreat, that it represents a determination to assert himself against the subtle coercions of Kate, Aunt Maud, and even of Milly. His growing purpose makes it impossible, therefore, that Milly visit him there: 'There were things she would never recognise, never feel, never catch in the air; but this made no difference to the fact that her brushing against them would do nobody any good' (p. 376). And when Kate has left, having honoured her bargain, it is as though the place is, like himself, completely possessed by her physical presence:

> What had come to pass within his walls lingered there as an obsession importunate to all his senses; it lived again, as a cluster of pleasant memories, at every hour and in every object; it made everything but itself irrelevant and tasteless. (p. 415)

It played for him – certainly in this prime after-glow – the part of a treasure kept at home in safety and sanctity, something he was sure of finding in its place when, with each return, he worked his heavy old key in the lock. The door had but to open for him to be with it again and for it to be all there; so intensely there that, as we say, no other act was possible to him than the renewed act, almost the hallucination, of intimacy. (p. 416)

Whether or not the sexual suggestiveness of the imagery of key and lock is consciously apprehended, the writing glows with the rapturous sense of desire at last appeased. The room makes a metaphor for what is there, in Kate, to be returned to, in actuality as in the enclosure of memory, each return a renewal. But its cost is implicit, too, in its privacy. Kate and Densher's passion, consummated by negotiation and locked away from the world they must both inhabit, is to be denied any lasting fulfilment. It shields Densher only momentarily from the conflict created between his deepest feelings and the public role he is committed to playing. The view Kate sees, 'beautiful' as it may seem to her in its reconciliation of their interests with Milly's needs, or with Aunt Maud's interests, is not, in the end, a view Densher is prepared to share. The commercial language that intrudes even on his rapture ('the quality of the article to be supplied', 'a service for which the price named by him had been magnificently paid' – p. 417) nevertheless conveys the corruption of his early feelings, and his entrapment by 'material things'.

Like Kate, Milly Theale is to be to those close to her, '*the* value'. Susan Shepherd Stringham's interest in her young companion has its own kind of calculation: 'The mine but needed working and would certainly yield a treasure. She wasn't thinking, either, of Milly's gold' (p. 120). As a contributor to the best magazines, she is thinking of the appealing romance of Milly's life:

it was rich, romantic, abysmal, to have, as was evident, thousands and thousands a year, to have youth and intelligence, and, if not beauty, at least in equal measure a high dim charming ambiguous oddity, which was even better, and then on top of all to enjoy boundless freedom, the freedom of the wind in the desert – it was unspeakably touching to be so equipped and yet to have been reduced by fortune to little humble-minded mistakes. (p. 108)

Affection and devotion can be glimpsed through the journalese in which, in Susie's reflections, Milly is introduced in Book Third. In Book First, Kate is presented within the frame of Mr Croy's shabby room; here, Milly is held within the frame of Susie's 'impenetrable deference', portrayed as the princess in an epic tale. Susie's response anticipates the response to Milly of London society, which will certainly be thinking of Milly as '*the* value', in accordance with what Milly comes to recognise as '*the* view' of her. Books First and Second have prepared for Milly's entrance a detailed social context. The social milieu revolving about Lancaster Gate is insistent in its repetitiousness, its decorum, its rigid stratifications. And it exacts, most notably from Kate and Densher, a measure of allegiance. The process of 'squaring' their deepest feelings with social forms and occasions inevitably entails the squandering of those feelings. The structure of these early books, alternating between the inner world of the perceiving consciousness and the social circumstances and occasions in which it finds itself, has at once explored Kate's situation and established her mode of surviving in the duplicitous medium that forms and contains her. Her capacity to survive depends on her shaping of outward appearances to produce by her mysterious and charming felicities, her 'impression'.

Milly's impression is made by those aids, both obvious and subtle, which appeal to Susie Stringham. They include not only the romance of her wealthy patrician New York background and sad history of bereavement, but also her pallor, her haggard delicate attractiveness, her high restlessness. These very accoutrements, which enhance Susie's sense of Milly's 'boundless freedom', begin to suggest the limiting contours of Milly's 'box'. Susie's course in Maeterlinck and Pater and Marbot and Gregorious, together with their jaunt to Europe, are designed to remedy 'the little humble-minded mistakes' that betray her young friend's deficiencies of culture. Her general air of vulnerability and innocence make Milly, for her companion, not a case of 'nerves', but a representative case (one of the 'finest' and 'rarest') of 'American intensity', 'the potential heiress of all the ages' (pp. 113, 108). This sense of Milly's importance calls out in Susie a devoted awe that holds Milly, despite her loneliness and her illness, at arm's length. Milly's own reticence and privacy, we are told, contribute in part to this effect:

> She worked – and seemingly quite without design – upon the sympathy, the curiosity, the fancy of her associates, and we shall

really ourselves scarce otherwise come close to her than by feeling
their impressions and sharing, if need be, their confusion.

(p. 113)

If James, too, is inclined to hold his 'unspotted princess' at arm's
length, it is at her own bidding, he seems to suggest. His creative
endeavour is, however, to show what it is in Milly and her situation
that makes for her such a reverential hush, and what more there is to
her than an idealising halo. Susie is tactfully silent about Milly's
visit to Sir Luke Strett, the great London physician whose very
name is enough to convince Merton Densher of the gravity of
Milly's illness, though, in James's characteristic way, its exact
nature is never specified. Milly charitably and not inaccurately
reflects that Susie's attitude has a great deal to do with her 'culture':

> It was definite for her, even if not quite solid, that to treat her as a
> princess was a positive need of her companion's mind; wherefore
> she couldn't help it if this lady had her transcendent view of the
> way the class in question were treated. Susan had read history,
> had read Gibbon and Froude and Saint-Simon; she had high
> lights as to the special allowances made for the class, and, since
> she saw them, when young, as effete and overtutored, inevitably
> ironic and infinitely refined, one must take it for amusing if she
> inclined to an indulgence verily Byzantine. If one could only be
> Byzantine! – wasn't that what she insidiously led one on to sigh?
> Milly tried to oblige her – for it really placed Susan herself so
> handsomely to be Byzantine now. The great ladies of that race –
> it would be somewhere in Gibbon – were apparently not ques-
> tioned about their mysteries. But oh poor Milly and hers! Susan at
> all events proved scarce more inquisitive than if she had been a
> mosaic at Ravenna. Susan was a porcelain monument to the
> old moral that consideration might, like cynicism, have
> abysses. (pp. 212–13)

'But oh poor Milly and hers!' – the phrase suggests a wry self-regard
on Milly's part, and an edge of intrusiveness on James's, perhaps, as
he enters with the absorption of the prefaces into intensities of
sensibility his art is shaping. The wondering, wide-eyed, perfectly
behaved tone and manner of Milly's reflections barely avoid
coyness and preciosity at times, recalling not so much the

innocence of Maisie Farrange as that of Pansy Osmond. Nevertheless, that fuss about Milly to which Leavis objects ('The fuss the other characters make about her as the "Dove" has the effect of an irritating sentimentality')[16] is firmly held in view, as originating in relationships like this one, where the ever-so-slightly complacent defencelessness of Milly feeds on, and is fed by, the romanticising devotion of a Susie. But Milly's analysis of this situation is perceptive, and it is to take on a more anguished note as she sees herself more irrevocably isolated within her role as princess. Like the great ladies of Byzantine art, or the lady she is to see in Bronzino's portrait, she is to be beyond the reach of relationship and of feeling. Doomed and isolated by circumstances that seem the antithesis of Kate's, she is confined like Kate, and like Isabel Archer, to the solitude and self-sufficiency of her own 'stirred intelligence' and heightened consciousness.

The art of being supremely aware may compensate in some measure for the fate of being doomed, though to put the emphasis in this way is to come closer to the perspective of Mrs Stringham's Pater than the novel ever does. James's exploration of the limitations made by that envelope of circumstances that shapes seeing as it shapes living is directed to what happens, in terms of relationship and event, within a densely textured and immediately absorbing real world. If Milly is to impress us as more than a lucid reflector or disembodied notion, she must be, as James himself saw, convincingly 'living'. As Book Third opens, Milly has forsaken the wonders of European culture, and those kingdoms of the earth Susan Shepherd Stringham sees spread out beneath the solitary figure poised among the Swiss Alps, to survey a more human 'scenery': 'the human, the English picture . . . the concrete world inferred so fondly from what one had read and dreamed' (p. 127). In this concrete world, and from within Milly's own consciousness, Milly's distinctive personality takes shape in terms of what she 'sees' (and doesn't see). In rendering Kate, James's emphasis is increasingly on Kate's making her impression on her world. 'Shadows of the world appear' as they are organised in the making of that impression, and Kate thinks and acts with the boldness, swiftness, and assuredness of a creature thoroughly at home in its setting. Milly's consciousness is rendered with a more continuous inwardness, focusing rather more on the impressions she takes, at first hesitatingly and bewilderedly, from a world that is strange and fascinating. Lacking the sophistication of Lancaster Gate, eager to participate and to learn the rules, Milly feels herself a child at the elder's dinner party, naïvely enthusiastic and 'for ever seeing things afterwards' (p. 140). That childlikeness is defensive; at best James does not indulge, but places, it. Milly is seen to grasp at consoling interpretations of threatening experience for example, as a child draws up its counterpane, 'tried it hard, for the time; pulled it over her . . . drew it up to her chin with energy' (p. 243).

Nevertheless, in the key scenes that mark the development of Milly's understanding of English society, we are also aware of Milly herself as object of society's interest. As in the opening glimpses of Kate, there is an alternation between seeing the world from Milly's vantage-point, and seeing Milly at the centre of the social composition. Furthermore, there develops between Milly and Kate, as an underlying aspect of their friendship, that sense of their being two sides of the one medal described in the Preface – mutually involved each in the other's story, set up 'side by side' as Aunt Maud complacently notes, for mutual benefit. Milly sees Kate's 'striking young person' as that of 'a heroine, felt it the only character in which she wouldn't be wasted', and commends her, in those terms, to the eligible Lord Mark (p. 153). Kate sees Milly as 'quite the nearest approach to a practical princess Bayswater could ever hope to know' (p. 154) and as heroine of the story she begins to compose. In the difficult drama of their lives, taking shape about the figure of Merton Densher, each is inclined, for her different reasons, to relinquish to the other the central role. As with Charlotte Brontë's Lucy Snowe and Dickens's Little Dorrit, this removal from the action is subtly motivated. It expresses the impotence of being each in her 'box', and a certain envy each has of the other – Kate of Milly's wealth and Milly of Kate's beauty and energetic self-assurance. Milly confides early to Susan Stringham her 'subtle guess' that Kate has a lover, and quickly registers that Kate has said nothing to her of knowing Merton Densher. From which Milly knows that there is a Kate who has been kept quite hidden during what had seemed a developing intimacy:

> Milly found herself seeing Kate, quite fixing her, in the light of the knowledge that it was a face on which Mr Densher's eyes had more or less familiarly rested and which, by the same token, had looked, rather *more* beautifully than less, into her own.   (p. 165)

In Book Third to Seventh, Milly's gathering 'knowledge', her capacity to interpret what she 'sees', is interwoven with what Kate sees and shows as she weaves her picture. But the focus is now on Milly. In the great historic house at Matcham, in Regent's Park and Lancaster Gate, at the National Gallery and in her Venetian palace, the dimensions of Milly's particular 'box' are progressively explored. In the process, it is possible to demonstrate, Milly is established as a rather more palpable and impressive presence in the novel than she is often taken to be.[17]

Milly begins by seeing 'the Watteau composition' at Matcham, through the cultural lens provided by Susie's enthusiasms,[18] as 'just that sort of frame' required by the rare impressiveness of Kate, who moves through the scene like 'a beautiful stranger' (p. 180). As Milly runs the gauntlet of the assembled company, however, she becomes sharply aware of the implications of such 'picturing'. She sees herself as 'framed' in her role: 'the awfully rich young American who was so queer to behold, but nice, by all accounts, to know' (p. 186). She is conscious of herself as that same 'exotic' who sat by Lord Mark at Aunt Maud's dinner table, to learn from him how she is being 'jumped at' by Mrs Lowder and her circle. The scene catches brilliantly the texture of social life as James sees it, in the flicker of shifting viewpoints and the presenting and receiving of impressions, both calculated and inadvertent. This is the medium within which portraits of ladies are made, the Bronzino portrait Lord Mark shows to Milly being an evocative symbol. For Milly, however, the portrait is charged with a special and personal significance. Like an image framed by a window, the figure within the picture-frame, caught up in Milly's reflections, makes a visual focus for them, distilling a sudden sharp perception:

> she found herself, for the first moment, looking at the mysterious portrait through tears. Perhaps it was her tears that made it just then so strange and fair – as wonderful as he had said: the face of a young woman, all splendidly drawn, down to the hands, and splendidly dressed; a face almost livid in hue, yet handsome in sadness and crowned with a mass of hair, rolled back and high, that must, before fading with time, have had a family resembl-ance to her own. The lady in question, at all events, with her slightly Michael-angelesque squareness, her eyes of other days, her full lips, her long neck, her recorded jewels, her brocaded and

wasted reds, was a very great personage – only unaccompanied
by a joy. And she was dead, dead, dead. Milly recognised her
exactly in words that had nothing to do with her. 'I shall never be
better than this.'

He smiled for her at the portrait. 'Than she? You'd scarce need
to be better, for surely that's well enough. But you *are*, one feels, as
it happens, better; because, splendid as she is, one doubts if she
was good.'

He hadn't understood. She was before the picture, but she had
turned to him, and she didn't care if for the minute he noticed her
tears. It was probably as good a moment as she should ever have
with him. It was perhaps as good as a moment as she should have
with any one, or have in any connexion whatever. 'I mean that
everything this afternoon has been too beautiful, and that perhaps
everything together will never be so right again. I'm very glad
therefore you've been a part of it.' (p. 187)

Milly's tears flow, yet the moment seems neither sentimental nor
contrived. In all her vivid grace, the pictured lady is 'dead, dead,
dead': 'her full lips, her long neck, her recorded jewels, her
brocaded and wasted reds' make evocative the inescapable 'box' of
life under sentence of time, fleetingly and partially captured by this
moment of art. Her picture, splendidly drawn in James's studied
prose, resembles Milly's in more than the physical details. It is
almost as though her sadness acknowledges the poignancy of never
having been fully 'known'. Bronzino's lady is, as Milly has felt
herself, 'fixed' for all time, held within the frame of contemplation
by gazers whose very compliments intensify her remoteness from
them: 'the likeness is so great . . . there you are, my dear, if you
want to know. And you're superb' (p. 188). Kate echoes Lord
Mark, while Lady Aldershaw 'looked at Milly quite as if Milly had
been the Bronzino and the Bronzino only Milly' (p. 189). Milly's
own 'recognition' is expressed in words that identify, in the portrait,
the ultimate significance of her own life: 'I shall never be better than
this' (emphasis added). The complexities of Milly's thought are the
complexities of her feeling. To be 'better' would be to be made well
again, in that sense of 'better' that flies, with such varying measures
of feeling, between Aunt Maud, Susie, Densher and Kate later in
the novel. Lord Mark's response seems almost to touch on that
possible meaning, but in the end 'He hadn't understood.' It is
perhaps just because the limits of his sensitivity are so clearly

discernible that Milly is prompted here, and crucially in Venice, to reveal more of her feelings to him than to anyone else. But he is content to stay within the comfortable limits of graceful compliment: if Milly is no more superb than the Bronzino she will look quite well enough, and she is, besides, morally 'better' than Bronzino's lady. Lord Mark's failure to see Milly, yet again, as anyone other than the innocent to be handled and helped paradoxically enables Milly's movement of self-recognition itself to become 'better'. The exchange of gallant courtesies elicited by her own deepest feelings is 'as good a moment as she should have with anyone' – a reflection more poignant than self-congratulatory. This kind of moment, this kind of social importance, precisely this degree of intimate exchange is what Milly can expect from her life. As she intuits and bears this knowledge, she deflects sadness and self-concern by her little speech of genuine gratefulness. Milly begins to be distinguished by her qualities of sensitivity, which extend beyond the impression she is making, beyond that surface of manners that increasingly preoccupies Kate, into a quickness of perception and a concern for the sensitivities of others. There unfolds in Milly an active intelligence coping with diffidence, hesitation, innocence and pain, determined not to dwell in self-pity, but to look outwards to the fullness and variety that surround her.

Commanded by the great Sir Luke to 'live' as one can only be commanded when life is to be in short supply, Milly wanders alone through the slums of London: 'No one in the world would have sufficiently entered into her state', 'her only company must be the human race at large' (p. 206). More essentially alone in her wanderings than ever Little Dorrit is, Milly comes at last to what she recognises as Regent's Park:

> Here were benches and smutty sheep; here were idle lads at games of ball, with their cries mild in the thick air; here were wanderers anxious and tired like herself; here doubtless were hundreds of others just in the same box. Their box, their great common anxiety, what was it, in this grim breathing-space, but the practical question of life? They could live if they would; that is, like herself, they had been told so: she saw them all about her, on seats, digesting the information, recognising it again as something in a slightly different shape familiar enough, the blessed old truth that they would live if they could. All she thus shared with them made her wish to sit in their company; which

she so far did that she looked for a bench that was empty,
eschewing a still emptier chair that she saw hard by and for which
she would have paid, with superiority, a fee.   (pp. 208–9)

Patrick Swinden, comparing this passage with the moment in
Dorothea Brooke's boudoir in Rome, where she anticipates, and
attempts to come to terms with, a painful future, criticises it for its
lack of a convincing sense of 'the physicality of Milly's pain'.[19]
Barbara Hardy, reading the same passage, stresses the dramatic
appropriateness with which, in its generalising and verbal play, the
passage both expresses Milly's 'sick obsession' and seeks to reach
beyond it, converting the world of the park 'into a subjective and
transparent world of appropriate appearances, metaphors for her
predicament which are not mere rhetorical identifications, con-
ceited and convenient, but the literal identifications of genuine
sympathy'.[20] The delicacy of the writing here seems to me to lie in
James's sense that, although Milly sees her 'box' as extending to
include suffering people all around her, she isn't able, any more
than Dorothea was, to 'share with them', however much she wishes
it. Milly can only see from within her box, and she is never more
isolated within it than here, alone in the middle of London, looking
out at strange people in a strange world. The metaphors and puns –
'They could live if they would', 'the practical question of life', 'with
superiority' – precisely define the differences that Milly, in her
momentary identification with any other poor girl 'with her rent to
pay . . . staring before her in a great city' (p. 211), needs to
minimise. Milly's 'box' makes a superiority she can never completely relinquish, just as the poor girl's box is made different by her
having, if not rent, then more of 'breathing-space'. The 'practical
question of life' makes exigencies that irrevocably separate Milly
from the poor girl and there can be only the most cerebral and
whimsical connections between them. Sentenced to a great
common anxiety, Milly is relieved of its most anxious cares, and this
the passage recognises in its quite unsentimental steadiness of tone.
She is also, at this painful moment, incapable of registering 'pain',
left with no greater resource than the rather laconic noting of
parallels, in the same detached way in which she reflects on the
kindly indirections of Sir Luke: 'She had him, with her little lonely
acuteness . . . in a cleft stick; she either mattered, and then she was
ill; or she didn't matter, and then she was well enough' (p. 210). The
connection between Milly's box and that of the poor girl with her

rent to pay is only made painfully real as Milly is brought face to face with it in her relationship with Kate Croy.

The ladies present to each other a series of pictures, in the sequences through which that relationship now develops. And each is seen, like Tennyson's lady, within her 'box' or 'cage',[21] condemned to scrutinise the world not for interpretations that will enable a fuller life, but compensate for its impossibility. There is Milly, poised at the French windows of her hotel balcony as Kate waits below her, in evocative impatience, for the change from her cab driver. There is the image thrown up at Milly by the smiling Kate, of 'the splendid young woman who looked so particularly handsome in impatience' (p. 213), and which conveys to Milly, in its confident physical assurance, the certainty that Densher has returned. There are the pictures presented as Milly counters Kate's solicitude about Sir Luke's diagnosis, in the somewhat irritating mode in which James renders the artificiality of manners that conceals inner thoughts: 'Oh it's all right. He's lovely' (p. 215). Kate's taking the measure of Milly's ambiguous answers about enjoying herself, knocking about, doing as she likes, is expressed in the equally ambiguous moment in which Kate seizes, kisses and blesses Milly. The narrative summary that 'Kate triumphed with gaiety' (p. 215) catches it exactly, for the gaiety registers Kate's surface pleasure at Milly's optimistic answers, her enjoyment of the game of optimism, and holds open the more sinister suggestion of that simple triumph of the healthy animal over the maimed, from which Milly's sensibility has cowed. It is a triumph that begins to take shape in Kate's 'using' of Milly's doom in the matter of squaring Aunt Maud.

Kate takes Milly's place at the balcony window some nights later, 'very handsome and upright, the outer dark framing in a highly favourable way her summery simplicities and lightnesses of dress'. (pp. 224–5). Her self-presentation underlines the element of deliberation in her withdrawal, a strategic retreat that enables, and suggests the direction of, the 'private' conversation Aunt Maud is about to have with Milly. For Aunt Maud's enlisting Milly's aid in sounding out Kate about whether she is again seeing Densher is a way, clearly, of eliciting Milly's own vulnerabilities and using them. This aspect of Mrs Lowder's design Milly partly sees. She is incapable of seeing the aspect that emerges in Mrs Lowder's lie about Kate's feelings – 'she doesn't care for him' (p. 219) – as anything other than the truth she needs to hear. Milly, capable of

meeting Aunt Maud's manipulation with an embarrassing directness, is not proof against the 'onyx eyes' which, basilisk-like, find the
point of weakness in her 'young friend'. For Milly's worry at Kate's
having concealed from her all mention of Densher provokes in turn
the worry that being worried may reveal what Milly herself would
conceal, her own love for Densher. In this exchange between
Jamesian 'super-subtle fry', Milly knows herself 'dealt with'
'handsomely, completely' (p. 226).

But it is Kate now, restlessly walking around the room, as 'caged'
as Milly has felt herself to be, who proceeds, with barely suppressed
irritation and almost with cynicism, to 'deal' with Milly to her face.
Kate reveals to Milly the extent of the box they inhabit together,
with a loathing that includes herself as victim, ('commercially'
whisked into the shop window set up for Lord Mark's bid), and
herself as predator. Kate's advice to 'drop us while you can', while it
seems to summarise a lesson in 'seeing things as they were', doesn't
as Milly reflects, include in its frank directness the question of
Densher (p. 231). The frightening note that comes with a jolt
through the semblance of caring friendship – 'you may very well
loathe me yet' – makes Milly feel herself alone 'with a creature who
paced like a panther' (p. 231). Kate, too, has a moment in which to
recognise her own part in what Milly apprehends as 'a rough
rehearsal of the possible big drama' (p. 226). She meets Milly's
direct question, 'Why do you say such things to me?', with a more or
less direct answer: 'Because you're a dove' (pp. 231–2). The word,
accompanied by Kate's embrace, implies affection, condescension,
insight. It seals, for Milly, the way in which she is to be set apart,
'partly as if, though a dove who would perch on a finger, one were
also a princess with whom forms were to be observed'. It has the
quality of inspiration and of 'revealed truth': '*That* was what was the
matter with her. She was a dove. Oh *wasn't* she?' For it identifies
how and why Milly is given her convenient social role, and she
instantly sees how she may shelter behind it, even while she suffers
from its obscuring her fullest self. With dove-like blandness she then
parries Aunt Maud's commission concerning Densher: 'I don't
think, dear lady, he's here' (p. 233), and meets Mrs Lowder's deep
unspoken criticism of such rebelliousness. But the great test of her
role as dove comes as she views, in the National Gallery, the picture
that has been veiled throughout this sequence of scenes and
conversations.

As Milly sits at the centre of the great salon, as composed herself as a picture, in that contemplative fatigue in which she dreads being 'flagrantly caught', it is the human pictures that most interest her. Here is the giving and taking of appearances on a grand scale, not only among the Titians and Turners, but also among the fellow pilgrims Milly is almost ashamed to find herself surveying down the vistas and approaches to her vantage-point, and 'placing' as to origin and status: 'cut out as by scissors, coloured, labelled, mounted' (p. 237). The American trio she so precisely interprets can be heard placing in turn a picture that impresses them as 'Handsome. . . . In the English style' (p. 238), a picture that Milly is to recognise first as Densher, and then, with a second shock, as Densher accompanied by Kate:

> he was standing there, standing long enough unconscious for her to fix him and then hesitate. These successions were swift, so that she could still ask herself in freedom if she had best let him see her. She could still reply to this that she shouldn't like him to catch her in the effort to prevent it; and she might further have decided that he was too preoccupied to see anything had not a perception intervened that surpassed the first in violence. She was unable to think afterwards how long she had looked at him before knowing herself as otherwise looked at; all she was coherently to put together was that she had had a second recognition without his having noticed her. The source of this latter shock was nobody less than Kate Croy – Kate Croy who was suddenly also in the line of vision and whose eyes met her eyes at their next movement. Kate was but two yards off – Mr Densher wasn't alone. Kate's face specifically said so, for after a stare as blank at first as Milly's it broke into a far smile. That was what, wonderfully – in addition to the marvel of their meeting – passed from her for Milly; the instant reduction to easy terms of the fact of their being there, the two young women, together.   (p. 239)

All three protagonists are posed among the small Dutch pictures, in a tableau that reveals the simple domestic truth that underlies their public relationship: Milly, solitary and excluded, Kate and Densher 'familiarly associated'. The picture Milly here confronts has a more disturbing power than the Bronzino portrait at Matcham, which spoke of something fixed and final. Kate and Densher make a picture that holds the visual impact and suggestiveness of art, but the key to its interpretation lies in a continuing process of action and relationship that immediately begins to claim Milly's attention. And, as she begins to piece together a 'story', she is aware that her own picture involves, for Densher and Kate, a similar process of interpretation. The contemplative act is inseparable from the other modes of action in which all are involved. The picture of Kate and Densher makes vivid the dilemma of lovers who have no place to take their love. A moment before Milly sees them, the private bond has threatened the public performance in the public place, a 'natural sign of the eyes or an accidental touch of the hand', as Densher reflects, displaying the mutual consciousness and uneasy appearance 'of persons who, infinitely engaged together, had been startled and were trying to look natural' (p. 252). Kate's smile at once acknowledges that Milly provides a testing circumstance for their capacity to present a picture that deceives, saying, as it tacitly does, 'Oh yes, our look's queer – but give me time' (p. 242). Milly's reading of the picture reflects involuntary pain and shock, giving way to a desire to find 'easy terms' for 'the marvel of their meeting' (p. 239). She is aware, yet again, of being 'dealt with' for her 'greater pleasure', but, again, not completely aware of the motivation for Kate's manipulating of the appearances, and happy, for her own reasons, to negotiate entirely at the level of smoothing out the social embarrassment arising from Kate's turning up 'on the very heels of their having separated without allusion to it' (p. 240), with the very person who has remained so markedly unmentioned between them. Kate 'deals' with the ensuing scene by skills Milly sees as at once feminine – 'women got out of predicaments better than men' – and supremely civilised: 'Whatever the facts, their perfect manners, all round, saw them through' (p. 241). Kate's stage-management, determining Densher's behaviour and the version of her relationship with him that is to satisfy and entrap Milly, is only one element. The other is Milly's deployment of her serviceable role of dove. In sounding the 'native wood-note' of the dove, she is spontaneous, American, kept aloft by pride, but also genuinely prepared to be led and to believe: 'Little by little indeed, under the vividness of Kate's behaviour, the probabilities fell back into their order. Merton Densher was in love and Kate couldn't help it – could only be sorry and kind' (p. 243). Absorbing actualities are transformed into the picture Milly wants to see, and the transformation is effected by all three figures.

In the exhausting social life of Venice, both Kate and Milly flourish 'masks' behind which their inner lives are hidden, not only from the world, but from each other: 'It was when they called each other's attention to their ceasing to pretend, it was then that what they were keeping back was most in the air' (p. 346). In a rare moment, the novel's rigorous scrutiny of pictures is suspended in admiration of its portraits of Milly and Kate 'in the likeness of some dim scene in a Maeterlinck play (p. 347). A dim twilight gathers about this tableau, which pictures not the complex relationships that have developed around the enclosed figures, but the emblematic romanticism of the princess imprisoned in the tower:

> we have positively the image, in the delicate dusk, of the figures so associated and yet so opposed, so mutually watchful: that of the angular pale princess, ostrich-plumed, black-robed, hung about with amulets, reminders, relics, mainly seated, mainly still, and that of the upright restless slow-circling lady of her court who exchanges with her, across the black water streaked with evening gleams, fitful questions and answers. The upright lady, with thick dark braids down her back, drawing over the grass a more embroidered train, makes the whole circuit, and makes it again, and the broken talk, brief and sparingly allusive, seems more to cover than to free their sense.

Attractive as that 'image' is, for James, it is one that is elsewhere subject to searching scrutiny. Here, briefly, it is simply admired; the itemising of the visual details that compose the portrait creates the stasis of Victorian genre painting. Certainly, these are the masks of aloof composure the ladies offer each other, but they are accepted here at their face value, in a passage that absolves the protagonists from all the ambiguities created by the portraits they offer to the world. In the dense and duplicitous social medium the novel creates, the endless responsibility of scrutinising appearances cannot be so lightly set aside. It is by this process, after all, that the novel has involved us in the difficult task that confronts the protagonists – the task of finding bearings by which to act and judge. Kate commends to Densher 'the beauty of what I see' (p. 267). And, although her 'seeing' entails distorting appearances, for herself as for others, her charm and candour enable the possibility that there is a certain beauty in her envisaging of happiness for Milly. In a society where truth seems best served by a lie, or where fidelity must express itself as the opposite, the protagonists are ensnared by, and ensnare others in, a series of more and less treacherous conspiracies. Milly's conspiracies with Susie, with Sir Luke, with Densher, that she is not 'ill', have a different quality from the conspiracies in which Aunt Maud and Kate are involved, but no character is free to speak and act quite openly. Milly and Densher, even in their moments of closeness, know themselves to be playing an elaborate game:

> They really as it went on *saw* each other at the game; she knowing he tried to keep her in tune with his conception, and he knowing she thus knew it. Add that he again knew she knew, and yet that nothing was spoiled by it, and we get a fair impression of the line they found most completely workable. (p. 430)

'Lines' and 'views' make difficult social relationships workable, and the master barely conceals his creative delight at the genuine subtleties this kind of writing can realise. But, increasingly, in what James describes as the 'deformed' second half of the novel, with its acceleration of incident, and the obscuring first of Kate's, and then of Milly's consciousness from direct apprehension, it becomes difficult for the reader as for the characters themselves to find bearings. After Lord Mark's visit Milly is sealed off, irrevocably, within the impenetrable ring fence of her consciousness and her palace. Her thoughts and feelings during the crisis that ends her life can only be inferred, or speculated about, by her actions and the reactions of others to her, as she moves into what many readers find an ultimate 'impalpability'. The focus of the novel moves to the consciousness of Densher, who is thus revealed and developed as his 'so manipulated state' yields to a more rigorous self-scrutiny, self-assertion and an unexpected toughness. More than either of the women, Densher feels the difficulty of squaring feeling with behaviour chaffing at the subtle deceptions he is forced to enact. In two notable scenes, Densher is locked in relationship with Milly and with Kate, each in her particular 'box', as the novel moves towards its complex conclusion.

Densher is announced, at the Palazzo Leporelli, as Lord Mark is taking his leave. The 'palpable self' that has been so subtly developing in Milly's relationship with Kate is extended now in relation to each of her suitors. To Lord Mark she has been adamant about her confinement: 'I don't move . . . I've not been out . . . I stay up' (p. 353). There is an illusion of directness created by the momentary lowering of her mask in the presence of this 'safe sympathiser', permitting Milly's confession, 'I'm very badly ill' (p. 359), and the rare release of tears. She is prompted for the first time to recognise her 'value' for a possible suitor: 'wouldn't her value, for the man who should marry her, be precisely in the ravage of her disease? *She* mightn't last, but her money would' (pp. 354–5). Her response is to cling to her solitude, to discourage Lord Mark without offending him. Manners, again, carry the awkwardness off: he is at pains to retreat gracefully, but taking in, on the way, Milly's view of the relationship between Kate and Densher. Bland and blunt, Lord Mark's solicitude scarcely conceals his astute assessment of Milly's value at its current market rate. He leaves knowing that Densher is outbidding him in Milly's affections, and that she is dying.

It is part of Densher's bargain with Kate that he visit Milly now in her great saloon, 'noble in its half-lighted beauty' (p. 420). And, as they endeavour to find a way of putting to themselves the significance of Densher's staying in Venice after the other ladies have gone, it emerges that Milly not only wants to leave her 'fortress' to go about with Densher as she has done in London, but that she wants most of all to visit him in his rooms, to enter that sanctuary in which Densher believes his deepest feelings to be inviolably sealed:

> casting about him in his anxiety for a middle way to meet her, he put his foot, with unhappy effect, just in the wrong place. 'Will it be safe for you to break into your custom of not leaving the house?'
>
> ' "Safe" – ?' She had for twenty seconds an exquisite pale glare. Oh but he didn't need it, by that time, to wince; he had winced for himself as soon as he had made his mistake. He had done what, so unforgettably, she had asked him in London not to do; he had touched, all alone with her here, the supersensitive nerve of which she had warned him. He had not, since the occasion in London, touched it again till now; but he saw himself freshly warned that it was able to bear still less. So for the moment he knew as little what to do as he had ever known it in his life. He couldn't emphasise that he thought of her as dying, yet he couldn't pretend he thought of her as indifferent to precautions. Meanwhile too she had narrowed his choice. 'You suppose me so awfully bad?'

He turned, in his pain, within himself; but by the time the colour had mounted to the roots of his hair he had found what he wanted. 'I'll believe whatever you tell me.'

'Well then, I'm splendid.'

'Oh I don't need you to tell me that.'

'I mean I'm capable of life.'

'I've never doubted it.'

'I mean', she went on, 'that I want so to live –!'

'Well?' he asked while she paused with the intensity of it.

'Well, that I know I *can*.'

'Whatever you do?' He shrank from solemnity about it.

'Whatever I do. If I want to.'

'If you want to do it?'

'If I want to live I *can*', Milly repeated.

He had clumsily brought it on himself, but he hesitated with all the pity of it. 'Ah then *that* I believe.'

'I will, I will', she declared; yet with the weight of it somehow turned for him to mere light and sound.

He felt himself smiling through a mist. 'You simply must!'

It brought her straight again to the fact. 'Well then, if you say it, why mayn't we pay you our visit?'

'Will it help you to live?'

'Every little helps', she laughed .... (pp. 422–4)

And Densher finds himself drained of everything 'but a sense of her own reality'. 'His great scruple suddenly broke: "You can come", he said, "when you like."' Although Milly, sensing a significance here that makes the visit inconvenient, now retreats from the idea, the point has been gained. Kate, in Densher's terms, has been betrayed. And yet, in Kate's terms, she has been doubly affirmed – in his sense of her being somehow present, in control, enabling and directing his relationship with Milly and in Milly's echoing of Kate's 'view' of their handling of her: 'we're making her want to live' (p. 405). Milly's request makes it impossible for him to sustain the paradox. Embarrassment prompts a moment of directness between them which, unlike the comparable moment with Lord Mark, touches sources of profound feeling. In writing of this kind, James's command of the conversational arts is brilliant. The rapidly paced surface of polite gallantry and courtesy is kept up, while its limitations and its usefulness are tested at every point. Through it there emerge feelings and qualities that make both characters

admirable, and which draw them each to the other. As with Kate
and Milly, there are many layers of social mask. 'I'm splendid' is
scarcely true, but nor does Milly expect Densher to believe it; only
to believe it as potentiality and aspiration. This conspiracy expresses
an emotional truth more profound than anything generated or ever
conceivable between Milly and Lord Mark. Densher's tears
respond to what Milly's sad little assertions voice: a determination
exceeding her capacity. Her 'I want so to live . . . I want to live'
reverberates, in all its accepted ambiguity, reverberates with the
impossibility as well as the intensity of it, turning at last to 'mere
light and sound'. Milly is sentenced to her fortress. Densher's tears
are for a doom he cannot prevent. He feels quite directly and
physically what is inherent in the symbolic suggestiveness of the
novel's successive enclosures. Milly's life is 'in his hands'; 'It was on
the cards for him that he might kill her' (p. 427). Milly's doom is
sealed by his being unable to free her from her room by admitting
her to his. And as the conversation continues he finds it impossible to
remain at the level of 'extravagant kind humour' (p. 424). Pity and
tenderness break in for Milly's gallantry and her lonely burden;
there is an impotence in his being unable to do more than respect
her way of bearing it. Despite the insoluble conflict in which he finds
himself, however, he feels himself to be 'doing what he liked' and
discovering what that means: struggling for an integrity of feeling
with less sense of things concealed or compromised than he ever feels
with Kate.

Milly, in this conversation, is not simply 'dove-like'. Her
vulnerability is registered, especially in the poignancy of her pauses
and rephrasings, but so is her quickness and firmness. As always
with Densher, there is a distinctive version of her 'native wood-
note' – the gaiety, enthusiasm, and unashamed interest in him that
she feels permitted by her American 'spontaneity'. And, while there
is a delicacy and consideration in the strategy that develops between
them that is quite different from the strategies Kate employs and
encourages, Milly is capable of her own kind of toughness and self-
assertion, with Densher as with Aunt Maud or Kate. Her bequest to
Densher is of course as much self-assertion as self-abnegation. It is
clear from the tone of this, the last meeting we see between them,
that Milly is capable, where Densher is concerned, of transcending
her own hurt, in large and imaginative efforts of understanding, and
that her final exchange with him as she lies dying will have
expressed her forgiveness, her sense of the joy of having been loved.

But the gift is a direct challenge to Kate, as Densher at last makes Kate see. Milly's 'transcendence' expresses generosity and forgiveness, perhaps, but it takes account of, and indeed underlines Kate's sense of Milly's 'value'. 'Her wings cover us', Kate piously declares (p. 538); it is only at the last that Kate realises how completely this is true. Milly's death comes at the end of a drama in which 'life', too, is a word charged with complex meanings. Milly's forfeiting of 'life' (the keen enjoyment of it as well as the sheer physical endurance that enjoyment makes possible) is profoundly entailed by Kate's deception. And Kate's forfeiting of life (that 'life' she has so abundantly represented for Densher) is no less entailed by Milly's final action.

The concluding sequences of *The Wings of the Dove* take place between Kate and Densher in her sister's small ugly house in Chelsea, in an atmosphere that recalls the novel's opening. Kate has been returned to this particular box, but now we see its ugliness through Densher's eyes, its making vivid for him, as never before, the conditions of her life:

> He had seen her but in places comparatively great; in her aunt's pompous house, under the high trees of Kensington and the storied ceilings of Venice. He had seen her, in Venice, on a great occasion, as the centre itself of the splendid Piazza: he had seen her there, on a still greater one, in his own poor rooms, which yet had consorted with her, having state and ancientry even in their poorness; but Mrs Condrip's interior, even by this best view of it and though not flagrantly mean, showed itself as a setting almost grotesquely inapt.   (pp. 508–9)

Densher reflects that '*He* could have lived in such a place'. But he cannot but see the poor room in the light of Kate's values and sense of self. His understanding of why Kate is 'exceptionally under the impression of that element of wealth in (Milly) which was a power' (p. 403) recalls the sympathy with which Kate has been seen in the novel's opening. Under the 'storied ceilings of Venice' Densher has grasped Kate's envy of Milly's pearls. Even after Milly's death has left him bitterly self-reproachful he is still able to allow a fineness in Kate that needs, for its fullest portrayal, the right surroundings and accessories. He is still able to see the intolerableness of Kate's 'box':

What a person she would be if they *had* been rich – with what a
genius for the so-called great life, what a presence for the so-called
great house, what a grace for the so-called great positions! He
might regret at once, while he was about it, that they weren't
princes or billionaires. She had treated him on their Christmas to
a softness that had struck him at the time as of the quality of fine
velvet, meant to fold thick, but stretched a little thin; at present,
however, she gave him the impression of a contact multitudinous
as only the superficial can be. She had throughout never a word
for what went on at home. She came out of that and she returned
to it, but her nearest reference was the look with which, each
time, she bade him good-bye. The look was her repeated
prohibition: 'It's what I *have* to see and to know – so don't touch
it. That but wakes up the old evil, which. I keep still, in my way,
by sitting by it. I go now – leave me alone! – to sit by it again. The
way to pity me – if that's what you want – is to believe in me. If we
could really *do* anything it would be another matter.'   (p. 531)

The stretching thin of Kate's fineness can be heard in the self-
dramatising stoicism of her voice here; it is a fineness that simply
needs the 'element of wealth' to sustain it. Her note is to become
more strident as she contends, against Densher's fineness of scruple
and discrimination, for that sustaining power.
	The ensuing conversation between them makes yet another of the
novel's interweaving parallels, recalling Densher's final conversation with Milly. He has come now to ask Kate yet again, at the last
possible moment, to take him 'just as he is', without waiting for
Milly's death and its probable legacy: 'Our marriage will –
fundamentally, somehow, don't you see? – right everything that's
wrong, and I can't express to you my impatience' (p. 497). Kate can
only take his impatience not as an expression of his still urgent
physical passion for her, nor as a final attempt to establish the
integrity of his regard for Milly, but (with a strange smile that
'nearly sickened him' – p. 498), as a sign that he is sure of the dying
girl's money. From this point his response to Kate is expressed almost
solely in terms of his testing her, eliciting her moral coarsening. He
comes to bring her, as a Christmas gift, the unopened letter from
Milly that has arrived for him on Christmas Eve:

	'I've asked myself for a tribute, for a sacrifice by which I can
	peculiarly recognise – '

'Peculiarly recognise what?' She demanded as he dropped.

'The admirable nature of your own sacrifice. You were capable in Venice of an act of splendid generosity.'

'And the privilege you offer me with that document is my reward?'

He made a movement. 'It's all I can do as a symbol of my attitude.'

She looked at him long. 'Your attitude, my dear, is that you're afraid of yourself. You've had to take yourself in hand. You've had to do yourself violence.'

'So it is then you meet me?'

She bent her eyes hard a moment to the letter, from which her hand still stayed itself. 'You absolutely *desire* me to take it?'

'I absolutely desire you to take it.'

'To do what I like with it?'

'Short of course of making known its terms. It must remain – pardon my making the point – between you and me.'

She had a last hesitation, but she presently broke it. 'Trust me.' Taking from him the sacred script she held it a little while her eyes again rested on those fine characters of Milly's that they had shortly before discussed. 'To hold it', she brought out, 'is to know.'

'Oh I *know*!' said Merton Densher.

'Well then if we both do – !' She had already turned to the fire, nearer to which she had moved, and with a quick gesture had jerked the thing into the flame. He started – but only half – as to undo her action: his arrest was as prompt as the latter had been decisive. He only watched, with her, the paper burn; after which their eyes again met. 'You'll have it all', Kate said, 'from New York.'   (pp. 525–6)

The dialogue is terse, but its ramifications are intricate. Densher's talk of 'playing fair' is seen to be specious. His 'tribute' to Kate is a travesty of the open-handed gift, and given a particularly unpleasant emphasis by the irony in Densher's reference to her 'sacrifice' in Venice. The inescapable medium of sordid bargaining, where 'giving' has its inevitable price and its inevitable self-interest, recalls not only the opening conversation with Mr Croy, but also the whole development of plot. Feelings are expressed by strategies in this, the starkest of the power-struggles between the lovers. That quality of watchful civility that has changed the tone of their conversations after Densher's return from Venice – 'pardon my making the point' – has an edge of brutality now. Densher's defence is simple and telling: 'It's all I can do as a symbol of my attitude.' A careful reading of the part he has been forced to play, of Kate's overriding of his scruples and her parrying of his passion, surely suggests that he has earned the right to his bitterness.[22] Densher wants to 'symbolise' what Milly's gift to him has meant by handing it directly to Kate, thus reversing, with stern deliberation, that irony in which he has been entrapped, where to earn Kate he must offer himself to Milly. As well as the implication that Milly's bequest is Kate's by right, the gesture carries the suggestion that Kate, who has shown more than a twinge of jealousy about the exact nature of Densher's relationship with Milly, ought properly to inspect the letter Milly has written him. Densher is insisting that Kate confront Milly's love for him as part of the price Kate must pay for what she has done.

Kate's destruction of the letter is the more brutal in view of what Densher has shown her of the delicacy of his feelings. She destroys it not as Densher might himself have done, as a ritual renunciation of the gift and the deception, but as a symbol of *her* attitude. For Densher the burning letter is 'like the sight of a priceless pearl cast before his eyes' (p. 532). '*The* value' of Milly, once manifested for the lovers in her fabulous pearls, is now for Densher beyond estimation. Kate re-enacts the destruction of her friend's happiness and her life: she needs to destroy all evidence of the feelings with which Milly's gift has come. She acts as though the fact of the gift itself is what matters, and there is almost nothing to redeem her action from this interpretation: 'To hold it . . . is to know'; 'You'll have it all . . . from New York.' What Densher 'knows' is different, but so hazily known as to cause him a grief that emerges powerfully between the lines. He can never quite know what he needs most fully to know, the exact tone with which Milly has expressed her understanding and forgiveness of the part he has played in the extinguishing of her hopes for life. Kate's 'brutality' is something she has always confessed to, but in the closing scenes it is the quality that most distinguishes her: 'she has had *all* she wanted', 'we've succeeded', 'She's dead?', 'Not yet?' (pp. 486, 474). Her accusation that Densher is afraid of himself and has had to do himself violence, is acute enough. It makes Kate no less prepared, however, to do violence to his feelings, and Densher no less prepared to keep insisting on them. When Kate opens the unopened letter he sends her from Milly's solicitors in New York, her opening it is, for

Densher, a measure of 'her departure from delicacy', as Kate resentfully sees (p. 534). His hope that Kate might begin to see, in the return of the unopened letter, the beauty of what he 'sees' is met by Kate's determination to make good the beauty of what she has seen. It is only by Densher's final ultimatum, that she choose between the money and him, that he makes her acknowledge what has been apparent in these conversations: that they will never again be as they were. The final bargaining is the expression of their wasted passion, their inability any longer 'to bury in the dark blindness of each other's arms the knowledge of each other that they couldn't undo' (p. 529).

'Really, ideally, relations stop nowhere',[23] James remarks. The area he has illumined, in *The Wings of the Dove*, finds a more open end, even, than in *The Portrait of a Lady*. The meaning and implications of Kate's final words are left to reverberate. Her 'We shall never be again as we were!' (p. 539) neither accepts nor refuses Densher's offer to marry her, though her headshake and her exit suggest its impossibility. Densher hasn't denied Kate's accusation: 'her memory's your love. You *want* no other' (p. 539). The question of where truth lies, in human relationships is, after all, the question held before us at every moment of the novel. If the outlines of the drama are clear, its edges are blurred, and the unanswered, unanswerable questions loom larger towards the end. Lord Mark's silent and watchful presence, waiting, with Aunt Maud's conniv- ance, just off-stage, suggests that he may hope to claim Kate and the money; Densher's last, private interview with Milly may have revealed to him a love 'worth' more than the check-mating of passion and subtle deceptiveness to which his love for Kate has been reduced. The lovers manoeuvre incessantly to discover the chang- ing truth about each other's feelings. Can Lord Mark's return to Venice to disillusion Milly be explained by Kate's having revealed to him her commitment to Densher? Has Densher known Milly more intimately than Kate can know? What motivated Lord Mark's revelation? Kate refutes Densher's view that she should have deceived Lord Mark, as vehemently as Densher refutes Kate's view that he should have agreed to marry Milly while knowing he could never do so. In the end, the novel seems to suggest, it is impossible adequately to inhabit or to construe another's 'box'. For

L. B. Holland, in somewhat mystical vein, this drift towards impalpability expresses what Milly, the novel's 'muse' and inspiration, represents for James's imagination:

> The novel tacitly acknowledges that it cannot completely or directly embrace the ultimate reality – neither the ultimate horror nor the ultimate beauty, neither the pulsating actuality of life beyond art, nor the completely imagined vision which was the novel's origin or muse. . . . But the novel is not content to acknowledge this by saying it. Instead it acts as if its vision lay within the presence but beyond the reach of language . . . acknowledges the fact in the contortions of expressive movement, the rhythm of approach and withdrawal as a tribute of devotion to what it leaves behind. As a gesture of love, the rhythmical form falls short of the full communion it manages none-the-less to intimate and celebrate; as an act of devotion it reveals by betraying the life and sacred presence it adores.[24]

But this is to apotheosise Milly. While it is true that in and through her James explores the inevitable failure of art to catch 'the pulsating actuality of life', that life from which Bronzino made his portrait, and which Kate possesses in such abundance, Milly's 'case' is, in the end, not essentially different from Kate's, or from Densher's. Each must inhabit the box of a general and representative human, social existence. What they are, the novel insists, can never be entirely 'known'. We are left at the end to infer what each protagonist feels, as we have been all along, by what they see and show. The 'beauty' of what Kate has seen, for all its shabbiness of deception, its manipulation of trust, is not without its potential fineness, in enabling for Milly the fulfilment that could have been available in no other way, in her loving Densher. The 'rightness' of what Densher comes to see, brutal though it may seem, and impotently face-saving, asserts a way of valuing Milly, and a hope of righting, in some now symbolic way, the wrong done to her. Milly's vision, expressed in her gift, is both open and ambiguous: she enables the lovers' freedom to respond as they wish. She accepts their intolerable dilemma and forgives their deception, but returns to them, consciously or unconsciously, that degree of moral responsibility the novel has allowed them all along.

Densher is intensely aware of Kate, at the last, as 'lady' – 'pale, grave and charming' (p. 509), like a princess in exile. And this, whatever happens, is what Kate will remain, her charming appearance kept up at the cost of finer feelings priced out of her reach, and knowing that, for the man she has loved, appearances can no longer be made to cover what she is and does. It is in the name of this self-portrait that Kate has acted. The sense of herself for which she contends defines something essential to the person she is in the box she must inhabit. Milly is in the end not simply, transcendently, the dove that Aunt Maud and Kate see, obligingly removing herself and leaving her useful wealth. Nor is she an idealised tribute to the memory of Minnie Temple. In the context created for her by the novel's developing design, she asserts a self that compels attention, not as a stereotype, or representative 'case' or 'view', but for what she is. Yet the assertion is enabled by, indeed determined by, her dying. She becomes the 'portrait' in death as Kate must remain the 'portrait' in life. Her quality cannot be felt by the intensity that is Kate's quick of being, but only by 'memory'. But the vital quick of life in both ladies is vanquished, as it is in Isabel Archer, by their confrontation with a reality beyond their web. And, unlike Little Dorrit or Dorothea Brooke, they are promised no fuller, more expansive life, as a consequence of discovering the limits of their own solipsism. James, like Hardy, rests less contentedly within the limits of the Victorian novel's romantic fable than Dickens or the George Eliot of *Middlemarch*, more conscious of the costs, in terms of human possibilities, inherent in its certain moral scheme.

In an essay contemporaneous with *The Wings of the Dove*, James writes of Emma Bovary's imagination as a consolation for 'the contracted cage in which she flutters' in the dreariness of provincial life: 'a case of . . . an intense and complex imagination, corrupt almost in germ . . . being pressed back upon itself with a force which makes explosion inevitable' and of 'Flaubert's having in this picture expressed something of his intimate self, given his heroine something of his own imagination'.[25] In James's novel, imagination, the ambiguous beauty of what his characters see, has a power that imitates the novelist's own, to create the wondrous silken webs that reflect subjective needs and preoccupations, reflecting and entangling the selves thus presented to the world. The novel explores how generously and creatively, as well as how selfishly and subversively, this contracted freedom may be experienced. Within their individual boxes, brief human lives take the shape given them by the Victorian novel's circumscribing fable, contained by it, though, as

James suggests, never quite fixed or wholly known. It is not a vision of life that prevents the enthusiastic desire to 'live', however. For it is with the demanding medium of acting and suffering, rather than with the contemplative detachment that savours the Paterian 'moment', that *The Wings of the Dove*, like the great Victorian novels that precede it, is most profoundly engaged.

6 'The Lady in the Looking-glass: some Reflections'

> Supposing the looking-glass smashes, the image disappears, and the romantic figure with the green of forest depths all about it is seen by other people – what an airless, shallow, bold, prominent world it becomes! A world not to be lived in. As we face each other in omnibuses and underground railways we are looking into the mirror; that accounts for the vagueness, the gleam of glassiness, in our eyes. And the novelists in future will realize more and more the importance of these reflections, for of course there is not one reflection but an almost infinite number; those are the depths they will explore, those the phantoms they will pursue, leaving the description of reality more and more out of their stories, taking a knowledge of it for granted, as the Greeks did and Shakespeare perhaps.
>
> (Virginia Woolf, 'A Mark on the Wall', in *A Haunted House and Other Stories*, p. 43)

The lady in the looking-glass and the web she weaves in a room of her own are recurring images of creativity in the essays, stories and novels of Virginia Woolf. In 'A Sketch of the Past' she locates her preoccupation with mirror-gazing in childhood guilt about her own body and her developing potentialities. In adolescence, the guilt is vivified by the dream of a fearful 'other face' appearing in the glass behind her own reflection. For the adult writer, this dream signifies the artist's creative shock of recognition:

> a token of some real thing behind appearances; and I make it real by putting it into words. It is only by putting it into words that I

make it whole; this wholeness means that it has lost its power to hurt me; it gives me, perhaps because by doing so I take away the pain, a great delight to put the severed parts together.

She supposes that all artists feel something like this ('Why did Dickens spend his entire life writing stories?'), searching out the hidden pattern that reveals the interconnectedness of lives, and the whole world as a work of art.[1] Weaving that pattern, we are all 'sealed vessels afloat on what it is convenient to call reality'.[2]

The 'mark on the wall', then, like the faces in the omnibus, is less a phenomenon to be grasped and identified than the occasion for speculations about the self and the nature of what it calls reality. In another of these speculative short pieces, 'The Lady in the Looking-glass: some Reflections', the glass reflects the untenanted domestic interior so appealing to the Georgian imagination, and somewhat coyly constructs the lady herself, prising her open and verifying her by degrees:

> her mind was like her room, in which lights advanced and retreated, came pirouetting and stepping delicately, spread their tails, picked their way; and then her whole being was suffused, like the room again, with a cloud of some profound knowledge, some unspoken regret, and then she was full of locked drawers, stuffed with letters, like her cabinets. To talk of 'prising her open' as if she were an oyster, to use any but the finest and subtlest and most pliable tools upon her was impious and absurd. One must imagine – here was she in the looking-glass. It made one start.   (*A Haunted House and Other Stories*, p. 91)

The imagination that has begun by entertaining rich possibilities for her proceeds to fix her in the glass, 'the woman herself', 'naked in that pitiless light': empty, old, isolated and self-centred. As allegories of the creative process, with its power to make and annihilate a person and a world, these short pieces are whimsical musings, somewhat uncertain in tone, on the status of fictional 'reality'.

The continuing importance of 'all that Lady of Shalott business' in shaping the novel's form and its history is indicated by its persistence in the work of twentieth-century writers as experimental as Lawrence and Virginia Woolf. For Lawrence, as I suggested at the outset, it identifies a self-consciousness he wants to repudiate. But Virginia Woolf makes this self-consciousness the very basis of her radical challenge to the Victorian novel. The mind 'at its upper window', separate, looking down to indulge its isolation or to 'embrace' or 'create' what is outside itself and beyond'[3] becomes her whole medium. The flow of consciousness charted by Henry James is, by comparison, selective and partial. Woolf's prose seeks to capture 'the atoms as they fall', with all the apparent randomness of individual experience. Her exploration of the 'depths' inhabited by the romantic figure in the looking-glass takes for granted that 'reality' defined by her reading of the Victorian novel as 'this appalling narrative business of the realist: getting on from lunch to dinner'.[4] Meditative passages in the Victorian novel foreshadow the ways in which, in Woolf's fiction, moments are saturated with the gathered significance of an individual history, revealing the distinctive patterns in which the mind shapes its world. But Woolf's interest lies in the 'quickened, multiplied consciousness' and in the evanescent impressions caught in its texture, rather than in the dense network of social relations and incident that challenges the consciousness of Victorian protagonists.

'The nature of women' and 'the nature of fiction', related questions explored in Woolf's extended essay *A Room of One's Own*, are questions that preoccupy her in each of her novels. Mrs Dalloway is not only a representative modern consciousness created through the outflowing of her mind on an ordinary day. She is an exemplary woman as well, endowed, still, with some of the emblematic virtues of her Victorian predecessors. It is not only her femininity, 'that woman's gift of making a world of her own wherever she happened to be', but something more mysterious, transcending her rather 'tinselly' brittleness, that impresses Peter Walsh, as well as her creator: 'For there she was' (*Mrs Dalloway*, p. 215). As Virginia Woolf prepares to write *To the Lighthouse*, she is again 'haunted by some semi-mystic nay profound life of a woman, which shall all be told on one occasion'.[5] The result is Mrs Ramsay, a much more impressive figure than Mrs Dalloway, but still, like E. M. Forster's maternal figures in these years, exerting a beauty and power that indeed seems 'mystic', triumphing even beyond death: 'it was this: it was this', reflects Charles Tansley, 'she was the most beautiful person he had ever seen' (*To the Lighthouse*, p. 17).

'If there isn't the woman there's nothing', is the view of Lawrence's Birkin (*Women in Love*, p. 51). For Lawrence, however, a special valuing of the woman entails freeing her from Victorian literary and social conventions. She is woman in love, passionate, and releasing an answering passion in her lovers. In Clarissa Dalloway, by contrast, there is represented that constricting of passion that is an aspect of the Lady of Shalott's imprisonment. There is about Clarissa a virginal quality that is essential to her inviolable selfhood. When she retreats to her attic room she is like 'a nun withdrawing' (*Mrs Dalloway*, p. 35). The moment defines her continuing retreat from the fullness of experience; she senses in herself the lack of 'something central which permeated; something warm which broke up surfaces and rippled the cold contact of man and woman, or of women together'. She recalls her timorous love for Sally Seton, a figure glimpsed through her recollections as the similar figures of Ginevra Fanshaw or Pet Meagles or Kate Croy are glimpsed through the enclosed consciousnesses of Charlotte Brontë's and Dickens's and James's novels, asserting a vitality and beauty from which the contemplative heroines feel themselves shut away. Clarissa Dalloway, caught in the tension between what seems fixed and definite in her inviolable self and the fluidity of its recollections and speculations, pauses to look at herself in the glass:

> Laying her brooch on the table, she had a sudden spasm, as if, while she mused, the icy claws had had the chance to fix in her. She was not old yet. She had just broken into her fifty-second year. Months and months of it were still untouched. June, July, August! Each still remained almost whole, and, as if to catch the falling drop, Clarissa (crossing to the dressing-table) plunged into the very heart of the moment, transfixed it, there – the moment of this June morning on which was the pressure of all the other mornings, seeing the glass, the dressing-table, and all the bottles afresh, collecting the whole of her at one point (as she looked into the glass), seeing the delicate pink face of the woman who was that very night to give a party; of Clarissa Dalloway; of herself. (pp. 41–2)

Clarissa is transfixed by this moment as George Eliot's Mrs Transome or Dorothea Brooke are transfixed in their boudoirs, portraits of ladies held in time like the framed ladies who line their walls, or Milly Theale, recognising in Bronzino's lady the significance of her own fleeting moment. For Clarissa, as for Milly or for Sue Bridehead, it is not only the 'icy claws' of time that transfix her, but also those qualities in herself and in her society that isolate her within her 'social mould': 'the woman who was that very night to give a party; of Clarissa Dalloway; of herself'. The drift of the passage, and of the whole novel, towards Clarissa's awareness of who that woman is, is summarised, as it is symbolised, in this moment in which she confronts her reflected self. But Clarissa's recognition of her own 'death of the soul' is partial only, just as Virginia Woolf's is:

> 'Oh, Lucy,' she said, 'the silver does look nice.'
> 'And how,' she said, turning the crystal dolphin to stand straight, 'how did you enjoy the play last night?' 'Oh, they had to go before the end!' she said. 'They had to be back at ten!' she said. 'So they don't know what happened', she said. 'That does seem hard luck', she said (for her servants stayed later, if they asked her). 'That does seem rather a shame', she said, taking the old bald-looking cushion in the middle of the sofa and putting it in Lucy's arms, and giving her a little push and crying:
> 'Take it away! Give it to Mrs Walker with my compliments! Take it away!' she cried.
> And Lucy stopped at the drawing-room door, holding the cushion, and said, very shyly, turning a little pink, couldn't she help to mend that dress?
> But, said Mrs Dalloway, she had enough on her hands already, quite enough of her own to do without that.
> 'But, thank you, Lucy, oh, thank you', said Mrs Dalloway, and thank you, thank you, she went on saying (sitting down on the sofa with her dress over her knees, her scissors, her silks), thank you, thank you, she went on saying in gratitude to her servants generally for helping her to be like this, to be what she wanted, gentle, generous-hearted. Her servants liked her. (pp. 43–4)

Mrs Dalloway's reflections evoke the cadences of Tennyson's Mariana in her moated grange:

> 'He cometh not', she said;
> She said, 'I am aweary, aweary,
> I would that I were dead!'

But the writing seems barely aware of the monotony and inertia that makes its plangent rhythms, giving the lie to Clarissa's little spurts of energy and enthusiasm. Mrs Dalloway's identity as mistress of the house and society hostess is subject to no very incisive criticism. Woolf's attempt to catch the flavour of contemporary upper-class life in the triviality of Clarissa's reflections[6] founders on the assumptions she shares with her heroine. Like Dorothea Brooke, Clarissa lives in a 'rarefied social air', looking down 'with imperfect discrimination on the belts of thicker life below' (*Middlemarch*, p. 346). The lady who has 'gone up into the tower alone' (*Mrs Dalloway*, p. 53) is as thoroughly cut off, in her high place, as the lady of Victorian courtly love. But Virginia Woolf lacks George Eliot's awareness of the debilitating effects of 'rarefied social air'. Clarissa's treatment of her servants gives voice to her isolation within a complacent self-image: 'Her servants liked her.' And the passage likes her, helping her, as her servants do, to be 'what she wanted, gentle, generous-hearted', offering her patronising tone and be- haviour as generosity, while presenting her, to the end, as the unattainable lady of Peter Walsh's life-long pursuit.

The web Clarissa's reflections make, the thin thread which, we are told, 'would stretch and stretch' (p. 124), is not challenged, as Dorothea's reflections, or Rosamond Vincy's 'gossamer web' are challenged, by an intractable world beyond 'the narrow chamber of the individual mind'. And, whereas in Dorothea, for example, or in Milly Theale, intensity of thought is intensity of feeling, touching the quick of a self in process and in relationships that reach out beyond self, Clarissa's consciousness reflects at worst triviality and at best a limiting concentration on the curious nature of the mind's processes.

Beyond Clarissa, certainly, there is outlined 'a world not to be lived in'. The strollers in Regent's Park continue to suggest, as for Milly Theale, a world where people have their rent to pay, their jobs to find, are in quest of the meanings variously noted in 'Einstein, speculation, mathematics, the Mendelian theory' or St Paul's Cathedral, 'all spirit, disembodied, ghostly' (p. 33). A swooping 'plane writes its enigmatic message to mankind, boring into the war-crazed ears of Septimus Warren-Smith and requiring him to look out at a world which is for him, quite literally, 'not to be lived in'. His is the complete solipsism of madness. His attempt to order the flux of his changing impressions is clearly intended as a contrast, as it is sometimes a near parody of, Clarissa's and the novelist's: 'he was attaching meanings to words of a symbolic kind' (p. 106), Sir William Bradshaw clinically notes. In his state of heightened sensory awareness, voices impinge on Septimus with a roughness

> like a grasshopper's, which rasped his spine deliciously and sent running up into his brain waves of sound which, concussing, broke. A marvellous discovery indeed – that the human voice in certain atmospheric conditions (for one must be scientific, above all scientific) can quicken trees into life! Happily Rezia put her hand with a tremendous weight on his knee so that he was weighted down, transfixed, or the excitement of the elm trees rising and falling, rising and falling, with all their leaves alight and the colour thinning and thickening from blue to the green of a hollow wave, like plume on horses' heads, feathers on ladies', so proudly they rose and fell, so superbly, would have sent him mad. But he would not go mad. He would shut his eyes; he would see no more.   (pp. 25–6)

The passage recalls Robert Graves's returned soldier, whose taut sensibility reflects a world where Georgian pastoral is stretched to breaking-point:

> His eyes are quickened so with grief
> He can watch a grass or leaf
> Every instant grow.

> ('Lost Love')

But the world Septimus inhabits is that same world of heightened sensibility as Clarissa Dalloway and Virginia Woolf inhabit: not a world inhospitable to imagination, but one which recreates the streets of London or the fields of Norfolk alike, with 'a quickened, multiplied consciousness' seizing its moments as they pass.

And, yet the world Virginia Woolf and Lawrence inhabit, the world of Einstein, aeroplanes, disembodied values, in the aftermath of war, surely brings to sharper focus than ever before that sense of the modern predicament shaping throughout the nineteenth century, of man as finite 'in an infinitely complex and contradictory world'. Carlyle's questions, 'What am I; and Whence; and Whither?' remain at the level of fanciful speculation for both Septimus and Clarissa. 'Sealed vessels afloat on what it is convenient to call reality', neither is brought to the edge of that 'ontological chaos' that confronts Nietzsche. In *The Waves*, Woolf's prose poem for six voices, she carries to the furthest possible point that 'soliloquy in solitude' she wanted the twentieth-century novel to be – a point from which the novel could only retreat, as Virginia Woolf herself retreats, in *Between the Acts*.

For Virginia Woolf, at the last, it was a world 'not to be lived in'. As for a significant number of women writers from the nineteenth century to the present day, the creative delight with which she transmuted its pain into art was not proof against the twofold burden of womanhood and creative sensibility. This 'novelist of the future' emancipating herself from the Victorian novel's 'reality' experiences the more fully the curse that imprisons the Lady of Shalott.

Notes

NOTES TO THE INTRODUCTION

1. 'The Lady of Shalott is evidently the Elaine of the Morte d'Arthur, but I do not think I had ever heard of the latter when I wrote the former' – quoted in G. O. Marshall Jr, *A Tennyson Handbook* (New York, 1963).

2. See L. S. Potwin, 'The Source of Tennyson's "The Lady of Shalott" ', *Modern Language Notes*, vol. XVII, no. 8 (Dec 1902) pp. 237–9.

3. Alice James lived 'an existence dominated by a mysterious illness for which no organic cause could be discovered and no cure found', sustained latterly by the diary in which she scribbled to 'clarify the density and shape the formless mass within'. See Jean Strouse, *Alice James: A Biography* (London, 1981).

4. Details of Hunt's five versions of the Lady of Shalott are supplied in the Walker Art Gallery's *Holman Hunt Exhibition Catalogue* (Liverpool, 1969).

5. Quoted in G. S. Layard, *Tennyson and his Pre-Raphaelite Illustrators* (London, 1894) p. 41.

6. Hunt's interpretation of its 'eternal truth' is reprinted in the *Hunt Catalogue*, p. 157.

7. The connection between *The Awakening Conscience* and 'The Lady of Shalott' is convincingly made by Samuel Wagstaff in 'Some Notes on Holman Hunt and the Lady of Shalott', *Wadsworth Atheneum Bulletin*, Summer 1962.

8. Martin Meisel, 'Half Sick of Shadows', in *Nature and the Victorian Imagination*, ed. U. C. Knoepflmacher and G. B. Tennyson (Berkeley, Calif., 1977) p. 337, sees this as evidence that Millais, unlike Hunt and Rossetti, abandons 'communally fostered anxieties over the adequacy of Art'.

9. See, for example, Whistler's paintings of the 1860s (influenced by his friendship with Rossetti), especially *The Little White Girl*, William Orpen's *The Mirror*, Walter Howell Deverell's *Lady Feeding a Bird*, Charles Allston Collins's *Convent Thoughts*, Burne-Jones's Von Borke watercolours, William Morris's *Queen Guinevere*.

10. Hugh Witemeyer, *George Eliot and the Visual Arts* (New Haven, Conn., 1975) p. 155, notes examples in the work of German painters, for example Friedrich and Schwind. The Dutch school admired by George Eliot also provides some notable examples.

11. Denis de Rougemont, *Passion and Society* (London, 1956) p. 18.

12. I am indebted to James Gribble for recalling this passage to my attention.

13. Letter to Edward Garnett, 5 June 1914, in D. H. Lawrence, *Selected Literary Criticism*, ed. A. Beal (London, 1961) p. 17; and 'A Study of Thomas Hardy', ibid., pp. 176–7.

14. G. Armour Craig, 'Self and Society in the Novel', in *English Institute Essays 1955*, ed. Mark Schorer (New York, 1956), provides one of the earliest discussions of the figure: 'in some of the worst novels as well as the best, from a high place and in solitude the heroine looks out on the world, and in her vision we see her differences from those around her' (p. 28).

15. Preface to *The Portrait of a Lady*, in Henry James, *The Art of the Novel*, ed. R. P. Blackmur (New York, 1937) p. 51.

16. As F. R. Leavis notes in *The Great Tradition* (London, 1962) p. 10, James must have seen that Jane Austen's presentation of everything through Emma's dramatised consciousness fulfils a prescription of his own. See also Susan Morgan, *In the Meantime* (Chicago, 1980) which discusses Jane Austen's 'romanticism', particularly her interest in the nature and value of perception.

17. John Bayley, *The Romantic Survival* (London, 1969) p. 15.

18. Northrop Frye, *Romanticism Reconsidered: English Institute Papers* (New York, 1963) p. 11. Though it is evident that 'readers as yet have no shared definition of a romantic tradition in fiction' (Morgan, *In the Meantime*, p. 3); (they probably have no shared definition of romanticism either), a number of recent articles and books have attempted to define one by drawing parallels between the preoccupations of poets and novelists. See, for example, Donald Stone, *The Romantic Impulse in Victorian Fiction* (Cambridge, Mass., 1980).

19. Peter Coveney, *The Image of Childhood in Nineteenth-Century Literature* (London, 1967) p. 31.

20. Northrop Frye, *The Ringers in the Tower* (London, 1971) p. 21.

21. George Lukács, *The Theory of the Novel* (London, 1963) pp. 60–80.

22. Michael Zeraffa, *Fictions: The Novel and Social Reality* (London, 1976) p. 90, provides a useful summary of Barthes's argument.

23. Tsvetan Todorov, 'The Structural Analysis of Literature: the Tales of Henry James', in *Structuralism: An Introduction*, ed. D. Robey (Oxford, 1973) pp. 73–104.

24. Ibid., p. 101.

25. See Gillian Beer, 'Myth and the Single Consciousness: *Middlemarch* and "The Lifted Veil"', in *Critical Essays on George Eliot* (London, 1970), and Joseph Wiesenfarth, *George Eliot's Mythmaking* (Heidelberg, 1977).

26. Northrop Frye, *Fables of Identity* (New York, 1963) p. 33.

27. Roland Barthes, *Writing Degree Zero* (London, 1967).

28. As Q. D. Leavis demonstrates, however, in comparing the solitary Roman meditations of Little Dorrit, Dorothea Brooke and Isabel Archer, in 'A Note on Literary Indebtedness', *Hudson Review*, vol. 8 (Fall 1955) pp. 422–8, deliberate borrowings from earlier writers may weaken rather than enlarge on the creative inspiration of the original.

29. Samuel Taylor Coleridge, *The Statesman's Manual* (London, 1852) p. 33.

30. T. B. Tomlinson, *The English Middle Class Novel* (London, 1976), argues that the kind of experience with which this study is concerned is dealt with badly, if at all, by the best nineteenth-century novels – a view which has stimulated my thinking at many points. See also R. Alter, *Partial Magic* (London, 1975) p. 87: 'the centre had shifted, broadly speaking, from consciousness and how it shaped the world around it to the world around it and how it impinged . . . on consciousness'.

31. John Ruskin, *Sesame and Lilies* (London, 1892) p. 168.

32. Leslie A. Feidler, *Love and Death in the American Novel* (London, 1967), provides a useful account of these traditions.
33. ' . . . something that holds one in one's place, makes it a standpoint in the universe which it is probably good not to forsake' – to Grace Norton, 28 July 1883, in *The Letters of Henry James*, ed. Percy Lubbock (London, 1920) vol. I, p. 101.
34. See, for example, Sandra M. Gilbert and Susan Gubar, *The Madwoman in the Attic* (New Haven, Conn., 1980), who assert (p. 86), that, although male writers in the nineteenth century deal with the imprisonment or enclosure of protagonists, 'the male writer is so much more comfortable with his literary role that he can usually elaborate upon his visionary theme more consciously and objectively than the female writer can'.
35. Lisa Appignanesi, *Femininity and the Creative Imagination* (London, 1973), identifies a 'myth of femininity' which associates creativity with the 'feminine', the unconscious, the internalisation of experience, and explores it in the work of three modern writers, James, Meusil and Proust.
36. Quoted by John Kilham, *Tennyson and the Princess: Reflections of an Age* (London, 1958) p. 78.
37. Arthur Hallam, 'The Influence of Italian upon English Literature', an oration of 16 Dec 1831; quoted ibid., p. 78.
38. Lionel Stevenson, 'The High-born Maiden Symbol in Tennyson', in *Critical Essays on the Poetry of Tennyson*, ed. John Kilham (London, 1964) p. 135.
39. Quoted in Edgar Finley Shannon Jr, *Tennyson and the Reviewers* (Cambridge, Mass., 1967) p. 93.
40. Mary Wollstonecraft, *A Vindication of the Rights of Man* (Gainsville, Fla., 1960) p. 13.
41. Mary Wollstonecraft, *A Vindication of the Rights of Woman*, Everyman edn (London, 1929) p. 62.
42. Ibid., p. 69.
43. George Eliot, 'Mary Wollstonecraft and Margaret Fuller', in *Essays of George Eliot*, ed. Thomas Pinney (London, 1963) p. 205.
44. Wollstonecraft, *The Rights of Woman*, p. 73.
45. Ibid., p. 122.
46. See discussion in Ch. 1, pp. 49–52.
47. Wollstonecraft, *The Rights of Woman*, p. 71.
48. F. R. Leavis, *The Great Tradition*, pp. 32, 41–2, draws attention to this.
49. *Daily News*, 3 Feb 1853; quoted in Laurence Lerner, *Love and Marriage: Literature and its Social Context* (London, 1958) p. 198.
50. To John Morley, 14 May 1867, in *The George Eliot Letters*, ed. Gordon S. Haight (New Haven, Conn., 1955) vol. IV, p. 364.
51. See discussion in Ch. 2, pp. 82–5.
52. Preface to *The Portrait of a Lady*, in James, *The Art of the Novel*, p. 49.
53. Quoted in Leon Edel, *Henry James: The Middle Years* (New York, 1962) p. 137.
54. Quoted in Philip Sicker, *Love and the Quest for Identity in the Fiction of Henry James* (Princeton, NJ, 1980) p. 18.
55. Julian Moynahan, 'Pastoralism as Culture and Counter-culture in English Fiction 1800–1928', in *Towards a Poetics of Fiction*, ed. Mark Spilka (Bloomington, Ind., 1977) pp. 242–4.
56. Jeanette King, *Tragedy and the Victorian Novel* (Cambridge, 1979) p. 17. As

R. L. P. Jackson notes in his review of King's book, in *Quadrant*, Apr 1979, p. 41, that way of characterising tragedy is in itself romantic.

57. *A Defence of Poetry*, in Percy Bysshe Shelley, *Works*, vol. VII (London, 1956) p. 118.

58. Elaine Showalter, *A Literature of their Own* (Princeton, NJ, 1977) p. 33. Showalter sees this as a development discernible from *Jane Eyre* onwards, and most noticeable by the end of the century. As I have argued in 'Jane Eyre's Imagination', *Nineteenth-century Fiction*, vol. 23, no. 3 (Dec 1968), Jane's room, far from being a flight or a retreat, nourishes an imaginative resourcefulness that empowers her to deal with the world of masculine (and feminine) aggressiveness.

59. Gilbert and Gubar, *The Madwoman in the Attic*, p. 87. See also Elizabeth Sabiston, 'Prison of Womanhood', *Comparative Literature*, vol. 25 (1973) p. 336.

60. Gilbert and Gubar, *The Madwoman in the Attic*, p. 87.

61. Lorenz Eitner, 'Cages, Prisons and Captives in Eighteenth-century Art', in *Images of Romanticism*, ed. K. Kroeber and W. Walling (New Haven, Conn., 1978) p. 17.

62. Victor Brombert, *The Romantic Prison* (Princeton, NJ, 1978), provides a detailed account of the prison as a romantic image.

63. Gilbert and Gubar, *The Madwoman in the Attic*, p. 87.

64. F. E. Hardy, *The Early Life of Thomas Hardy 1840–81* (London, 1928) p. 224.

65. Ellen Moers, *Literary Women* (New York, 1976) p. 249. See also King, *Tragedy and the Victorian Novel*, p. 120: 'Hardy repeatedly uses the image of the bird – the archetypal image of the soul – for women, suggesting that the woman's tragedy is a type of the tragedy of human life.' Elaine Showalter in 'Towards a Feminist Poetics', in *Women Writing and Writing about Women*, ed. Mary Jacobus (London, 1979), finds the women characters 'somewhat idealized and melancholy projections of a repressed male self', less adequately achieved than Henchard. This view takes no account of the novel's images of enclosure and I think underestimates the finely realised comparisons to which these direct us, between the social and psychological deprivations shared by both male and female characters.

66. Peter Conrad, *The Victorian Treasure House* (London, 1973) p. 72, sees the domestic interior as a 'fortress' for 'the angelic woman', and a kind of 'exoskeleton' for the personality. Michael Irwin, in *Picturing: Description and Illusion in the Nineteenth-century Novel* (London, 1979) p. 4, argues that such extended descriptions of interiors are essentially 'static', set-pieces that may provide relevant prelude to the dramatic scene, but 'can scarcely be accommodated within one'.

67. James, *The Art of the Novel*, p. xxix.

68. Henry James, *The Painter's Eye*, selected and edited by J. L. Sweeney (London, 1956) p. 181.

69. Preface to *The Portrait of a Lady*, in James, *The Art of the Novel*, p. 46.

70. 3 Aug 1891, *The Notebooks of Henry James* (Oxford, 1947) p. 111.

71. Preface to *The Portrait of a Lady*, in James, *The Art of the Novel*, p. 48.

72. See, for example, Gilbert and Gubar, *The Madwoman in the Attic*, pp. 13–14.

73. Preface to *Roderick Hudson*, in James, *The Art of the Novel*, p. 5.

74. Ian Gregor, *The Great Web* (London, 1974) p. 24.

75. Cf. Keats's view of the world as 'the Mind's experience . . . the teat from

which the Mind or Intelligence sucks its identity' – *Letters*, ed. H. E. Rollins (Cambridge, 1958) p. 102 – a possible source for George Eliot's striking metaphor.
76. Isaiah Berlin, *Four Essays on Liberty* (London, 1969) p. 131.
77. Morton Zabel, Introduction to Henry James, *In the Cage and Other Tales* (London, 1958) p. 12. See also L. C. Knights, 'Henry James and the Trapped Spectator', in *Explorations* (London, 1964).
78. Walter Pater, *The Renaissance*, Fontana edn (London, 1971) p. 221.
79. Virginia Woolf, 'Modern Fiction', *The Common Reader* (London, 1929) p. 191.
80. Robert Kiely, *The Romantic Novel* (Cambridge, Mass., 1972) p. 19.
81. See F. E. Hardy, *The Early Life of Thomas Hardy* (4 March 1885) (London, 1928) p. 232; the Preface to *Roderick Hudson* in James, *The Art of the Novel*, p. 5; and *The Future of the Novel*, in *Theory of Fiction: Henry James*, ed. J. E. Miller (Nebraska, 1972) p. 336.
82. As Christopher Ricks suggests in *Tennyson* (London, 1972) p. 80.
83. Preface to *The Princess Casamassima*, in James, *The Art of the Novel*, p. 70.
84. *Westminster Review*, vol. XXXIX (May 1843). Hilda M. Hume, 'The Language of the Novel: Imagery', in *Middlemarch: Critical Approaches to the Novel*, ed. Barbara Hardy (London, 1967), draws attention to this passage, which seems a more likely source for the 'eminent philosophers' than Herbert Spencer and the passage of Ruskin cited by N. N. Feltes in 'George Eliot's Pier-glass: the Development of a Metaphor', *Modern Philology*, vol. 67, no. 1 (Aug 1969) pp. 69–71, relevant though some of Ruskin's phrases are to perceptual imagery elsewhere in the novel.
85. Jessie Chambers, 'A Personal Record', in H. Coombes, *D. H. Lawrence: Critical Anthology* (London, 1973) p. 289.
86. Preface to *The Princess Casamassima*, in James, *The Art of the Novel*, p. 70.
87. Preface to *The Portrait of a Lady*, ibid., p. 46.
88. Ibid., p. 57.
89. Stuart Hutchinson, 'Beyond the Victorians: *The Portrait of a Lady*', in *Reading the Victorian Novel: Detail into Form*, ed. Ian Gregor (London, 1980) p. 283, sees Ch. 42 as signalling James's growing conviction that it was in the consciousness that the individual must really live.
90. Preface to *What Maisie Knew*, in James, *The Art of the Novel*, p. 164.
91. Todorov, in *Structuralism*, ed. Robey, pp. 79, 78.
92. In Todorov's view, ibid., the 'essence' of the Captain's character remains concealed.
93. 'Gustave Flaubert' (1902), in Henry James, *Selected Literary Criticism*, ed. Morris Schapira (London, 1962) p. 262.
94. Friedrich Nietzsche, *The Will to Power*; quoted in Anne K. Mellor, *English Romantic Irony* (Cambridge, Mass., 1980) p. 185.
95. See Friedrich von Schlegel, *Dialogue on Poetry*, quoted by Anne K. Mellor, *English Romantic Irony*, p. 19, and Fragment no. 116, in Friedrich von Schlegel, *European Romanticism: Self-Definition*, ed. Lilian R. Furst (London, 1980) p. 136.
96. D. C. Meucke, *The Compass of Irony* (London, 1969) p. 215.
97. A view I put forward in 'The Ambiguous Life of Doctor Faustus', *Critical Review*, 1960.
98. Thomas Carlyle, 'Characteristics', *Critical and Miscellaneous Essays*, vol. III (London, 1899) p. 25.

99. Ibid., p. 10.
100. Matthew Arnold, 'Religion Given', *Dissent and Dogma*, ed. R. H. Super (Ann Arbor, Mich., 1968) p. 178.

NOTES TO CHAPTER I SENSE AND SENSIBILITY: LUCY SNOWE'S CONVENT THOUGHTS

1. Quoted in Winifred Gérin, *Charlotte Brontë* (Oxford, 1967) p. 510.
2. See Ch. 2, pp. 87–90.
3. 'The Lesson of Balzac', in James, *Selected Literary Criticism*.
4. Fanny Ratchford, *The Brontës' Web of Childhood* (New York, 1941), discusses the relationship between the Brontë juvenilia and the mature work.
5. See Coral Anne Howells, *Love, Mystery and Misery: Feeling in Gothic Fiction* (London, 1978) p. 8.
6. 9 Jan 1845, quoted in Gérin, *Charlotte Brontë*, p. 278.
7. July 1852, quoted in Kathleen Adams, *Those of Us Who Loved Her* (Warwick, 1980).
8. In *The George Eliot Letters*, ed. Haight, vol. II, p. 87.
9. Quoted in Mellor, *English Romantic Irony*, p. 15.
10. Jan 1876, in *The George Eliot Letters*, vol. VII, p. 216.
11. To A. W. McLeod, Oct 1913, in Coombes *D. H. Lawrence: A Critical Anthology*, p. 80.
12. To George Smith, 3 Nov 1852, in *The Brontës: Their Lives, Friendships and Correspondences*, ed. Thomas J. Wise and J. Alexander Symington, Shakespeare Head edn (Oxford, 1932) vol. IV, p. 16.
13. The phrases are Terry Eagleton's, in *Myths of Power: A Marxist Study of the Brontës* (London, 1975) p. 88.
14. To W. S. Williams, 12 Apr 1850, in *The Brontës: Lives, Friendships and Correspondences*, vol. III, p. 99.
15. 'Regulated Hatred', *Scrutiny*, vol. VIII (1940) pp. 351, 356.
16. Jean H. Hagstrum, *Sex and Sensibility* (Chicago, 1980) p. 9, offers a useful discussion of this question.
17. C. S. Lewis, *Studies in Words*; quoted ibid.
18. Quoted ibid., p. 270.
19. Johnson's *Rasselas*, Rousseau's *La Nouvelle Héloïse*, Mrs Radcliffe's *The Mysteries of Udolpho* and the poetry of Cowper are some of the most significant examples of shared reading.
20. To G. H. Lewes, 6 Nov 1847, in *The Brontës: Lives, Friendships and Correspondences*, vol. II, p. 153.
21. For example, Matthew Arnold, letter to Mrs Forster, 14 Apr 1853, in *The Brontës: The Critical Heritage*, ed. Miriam Allott (London, 1974) p. 201: 'the writer's mind contains nothing but hunger, rebellion and rage, and therefore that is all she can, in fact, put into her book'. Craig, in *English Institute Essays 1955*, p. 40, describes *Jane Eyre* as 'the reduction of the world to the terms of a single vision'. Raymond Williams writes of *Villette*, 'persons outside the shaping longing demanding consciousness have reality only as they contribute to the landscape, the emotional landscape, of the special, the pleading, the recommending character' – *The English Novel from Dickens to Lawrence* (London, 1974) p. 61.

22. Eagleton, *Myths of Power*.
23. Kate Millett, *Sexual Politics* (London, 1979) pp. 140–7.
24. Mary Jacobus, 'Villette's Buried Letter', *Essays in Criticism*, vol. XXVIII, no. 3 (July 1978) pp. 228–44.
25. Eagleton, *Myths of Power*, p. 26.
26. Millett, *Sexual Politics*, p. 146.
27. Jacobus, in *Essays in Criticism*, vol. XXVIII, no. 3, p. 229.
28. To George Henry Lewes, 17 Oct 1850, in *The Brontës: Lives, Friendships and Correspondences*, vol. III, p. 72.
29. The phrase is Robert Heilman's, in 'Charlotte Brontë's "New" Gothic in *Jane Eyre* and *Villette*', *Charlotte Brontë: 'Jane Eyre' and 'Villette': A Casebook*, ed. Miriam Allott (London, 1973).
30. Jacobus, in *Essays in Criticism*, vol. XXVIII, no. 3, pp. 235–6.
31. Ibid., p. 238.
32. To W. S. Williams, 6 Nov 1852, in *The Brontës: Their Lives, Friendships and Correspondences*, vol. IV, p. 18.
33. Samuel Taylor Coleridge, *Biographia Literaria*, ed. J. Shawcross (Oxford, 1907) Ch. 14.

NOTES TO CHAPTER 2   LITTLE DORRIT'S PRISON

1. Harry Stone, *Dickens and the Invisible World* (London, 1979) p. 53, draws attention to the similarity between this passage from 'George Silverman's Explanation' and many passages in Dickens's letters.
2. *All the Year Round*, vol. XVIII (27 July 1867) p. 119.
3. William Wordsworth, *Essay Supplementary to the Preface* (1815).
4. Stone, *Dickens and the Invisible World*, p. 60.
5. From Henry James, 'Talks with Tolstoy', epigraph to H. L. Daleski, *Dickens and the Art of Analogy* (London, 1970).
6. G. Tillotson and J. Butt, *Dickens at Work* (London, 1957) pp. 223–5.
7. Robert Garis, *The Dickens Theatre* (Oxford, 1965) p. 183.
8. Lionel Trilling, '*Little Dorrit*', in *The Dickens Critics*, ed. G. H. Ford and L. Lane (New York, 1966) p. 293.
9. Raymond Williams, 'Social Criticism in Dickens', *Critical Quarterly*, vol. 6, no. 3 (1964) p. 224.
10. Ross Dabney, *Love and Property in the Novels of Dickens* (London, 1967) p. 108.
11. F. R. Leavis, 'Dickens and Blake: *Little Dorrit*', in F. R. and Q. D. Leavis, *Dickens the Novelist* (London, 1970).
12. John Bayley, *The Uses of Division* (London, 1976) p. 100.
13. See Q. D. Leavis's persuasive argument on the question of Esther's tone, in *Dickens the Novelist*, pp. 155–60.
14. Le Duchat, *Dictionnaire* (1725), in describing this roundelay, notes that it was 'in ancient times, the custom with the burgesses to put on the window of the room inhabited by the daughters of the house a pot of majolaine . . . a good pretext for a coquette to make her appearance at the window, under the pretence of watering her thirsty plants, and to show herself to the "compagnons de la majolaine" (le chevalier du guet, or mounted watchman) patrolling the street' – *The Dickensian*, vol. 5 (1909) p. 44.

15. See, for example, John Wain, '*Little Dorrit*', in *Dickens and the Twentieth Century*, ed. John Gross and Gabriel Pearson (London, 1962) p. 175: 'it is his most stationary novel . . . for all the scurry of event on its surface, it never for a moment suggests genuine movement'.
16. Philip Collins, in *Dickens and Crime* (London, 1962), gives a useful account of Dickens's involvement in the Urania Cottage project.
17. Letter to Miss Coutts, quoted ibid., p. 105.
18. Barbara Hardy, *Tellers and Listeners* (London, 1975) pp. 171–3, notes that the story is adapted 'to the expressed and unexpressed needs of the listener and the teller'. Her account emphasises Little Dorrit's needs rather than the novel's implicit sense of her limitations.
19. Harvey Sucksmith, in his Introduction to the Oxford edition (1979) p. xviii, argues that, 'apart from the prison metaphor, no true unifying idea had yet emerged'.
20. Peter Coveney, *The Image of Childhood in Nineteenth-Century Literature*, discusses this preoccupation in Dickens and other nineteenth-century writers.
21. Wollstonecraft, *Vindication*, p. 62.
22. Letter to Forster, 1856, in *Charles Dickens: A Critical Anthology*, ed. Stephen Wall (London, 1970).
23. Number plan for Ch. 20 in *Little Dorrit*, ed. Sucksmith, p. 822.
24. Speech in Leeds 1847, quoted in Alexander Walsh, *The City of Dickens* (Oxford, 1971) p. 155.
25. See F. R. Leavis, 'Dickens and Blake', in *Dickens the Novelist*.
26. David Gervais, 'The Poetry of *Little Dorrit*', *Cambridge Quarterly*, vol. IV, no. 1 (1968) pp. 46–7, argues to the contrary. While I agree that Clennam's feelings are often 'latent in the author's view of his surroundings', Gervais overlooks some delicate explorations of interior struggle in Clennam: between what is just and unjust resentment of the Gowans, for example, and in his searching self-analysis about the meaning and purpose of life.
27. The section beginning 'Blest the infant Babe', in *The Prelude* (1850), Book II, lines 232–64.
28. Trilling, in *The Dickens Critics*, offers an interesting account of Clennam's mental processes in Ch. 8 of Book the First.
29. J. S. Mill, *On the Subjection of Women* (London, 1929) p. 309.

NOTES TO CHAPTER 3   GEORGE ELIOT'S WEB

1. Some of these are discussed in Barbara Hardy, *The Novels of George Eliot* (London, 1962) pp. 198–200; D. R. Carroll, 'An Image of Disenchantment in the Novels of George Eliot', *Review of English Studies*, new ser., vol. XI (1960) pp. 29–41; and John Halperin, *The Language of Meditation: Four Studies in Nineteenth-Century Fiction* (Ilfracombe, 1973).
2. For Raymond Williams, George Eliot is finally incapable of rendering the rural community, recording 'an England in which only certain histories matter, and to which the sensibility – the bitter and frank sensibility of the isolated moral observer can be made appropriate' – 'The Knowable Community in George Eliot's Novels', in *The Poetics of Fiction*, p. 238.

3. Jerome Beaty, *Middlemarch from Notebook to Novel* (Urbana, Ill., 1960), shows how meticulously the two stories were woven together.
4. Unsigned review in *Galaxy*, Mar 1873, pp. 424–8, in *George Eliot: The Critical Heritage* (London, 1971) p. 359.
5. Ibid., p. 359.
6. See Introduction, pp. 31–2.
7. J. S. Mill, *System of Logic*; quoted in Bernard J. Paris, *Experiments in Life* (Detroit, 1965) p. 31.
8. R. T. Jones, *Philosophy and the Novel* (Oxford, 1975) pp. 26–7, and J. Hillis Miller, 'Optic and Semiotic in *Middlemarch*', in *The Worlds of Victorian Fiction* (Cambridge, Mass., 1975), deal with the question of how the narrator may be said to escape the narrowed vision implicit in the pier-glass metaphor. Inevitably, as each concludes, she can only strive for a perspective larger than those of her characters. And there are many narrative passages (see, for example, p. 451, discussed on p. 119 of this chapter) in which she recognises this.
9. E. Duncan Jones first identified the critic as Hazlitt, in 'Hazlitt's Mistake', *TLS*, 27 Jan 1966, p. 68.
10. Gillian Beer, in *Critical Essays on George Eliot*, p. 104, notes that the theories of Naumann and his friends are based on those of the Nazarenes, whom many art historians see as precursors of the Pre-Raphaelites.
11. See Joseph Wiesenfarth, Introduction to *George Eliot: A Writer's Notebook* (Virginia, 1981) pp. xxxiii–xxxiv, for a useful discussion of both interests.
12. Pater, *The Renaissance*, p. 218.
13. See discussion in the Introduction, pp. 28–9.
14. Trenchantly put by Jenni Calder, in *Women and Marriage in Victorian Fiction* (London, 1976) p. 158: 'Does she not excite our interest . . . and then deftly dam up and fence round the momentum she has so powerfully created? She diagnoses so brilliantly "the common yearning of womanhood", and then cures it, sometimes drastically, as if it were a disease.'
15. Leavis, *The Great Tradition*, pp. 32, 41–2.
16. 'Three Novels', in *Essays of George Eliot*, p. 334.
17. Cf. Leavis, *The Great Tradition*, p. 65: 'Dorothea . . . doesn't represent her author's strength'; and Laurence Lerner, *The Truth Tellers* (London, 1967) p. 269: 'the presence of a noble nature, generous in its wishes, ardent in its charity, *does* change the lights for us'.
18. Michael Irwin, in *Picturing*, p. 125, argues, I think wrongly, that Dorothea's myopia and heedlessness of her surroundings 'makes her less amenable to Eliot's characteristic method of fictional portrayal'.
19. E. D. H. Johnson's conclusion, in 'The Truer Measure: Setting in *Emma*, *Middlemarch*, and *Howard's End*', in *Romantic and Modern: Revaluations of Literary Tradition*, ed. George Bornstein (Pittsburgh, 1977) p. 200, that the view from Dorothea's window is an 'index to her moods' fails to take account of this.
20. See note 1 above.
21. Achieved, as Derek Oldfield points out in 'The Language of the Novel: the Character of Dorothea', in *Middlemarch: Critical Approaches to the Novel*, pp. 63–86, by Eliot's characteristic use of *erblete Rede*.
22. Hugh Witemeyer, *George Eliot and the Visual Arts*, p. 43, discusses Eliot's habit of using 'memory pictures' as aids to 'secular meditation'.

23. Witemeyer, who draws attention to the 'composed' element – the picture-frame, the placing of the figures, the perspectives and lighting – suggests (ibid., p. 154) that the 'objective reality' of the scene affords Dorothea an alternative to self-pity. The scene surely insists, however, that it is only Dorothea's 'cleansed seeing' that enables her to look out, and to find a significance (scarcely 'objective') in the figures outside her window.

24. John Ruskin, *Modern Painters* (1843–60), vol. IV, pt V, ch. 1. Witemeyer, in *George Eliot and the Visual Arts*, p. 155, notes the similarity between the two passages.

NOTES TO CHAPTER 4   JUDE, SUE AND 'SOCIAL MOULDS'

1. Ian Ousley, in 'Love–Hate Relations: Bathsheba, Hardy and the Men in *Far From the Madding Crowd*', *Cambridge Quarterly*, vol. X, no. 1 (1981) p. 32, argues that the *tableau vivant* of Bathsheba looking at herself in the mirror draws on a misogynist tradition which mingles with personal 'memories, dreams, desires' in Hardy to make heroines like her 'always remain fractionally outside his grasp, the objects of fascinated but inconclusive scrutiny'. Sue, I shall argue, comes within Hardy's grasp.

2. 'A Study of Thomas Hardy', in Lawrence, *Selected Literary Criticism*, p. 217.

3. Letter, 20 Nov 1895, in F. E. Hardy, *The Later Years of Thomas Hardy* (London, 1930) p. 42.

4. Lois Deacon and Terry Coleman, *Providence and Mr Hardy* (London, 1966), argue convincingly that both Elfride and Sue are modelled on Hardy's 'lost love', Tryphena Sparks, the cousin to whom Hardy was secretly engaged for five years, prior to his first marriage.

5. Lascelles Abercrombie, *Thomas Hardy: A Critical Study* (London, 1912) p. 85.

6. Lawrence, *Selected Literary Criticism*, p. 205.

7. Kate Millett, who sees Sue's revolt against convention as 'uncertain, confused, and imperfectly convincing', and Hardy's grasp on her as 'unsure', is nevertheless inclined to read her feminism as the explanation of her destruction: 'she is only too logical. She has understood the world, absorbed its propositions' (*Sexual Politics*, p. 133). Mary Jacobus's sensitive account of the split in Sue 'between belief and instinctive behaviour' nevertheless finds Hardy's intention in the end 'incompletely realized' – 'Sue the Obscure', *Essays in Criticism*, vol. XXV, no. 3 (July 1975). John Goode, in 'Sue Bridehead and the New Woman', in *Women Writing and Writing about Women*, argues (p. 107) that Sue's 'function' is that of 'an image carrying its own logic which is not the logic of the understandable, comprising both what she utters and what she seems, the gap between them and the collusion they make'. His analysis sometimes gives undue emphasis, I think (see, for example, the passage cited in note 13) to what Sue utters.

8. Ibid., p. 105.

9. Burke suggests, in Wollstonecraft's view *The Rights of Man*, p. 112), that 'the supreme Being, in giving woman beauty in the most supereminent degree, seemed to command them, by the powerful voice of Nature, not to cultivate the moral virtues that might chance to excite respect, and interfere with the pleasing sensations they were created to inspire'.

10. F. E. Hardy, *The Later Years of Thomas Hardy*, p. 42.
11. Gregor, *The Great Web*, pp. 220–6, offers a persuasive reading of the role of Little Father Time in the novel.

NOTES TO CHAPTER 5   PORTRAITS OF LADIES: 'THE WINGS OF THE DOVE'

1. Leon Edel, in *The Untried Years 1843–70* (London, 1953) p. 336, discusses the relationship between Isabel, Milly and Minnie Temple.
2. 3 Nov 1894, *The Notebooks of Henry James* (Oxford, 1947) p. 169.
3. Ibid., p. 15.
4. Henry James, *Notes of a Son and Brother* (London, 1914) p. 73.
5. Quoted in Edel, *The Untried Years*, p. 331.
6. Ibid., p. 334.
7. Review of *Far From the Madding Crowd*, in *Nation*, 24 Dec 1874.
8. See, for example, Showalter, in *Women Writing and Writing about Women*, p. 27.
9. F. C. Crews, *The Tragedy of Manners* (New Haven, Conn., 1975) p. 75, who makes the comparison, believes that Milly, like Tennyson's Lady, 'has never had the capacity for genuine social contact'.
10. See the Preface to *The Tragic Muse*, where James describes this as 'One of the half-dozen great primary motives' of art.
11. James might well have found suggestive the pairing of two female figures in one of the most widely exhibited of these paintings, Millais's *Return of the Dove to the Ark*.
12. James was critical of 'faint, pale, embarrassed, exquisite Pater', but steeped himself in *The Renaissance* shortly after its publication. He must surely have noted Pater's comment on Giorgione's Venice: 'all the fulness of existence . . . some consummate extract or quintessence of life' (p. 141).
13. Ibid., p. 224.
14. The phrase is used in Ruth Yeazell, *Language and Knowledge in the Late Novels of Henry James* (Chicago, 1976) p. 71.
15. Leo Bersani, 'The Narrator as Center in *The Wings of the Dove*', *Modern Fiction Studies*, vol. 6 (1960–1) pp. 135, 138.
16. Leavis, *The Great Tradition*, p. 158.
17. Crews's view, in *The Tragedy of Manners*, p. 59 – 'even when exerting her power, Milly is somehow passive and intangible; her status as a symbol always prevails' – is not unrepresentative.
18. Viola Hopkins Winner, 'Visual Art Devices and Parallels in the Fiction of Henry James', in *Henry James: Modern Judgements*, ed. Tony Tanner (London, 1968) p. 102, notes James's response to the Watteaus in the Wallace Collection – 'his irresistible air of believing in these visionary picnics' – as idealising, as Milly does, the social scene.
19. Patrick Swinden, *Unofficial Selves* (London, 1973) p. 111.
20. Barbara Hardy, *The Appropriate Form: An Essay on the Novel* (London, 1964) p. 23.
21. The two words occur interchangeably here, and recur in later James novels. See Introduction, sections I and II.
22. Sally Sears, *The Negative Imagination: Form and Perspective in the Novels of Henry*

James (Ithaca, NY, 1963), refers on p. 95 to Densher's 'sanctimonious viciousness'.

23. Preface to *Roderick Hudson*, in James, *The Art of the Novel*, p. 5.
24. L. B. Holland, *The Expense of Vision* (Princeton, NJ, 1964) p. 320.
25. 'Gustave Flaubert' (1902), in James, *Selected Literary Criticism*, p. 222.

NOTES TO CHAPTER 6 'THE LADY IN THE LOOKING-GLASS: SOME REFLECTIONS'

1. Virginia Woolf, *Moments of Being: Unpublished Autobiographical Writings*, ed. Jeanne Schulkind (London, 1976) pp. 69–72.
2. Ibid., p. 222.
3. James Naremore, *The World Without a Self: Virginia Woolf and the Novel* (New Haven, Conn., 1973) rightly notes (p. 74), in quoting from 'Modern Fiction', that Woolf's novels are not always clear about the distinction between 'embrace' and 'create'.
4. 28 Nov 1928, *A Writer's Diary*, ed. Leonard Woolf (London, 1954) p. 139.
5. 26 Nov 1926, ibid.
6. Cf. A. D. Moody, *Virginia Woolf* (London, 1963) p. 20: 'she is shown to be of not much interest in herself; she has to offer only a sharp awareness of the surface of her world and its people. This makes her something of an animated mirror, having a life made up of the world she reflects. But to be and do that is precisely her function for the novel: she is a living image of the surface of society Virginia Woolf was concerned with.'

Index

Women (*Contd.*)
  writers, 12, 21–2
  see also Lady, the
Woolf, Leonard, 216n4
Woolf, Virginia, 6, 29, 197–204
  Mrs Dalloway, 199–203
  A Haunted House and Other Stories, 198
  'The Lady in the Looking Glass:
    Some Reflections', 198
  'A Mark on the Wall', 197–8
  A Room of One's Own, 199
  'A Sketch of the Past', 197

To the Lighthouse, 199
Wordsworth, William, 30, 77–8
  'Intimations of Immortality', 58
  'The Old Cumberland Beggar',
    127–8
  'The Prelude', 101
  'The Ruined Cottage', 39

Yeazell, Ruth, 215n14

Zabel, Morton, 209n77
Zeraffa, Michael, 206n22